Young Blood

YOUNG BLOOD

BRIAN STABLEFORD

SIMON & SCHUSTER

LONDON·SYDNEY·NEW YORK·TOKYO·SINGAPORE·TORONTO

For Jon and Bev James

First published in Great Britain by
Simon & Schuster Ltd in 1992
A Paramount Communications Company

Simon & Schuster Ltd
West Garden Place
Kendal Street
London W2 2AQ

Simon & Schuster of Australia Pty Ltd
Sydney

A CIP catalogue record for this book is
available from the British Library
ISBN 0–671–71757-X

Typeset by Hewer Text Composition Services, Edinburgh
Printed and bound in Great Britain by
Butler & Tanner Ltd, Frome and London

CONTENTS

Primary Phase:
Impuissance

I

I let it happen. I wanted it to happen.

I could say that I was under some kind of magic spell, or that I was mesmerized, that I couldn't help myself, but Dr Gray would call that fudging. According to Dr Gray – and he's right – words like 'magic spell' and 'mesmerized' aren't proper explanations at all; they're just empty concepts, lame excuses for not looking any further for real explanations.

I *let it happen*, even though I was afraid. I wanted it to happen. I wanted *him*, more than anything on Earth ... I mean, more than anything *else* on Earth.

I wanted him, and Maldureve took me. He drew me a little way into his own world, which overlaps with ours but isn't really ours. He came out of the shadows and acquired flesh. He needed blood, and the blood he wanted most was mine, and I gave it to him. Knowing that it was impossible, knowing that *he* was impossible, I gave him my blood to drink. I can't really explain it. I have no excuse, if an excuse is what I need. I wanted it to happen, desperately. I needed it to happen. Why an ordinary person like me should need something like that, I don't know, but I did.

Maybe it would have been more appropriate, in a way, if we had done it out of doors, while dark shadows lay upon the world like a great blanket of mystery. Perhaps I should have laid myself down in that soft leaf-litter which carpeted the ground beneath the gnarled trees in the Marquis of Membury's Garden: the exotic, foreign trees which didn't really belong there. Perhaps

we should have made love in the heart of the moon-shadow cast
by one of the gabled attics of Wombwell House.

If he'd been hungrier, more desperate, I suppose it might
have been like that. But Maldureve was very patient – even
more patient than Gil. He was a gentleman, very scrupulous
about touching, pressuring. I suppose he had to be, when he
was only shadow and hadn't yet found substance, but even when
he'd put on flesh, he didn't pressure me. He knew that I would
give him what he wanted – what he needed – in my own time,
and he wanted to wait, for my sake. He lived with his hunger
until I was ready to appease it.

We did it, in the end, in a very ordinary place, which seemed
to me to be a million miles away from the shadowy world from
which he'd come, but wasn't. The borderlands are everywhere.
By that time, he could tolerate dull daylight. Even the glare of
the electric lights wouldn't have hurt or dissolved him, but we
steered clear of those anyhow.

It was in my room in Brennan Hall, which wasn't even in the
old part of the campus, although it was on the edge opposite to
the science blocks. We used the same bed on which I'd sweated
and wriggled and shuffled and shoved with Gil without – as yet
– going all the way. The light was off, but the curtains were
half-open. There was a yellow sodium light just outside, and
although the bulb was below the level of the sill, and had a
hood on it to reflect its light downwards, it still leaked a muted
fiery glow into the room. So we weren't exactly doing it in the
dark; once my eyes had adjusted to the dimness, I could see the
contours of his face.

I went into it, you see, with my eyes open. I knew exactly what
I was doing. I wasn't hypnotized.

It was very different from what I had expected sex to be like,
and from what sex eventually turned out to be like. It seems
slightly absurd to say that, given that it wasn't sex at all, and
there was no reason to think that it should be in any way similar
– but it *was* similar, in some ways. It wasn't sex, but it felt sexy.
In fact, although Dr Gray might consider it an incoherent thing
to say, it felt much sexier than sex. Perhaps what I really mean is
that Maldureve made me feel all the things that sex is supposed
to make you feel, whereas being screwed by Gil, when I finally

let him do it, didn't. Being screwed by Gil, even though we were civilized and gentle about it, felt much more like what I'd imagined Sharon must have felt, being screwed up against the back garden wall by some scrawny sixteen-year-old goth. She'd told me that it wasn't so bad, but she'd also confessed that she was high on ecstasy, so I knew that she probably hadn't a clue what it really had been like.

I'd never taken ecstasy or anything else. I valued my clarity of mind too much.

There was no real need for us to be naked, but we were. We both wanted to be. It must have been like sex for Maldureve too, although he didn't get excited in any recognizable way. He didn't have an erection. He didn't do anything with *that* at all – but he caressed me with his silky hands, lightly, affectionately. He touched my breasts, my shoulders, my back, my thighs, but he didn't touch me between my legs. It wasn't actual sex, but it was unbelievably sensuous.

His body was as silky as his hands: smooth, flawless, beautifully shaped. It wasn't soft, but its hardness wasn't coarse, like Gil's. Maldureve's body was like a work of art: something patiently carved out of some strange, exotic substance; like wood, but not wood; like marble, but not marble. He was massive, but he didn't seem oppressive. Somehow, he supported most of his own weight, the way Gil tried to but couldn't ever quite sustain, even when we were only messing about. I didn't feel uncomfortable under Maldureve – pinned down, yes; imprisoned, yes; but not trapped. It was like being tied up with rope so gentle and so velvety that the restraint was sheer delight.

I kissed him a lot, mostly around the neck and the shoulders. I think he liked being kissed on the neck best of all. I think that *meant* more to him. He kissed me, too. Eyes, mouth, neck, breasts – nothing lower down. His kisses were very gentle, but not weak. He didn't try to force his tongue into my mouth, but there was nothing damp and feeble about his kissing. They were strong kisses, insistent in their way.

I got very hot, I *burned* . . . long before he actually did anything . . . anything that could be thought of as a climax, as *it* . . . I was swimming in supernatural heat, in fervour, in tides of pleasure, the way I never had done in damp and distant dreams, or when

I brought myself off. Long before we got to the actual point of
it all, I felt that I was in another world, and that it was a better
world, where it felt better simply to *be* . . . the kind of world we
ought to be in all the time.

I don't mean to imply that I wasn't frightened. I was. But the
fear – even the thought of my blood being let – was just part
of it. I thought it would hurt more than it actually did, but the
thought of being hurt was just part of it, another dimension
of excitement. The fear was part of the thrill, as it always had
been with Maldureve. That was Maldureve's magic, if he had
any magic at all: the ability to transmute fear into something
welcome, something sexy.

I had never felt like that before, but once I'd had a taste of it,
I didn't ever want to go back. I felt that I was only just waking
up from a lifelong sleep.

When you think about it, there's no real reason why ordinary,
everyday consciousness should be as dull, as empty, as desolate,
as near to being nothingness as it is. We might be permanently
high on our own endorphins, if only natural selection had made
a better job of shaping our minds; but we're not, and that's
why we have to go searching for sensation, even in the most
absurd places: in pills and powders, mushrooms and weeds; in
the further reaches of the imagination; in relationships; in sex.

Maybe sex does deliver, for some. Maybe Jackie Collins really
can scale those heights of ecstasy she writes about. Maybe
Barbara Cartland really can get blown away simply by being
in love. Maybe I could have followed that route, if only I had
found the right man (not Gil), but I don't think so. I certainly
don't think that Maldureve was simply the right man: my Lord
Byron, my Rhett Butler. He got me to where I wanted to be
not because he was handsome, charming or overpowering, or
because I was 'in love' with him, and certainly not by virtue of
the awesome power of his utterly uninterested phallus. I was hot
and high long before he did *it*, but that was because of what he
was, and because of what *it* was, not because of the masculinity of
the form he'd taken on when he came out of the borderlands.

Maldureve really made me *live*, the way nothing ever had
before.

I have to say all this now because I still have to make it clear in my own mind. A lot has happened since that first fateful night in Brennan Hall, but I have to be certain that the memory I have of it is true and accurate and insightful. I have to be quite certain that I know what I did, and how it felt, because I have to be quite certain about what I am. I have to understand what happened to me, and how, and why, so that I can carry my life forward positively and authoritatively.

Being with Maldureve, and making love to Maldureve, was the peak experience of my life. It was so infinitely pleasurable, so fabulously intense, that had I been able to anticipate it in advance it would inevitably have become the only worthwhile goal of my future existence, even if it had been necessary for me to override all moral considerations, and all considerations of sanity and reason. Maldureve accomplished my awakening purely and simply by virtue of what he was and what he *did*.

I didn't know, at first, exactly what it was all leading up to. I knew what he was going to do, but I didn't know precisely how. I only knew that what I thought I knew – derived from all those stupidly gory books and ridiculously camp films – couldn't possibly be right. Vampires have no fangs.

Recording that, even now, seems like a descent from the sublime to the ridiculous. But it only seems that way because the words come trailing tattered clouds of association, like dusty cobwebs, which can never entirely be shaken off. Write 'vampire', think Christopher Lee, Bela Lugosi or – these days – any one of a hundred others. But it isn't like that. Not really – if 'really' is a word that I'm entitled to use here. Dr Gray would say not; but *Dr Gray doesn't know*. I do mean 'really', and I don't just mean 'real for me' or any other weak and cowardly evasion of authentic assertion. I mean *really*. Maldureve was a *real* vampire.

Maldureve came from the shadows and put on substance by slow degrees, but when he first drank my blood he was no longer a shadow, and he certainly was not a dream. He was on my bed in Brennan Hall, faintly illuminated by that inconvenient sodium light, holding me down and bringing me up . . . up as high as a kite, as high as a shooting star, as high as Heaven itself.

Cliché, I know, cliché, cliché, cliché . . . but what other words do we have for talking about our emotional ascents to the limits and beyond, except those which have been crudely hacked to death by romantic novelists for hundreds of years?

That's irrelevant, of course. It doesn't matter how others have abused the words; I must do the best I can to describe how I felt, and what it meant to me. I need to remember, to analyse, to understand.

At first, it was like a long kiss. He did use his teeth, but they were perfectly ordinary teeth – white and neat, with canines no longer or sharper than the average. And yes, he used the side of my neck, where – I suppose – the jugular vein is. But he didn't puncture the vein with his teeth, and he didn't shoot in any kind of hypodermic syringe, mosquito-fashion. What he did was to make my flesh change. By means of the teasing of his teeth and the seductive pressure of his lips he reconstructed my tissues so that they would yield what he wanted, what he needed, what he couldn't live without.

I felt my flesh changing, but it's difficult to describe because there's nothing to liken it to. I suppose a man might think of his prick becoming erect, but that's just a matter of inflation; this was much more complicated. If I'd been able to see what was happening, I could probably have organized my sensations better, but I couldn't see – not then. I could only lay my head back to bare my neck and study the delicate play of light and shadow on the ceiling.

Vampires can change their shape, within limits. It would take enormous effort and artistry to become a bat or a wolf, but lesser changes are easy enough. The flesh of a vampire isn't as fixed as human flesh, and when one feeds, he or she can communicate that relative fluidity, that power of change. Under the pressure of Maldureve's special kiss, the flesh of my neck seemed to flow, like some viscous liquid.

The sensation of flow was absolutely delicious.

When we speak of melting into someone's arms, we're trying to express the inexpressible by means of metaphor, but on those magical occasions when our world is infected by the world from which Maldureve emerged, we really can acquire the ability to melt under the pressure of a lover's kiss, and it really is a passionate experience: hot, beautiful, like floating beneath the surface of an ocean of pure calmness.

It must be wonderful, I thought, to melt like this entirely: to become lava, pure flux, glowing with internal fire . . .

I don't know what men feel when they come – when the semen spurts out of them – but it can't be smooth. It's spasmodic, interrupted, jagged. My orgasms tend that way, too, when I bring myself off. The flow of blood, when Maldureve began to feed, wasn't like that. Not only was it perfectly smooth, but there wasn't any sensation of expulsion through a channel or duct. However Maldureve's kiss had restructured the flesh of my neck, it hadn't turned it into any kind of tap or fountain, or even a tit, although it must have been something not too unlike a tit. Perhaps the process is more like a kind of osmosis, with the red blood cells migrating across some specially constituted membrane. It didn't feel as though he were *drinking* my blood; it felt as if my blood were somehow *reaching out* to him. The manner of our connection was quite unique, nothing at all like what you read in *Dracula* or see on the screen.

It was infinitely better, of course.

It was as if that connection – which was sustained, I suppose, for seven or eight minutes – affected all the blood in my body, and hence all the places in my body that my blood could reach while my heart pumped it round and round and round. The feeling filled me up, from top to toe. I can only call it ecstasy, though I certainly don't mean the stuff that Sharon and her goth had popped at the party; I mean the real thing.

I don't know how much blood Maldureve actually took – maybe less than a pint, maybe more – but he gave such an unimaginable thrill to all that remained that I couldn't have cared even if he'd taken it all. Even though it felt better simply to *be* than ever before, I think I could have been content to die while he was feeding off me.

Afterwards, of course, it was different. Afterwards, I felt good in a more relaxed sort of way, and though I knew that I'd want to do it again, eventually, there was nothing urgent about the feeling. But while it was happening, I was out of this world, untouchable by any fear of pain or injury or death.

I remember thinking that when I died, I wanted to die in that way. I instructed myself, quite earnestly, that I was to make certain that I died in the arms of a vampire lover:

weighed down but not oppressed; imprisoned by gentle, sensuous bonds.

If I died, that is.

While I lay beneath Maldureve, that night, I didn't want to die for a long time. *Being* had become so intoxicating, so lovely, so full of pleasure, now that I actually knew *how to be* . . .

That's what I learned, that night in my room, while Maldureve made love to me by the mute overflow of the yellow light that was supposed to make the pathway beside the Hall safe – safe from the kind of predator that waits in darkness near places where succulent young girls live and sleep, with the bright, sweet blood pulsing through their satin flesh . . .

That's what I learned, when I let the vampire feed on my blood. I learned *to be*. Maybe I should have known that before, but I never had. In spite of all the practice I'd had, between birth and being eighteen, I never had. Even Sharon had been better at it than I had, despite the fact that I'd had two years start on her; but I'd certainly made up for that now. I was way ahead of the field. I'd gone from last to first in one single, devastating swoop.

And I never looked back. If I'm looking back now, it's simply because I need to understand as fully as I can, before I can go forward again into the *terra incognita* of experience.

In spite of all that was later to happen – and I had already sensed, even then, that Maldureve knew fear as intimately and as keenly as he knew joy – I never once regretted what I'd done. I never for an instant wanted to be what I'd been before.

2

Going to university seemed to have been the one goal of my existence since I was fourteen or fifteen. Mum and Dad certainly took it for granted that it was a necessary next step in life, and did everything they could to make sure that I didn't miss my chance. They took great care to explain to me exactly

why it was so vital, and why I mustn't let anything distract me
from my school work. They seemed desperately afraid that I'd
let things slide if I got too interested in boys, and I saw that they
were right to be afraid when I watched what happened to some
of my friends.

They didn't seem to have such high expectations of Sharon,
maybe because they took it for granted that a younger sister
would make every effort to be different, to avoid being caught
up in a lifelong competition in which she'd always be two years
behind. Sometimes I envied Sharon, just a little. I didn't approve
when she dyed her hair black, and I certainly didn't approve
when she lost her virginity up against the wall, before she'd even
reached the age of consent, but there was something about being
a goth, about running just a little bit wild, which I couldn't help
but envy.

I wasn't tempted, though. I was careful not to get distracted,
to make sure that I kept the course of my life on the right
track. I knew that Mum and Dad were right, even if everything
that Sharon said about them was true. They were boring and
conventional, but they were right about education, about making
the most of one's opportunities. I wanted to make the most of
my opportunities. I wanted to build my life on a secure basis.
I was prepared to be patient.

University was the end I always had in mind, from the time I
first went to secondary school. I didn't ever want to be a rebel;
I wanted to be a swot.

Oddly enough, when I actually got to university – when Dad
waved goodbye after unloading all the stuff from the back of the
car into my room in Brennan Hall – I felt a sudden shock of panic,
and a sense of terrible unease, simply because I realized that I
didn't know what to do next. There were other goals already
about to replace the one I had just attained – first-year exams,
second-year exams, finals – but somehow, they didn't seem quite
important enough to fill the void. I tried to explain it to Mum
when I phoned home that first night, but she said I was just
nervous and would get over it soon enough. What else could
she say? I had every right to be nervous, after all the warnings
she'd been careful to remind me of on the way down. She was
nervous, too, of all the things that might happen to me now that

I was out of sight and there was no one to insist that I be safe indoors by eleven at the latest.

They were good parents, Mum and Dad. They loved their kids, and they still quite liked one another, after a fashion. They were the kind of parents who made it difficult to believe in things like divorce and child abuse. They stuck to the script, and they played their parts with real conviction. They weren't ashamed to be conventional; in fact, they were proud of being ordinary, of having all the ordinary ambitions. They thought that if everybody in the world could think like them and live like them, everything would be okay: no hatred, no violence, no evil. All it took, they thought, was decency. They were decent about everything, including Sharon's hair. They expected a certain amount of adolescent rebellion. 'It's only young blood,' Dad would say. They'd expected it from me but they hadn't got it, and that really pleased them. 'You've an old head on young shoulders,' Dad told me, when I was packing to leave. 'You'll go far.' I was really pleased. 'Make sure you eat properly' was all Mum said, but I knew what she meant.

In spite of Mum's reassurances, I didn't get any less nervous during the first few days. If I hadn't been terrified enough already, my first meeting with my tutor would have done the job.

Dr Gray was over sixty, and not very well preserved. His hair was wispy, and he looked as if he had once been a much taller man who was now slowly crumpling and collapsing into a shortness he was unprepared to tolerate. He was nearly as thin as I, but his skin was so slack that he must once have been much fuller of face and figure. His office, which was on the third floor, right under the eaves of Wombwell House, was full of books and dust. Some people might have said it was full of character, too, but Mum would have said it was disgracefully scruffy. Unlike the offices on the lower floors, it had a carpet, and its thick red curtains were not in the conventional university style. The fireplace had never been bricked up, and the grate was still in it, although the room was centrally heated. Dr Gray didn't seem out of place as long as he was in his office, but he and his office taken together seemed to be not only out of place but out of time. What decade or century they really belonged to I couldn't tell, but I knew that it wasn't mine.

'Charet,' he said, when I first told him my surname. 'Is that French in origin?'

'I don't know,' I said, and immediately felt that the answer was inadequate. 'I don't have any French relatives. My father says that there was an inquisitor named Clement Charet in the sixteenth century, who burned witches in the south of France, but that he can't have been an ancestor of ours because he was a Dominican monk and wouldn't have been able to get married.'

'Quite so,' he said. 'It would not have been a matter for undue anxiety in any case, given that a propensity for witch-burning is highly unlikely to be hereditary. Long before the university received its royal charter it was a theological college, and probably produced its fair share of inquisitors, so we start even on that score. But I shouldn't mock – it's because the philosophy department was once affiliated to the theology department that it had sufficient prestige to be allotted Wombwell House when the family petered out and abandoned its estates to become a university campus. Wombwell is the family name of the Marquis of Membury, as you probably know. That little woodland behind the house is still known as the Marquis of Membury's Garden, after a nineteenth-century scion of the family who persisted in bringing back seeds from his various foreign tours, which he then flung about at random, to see which would germinate and which would not. The wood has several exotic trees found nowhere else in the northern hemisphere. Were you interviewed before being accepted?'

'No,' I said, wishing that I had been. 'I got a conditional offer on my A levels. Three Cs. I got three As.'

He sighed. 'I wish we could interview all our applicants,' he said. 'So many of them apply to us in the mistaken belief that philosophy is all about learning to run one's life, or selecting some kind of mystical faith that might make one feel happy.'

My cheeks must have been burning. I felt that I was there under false pretences. I didn't say anything, because I didn't know what to say.

'No matter,' he went on, sadly. 'My job, as your tutor, is to monitor your academic progress, and to provide you with a point of contact within the department should you experience any problems. Many years ago, tutors stood *in loco parentis* to their students, but ever since the government obligingly lowered the age of majority to eighteen, students have been assumed to be adults and are held to be responsible for their own moral safety. Older members of staff like myself, however, for whom obsolete ideas die hard, still feel a certain obligation to pry in the interests of our tutees' welfare. May I enquire whether you are a sufferer from the complaint known as anorexia nervosa?'

'No,' I said, startled by the question although it was by no means the first time I'd been asked. 'I'm just thin.'

'I'm glad to hear it,' he said. 'Although I suppose I shouldn't be entirely content with such an answer, given that one of the symptoms of the disease is rumoured to be a reluctance to admit to suffering from it. I don't mean to imply that you are in any way dishonest, but I do feel obliged to mention that were you, in fact, to be suffering from any such disorder, you would be unable to rely on me to interfere with its course. I could not claim to understand or sympathize with a desire on your part to starve yourself, but as an old-fashioned liberal I would defend to the death – anyone's death – your right to do so.'

What could I say to that? I was eighteen years old, away from home for the first time, utterly intimidated, and out of my depth. I just blushed and wished that I were somewhere else. Dr Gray scared me. He was uncontrollable. He could say what he liked, and he had a licence to be clever at my expense. I wasn't sure he actually cared whether I was anorexic or not.

I wasn't. I was just thin.

Things didn't seem to be getting any easier when I was introduced, a little later, to the other two members of my tutorial group, in whose company I would have to face Dr Gray once a week, so that he could discuss our essays with us. One was a boy named Daniel Calvert, who was trying to grow a beard and not having much luck with it; he seemed bright and rather argumentative, but easily flustered and confused. His manner veered from awkward aggression to defensive sullenness and back again with bewildering rapidity as Dr Gray smoothly tied him in knots. The other was a rather plain and stout mature student in her late twenties, named Cynthia Leigh. She wore

a GAY PRIDE badge which featured two overlapping white circles
with pendant crosses. She was discreet enough not to try to be
clever, and thus avoided the more sarcastic edge of Dr Gray's
tongue, but he seemed slightly pained when she made a point of
informing us all that she was a single parent and that she hoped
he would bear in mind the occasional difficulties that might arise
from her situation.

We all listened politely while Dr Gray tried to explain to us
that his job was not to tell us the truth, but merely to challenge
whatever beliefs we happened to have or to adopt, in order to
subject them to a proper trial by ordeal. I didn't understand.
I simply assumed, on the basis of common sense and past
experience, that what a teacher was supposed to do was to tell
you the truth and explain it carefully, so that you'd know why it
was true. Even though I did know – in spite of Dr Gray's fears
– that much of philosophy had to do with trying to decide what
the word 'truth' actually meant and what 'an explanation' actually
was, I was still slow to understand that Dr Gray's method of
teaching really was teaching, and not cruel mockery.

In time, I began to see why it all made sense, and that Dr Gray
wasn't quite the ogre that he seemed, but after that first dismal
introductory session I went back to my room convinced that I
had made a dreadful mistake, and that I was not cut out for
university at all.

The freshers' dance was that evening. I wasn't sure that I
ought to go. One of Mum's many warnings had concerned the
number of older boys who would be avid for every opportunity
to take advantage of me, and who would regard the dance as a
kind of meat-market. I knew that she was right, and that the
darkness beyond the madly flashing strobe lights would be full
of predators on the lookout, all determined to score with some
innocent new girl who would be carried away by the excitement
of it all. On the other hand, I didn't want to be left out, and I
didn't want to be a coward. Sharon, for one, would have been
utterly contemptuous if I'd missed it – all the more so because
the group that was playing was a minor gothic band called the
Night Land who normally did the northern circuit. She'd seen
them on one of her trips to Leeds.

I'd never been with Sharon on any of her outings, and I

didn't really share her taste in music. Music was one of the things I'd always set aside, one of the things I didn't want to be interested in. That might have had something to do with Sharon's enthusiasm. I always bought her a tape for Christmas and her birthday, and she always took care to ask me to get her the one she really wanted. Mostly she played them to herself, using her Walkman so as not to disturb Mum and Dad, but during the summer holidays, when we were both at home, she'd use Dad's midi system whenever Mum was out shopping, playing her favourites at full blast. She said that was the only way to hear them properly – to fill the room with sound and let the drumbeat resonate your ribcage. This summer's favourite had been *Vision Thing* by the Sisters of Mercy. Last summer's – that was before she'd become a dedicated goth – had been *Stay Sick* by the Cramps. I could still hum most of the choruses from both records; they'd seeped into my consciousness. In future years, I thought, I'd still be able to remember those summers every time I heard any track off the relevant tape.

I knew that I had to go to the dance, for Sharon's sake. It would be something to connect us.

I went with a group of girls who lived on the same corridor in Brennan Hall. The girl who lived next door to me was called Karen, and though she was very friendly she seemed very different from me. She told me that she'd never been north of Watford, and though she was only being flippant I felt put down. Everybody else I met seemed to be from the south too; I felt like an outsider, and was suddenly self-conscious about my accent. The other girls and I didn't have much chance to get to know one another once we were at the dance, because the pauses in between the music weren't long enough to fit in more than a couple of questions and answers. Over the course of the evening the group dissolved by slow degrees as its members were picked off by the predators. I felt slightly hurt that I was nearly the last to be targeted.

I knew, and understood perfectly well, that meeting Gil was just a freak of random chance. There was a sense, to be sure, in which he selected me: he saw, he found me acceptable, he moved in – but I could have been anyone, really. Anyone not too sour of face. It didn't even matter that I was averagely pretty, and not fat; he didn't look at me and ask himself, 'Is she beautiful?' he looked at me and asked himself, 'Is she the type to spread her legs?' If he'd been certain that I would let him screw me, it wouldn't have mattered if I'd had a paper bag over my head and twenty pounds of lard on my hips. I knew that even then, but there wasn't anything I could do about it. It was, as Dad would have said, the way of the world.

Not that there was anything wrong with Gil. He was better than anything I could reasonably have expected. He was tall, handsome and a lot older than most of the boys skulking in the shadows. He was mature and self-assured, and his accent was even more exotic than mine. Sharon would have said that I was lucky, and she'd have been right. In spite of everything, she'd have been right.

Right from the beginning, he pressured me – literally pressured me. The dance floor was crowded, its margins even more so. Circumstances licensed his pushing up against me, thigh to thigh, hand to arm. I didn't like his touching me, at first – I'd never liked being touched, and ours wasn't a very physical family – but I knew I'd have to get used to it, if I was going to go to bed with him. And I was. Not right away, but eventually. From the very beginning, I knew that.

When temporary quietness gave him his chance, the first thing he said was: 'You look lost.'

'Not as lost as you sound,' I said, trying desperately to figure out which way was west. 'I think America's over there.' He grinned, not so much at the joke as at the pleasure of having his accent recognized. He was proud of being an American.

'What's your name?' he asked.

'Anne Charet.'

'Is that French?'

'No. I'm from Yorkshire. Near Sheffield.'

'I think this band's from Yorkshire. Are they what you'd call a gothic band?'

'Yes. My sister saw them play once. She's got all the gear – black jacket, black jeans, black hair.' I pointed to the place by the stage where the few goths in the audience had congregated. There were only half a dozen, and I think they'd come in from off-campus. I couldn't believe that there'd be any goths among the students. He looked at them vaguely, but he wasn't really interested

'I'm Gil Molari,' he said.

'Is that Italian?'

'No – not any more, anyhow. I'm from California, a small town south of LA. Are you new here?'

'Yes.'

'Me too. I'm a postgrad, doing research in psychology. Where d'you live?'

'Brennan Hall.'

'I've got a flat on some kind of off-campus estate. It's run by something called a housing association, but it's all university people – staff, technicians, postgrads. D'you want a drink?'

He only just managed to get the last question in before the music started again. I had to answer with a nod.

He grinned when I accepted the drink. It was supposed to be a friendly smile, but it showed that he couldn't suppress his satisfaction at the thought that I'd taken the first step on the slippery slope.

I let him pay for the drink – and the others. It was what he seemed to expect, though I don't suppose a local boy would have done. We didn't dance much. Being American, he didn't really know what a gothic band was, and tried to make a joke of it.

'The lead singer does look a bit like Frankenstein's monster,' he said, inaccurately, when there was further space for talk. He didn't listen to what I said in reply. I suppose he figured that we could talk any old time, once the vital business of the night was out of the way.

He was so transparent that he might as well have come straight out with 'Your place or mine?' or 'How about it?' but he figured that he ought to be subtle, to creep up on me, to pressure me inch by inch. He was ready to fail, though – he was by no means certain then that he would make enough progress to make the eventual end inevitable, a week or a month later. He just kept making hopeful contact, one nudge at a time, one grope at a time, one question or tawdry joke at a time.

'You're not anorexic, are you?'

'No, just thin.'

'Do you want another drink?'

'All right.'

'Is this your first time away from home?'

'Yes – is it yours?'

'Hell, no. What d'you think of the campus?'

'The old part of it's nice. My tutor's office is in one of the oldest buldings – Wombwell House.'

'I saw it – weird place. Nothing like that on our campuses back home. My lab's over this side, in the newest building of all. I'll feel at home there all right. What's a tutor do?'

'Teaches tutorials. At Oxford or Cambridge every student has individual tutorials, I think. Here, we have groups of three or four. We have to do an essay every week, and we discuss them with our tutors. We have lectures as well, of course.'

'It's different back home. The classes are much bigger, even when you're a postgrad. Here, there's just me and my supervisor – and the test tubes.'

'Test tubes? I thought you were a psychologist.'

'Not a couch potato, a hands-on psychologist. Brain chemistry. Very messy. Some animal work – rats, rabbits, cats – but mostly tissue-culture stuff, electrophoresis and chromatography. D'you want another drink?'

And so on. Just a series of sound bites, squeezed between the band's pauses.

When he walked me home, the pressure intensified. He put his arm round me, as though to protect me from the creatures of the night, staking his claim so that any freaks and rapists waiting in the bushes would know that they had to stay away.

It was a fairly long walk. The Students' Union was in the corner of the campus furthest away from Brennan Hall, near the main road into the city. We had to pass between the various sets of science labs, and the buildings which housed the main lecture halls. A lot of the rooms in the science labs were still lit up inside, even though it was past midnight. Some were always lit up, even when they were empty, shining through the darkest night like beacons, because their blinds were never drawn. Beyond them, there was an area of near-Stygian gloom, which included Wombwell House and the little wood known as the Marquis of Membury's Garden.

Gil kissed me for the first time – wetly, weakly – on the bridge over the stream, and with that kiss we sealed our tacit compact, although he knew well enough that it wasn't going any further that night. As we passed from the part of the campus to which he belonged to the part to which I belonged, past the hulking shadow of Wombwell House – behind whose curtained windows not a single bright light blazed – and back on to the concrete path which led to Brennan Hall, we were already committed to one another: not just to one forgettable screw (he was too honourable a man for that) but to an evolving relationship of a perfectly ordinary kind.

I was more pleased with that assumed commitment than with anything else that had happened that day, or anything else that happened in the week which followed. I didn't really expect very much from the relationship, but I was content with it.

It was what there was. It was life.

I didn't believe in vampires, then.

3

At first, naturally enough, I thought Maldureve was a phantom of my own imagination. Even when I became convinced that he wasn't – which didn't take long – I knew that I would never be able to convince anyone else of the objective reality of my situation. I knew that he would have to remain a secret, not merely from Gil and Mum and Dad but even from Sharon. It was a pity, but there was simply no way around it.

It is unfortunately true, as Dr Gray once observed in one of his little homilies, that there are facts which one person can know for certain, without ever being able to assemble evidence adequate to prove the fact to another. These are mostly of two kinds. One consists of external events which leave no unambiguous physical traces, to which one person is a sole witness; the other consists of events internal to consciousness, like thoughts, feelings, flights of fancy and dreams. Dr Gray went on to point out that people to whom events of the first kind are reported always have the option, if they wish to deny the fact while accepting the truthfulness of the believer, of suggesting that an event of the second kind has mistakenly been taken for an event of the first kind. He added, sarcastically, that it is fashionable nowadays to use this strategy to account for all sightings of ghosts and all accounts of abduction by alien spaceships. I knew that an encounter with a vampire would be treated in the same way, and that I would be thought to be at best deluded or at worst mad if I tried to tell anyone about Maldureve – especially Gil, and most especially of all Dr Gray.

So I kept silent. I was powerless to do otherwise.

It was difficult enough, at the very beginning, to convince myself that I was neither mad nor deluded. Mercifully, I didn't try too hard. Some people wouldn't have had the mental flexibility. Some people, in similar circumstances, could easily have convinced themselves that they *were* mad. Someone like that would have turned her back on Maldureve and refused to see him. Someone like that would have refused point-blank to help him emerge from the borderlands. Someone like that would never have known what she was missing.

I take no credit for being different. It wasn't that I was unusually brave or unusually intelligent. It was just the way I was made: a quirk of nature. Everybody's different, one way or another. I just happened to be different in the right sort of way.

I first met Maldureve in the curious little patch of woodland behind Wombwell House, which Dr Gray had called the Marquis of Membury's Garden. Given Dr Gray's account of its origins, the wood can't have been very old, but that wasn't relevant; Maldureve was neither an echo of some remote antiquity nor an effusion of the alien vegetation. He didn't need a time-hallowed tomb for a point of origin. He just needed someone who could see him.

The stream which divides the campus into two runs through the wood from north to south. One of the footpaths connecting the two halves runs from east to west along its southern edge. That path is the most convenient one connecting the eastern part of the campus to Wombwell House and Brennan Hall, and is in almost constant use during the day, but at that time many students avoided it by night because it was so poorly lit. The lamps illuminating the pathway were discreet by comparison with those on the other paths; although they were electric, they were mounted on the same Victorian wrought-iron columns that once housed gas lamps.

When I first arrived, I was inclined to avoid the path myself. Like most other people – boys as well as girls – I tended to walk from the Students' Union to the Hall by way of the road which ran around the perimeter of the campus, unless I was in a group. Once or twice, though, I found myself taking the path, quite unthinkingly.

I'm sure there was nothing sinister in this. I've always been the kind of person who can easily get lost in thought, and when you're not really paying attention to what you're doing you tend to be guided by habit. My legs trod the path often enough in daylight to take it automatically by night, if I didn't make a conscious decision to go another way. That's all it was. I wasn't *drawn* to the path. Maldureve didn't *summon* me.

Usually, when I took the footpath by night, I realized what I'd done as soon I came to the dimly lit stretch by the bridge. Sometimes, if there was a group of people ahead of me or behind me, I'd hurry or dawdle in order to mingle with them until we reached the brighter glare of the sodium lights. When there wasn't – more often than not there wasn't – I'd just grit my teeth and carry on, walking quickly but refusing to be panicked into breaking into a run.

The night I encountered Maldureve for the first time was only slightly unusual. I must have been tired and particularly deep in thought, because I didn't even notice that I was on the path until I was over the bridge and passing by the border of the wood, and I must have been moving fairly sluggishly, because when I looked up – when my attention was caught – there was no inertia to carry me on; I was practically standing still. There was a tune going through my head, just a chorus repeating over and over. It was something from *Vision Thing*, but I can't remember what. It died away when I realized where I was, fading out to leave me all alone.

It wasn't a sound that had made me stop. There were always sounds in the wood, by day and by night: birds and animals in the undergrowth. Gil told me that there were rats and mice, and possibly weasels, but I'd only ever seen blackbirds. Maldureve made no sound at all – not to begin with. Even when he began to talk to me, he may not have made any actual sound, because his voice always sounded like a fainter-than-faint whisper, more inside the ear than out.

That first time, he didn't say a word.

He can't have caught my eye, either, though it was certainly what I saw that held me to the spot once I'd stopped. He was so very elusive to the eye, at that time, that it was easier to take him for a trick of the shadows than an actual presence. He wasn't a *solid* presence – not then.

It's tempting to say that my awareness of him must have been by extrasensory perception or some kind of sixth sense, simply because it was at first subconscious; but in retrospect, I think it was simply the odour of him that reached me. Our sense of smell is better than we think; it's just that we've lost the habit of paying attention to its signals. If you concentrate hard, it's possible to train your sense of smell to make very delicate distinctions between different perfumes or wines; so it's reasonable to assume, I think, that odours play a greater part in the business of recognition than we're consciously aware of. I'm sure, now, that it was that scent of Maldureve's, which I'd never encountered before, that made me stop.

When I became more familiar with it, I virtually stopped noticing it, but it was easy enough to make myself pay attention long enough to search for a description. It was a subtle smell, more pleasant than unpleasant; it was sweet but not at all sickly, and flowery rather than musky. It wasn't the smell of blood, nor was it that slightly honeyish smell which sometimes hovers around diabetics. It had a kind of cleanness about it, but it wasn't sharp like ammonia or warm like menthol. That was what brought me to a standstill, and made me look around at the trees.

It was mid-October. The weather hadn't yet turned cold. All the deciduous trees were losing their foliage, but there were evergreens mixed in with the others – some holly bushes and some kinds of pine or fir – and the pattern of shadows made by the various kinds of branches, so palely illuminated by the wan light trickling down from the tops of the old lampposts, was incredibly complicated. There was a light wind, which stirred the branches just enough to make the shadows quiver and quake.

I saw him instantly – although, as I said, I wasn't sure at first that he was anything more than an optical illusion.

He was tall, but it wasn't possible to make out how stoutly built he was because of the cloak he was wearing, or seemed to be wearing. The shapelessness of the hanging cloak was what suggested most strongly that he wasn't there at all – that he was just something my startled imagination had conjured out of a haphazard mess of shadows – but it was the face that I looked at, as anyone would. The face became clearer as I looked at it. The eyes didn't disappear or dissolve as I tried to meet their gaze, as they would have done if he'd only been some caprice of the branches and their shadows.

I looked at him and he looked back – not threateningly, mournfully, or any of the ways that a spectral creature is supposed to look, nor even lovingly, but simply interestedly, as though I'd caught his attention as surprisingly as he'd caught mine.

There was one crucial moment when my startlement might have turned to shock, and my shock to fear. In a sense, that would have been the natural progression. The newborn fear could easily have fed on itself, escalating into panic, forcing me to run away. I think my whole life turned upon that single moment, because that entirely natural and rational process was somehow caught and held.

I was afraid – more than a little – but there was no escalation, no further fear feeding on that first seed of alarm.

Perhaps I should have panicked. Most people would have done, and I'd always been more than averagely frightened by everything to which one might reasonably react with fear. It would have been quite reasonable to be terrified – if there *were* a man in the woodland, at that time of night, lying in wait, then the overwhelming probability was that he was up to no good. A university campus, like a hospital nurses' home, is the kind of place which draws would-be rapists and assorted lesser freaks like a magnet. Then again, there's nothing unreasonable about being frightened of the dark itself; the dark makes us vulnerable in every possible way, physically and psychologically.

Perhaps I should have been terrified, but I wasn't.

My lack of fear isn't just an incidental fact worth mentioning, an oddity to be noted. It's something more vital than that. Put yourself in my place: imagine yourself as a lightly built eighteen-year-old girl on a lonely, dimly lit pathway, at dead of night, with trees stirring in a light wind. You've been lost in thought, and now you've snapped out of it you're slightly bewildered, because you don't quite remember how you came to be there. You look round, responding to some signal you're not fully aware of, and you see a man – or what might be a man – looking back at you from the shadows, *interestedly*.

And you find, perversely, that your heart isn't leaping into your mouth, that your throat isn't constricting in sudden anxiety. The single most astonishing, unreasonable, incredible fact about this situation is that you don't panic.

The absence of terror seemed to me, as it would to you, like some kind of miracle, a liberation. It caught and held me much more effectively than the kind of terror which is supposed to root you to the spot.

Now, looking back, it's easy enough to find in that perverse reaction some kind of echo or premonition of that intense intoxicating pleasure which was ultimately to be mine by virtue of my acquaintance – my intimate acquaintance – with Maldureve. Perhaps, even then, he had already reached out to touch something elementary and fundamental in my state of being. At the time, it was very puzzling.

I suppose that if I'd had to put a name to it then, I would have called it a kind of tranquillization, but it wasn't at all like the effect of the Valium I'd had to take when I first started having periods, and again before my A levels. Valium flattens out your feelings, but it's like a heavy roller ironing them out; it weighs down on you; you can feel the sinuses in your face; the moment you relax, you become drowsy. This was something light and airy, not at all oppressive.

'Who are you?' I said, uncertainly. I was uncertain because I wasn't sure that there was anyone there, not because I was afraid.

He didn't answer, but I could see his face perfectly clearly,

or the eyes at least, and I knew that he was really looking at me
– *really* looking, *at me*.

'I'm not afraid,' I said. I suppose I'd have said the same if I *had*
been, and I still was, just a little – but it wasn't the sort of fear to
make me run; it was more like a thrill of pure excitement.

Again, he said nothing, but he was still looking. It didn't seem
that he was staring, but he didn't look away. I could see the line
of his shoulder quite clearly, and I could make out the texture of
that dark cloak. It was a long cloak, jet black in colour and very
plain. It was the cloak, and only the cloak, that made me think of
vampires – I did think of vampires even then, but I didn't think
he was one, only that the cloak somehow made him seem like
one. But the cloak didn't seem anachronistic – it didn't make
me think that he might be a refugee from some other time, like
the ghost of someone long departed.

I don't know how long I stood there, watching him. Perhaps
it was only a few seconds. Our memories of time are so easily
distorted, and common sense suggests that the whole thing must
have been over very quickly; though common sense, I suppose,
would also be likely to declare that nothing happened at all. It
seemed like longer. It seemed like four or five minutes, at the
very least.

Why should I stand so long, watching a man who was too
impolite to answer my questions? *Because I wasn't terrified*. The
sensation of not being terrified, because it was so very unlikely
and inappropriate, was both a mystery and a luxury; it was a state
of mind I wanted to savour, to cling to, to practise. I felt that if
I rushed away, behaving exactly as I would have if I'd panicked,
I'd lose the feeling for ever, and never find it again. So I stayed,
and I looked at the man in the dark cloak, and I let him look at
me. I hoped that I'd see him again, even before I decided that
it was all too absurd, and that I had to go.

'I'm sorry,' I said to him, out loud. 'It's late, and I have to
go.'

He didn't say a word, but I had the impression that he accepted
my apology. Perhaps he bowed, ever so slightly. Perhaps he
dropped his gaze, just for an instant. Perhaps he became slightly
less distinct, even before I turned away.

Then I walked on. After twelve or fourteen paces – slow,

unhurried paces – I looked back, suddenly quite uncertain of what I'd seen. There was no sign of him, but that wasn't surprising. The angle was different, the light was different, the shadows were all over the place. If he'd been as solid as I was, and still standing there in the same place, watching me walk away, I might easily have been unable to see him. I knew that. I also knew that *something* had happened, because I was only just, by degrees, becoming anxious again. My very ordinary, very understandable fear of the dark was beginning to come back.

The tune I'd briefly lost started repeating again in my head, as though the band had come to play a concert in the privacy of my head. I could hear the voice of Andrew Eldritch, the lead singer of the Sisters of Mercy, and even though I knew that he was only a memory impressed upon my mind by Sharon's tape during the lazy weeks of summer, he seemed almost to be there, singing just for me. My heart was thumping like a drum – which was oddly appropriate, in a way, because Sharon had told me more than once that the person who played the drums for the Sisters of Mercy wasn't really a person at all. He was a machine called Doktor Avalanche.

The song that the man in my head and the machine in my heart were playing together was called 'I Don't Exist When You Don't See Me'. But they did exist. They came from Leeds.

By the time I got back to the Hall, the cold unease of my everyday anxieties had fully returned, but its presence only served to make me aware of how remarkable and how exciting it had been to be without it, even for a few moments.

Perhaps I'm making too much of a mere absence, a state of mind, but I don't think so. There's probably nothing in us that is further from conscious control than fear. Like pain, it's an irresistible sensation, a dreadful monster which lives in the darkness within, emerging whenever circumstance calls it forth to torment us. Like pain, it can be anaesthetized, but only by such brute force as will simultaneously deaden our thoughts and our spirits. The other emotions aren't really like that, although we sometimes pretend that they are. Loving, and even grieving, are things that we have to *do*, even though their force is sometimes compelling. Fear, on the other hand, is something that just *happens* to us; it surges up, and may render us utterly helpless as easily as it forces us to panic-stricken action. Brave men may learn to live with fear, and fools may blind themselves to some of their own dangers, but no one – *no one* – can tame and domesticate fear and render it impotent. There's nothing quite so frightening as fear itself. I really believe that.

I had always been a fearful child – always small, thin, shy, lonely. When I was very small, I thought I was a coward; but the older I got, the more I came to suspect that other people knew fear far more intimately than they ever had the courage to admit. I began to see evidence which told me that my mum knew fear, that my dad knew fear, that even the bullies in the schoolyard and the heroes on the TV news knew fear. Maybe they coped better than I did, but they *knew*.

You know, too, and I know that you know. So you ought to understand me when I tell you how good it felt to be in a situation where any ordinary mortal would have felt sheer terror, and yet to be unclaimed and unhurt by fear. And you ought to understand, too, how I knew that it was real, and not just a figment of my imagination, not just an optical illusion taken for reality by mistake. If it had been a product of my own disordered, frightened mind, I couldn't possibly have confronted it as I did, quite calmly.

I didn't accept that conclusion readily; I told myself that what I had seen was only an illusion and that my reaction had just been folly, but I think I knew deep down, even then, that the man in the cloak had to be real, and *powerful* – powerful enough, and magical enough, to make me unafraid.

People take it too much for granted that encounters with the supernatural are terrifying. Actually, there's nothing more natural than terror. It's when the terror doesn't come, when the seed of fear is containable and thrilling, that you have good reason to believe that you've entered the borderlands, or glimpsed something in there, which might – with the proper encouragement – come out. I know this now, and I was on my way to this understanding from the crucial moment of that first brief encounter.

Anyone who had ever been any sort of coward – *anyone* – would have understood why I felt a need to seek out the man in the cloak again, to find him, to become intimate with him, to offer him anything I had if only he would make me unafraid for ever.

Alas, he was not unafraid himself. He was real, he was powerful and he was magical, but he was not unafraid.

4

I knew that I'd have to let Gil screw me eventually. It was just part of the dynamic of the situation. He was always polite, but his politeness was based in expectation; the pressure he put on was steady but relentless. He knew that in a way I'd already consented, and he was eager to push the process through to its appointed end. As Sharon would have said, he was panting to get inside my knickers. He wanted to do it in his flat but I decided that I would rather it happened in my room, at least the first time.

It might all have been different, I think, if it had been summer instead of winter, but the university year starts in October, and there are two terms of winter before you ever get to the long, warm days when you can spend more time in the open air. I think things got set up that way because the long vacation was originally arranged to coincide with the harvest; only when the serious business of laying in an adequate store of the necessities of life was taken care of could people's thoughts turn to education. Whatever the reason, the effect is that life in university begins indoors, and stays there as the nights darken and the wind blows icier.

It wasn't a particularly cold winter – it was mild enough to lend a little support to everyone's anxieties about the greenhouse effect – but it was still winter, grey and unpleasant. It forced relationships into places where they were surrounded by walls – into corners, under the dead glare of artificial light. If we'd been able to walk about more, in the afternoon sun, with greenery all around us and the scent of flowers, I think I could have found more pleasure in being with Gil: more delight, more comfort. But winter casts a pall over daylit life, stealing its colour.

Gil was the kind of person who would have blossomed in the sun. He was quite intrigued by the phenomena of the English winter – in California, he said, things are pretty much the same all the year round – and he professed to like it. But he didn't really like it at all. His tan faded by imperceptible degrees and, almost as if he were a chameleon, his Californian buoyancy cooled into a reasonable imitation of English sobriety. He said that he didn't mind the cold, but he felt it. He always had the central heating in his flat turned up a few degrees too high, and he wore some kind of flying jacket all the time, even indoors. He spent more time than was strictly necessary at the labs where he worked, and I think that it was because they were always warm. He said that it was because he was fascinated by his experiments, and got separation anxiety if he was away from his animals and his purple blotches for too long, but I didn't believe him. In the heat of summer, he'd have been outdoors all the time, with his shirt half unbuttoned, soaking up the radiation, and he'd have laughed more and bounced with enthusiasm. I didn't see the best of him.

I never saw the best of him.

I asked him once why he hadn't stayed in California to do his research.

'It's a better system here,' he said. 'I already did some postgrad back in the States. It was mostly programmed classroom work. Course after course. Here, it's just the research project, and I'll get much more freedom to design my experiments once Viners has shown me the ropes. Anyway, there are problems back home getting licences to do the kind of work I'm doing – there's a lot of very vocal opposition to experiments using live animals and research on viruses, and when you've got both together things get completely tied up in red tape. Viners doesn't seem to have too much of that kind of crap holding him back.'

'People here get angry about animal experiments too,' I said.

'Yeah, but you don't have a Freedom of Information Act which means that you have to tell every sucker and his cousin exactly what you're doing, and a University Ethics Committee to sit in judgement on every experiment. In ninety-nine fields out of a hundred the US is ahead of Britain because we spend more money, but in psychotropic genetics Mike Viners is way ahead of anyone else. When I heard him speak at a conference in LA I knew he was doing the kind of stuff I wanted to be in on. My dad pulled a few strings for me – he knew some guys at the foundation that paid me to come over. They expect me to go back in three years' time with a lot of useful data, ready to kick-start some kind of project at CalTech. It's a big break for me. There's an element of scholarly espionage in what I'm doing – not that it's secret or criminal or anything. Viners knows that I'm here to plunder his expertise and take what I learn back home, but he just wants to get the work done, and your SERC or whatever won't fund the number of research assistants he thinks he needs.'

I found it difficult to understand exactly what it was that Gil was doing, although I tried hard to be interested. I hadn't done enough science at school to follow all the jargon, and though he tried to explain it in easy terms he simply couldn't do it without using the private language of his subject. It wasn't easy to follow his arguments all the way through.

'Psychotropic means mind-altering,' he told me. 'Intoxicants like pot and alcohol, hallucinogens like LSD and psilocybin – they're all psychotropics. The familiar ones are chemicals produced by plants. Heaven alone knows what good they are to the plants which make them; I don't think anyone has ever managed to find out what opium does for the poppy or psilocybin for the magic mushroom. Since we invented organic chemistry and started messing about with the natural psychotropics, we've been able to devise new variants of the traditional compounds and invent dozens more but it's a pretty hazardous business trying to figure out exactly what psychotropic properties new substances have. A lot of them are highly toxic, and there are ethical problems inhibiting experimentation.

'What makes a substance psychotropic is that it interferes in some way with the ordinary chemistry of the brain. Some drugs enhance or inhibit the passage of information across the synapses, promoting hallucinations or inducing a kind of remote, spaced-out feeling. Morphine and other opium derivatives mimic a class of chemicals which the body itself uses to control the activity of the nervous system – the endorphins. Now we're beginning to understand the chemistry of the nervous system, we're beginning to understand why various kinds of psychotropics have the effects they do, and we're better able to use our knowledge of chemistry to design new psychotropics from scratch.

'Psychotropic genetics is a fancy name for the study of the mind-changing capabilities of DNA. It started out as a way of trying to investigate the hereditary components of certain mental illnesses – manic depression, schizophrenia and so on. Mental aberrations like those do seem to have a brain-chemistry component, although there's a lot of argument about whether the chemical changes in the brain are a cause or a consequence, or sometimes one and sometimes the other. Anyway, it went on from there to study the mental states associated with diseases – if you like, the psychotropics of nausea, of induced coma, of feverish delirium or of simply feeling ill. Psychotropic theory isn't all to do with getting stoned.

'Viners is interested in the psychotropic effects of fairly ordinary viruses – ones that cause mild fevers. They're all naturally occurring viruses, but he's imported some of them from the tropics. Some of them are animal viruses, but most are viruses that can affect lots of species, including humans. We're trying to study the effects the viruses have on the brain chemistry of the animals, in the hope of getting a better understanding of the way our dreams and our everyday consciousness are linked to brain chemistry and the genes.'

'Do you have to do vivisections?' I asked.

He shrugged. 'We sometimes have to operate on the animals,' he said, with carefully calculated vagueness. 'But we don't hurt them. We use anaesthetics. We aren't in the torture business.'

'Isn't it dangerous, working with viruses?'

'Not really. I'll take you to the lab some day – there's a special sterile section, where I do most of my work. You can watch me through the observation window. I wear a mask and rubber gloves whenever I'm handling infected animals. But the viruses aren't killers – most of them produce the same symptoms as a cold in the head or a bout of flu, along with a few bad dreams. If I caught anything, I'd be better inside a fortnight.'

'Be sure to let me know if you do,' I said.

'I will,' he promised. 'It's worth the risk. The work's pretty tedious, but it has some very interesting theoretical ramifications. It opens up some possibilities which are so way out as to be positively wacky. Some of his colleagues seem to think that Viners is lost in the further reaches of unorthodoxy – but that's only because nobody ever heard of *me* yet. When I start to publish my stuff, they'll see something wild and wonderful. Back home, I doubt if I'd be able to get anything really interesting approved as a subject for a doctoral thesis, but here it's all so relaxed – no limits. I like that.'

I asked him what he and Professor Viners actually did to their experimental animals, but he wouldn't go into detail. It wasn't that he didn't trust me; he was simply obeying an undertaking he'd given to Professor Viners.

'People overreact,' he told me. 'Viners is very anxious about the possibility of wild rumours getting started. People don't mind about the rats, but they sometimes get funny about cats and rabbits. It's not *Son of Frankenstein* up there, believe me.'

He didn't expect me to understand all the stuff about DNA, and in a way he might have been disappointed if I had done, because he liked to feel that he was on a higher intellectual plane than I was. He felt comfortable with my youth, my ignorance, my innocence and my helplessness. He could never have been quite as comfortable with me if I'd known what he was talking about as well as he did . . . or as well as he thought he did. Like me, he'd had a fairly narrow upbringing, pushed hard by his parents to be a high achiever. And no matter what he said, this was the first time that he'd really been away from home, even though he was five years older than me.

Gil thought he was doing me a favour by patiently going out with me, easing me along, and treating me gently when I finally let him screw me. He needed to feel like that, maybe because he didn't have quite enough confidence in himself to handle a relationship with someone from whom he could only accept favours, without giving any of his own in return. He desperately wanted to feel that he was managing the affair, that he was in complete control of his life. He wanted a girlfriend who was young, shy and a virgin. It made it easier for him.

It wasn't at all like that with Maldureve. I gave Gil far less than I gave Maldureve – I'd never in a million years have wondered whether it was worth dying for the sake of what I did with Gil – but what Maldureve offered me in return was never offered with condescension, never as a favour. Maldureve didn't pick me because I was young, no more than averagely pretty, and not quite clever enough to understand all the things he said. Maldureve wasn't a creature of summer fading in the grey light of a foreign winter; he was a creature of night emerging from the shadows into strength and solidity, thanks to the power of *my* eyes.

Even so, I had to go to bed with Gil just as I had to go to bed with Maldureve. I had to let him screw me just as I had to let Maldureve suck my blood. It was dull by comparison, but it wasn't bad. It didn't hurt as much as I'd feared, and it wasn't as undignified as it must have been for Sharon, backed up against that wall.

Before we actually did it, Gil asked me if I was on the Pill. It was as if he hoped – perhaps he had – that I'd gone to the doctor immediately after meeting him, making preparations for the big occasion.

'No,' I said. 'I'm sorry.' I felt foolish, because I *had* known that it was going to happen, and approximately when, and hadn't done anything at all to prepare for it, despite all Mum's lectures about the importance of being prepared, and not being ashamed to seem calculating, and how an intelligent girl like me ought to know how to take care of herself far better than all the stupid ones who ended up as teenage mums.

'It's okay,' he said. 'I got something from the machine in the rest room.' He meant the gents'.

I felt stupidly glad to be rescued from looming embarrassment. For a moment, he didn't seem quite so much like a sordid counter of unhatched chickens – more like a knight in glistening armour.

He was pathetically patient about the time it took him to get into me – which was understandable, even though I didn't any longer consider myself to be an authentic virgin – and humbly awkward about the way he couldn't help bearing down on me. Maybe he thought I might break, being so very pale and fragile, and not at all like a brown, busty, gum-chewing California girl.

His fingers were unexpectedly rough when they touched the sensitive parts his gropings had never quite reached before, and I was surprised by the coarseness of the hair on his body that I'd never felt before, some of which was only on his back and legs. He seemed much coarser than Maldureve, much more animal. He wasn't really clumsy – no clumsier, at any rate, than anyone else would have been – but after Maldureve's unearthly gentility he seemed unfortunately ham-fisted. It was while he was on top of me that I realized how ill-designed the human body is for sex. Our limbs are shaped for walking and tool-using, our heads for sight and hearing; when it comes to sex we just make do as best we can. I suppose that it's not quite as difficult for us as it is for elephants or dolphins, but it's difficult nevertheless to overlook our essential awkwardness when push comes to shove.

Gil didn't say much, perhaps because he didn't know what, if anything, he was supposed to say. I was grateful for his silence, even though I couldn't help wondering whether it was slightly inadequate, because I didn't know what he was supposed to say either, if anything.

It wasn't bad. It wasn't bad at all. It was even possible to see how one might get to like it, once it was unburdened of all its fearful anxieties. But it wasn't a feast of blood. It wasn't ecstatic, enfeebling, glorious and devouring. It was difficult, pressurized, wintry and fake. Not that I faked anything – I didn't even know how. I knew that it wasn't enough just to groan, the way they do on TV; I knew that there had to be something beyond the groaning, something which the groaning only signified, but whatever it was, I didn't know how to fake it and I didn't even try. If he cared about that, he didn't let it show.

Gil could have abandoned me once he'd had what he wanted, once he'd made his score, but he didn't. I'd known all along that he wouldn't. He wasn't the type. Doing it just confirmed in his mind the fact that I was his girlfriend, and that he was the central sun around which my emotional life must henceforth describe its orbit. He wanted that; he wanted an orbiting satellite as well as just a score. But he didn't want me to circle him too closely – at least, not yet.

He never said he loved me, that night in my room, but I think
it was embarrassment that prevented him, not scrupulousness.
He didn't say 'fuck' either, or even 'hell' – it was an evening
unusually free of commonplace expletives, we spoke plainly to
one another when we did speak, even though we didn't have
very much to say.

5

I didn't make any particular effort to return to the spot where
I'd seen Maldureve, after the first time I caught sight of him.
When I did pass by, in daylight or after dark, I looked into the
shadows, curiously, but I didn't stop. Usually, I was with Gil; he
had enough of a proprietorial claim on me even then to insist
that he should walk me home, and he wanted to do so as often
as possible, ever hopeful that he might not have to walk back
again. I wasn't with Gil every night, though. I wouldn't have
wanted to be, even if his experiments hadn't sometimes made
it necessary for him to work late in the labs. As things were,
he had to work late into the night twice or three times a week,
sometimes because his experimental animals had to be observed
intensively, and sometimes because his tissue cultures had to be
monitored.

'Brain tissue's difficult to culture,' he explained. 'When we
get fresh material in – whether it's from our own animals or
the local abattoir – we have to put it through its paces while
it's fresh. Otherwise, the tide of corruption would carry away
the short-lived proteins we're trying to track.'

Sometimes he had to work all night, in which case I wouldn't
see much of him during the daytime either. I went up to the
labs three or four times but he couldn't let me in because of
the security procedures, and he wasn't able to spare more than
fifteen minutes at a time to come out and chat. There was
a double-glazed window mounted in the wall so that people
outside could see about half the laboratory, and signal to those

within, but the animals were always out of sight, and watching Gil play about with Petri dishes and test tubes, or peer down his binocular microscope, left much to be desired as a spectator sport. Usually, he wasn't alone – sometimes Profesor Viners would be in with him, but more often it was a lab assistant – and I felt very self-conscious about hanging around outside while they were trying to get on with their work. The lab assistant was a dark-haired girl named Teresa, not much older than me, who didn't seem to appreciate my turning up, so I mostly refused Gil's invitations to visit him at the lab.

On the nights when he had to work, therefore, I had the opportunity to walk home alone – although I didn't think of it, at first, as an opportunity.

I walked the path more than once and saw nothing, but there were other people about on those occasions. Some time passed before an incident occurred which might have made me avoid the path for ever.

In the end, nothing actually happened. If I'd described the event to anyone, they would probably have said that it was nothing at all, certainly nothing to worry about. Dad would have reassured me that however unpleasant it might have seemed, I'd never been in real danger. 'Boys do things like that,' he would have said. 'It's not nice, but they don't really mean it. It's only young blood.'

Dad used phrases like 'young blood' all the time, mostly because he didn't know the proper jargon; the only thing he knew about hormones was the old joke about the difference between a hormone and an enzyme (when you're asked, you're supposed to say 'I don't know; I never heard an enzyme').

Maybe Dad would have been right. Nobody waved a knife about or threatened me with death – but what happened would have been terrifying and deeply unsettling nevertheless, and would surely have made me avoid the path for the rest of my time at the university, if it hadn't been for Maldureve's intervention.

I brought it on myself, in a way. When I set off from the Union building, there was a mixed group in front of me. There were five or six people, including at least two girls. They were boisterously drunk, but good-humoured. I could have hurried to catch up with them and walk close to them, if not actually with

them, but I didn't. Instead, I dawdled, letting them get further
in front of me, out of sight if not quite out of earshot. I didn't
consciously do that because I hoped to see Maldureve again – if
I offered myself any reason at all I must have told myself that they
were too loud, too playful, too likely to turn and say something to
me if I were close behind them. By dawdling, though, I let three
other people come up behind me without even noticing that they
were there. They were even drunker, and less good-humoured
in their drunkenness – and they were all male.

I don't remember what one of them first called out to me.
It was probably something reasonably harmless, like 'Hello,
darling'. But I hadn't known they were there, and I nearly
jumped out of my skin – which was probably what the one
who'd called out had intended. Reflexively, I looked round –
and equally reflexively, I speeded up. That amused them, and
they all started calling out.

'Don't run away, darling, we won't hurt you.'

'Only if you want us to.'

'You'll love it. We're the best on campus.'

'The best in the world.'

It was all punctuated by laughter, but it was dark, dirty
laughter, forced and aggressive. They wanted to pretend that
it was all in fun, but they also wanted to make it clear that they
were just *pretending*. The threat seemed all the greater because
they were pretending so half-heartedly that it wasn't a threat. The
fact that the double bluff was really a triple bluff, and that they
didn't really intend any harm at all, was in danger of becoming
lost in the confusion – theirs as well as mine.

I was frightened. I ran.

Mum always said that I shouldn't run away from bothersome
dogs, because it would only make them more excited and they
would chase me. Because of that, I'd always frozen stiff when
a big dog frightened me, and let him sniff around me until
the owner called him away. Perhaps I should have frozen
stiff when the boys started taunting me, and let them cluster
round me, refusing to react until they got bored and went
on their drunken way, but I couldn't. I was too afraid that
they'd start pawing me and trying to kiss me, all the while
pretending – maybe even to themselves – that they were only

being nice, or could at least say later that that was what they'd
been trying to be.

I ran across the bridge, and they ran after me.

'Hey, wait!'

'What are you, a virgin?'

'This is your big chance!'

'We won't hurt you!'

'We got the biggest and the best in the whole fucking
universe!'

'You'll love it!'

I ran across the bridge and on to the section of the path that was
bordered by the wood. I knew I couldn't outrun them. They were
too tall and too strong, probably sportsmen. They were nearly
at my heels already. The nearest one reached out as if to grab
me, or at least to touch my hair. Anticipation of that touch sent
a shock of anguish through my whole body.

And then the shadows reached out for *them*.

The electric bulb in one of the lamps abruptly went out, and
that entire section of the path became dark. It was a cloudy night
and there was no moon, so the shadow which pounced on them
was very black and deep. It was also *inhabited*.

The darkness enfolded itself around me just as it enfolded itself
around them, but I could feel its tenderness, its protectiveness.
To them, it was hostile, ominous and dangerous. Maldureve was
still a thing of shadow then, without any but the most phantasmal
substance, but he was real. He was still in the borderlands, at
the interface of his world and ours, unable to cross over. He
couldn't have hurt them – not physically. He certainly couldn't
have sucked the blood out of them, the way I wished he would.
But because he was a thing of shadow, he was more easily able
to reach into that private darkness which was the unillumined
arena of their filthy, monstrous thoughts. He was able to pierce
their souls with black arrows of hatred, and he did.

'Fucking hell!' said one, as the darkness burst over him. I
heard one of the others gasp wordlessly. They all jumped, every
bit as nervously as I had jumped when they first made their
presence known.

I realized then that they were almost as wound up as I
was. I understood that their carelessness of the dark was a

pretence of much the same kind as their pretence of exaggerated confidence in their sexual prowess: something that came from their competitive solidarity with one another, something deeply and essentially confused.

They ran on, desperate to get back to the light, hurried on their way by Maldureve's presence. They didn't know who or what he was, but they knew that he was not something they could confront.

One of them flicked my hair as he ran past. It was a casual, contemptuous and childish gesture, but it was also defensive and defeated. It was all he dared to do, now.

It wasn't until they were out of the deepened shadow, five or six paces ahead of me and still running, that one of them plucked up the courage to turn back and shout: 'Can't rape you tonight, darling – in a hurry.'

Another added: 'Sorry, girlie – some other time.'

The third chipped in, belatedly, with: 'Anyway, you're too fucking thin.'

I stopped, in the midst of the comforting darkness. I stood quite still while my hammering heart slowed down and the sickening panic ebbed away. Within thirty seconds, it was completely gone, and I felt almost delirious with the lack of it.

That was when Maldureve first whispered in my ear.

'Look at me,' he said – not pleadingly, but not commandingly either. 'See me.'

I looked at him – and I saw him. This time, he was near enough to touch. It was so very dark that I could hardly see the shape of his cloak, but I could see his face. I could see his beautiful eyes, his slightly thick-lipped mouth and his nose. I don't know what the word 'aquiline' actually means, but it's such a lovely word that his nose must have been aquiline. I was hardly aware of the scent of him, but it was there, soft and sweet and soothing.

'Each time you look at me,' he said to me, 'I come a little closer. Each time you see me, it enhances my existence.'

'Who are you?' I asked.

'Maldureve,' he told me. He pronounced it to rhyme with 'receive', but I was never in doubt how to spell it; I always thought of it as a word with a single uncomplicated 'e'.

'*What* are you?' I asked. I still thought that he might, after all, be just a ghost. I wondered whether he might be the Marquis of Membury who'd planted the garden of exotic trees.

'A vampire,' he whispered. 'A haunter of the dark. But to me, darkness isn't dark at all, because my powers of sight aren't like yours. If you will only let me touch you, you will begin to learn the art of the invisible. If you will only let me love you, I can show you the worlds which lie beyond the world. If you will only consent to feed me, you will begin to learn what it really is to *be.*'

There was no pretence in him; no pretence at all. Although he knew full well that I would think his claims impossible – that I could not accommodate him at all within my everyday world – he spoke frankly and with perfect honesty. Nor did he attempt to conceal the edge of anxiety in his voice, which told me even then that there was danger in this business, and that all his promises, no matter how sincere they might be, were edged with hazard.

He was not ashamed to let me see that he was not without fear.

'I'm not afraid,' I said to him – because I wasn't *too* afraid. I was just afraid enough. I trusted him, perhaps more than he trusted himself. Simply to be with him was to participate in a miracle; when he was there, *I wasn't afraid.* Not of the dark, nor of what the dark might conceal, nor of drunken freaks with bloated, diseased pricks and bloated, diseased egos. The promises he had made had already begun to come true. I had already begun to learn the art of the invisible, to see what I had never been able to see before, because of the black and choking cloak of fear. There was danger in it, I knew, but it was thrilling danger.

'I'm not afraid,' I said again; and I saw the gratitude in his eyes, the joy in his smile. I knew then that the world would never be the same again. I knew that I had taken a vital step in choosing to look into the borderlands.

The world in which we find ourselves, as Dr Chapman asserted adamantly in one of his introductory lectures, is something we take too much for granted. 'We are too ready to accept that what we see is what *is*,' he read out from his notes, in a tone rather less melodramatic than the one which must have hummed in his head when he first wrote them down. 'In fact, we are prisoners of our senses, doomed to experience nothing

of the greater spectrum of electromagnetic wavelengths but that
pathetically narrow band which we call the visual spectrum. Sight
is a mere slit, which excludes far more than it perceives, and
hearing is no better – and as for the sense of smell, how
utterly pathetic it is, even by comparison with the faculties of
chemoreception possessed by bees and sharks! *Their* perceived
world is very different from ours, although we feel compelled to
assume that we share precisely the same underlying reality.'

Maldureve had the subtlest imaginable odour, by our standards, but I knew that there was infinitely more to him than my
poor eyes could see or my poor ears could hear. He belonged to
that greater spectrum of sensory possibility, to the greater realm
of the real rather than the narrow realm of the apprehended. I
believed with all my heart that he could enrich me, teach me
the true nature of reality and show me how to live. I wanted
to welcome him into my world, to help him come out of the
borderlands.

'I'm not afraid,' I said to him, for the third time; and I reached
up to touch his beautiful face.

The face wasn't there – not in the solid, material sense
which communicates there-ness to poor sense-imprisoned human
beings. I couldn't feel its fleshiness at all; all I could feel was a
softness beyond softness, and a wealth of promises. But I could
still see him within the velvet darkness.

'Never allow yourself to be conquered by fear, Anne,' he said.
'We cannot help feeling it – my kind as well as yours – but we
need never be overcome by it. Whatever else you may fear, don't
be afraid to look at me, or to see me, or to touch me. Seek me, and
I am here to be found. Come to me, and I will come to you.'

'Thank you,' I said, as he faded back into the deeper recesses
of the shadows, into the gloomy borderlands which separated his
perceived world from mine. 'Thank you.'

It wasn't long after that meeting that I first began to leave the
Hall in the early hours, in search of that deeper darkness which
proverbial wisdom assures us can be found just before the dawn.
Once or twice I failed to find him; he couldn't always come to
me – but every time he did, he became just a little more solid,
a little more powerful, a little more beautiful.

I didn't *fall* in love. Things which fall can't help themselves;

they're dragged down by gravity, whether they like it or not. I leaped into love, or dived into love, or ran headlong into love, knowing every inch of the way exactly what it was I was doing and how and why. Could I have stopped, once I'd started? Perhaps. But I didn't want to stop; I wanted to go on.

I wanted to go all the way.

I wanted to *be*.

6

It wasn't until I'd made love with Maldureve for the third time that people began to notice anything different about me. Nobody saw the real transformation; nobody saw the joy, the contentment, the delight in being alive. The only change anyone could see was another kind of change altogether, and they couldn't understand why it irritated me so much; they couldn't understand how stupid it was that they could only see unfortunate and downbeat things when there was so much that was good, wonderful and magical.

'I want to take you out to dinner Friday,' Gil said, when he walked me home after the firework party on 5 November. 'We can go to that little Italian restaurant in the old Market Square. They do great pasta, and we can get a bottle of good wine.'

'My meal in Hall is all paid for,' I told him. 'It's all included in the fee.'

'You don't *have* to eat in Hall. It's not compulsory.'

'But it's a waste not to. The food's already bought and paid for, so why buy more? Let's go to the pictures instead – there must be something on.'

'Only serial killers and vampires. Anyhow, it's my money. I like to eat out, even though it's so unbelievably expensive in this tight little island of yours.'

'You just got the habit back home – now you're here you'll just have to break the addiction. It's too expensive, as you say.'

'I can afford it. Hell, Anne, what's the big deal? It's only a meal.'

'Exactly. What's the big deal? Why does it matter so much that I want to do something different?'

'Oh hell! Well, if you really want to know, I'm worried that you're not eating properly – or even at all. I mean, have you looked in a mirror recently? You're fading away, Anne – you're as pale as a ghost. I know you don't like me making anorexic jokes, but hell, Anne, it's getting past a joke.'

'I don't have anorexia. I've told you a dozen times. I'm just naturally thin. I eat, like anybody else. If you want to check up on me, come watch me. I'll buy you a ticket for dinner in Hall, and you can sit with me and monitor every mouthful.'

'I might just do that, Anne.'

'Then do it. If you can't believe me, check it out. It's a simple matter of fact. Dr Gray would approve – if all else fails, try it and see. You can come and watch me eat *all* my meals if you want to, just to make sure. After all, I wouldn't want you to think that I was making a special effort just for the one occasion.'

'Okay, I'll come – even if it makes you angry. I'm not prepared to back off on this, Anne. I care about you, and I want to make sure that you care about yourself. No matter how much it freaks you out, I'm going to make sure that you *are* eating. It isn't that I don't trust you, it's just that I have to make sure, because if you do have anorexia somebody has to make sure that you get cured before you starve yourself to death.'

He didn't trust me, but after his fashion, he did care. He bought himself a ticket, and came to watch me eat my dinner in Hall.

I didn't put on any kind of a show; I got the vegetarian salad, just as I always did, and the fruit for dessert, and I didn't eat the things I didn't like, but I had *enough*. Even he had to admit that I had enough.

'That's really what you always eat?' he asked. 'Amount-wise, I mean? You're really not just putting on a show?'

'I eat,' I told him. 'I always have and I always will. It isn't the greatest joy in my life, but it's not repulsive. I'm not anorexic, I'm just naturally thin.'

'Like hell,' he said. 'Maybe at the beginning of term you were naturally thin – I'd never have mentioned anorexia in the first place if I'd really thought you had it – but *now* you're in trouble. If you haven't got anorexia, you've got a hyperactive thyroid.'

'What the hell's a hyperactive thyroid?'

'The thyroid gland produces a hormone which helps to regulate your metabolism. An underactive thyroid gives you a thick neck – goitre, it's called. It used to be quite common in the days when people had lousy diets, because sometimes they got no iodine. Iodine's a trace element you need to make the hormone. A hyperactive thyroid makes you burn up all your calories far too fast, so that whatever you eat you never put on any weight. It's serious, Anne, if that's what you've got. You have to see a doctor to check it out.'

'It sounds to me like the kind of disease most girls would kill to get infected with. You can never be too rich or too thin, right?'

'Wrong. Too rich I wouldn't know about, but too thin is definitely on the cards. It isn't making you any more attractive, Anne – believe me, I know.'

'Oh, well, if *that's* all that's bothering you, it's no trouble at all. Look around, Mr Macho – there are half a hundred girls in this very room who'd just love to let you fondle their ample flesh. You don't need *me*. If you like cellulite, just go grab yourself a fistful – there's plenty of it around.'

'Anne, you're *ill*. You mustn't let this ludicrous feminine pride in being thin make you oblivious to that fact. If you do have a hyperactive thyroid, you really are in danger. I can *see* you getting thinner and paler with every week that passes. What's your mother going to say when you go home for Christmas? Hell, Anne, even if you don't believe me, you have to check it out. You have to see the doctor just in case. Maybe he can set your mind at rest – maybe he can set *my* mind at rest – but you have to ask him about it. Weren't you going to see him anyway, to see about going on the Pill?'

'Is *that* what this is all about? You want me to go to see the doctor because you think I'm dragging my heels about the other thing? Aren't you getting enough? Or is it just that it detracts from the quality of the experience – like eating a sweet with the wrapper on, isn't that what they say?'

'Oh, shit! I shouldn't have . . . Anne, you have to believe me,

I'm not just making this up. You're not well, and you know it. It's not just being thin; you're twitchy, too. You can hardly sit still for five minutes. That patch of skin on your neck you keep picking at is coming up like a blood-blister. For fuck's sake, Anne, look at yourself in the mirror.'

For fuck's sake. That was what it was, really. That was all it was. In his way, Gil did care about me, as much as he could care about anybody, but he used the word 'fuck' a lot more readily than he used the word 'love', even though we were usually polite with one another, limiting ourselves to 'hell' for the sake of some fragile phantom of decorum. But what he cared about was *having* a girl, in the literal as well as the metaphorical sense.

In Gil's way of thinking, and of being, a girl was a necessary accessory, like a pair of brand-name trainers, only more so. It didn't really matter to him that it was *me*; it could have been anybody – except that once the anybody became his, he acquired certain responsibilities: to see that I looked nice for him to show off. It could really ruin a guy's image if his girlfriend got hospitalized with anorexia – it was the next worst thing to a suicide attempt. It would reflect on *him*, because not being able to save a girl from wasting away was just as bad, in its way, as driving her to slit her wrists. It was the kind of thing that reflected badly on the magical potency of a guy's prick, which was supposed to keep a girl happy as well as getting its regular exercise.

Gil cared, all right, but not really for me. I was only a little piece of the jigsaw, becoming too thin to fit the gap in his life.

To keep him happy, I went to the doctor. I let him do a blood test, and reported back for the results. I got a prescription for the lowest-dose Pill and for some iron tablets.

'I shouldn't really be giving you this,' the doctor said, about the Pill. 'It's not advisable for people with anemia, and you are anemic. Whatever your boyfriend says – and a Master's in psychology isn't exactly a medical qualification, especially when it's from an American university – I can't find any evidence of thyroid abnormality, but your red count is low. Are you sure you're eating properly?'

The university doctor saw a lot of patients. Most of the female ones wanted the Pill, and the university wanted as few

pregnancies as possible. It was rumoured that you could go in
with a broken arm and he'd still offer you the Pill, presumably
assuming that you'd only broken your arm as a pretext to go
in, but were still too shy to say what it was you really wanted.
Having cleared me on the charge of thyroid hyperactivity, he
wasn't really interested in anything else. He thought the real
problem was solved, and that the iron tablets would take care
of the trivia.

I wasn't at all surprised by the revelation that I was anemic.
I'd have been surprised if I wasn't. I wasn't absolutely sure that
I wanted to be cured, at that point in time, but I was absolutely
sure that the iron tablets weren't going to do the trick. I took
them anyway. They were like coloured bullets. It might have
been easier, and much more orally gratifying, to suck a nail, but
they were useful as a kind of talisman to show to Gil.

'I'm anemic,' I told him. 'I have to take iron tablets. That's why
I look pale: common or garden anemia. I've been to the doctor
and he gave me these – a charm powerful enough to ward off
the nastiest of all evil spirits. He's checked my thyroid, and it's
perfectly okay. It's busy but stable, definitely not running amok.
Are you satisfied now?'

'Anemia?' he said, sceptically. 'Just anemia? He didn't say what
might have *caused* the anemia?'

'No,' I said, without further elaboration.

He sighed, and raised his eyes heavenwards.

Gil secretly thought that all doctors were quacks, and that his
Master's in psychology was worth a dozen MDs. He was shy
enough with me, but when he contemplated his own intellect his
ego knew no bounds. Maybe he was entitled to think of himself
as a future Nobel Prize winner. After all, he was certainly doing
cutting-edge research. He spent half his life slicing up brains and
doing all kinds of weird analyses which involved sheets of blotting
paper mottled with purple splodges. And when he wasn't doing
that he was doing mysterious things with cats and rats and rabbits
that would probably have had animal rights activists daubing red
paint all over the door of his flat if they'd only known about it.
I'd seen him looking sinister, with his surgeon's mask and his
white plastic gloves, and his curly hair bound up in something
that looked like an oversized shower cap.

Even so, he didn't know anything at all about what was going on inside *my* brain and *my* body. If I'd told him the truth, he wouldn't have believed me. He couldn't have.

'Look, Gil,' I said severely, 'I've done everything you asked. I've let you watch me eat, so that you know I'm not starving myself to death. I've been to the doctor so that I could get a check-up and go on the Pill, and he says that all I need is a little extra iron to boost my red count. Let's make a deal, hey? I'll put the iron in my body if you put the iron in your soul. Stop nagging me about it. Stop worrying about it. If you don't, your hair will probably fall out.'

He had no alternative but to agree, but he shrugged his shoulders overdramatically, as if the gesture constituted some kind of Parthian shot.

'It's very rarely possible to win an argument by a submission, even if you can get a fall,' Dr Gray once told us, in his usual picturesque fashion. 'Even if you prove your point with all the majesty and inescapability of a Euclidean theorem, your opponent will want to make it clear that he's just ordering a temporary tactical retreat, and hasn't really been beaten. He'll fire Parthian shots at you as he gallops off into the distance. But a philosopher always knows that he's won – why else would anybody want to be one?'

The Parthians, Dr Gray had then explained, in answer to Daniel's request, were the first mounted warriors to perfect the art of firing arrows backwards from the saddle, so that they could continue to shoot at their enemies even while they were fleeing in disarray.

Dr Gray noticed that I was getting thinner, too, and once asked me to stay for a moment after a particularly boring tutorial, so that he could ask me about it gently, with all the pseudo-parental concern he could muster – which wasn't much.

'Are you poorly?' he asked. 'I'm sorry to be indelicate, but you really don't look well.'

'I feel all right,' I said. 'I went to the doctor, and he says I'm just anemic. He put me on iron tablets.'

'Are you eating properly?'

'I don't have anorexia,' I told him, with infinite patience. 'I'm just thin.'

'As a philosopher,' he said, 'I'm bound to confess that I don't quite see the difference. I'm always slightly suspicious when people classify as diseases conditions which have no particular physical causes. When we didn't know about bacteria and viruses and cancers, it was understandably difficult to decide what could qualify as a disease and what couldn't, but now that we do it seems to me slightly irresponsible to force patterns of behaviour into the same medical frameworks as infections and biochemical malfunctions. There's something uncomfortably fuzzy about a concept of illness which can accommodate being depressed and not eating properly as comfortably as the common cold and the Black Death. The point is not whether you do or do not qualify for the label 'anorexic', but whether you're receiving sufficient nutrition to maintain you in a reasonably healthy state. I suspect that you aren't, and if that's a matter of choice, I really think that you ought to examine your motives very carefully. You are, after all, a philosopher-in-embryo, and ought by now to have mastered the elementary principles of self-analysis.'

I had already come to the conclusion that Dr Gray was a world-class bullshitter. The day they established it as an Olympic event, I thought, everyone else would be competing for the silver. I didn't particularly like the way he was always trying to overwhelm me with floods of clever words, but I knew it was a game I'd have to learn to play, eventually.

'I'm all right, Dr Gray,' I assured him. I knew better than to add anything about being a little 'run down'. He wouldn't have been able to resist the opportunity to spend another five minutes dissecting and demolishing the cliché.

'I hope you are. We really wouldn't like to lose you. We have our staff/student ratio to think about, after all. Unlikely as it may seem, there are many other departments in the university who envy us our humble little niche in Wombwell House, and would love to turn this quiet little corridor into one more plasticated nest of computers. Dropping out is such a selfish thing to do, in these dark days of cutbacks and arguments about practical relevance.'

'I'm not going to drop out,' I assured him. 'I like it here.'

In private, of course, I wasn't quite so stubbornly reasonable. I did look in the mirror, as Gil asked me to. I studied my thighs and my tits, and every contour and shadow of my face. Yes, I was getting thinner; yes, I was very pale – and the iron tablets made no obvious difference. I was careful to say nothing out loud to signify that I was worried, but in the privacy of my own thoughts I was free to entertain any and all possibilities.

I was free to ask myself: Am I prepared to die for love of Maldureve?

The idea of dying was strangely attractive, in some ways. I'd often had fantasies about it. I'd always been able to take a certain perverse pleasure in contemplating myself lying in my coffin, very pale and ethereally beautiful, surrounded by grieving relatives. There was a certain delicious sadness in imagining what the vicar might say about me at the funeral service – tragic death of one so young and all that stuff – and how the people listening would feel. Mum, Dad, Sharon, Gil . . . everyone. My daydreams used to drift on until they became quite ridiculous. I couldn't help imagining how the nine o'clock news might report the funeral, and what my obituary in the *Guardian* might say, even though I knew perfectly well that hundreds of people died every day, maybe thousands, and that nobody was in the least interested or cared at all, unless the person had been on TV and had become a familiar face. But that kind of daydreaming was just playing around. Now, I had to make the effort to come down to earth, back to reality. I had to confront the real questions: did I *mind* dying, if dying was the price I had to pay for being loved by Maldureve? Was it worth it? Was it sensible to sacrifice forty or fifty years of ordinary life in exchange for a dozen nights of unimaginable bliss? I kept telling myself *yes*, but I couldn't help having doubts.

One night – I'd been taking the iron tablets for over a week – I said to Maldureve: 'Is this killing me? I'm not afraid, but I need to know. I'm anemic – I'm not regenerating the blood as fast as I'm giving it to you. Am I going to die?' I didn't like to ask him what had happened in the past. I didn't like to think about the others who had preceded me, although I shouldn't have been so weak-kneed about it. Of course there had been others; maybe there still were. Should it have mattered so much?

'Anne, my beloved,' he said, in that thrilling whisper that was right inside my head and yet seemed to come from a million miles away, 'you don't have to die. There's another way.'

I'd known that, really. All along – maybe from that very first moment when he began to come out of the shadows, across the borderlands between the worlds – I'd known.

'How?' I asked him, knowing that he knew what I meant, without my having to say it. I meant: *How do I become a vampire? How do I save myself from dying by joining the ranks of the undead?*

In some books I'd read, a vampire's victims have to drink the vampire's blood in order to become vampires themselves – otherwise, they just fade away and die. Some writers made that a rule because it wasn't logical to presume, as most of the older ones did, that *all* a vampire's victims would rise from the grave to become vampires themselves; if that were so their number would increase so fast – like compound interest – that there soon wouldn't be any victims left to feed the vast host of vampires. I suppose, because of what I'd read, I half expected Maldureve to offer me his own blood. But he didn't.

'The answer,' he said, 'is in your own heart. You must find the strength to live. If you accept death, you will certainly die – but if you're strong, you can live for ever.'

Dr Gray would have called that 'impotent circumlocution' or just plain 'fudging', depending on his mood, but I knew better. Maldureve and I had an understanding. It wasn't that we didn't need words, but the words were only ever the smallest part of it. I trusted Maldureve then, far more than Gil or anyone else of *his* kind would ever trust *me*. I knew that Maldureve was telling me the truth, and that all I had to do was to decide not to die, and to find the strength to do what I had to do to stay alive. I knew that the choice was mine, and that if I didn't want to be a corpse, I could be a vampire. If I wanted to, I could be free to roam the borderlands between the worlds.

That was the beginning and the end of it. *I could be free.* All the world of shadows could be mine, if I were strong enough and unafraid.

'But I must warn you, my love,' he said, speaking very, very softly, 'that ours is not the life of angels in Heaven. We are like the bats which love the night, and darkness is our security, but there are others, which hide in light, sometimes invisible to our dark-accustomed eyes. Those are the staring ones, which screech like demons: *the owls*. You must be brave, beloved, if you join our company, for you will rediscover fear.'

I saw, then, why the choice was really a choice, and why it wasn't as simple as I'd thought and hoped. I understood that if I wanted joy, ecstasy and never to be afraid, then I would have to die. If I wanted joy, ecstasy and *life*, then I would have to take up once again that burden of fear which I'd so eagerly laid down.

I suppose it was only fair. Nothing in life is really free, even in the borderlands.

7

I didn't need to know what Dr Gray thought about vampires; I could easily have done without it. What he thought was bound to be irrelevant to my relationship with Maldureve because, when all was said and done, Dr Gray had no experience of vampires. His ideas were all hypothetical, and of course sceptical.

Even so, I could hardly help being curious, and I wondered about it, even when I thought I'd never be able to ask. But then the opening came up, quite by chance, and I was able to slip the question in without it seeming in the least out of place. I didn't even have to make it sound like a joke.

Daniel had been arguing with Dr Gray about the paranormal in general. He was trying to argue that there was as much statistical evidence on record for things like telepathy and psychokinesis as there was for a lot of ideas in physics that people accepted without a qualm. Wasn't it simple prejudice, he asked, that made people assume that the evidence for such things had to be corrupt, or that the people being tested were cheats, when no one would ever bother to wonder whether a physicist might have faked his results?

'Evidence doesn't exist in a vacuum,' Dr Gray said. 'One problem is that if our minds really did have the power to communicate directly with other minds, or act upon material objects at a distance, we'd expect them to be capable of much more than making hits when guessing Zener cards or bending spoons. We're entitled to wonder why, if psychics aren't simply dishonest conjurers, they only seem to be able to do the kinds of things that honest conjurers do.

'Then again, we can't just stop with evidence that something happens; we have to go on from there and ask *how* it happens – to find evidence of some kind of physical mechanism. We have to ask what, exactly, is happening when the mind supposedly communicates with another mind – and it's very difficult to come up with any kind of hypothesis about the means by which the information is being communicated that we could then subject to a test. Some of the things physicists have discovered are very peculiar, and not easy to fit into our way of thinking, but each discovery has led on to further ones, by pointing out new ways in which we might look for confirmatory evidence.

'Another thing to bear in mind is that it's really quite easy to account for the *plausibility* of ideas like telepathy and psychokinesis without having to concede their *possibility*. Because I can talk silently to myself, so that I seem to be hearing my own thoughts, it seems entirely reasonable that someone else might be able to eavesdrop on those thoughts. When I send out a mental instruction to my arm, I can't feel the electrical impulse which moves from my brain along my nerves. It's easy enough to imagine the action as an apparently magical response to a silent command, and if I do that my imagination has no trouble at all in jumping to the conclusion that if only I could get the hang of it I could raise external objects as easily as my arm. In a way, it's difficult *not* to believe in magical power, even though the notion is rationally unacceptable, and that's why such ideas have survived the decay of general magical belief, reappearing with a new supportive jargon which tries to accommodate them, however ineptly, to the scientific world-view.'

Daniel wasn't the kind to accept correction graciously, even though he hadn't yet mastered the art of the argumentative Parthian shot. 'Just because something's plausible doesn't mean to say it's not possible,' he said awkwardly. 'And anyway, lots of the things that people still believe in, in spite of all the scorn that scientists and philosophers pour on them, aren't at all plausible

– astrology, for instance. I can't see any way to account for the *illusion* that people's personalities are influenced by their natal charts, so why shouldn't I believe the people who say they believe it simply because it works?'

'It depends what you mean by *works*,' said Dr Gray. 'We're all terribly dependent – and I mean *terribly*, because it's a frightening thought, in some ways – on our limited and fallible power to predict the future. Unless we can calculate what the outcomes of our actions will be, we can't rationally decide which action to choose. Unless we can anticipate how the situations which surround us will develop, we can't exert our admittedly limited power to manipulate and control those situations to our advantage. And yet, choice and manipulation are the very essence of *human* being – of rationality, of consciousness. We're always avid to discover a new procedure which will increase out power to foresee the future, or a new method which will enhance our strategies of choice. It's uncomfortable in the extreme to confront the vicissitudes of chance, knowing that your foresight is limited and your choices are gambles against the odds. Even false oracles, provided that they can disguise their falseness with vagueness and enigma, have the power to command our attention, and our unwary belief, simply because they serve a psychological function in allowing us to believe that we have more foresight, more control and more power than we actually have. Most magic, like most medicine, can make us feel better even when it has no real effect, but its power to make us feel better is unfortunately dependent on its power to convince us that it does have a real effect. Philosophy, which certainly makes us wiser, can also make us feel uneasy – that's why so many people fear it.'

I could see that Dr Gray was enjoying himself. Usually he found tutorials boring, perhaps because he'd been going back and forth over the same arguments for thirty-five years, but he always warmed up when we left the syllabus behind and got on to something that allowed improvisation. I couldn't tell how good he really was as a philosopher, but I could see that he took a real pleasure in fanciful argument for argument's sake. It brought him to life.

'But not all the ideas that have survived the supposed decay of magical beliefs are comforting ones,' Cynthia objected. 'Some of them are really very scary.'

Cynthia, like Daniel, had a certain affection for oddball beliefs. She was apparently half convinced that technology, science and the kind of philosophy which Dr Gray taught were all by-products of the ruthless and insane male quest for domination. Once, when I'd vaguely mentioned what Gil did, she'd told me that science was just the mind-fucking aspect of men's ongoing rape of the world, but that had been well out of earshot of any of the lecturers. She'd never have had the nerve to say anything like that to Dr Gray.

'Can you give me an example?' Dr Gray asked her, in his best tutorial manner. That was my cue.

'Vampires,' I said, diving in before Cynthia could offer an example of her own. 'Maybe people don't believe in them, but the idea is as powerful now as it ever was – maybe more so. Given all the books and films, it's obvious that vampires still have the power to scare people. People may say that they don't believe in anything supernatural, that it's all just fiction and fun, but there's obviously a fascination in the idea of vampires – something which makes people uneasy. Why, if it's not plausible, not comforting, and not rational, should the idea affect us at all?'

It was the longest question I'd ever asked, and probably the best. Dr Gray looked at me approvingly through his thick-lensed spectacles, and I could feel the envy radiating from the other two. They probably thought that Dr Gray was easy on me because he fancied me, but I couldn't believe that.

'It's an interesting example,' he said, slowly, as though he were stalling while he thought of an answer, although I could tell that he wasn't. He really liked playing the game. 'It's all the more interesting because the kind of vampires that fascinate us now aren't at all like the vampires that people used to believe in, when people did believe in vampires.

'The vampire of folklore is a hideously unpleasant thing: a walking corpse. The vampire of folklore reeks of decay – and no wonder, when you bear in mind that many of his attributes are simply those which corpses acquire as they putrefy. Dead bodies, spared the embalmer's cunning artifice, undergo some pretty horrible changes. They swell up and become discoloured.

Some tissues are liquefied and others give off gas, so that horrid stuff may leak from the mouth. A decaying body – especially when it's penetrated by a wooden stake – is likely to belch and groan. That's what the vampires people once believed in were like: dead people strangely animated by natural processes they couldn't begin to understand.

'But the vampires we see in films aren't like that, are they? The vampires which fascinate *us* are rather different from the ones which used to terrify our ancestors. They're aristocratic, handsome, hypnotic . . . and sexy. They threaten to drink our blood, as the old vampires used to do, but they don't threaten to drown us in filth and corruption. Theirs is a much more subtle threat, a nakedly sexual threat.'

'So what?' said Daniel. 'That doesn't explain anything. It's just poetic licence.'

'A lovely phrase, that,' said Dr Gray, almost lasciviously. 'Poetic licence. Who grants poets a licence, and why? Why did we allow Bram Stoker to make Dracula into a terribly charming – and I do mean *terribly* and *charming* – count, who had the power to turn innocent young Victorian maidens into ravening bloodthirsty monsters? Did you ever notice that Stoker's favourite adjective is "voluptuous", that he uses it over and over again when describing his female vampires?'

I don't suppose any of us had. I certainly hadn't.

'I still don't see . . .' Cynthia began, but stopped when Dr Gray fixed his gaze upon her.

'The Victorians did tend to see sex as something monstrous,' Dr Gray went on. 'They tried ever so hard to believe that women didn't have any sexual feelings – or, rather, that all sexual feeling in a woman was unnatural. The idea of the sexually demanding woman, with an appetite to be fed, was something they tried to reject, and one of their strategies of rejection was demonization. In fiction, female sexuality became the prerogative of lamias and vampires; in reality, the Victorians committed young girls to lunatic asylums for confessing that they wanted sex.'

'But *we* don't think like that,' said Daniel, aggressively – Cynthia, I suspect, wasn't so sure –' and yet Dracula is more popular now than ever.'

'And more attractive now than ever,' Dr Gray countered.

'You're quite right, of course. There must be something deeper, mustn't there? There must be something else which sustains the vampire myth so powerfully in an age of non-belief. What can it possibly be?'

He looked around, hopefully, the way he sometimes did – but nobody had any ideas. Not even me.

'I wonder,' he said, putting on his most teasing expression, 'whether it might have anything to do with the fact that each and every one of us actually begins life as a vampire, sustained in the blissful safety of the womb by the constant flow of our mother's blood? We had no teeth then, of course, but I rather think that the vampire's fangs are just for show, don't you? We can all see that Christopher Lee's canines are at least two inches apart, and the two holes in the girl's neck are never more than half an inch from one another – there's no real pretence, is there? But the silk-lined coffin in which the vampire is required to rest, upon the soil of his homeland – isn't that rather reminiscent of the womb?'

Is it? I wondered. Maldureve had no silk-lined coffin, so far as I knew. Nor had he any fangs.

'Even after we're born,' Dr Gray continued, thrilled to bits with his own ingenuity, 'we continue to suckle at our mother's breast, drawing her to us magnetically with the power of our cries. Perhaps – just perhaps – what we see in the literary and cinematic vampire is an echo of ourselves: imperious, irresistible, locked into an unsurpassable intimacy with our loving victim. And perhaps we can't help feeling disturbed by the confrontation with what we once were; perhaps we're guilty, uneasy, unwilling to look ourselves in the face. Vampires are invisible in mirrors, aren't they? Perhaps that's because, when we look into the mirror, we only want to see ourselves as we are, and are intent on refusing any confrontation with our tiny, incestuous, vampiric selves, lest we should feel desperately nostalgic for that lovely limbo of pre-consciousness which was the womb.'

I hadn't expected to hear him say anything like that, and it sent all kinds of shivers up and down my spine. He was wrong, of course. Completely wrong. Maldureve wasn't me, and I wasn't trying to be my own mother. Whatever that bliss was which possessed me when he fed on me, it wasn't the syrupy liquidity of the womb.

All in all, though, I had to admit that it was still a hell of a theory.

It left Daniel and Cynthia completely cold, though. I was the only one who got a buzz out of it, and I think Dr Gray knew it, though he couldn't have begun to understand the reason. He wasn't so gross as to wink at me, but if it's possible to twinkle an eye deliberately he twinkled his at me while the others gave their verdict.

'That's *sick*,' said Cynthia. 'It's utterly repulsive.'

'It's ridiculous,' Daniel agreed. 'Crazy.'

'I'm glad you think so,' said Dr Gray smoothly – no Parthian shot, this – 'because, you see, the argument couldn't possibly be true unless it provoked exactly that kind of alarm and unease. If you were able just to say *ho hum* the way you can a dozen times in every other tutorial, I'd have to concede that I was wrong, wouldn't I? If I were right, you'd *have* to consider the idea sick, ridiculous, repulsive, crazy. You'd have to thrust it away from you violently, because you couldn't bring yourselves to contemplate it with equanimity. Maybe, if you could accept it, you wouldn't find anything to move you, disturb you or frighten you in horror films. All the real horrors, you see, are inside us – but it's so dark inside us that we can only really see them, and get them in focus, by imagining them *outside*, and then trying to deny that they mean anything at all. Do you have your essay topics for next week?'

It was world class – an easy gold in the freestyle section. But it wasn't, in the end, much help to me. I remember thinking then that that was the trouble with philosophy – it was so impractical. Everybody thinks that, when they're only just beginning to get the hang of it.

I still had a lot to learn. Maldureve had taught me a lot, and even Dr Gray had taught me a little, but I'd hardly begun to cultivate wisdom. I didn't yet know what it would take to make that beginning.

8

Deciding to live instead of dying wasn't a momentary thing. I didn't sit down to think it over, listing the pros and cons on a piece of paper, and then suddenly stand up at the end of half an hour's intensive brooding, with the opening chords of Strauss's *Also Sprach Zarathustra* playing in the background of my imagination, and say: 'I've decided – I'm going to be a vampire. *I'm going to live!*' Life doesn't imitate art to that extent.

It's not that there weren't pros and cons to be weighed up; it wasn't as easy a decision as you might think. The mysterious owls of which Maldureve had spoken with trepidation hardly figured in my calculations at all, but when I coolly and honestly tried to weigh up the advantages of life vis-à-vis death, I found disincentives as well as pluses. I'm not one of those people who think suicide is always a cop-out or a symptom of insanity; I'm always surprised that more people don't do it.

First of all, I had to get past the idea that there was something intrinsically romantic about dying. Sometimes, when I used to look at myself in the mirror – and this was long before I came to university or met Maldureve – I used to think: there's the face of someone who was born to die young. When Miss Lawrence, the English teacher, told me I had authentic talent as a writer, what the word 'talent' conjured up for me was the idea of Sylvia Plath and Stevie Smith, making art out of despair. That was before Miss Lawrence started being sarcastic about the 'myth of tragic beauty' – I wonder what Dr Gray would have to say about *that*! – but it wasn't really the beauty bit of it that was important to me; I've never been more than averagely pretty. I think it had more to do with ideas of innocence. When I was fifteen, if I could have been anyone in the entire history of the world I'd have chosen to be St Teresa of Avila. I'd grown out of that, but not entirely.

Maybe if I'd still been a virgin, in the stricter sense –

meaning that Maldureve didn't count, only Gil – when my chance came to fade gently into oblivion, buoyed up by the ecstatic tide of Maldureve's intimate attentions, I might actually have decided to die.

But I wasn't, and I didn't.

Even if it had just been ordinary life I was choosing, with all its shabbiness, dirt and stress, and all its petty obligations, indignities and anxieties; even if it had just been sleep and alcohol, shitting and periods, tutorials and phoning home, sex and kissing, vegetarian salads and iron tablets, I think I might still have carried on. What really clinched it, though, was that life had become much more than that, for me. It wasn't just the way Maldureve made me feel, because I knew that would be a temporary thing. I had figured out, without his having to tell me, that once I became a full-fledged vampire myself, he'd have no further use for me. I knew my affair with him was doomed whatever I did. But I was gradually becoming excited by the prospect of turning into something like Maldureve, of becoming a haunter of the dark, a creature of the borderlands: a vampire.

The prospect of being able to enter the borderlands, whatever perils might be lurking in wait there, and being able to hide, dissolved in shadow, was very attractive to me. Even more attractive, above all else – above *all* else – was the prospect of being able to find donors of my own.

I had no idea, then, whether Maldureve felt the same emotions I did when we made love. I had no guarantee at all that becoming a vampire myself would compensate me for the loss of that special ecstasy, but the idea was incredibly thrilling anyway. I wanted to be able to bring about that miraculous transformation of the flesh: that magical lovebite which created an interface between body and body, essence and essence, soul and soul.

Essence and essence, soul and soul. That was how I represented it to myself. I knew that Dr Gray would disapprove of the empty concepts but I also knew that sometimes you have to use words to reach out beyond the concepts you can fill, to capture a little something of that elusive world-as-it-is which lies beyond the grasp of our enfeebled powers of perception. I knew that it was possible to be something more than human, and I believed that in being something more than human there was a very precious kind of joy. I wanted that. I wanted to leave my old self behind, but not just to let it wither and decay. I wanted to make use of the potential that was in it, and had somehow never managed to flourish and mature.

So, weighing everything in the balance, I decided that I had to choose life instead of death.

By the time I got it straight in my mind, my body had already made the decision to grow stronger. It hadn't bothered to wait for that silent speaker, my conscious mind, to get up on an imaginary podium and make its declaration of intent. I was already getting stronger. In fact, by the time I was settled in my mind I felt so healthy that I wondered whether that silent speaker might not be just like all politicians and other such monsters of ego, eager to credit itself with an authority it didn't really have. Perhaps, I realized, the decision of the flesh had come first and the decision of consciousness had merely fallen into line. I knew what it was that I was deciding, but the actual decision was made somewhere deep inside me, at a gut level. It was my gut that sent my mind the message confirming that the decision had been made.

It had to be my gut, because the result of the decision was *hunger*.

I'd never been a hungry person. Appetites are very variable, and mine had always been on the low side. There had never been anything courageous about my thinness; it hadn't been won by means of some heroic struggle against the ambitions of my body to grow fat. My body had never wanted to be fat, and was never very enthusiastic about being fed. Mostly, I didn't care at all whether I ate or not.

'You're lucky,' Sharon once told me. 'You're easily satisfied. I'm not. I could stuff myself to bursting, and still have greed-lights in my eyes. You're so lucky.'

I knew that she meant it, but I wasn't grateful. I didn't feel lucky. I always envied Sharon her appetites, because I always suspected that she found so much more pleasure in things than I could.

I suppose it was the same with my sex drive. Some of the girls at school were knocked for six when puberty hit them. My friend Mary told me once that she could wet her knickers with desire just sitting on a bus, when the hormones got to work on her. Sharon was the same when the curse descended on her. Wild music, black hair, pill parties and giving it away against the garden wall. 'Young blood,' Dad said, with a mournful shake of the head, never knowing the half of it. He'd never said that about me. I was always a stranger to greed and a stranger to lust. I never had that kind of trouble at all.

That's one of the reasons why I did so well at school, I suppose. A lot of the girls couldn't concentrate once they were swamped by all that sort of stuff. I think boys are better able to divide their attention, thanks to the nature of their equipment, but a lot of the girls just switched their minds off and gave themselves over to obsession. Not me. The hormones didn't bother me at all. I got far more of a buzz out of writing stories. Not that writing was any kind of substitute or sublimation. I was certainly never *hungry* to write. It was just that making things up was the only buzz I had. No greed, no lust; just imagination.

'I wish I had your imagination,' Sharon said to me once. But that was just because I was her big sister. She wished that she had everything of mine, from time to time.

Even with Maldureve, and all the glorious feelings I had when we made love, I never became physically hungry for more. My desire for Maldureve never became the kind of appetite which would build up and up and up if it wasn't satisfied, until it became desperate. The joy I had with Maldureve was a purified joy – infinitely desirable, but not in any sense a physical addiction. I *wanted* it, more than anything else in the world, but I didn't *need* it.

I always told myself that my way was best, even though I didn't feel lucky. I told myself that if only everyone were like me, the world wouldn't be such an awful place. Mum and Dad were like me, I thought, and Sharon would be too, when her young blood matured. It was the best way to be, even if it was dull. I still told myself that, even after I first met Maldureve and realized how many more things there were in Heaven and Earth than I'd dared to dream of. On the other hand, I could see well enough by then why natural selection had taken such care to booby-trap all creatures great and small with ferocious hungers and souped-up drives. We weren't timetabled to do

Schopenhauer until the second year, but I'd read enough in the textbook to have every sympathy with his comments about the necessary absurdity of the inbuilt will to live.

So I understood, at least in an intellectual sort of way, the kind of hunger which I acquired, for the first time, when I decided to live.

The new hunger wasn't any ordinary hunger, and there was never any possibility or danger of soothing its pangs in any ordinary or compromising fashion. I didn't have the least desire to abandon my vegetarian salads in favour of undercooked steak. The kind of blood which is let in abattoirs wasn't of any interest to me at all; my hunger was very specifically focused.

I was hungry for human blood, to be taken from living people, *with love.*

I emphasize that last part because it really was a vital part of the appetite, intrinsic to the hunger. Maybe there are other vampires who don't experience their appetite the same way – I have reason now to suspect that there are – but that's not the way I was taken. I claim no moral credit for this, because it wasn't the result of a moral decision to place limits or curbs on my desires; it was simply something in the desire itself. I had not the slightest inclination to be a rapist vampire, skulking in alleyway shadows, waiting to pounce on passers-by. Nor had I any desire to be a Svengali-like vampire, putting my enslaving spell on helpless innocents.

There was never the least possibility of my choosing anyone but Gil to be my sustenance, my source of life.

I knew, of course, that I would have to be subtle about it. I couldn't just happen to mention one night, while we were slipping our clothes off, that I wanted to try a new variation. 'By the way, Gil, I'm a vampire, and tonight I'd like to suck a little of your blood.' Sometimes, you just can't communicate by telling the truth. It's no good being honest with someone if they can't possibly believe what you say, and are bound to treat it either as a bizarre joke or a sign of madness. I knew that even if Gil were to say: 'Hey, that's okay. I like it; let's do it' – which he never would, because it wasn't his style at all – he wouldn't really be consenting, because he'd have taken entirely the wrong inference from the words. So I knew I had to approach the issue in a different way. I knew that I'd first have to show him, in order to widen his conceptual horizons to take in things he'd never dreamed of, before he'd be capable of making any kind of decision himself. In order to put him in a position where he could offer his sincere and meaningful consent, I'd first have to suck his blood without any warning at all. It sounds paradoxical, I know, but as Dr Gray is fond of sadly pointing out, there *are* such things as moral paradoxes, no matter how much we would like to believe that there aren't.

When the hunger grew to the point where I had to satisfy it, I made my move. I planned the whole thing very carefully, because I wanted him to be in the right sort of mood. I wanted it to be special. I decided that it ought to be his flat rather than my room, because I wanted him to feel at home, and I didn't want the beautiful feelings which he was going to experience – which would certainly be better than any he'd ever experienced before – to be undermined by his having to get up and walk home through the damp and icy night afterwards. So I volunteered to cook him a meal – a *big* meal.

'What's the occasion?' he said. 'My birthday isn't till March.'

'Birthdays are accidental,' I told him. 'They're just things we inherit, like Christmas and Easter. We ought to save our real celebrations for commemorating things we *do* – decisions we make that change the course of our lives.'

'I haven't made any decisions,' he said, raising his eyebrows to show that he was only joking and knew perfectly well that I was talking about something *I'd* decided.

'You will,' I told him. 'You don't know it yet, but you will.'

I was glad to see that he got ever so slightly anxious, wondering whether I was planning to hustle him into an engagement, or tell him that I was pregnant.

'You're not going to make me into a vegetarian,' he said, choosing the least threatening and most jokey alternative. 'I don't care how big the meal is, and how delicious, it won't make me abandon meat for ever. I *love* animals, no matter what the animal-rights people may suspect, and what I love about them best of all is the way they taste when they're roasted. Don't get me wrong – I'll eat your nut cutlet or your green lasagne, and enjoy every mouthful, but I'll still be an unrepentant heretic the morning after.'

'I wouldn't dream of trying to wean you away from flesh and blood,' I assured him, more sincerely than he knew. 'In fact, I'm going to roast some leg of lamb and eat it with you. I'm going on a new diet, to gain weight. I'm fed up with iron tablets and people thinking I'm anorexic. I'm going to demonstrate that I can eat just as heartily as anyone else. By Christmas, I'm going to be disgustingly fat. You'll probably go off me completely, and you'll be longing to have the old Anne back again, to feel her hips and touch her cheekbones – but it'll be too late.'

'It'd take a hell of a lot of lambs to make you fat by Christmas,' he said. 'Not to mention a litter of sucking pigs and a sizeable herd of best Texan steers. I bet you a dollar that you can't get to one-twenty pounds by the end of February.'

'What's that in real money and good honest stones?' I said.

'About fifty-five pence and eight stone eight,' he said promptly, just to show me what a mathematical wizard he was.

'Make it a round fifty pee and an even hundredweight,' I said, 'and I'll make it by the end of January.'

'Fifty pees aren't round,' he pointed out. 'They have seven sides, though there's no earthly reason why they should. I also can't imagine why your crazy antique system of weights calls a hundredweight a hundredweight when it has a hundred and twelve pounds in it, but you have a bet. I'll even buy a set of bathroom scales, so that you don't have to stand naked on the one outside the drugstore – sorry, the chemist's – and put a coin in the slot before we can figure out who won.'

And so the vital tryst was made, as easily as that.

For me, it was an appointment with destiny, because I knew that my decision to live wouldn't mean a thing – that it couldn't even count as a decision – until I actually began to satisfy my new-found hunger.

And though he didn't know it yet, it was an appointment with destiny for Gil, too, because the inevitable result of his choosing to feed me with his life's blood – and I had no doubt that he *would* choose to do that, once he'd had a taste of the inexpressible joy of the true joining of flesh to flesh – would be that he too, in his own good time, would have to make the same decision I had.

He'd have to decide whether he was going to be a vampire, and live, or whether he was going to be a victim, and die.

9

I tried not to leave anything to chance. I didn't just take it for granted that I'd know what to do, and exactly how to go about it, when I started to feed off Gil's blood. I was careful to ask Maldureve whether there was any special knack to it.

By this time, Maldureve was able to walk abroad in cloudy daylight, free from the shadows. Solidity was good for him. He was a very handsome man, but he wasn't like Gil. He was gaunt and bony; he looked like a man who had undergone terrible experiences, had borne his troubles with grace and dignity, and had come through it all stronger. He had learned the art of equanimity, and knew himself as well as any man alive – or so it seemed to me, lost as I was in hero-worship.

The wan white winter light suited him far better than the yellow glare of summer sun could ever have done, even if he hadn't had reason enough to shun the unbearable glare of the sun. His skin was like ivory, paler than mine, and his hair was uncannily streaked with polished silver. His eyes were deep-set and brooding; I knew how easily they might have seemed stark and menacing, but when he looked down at me they were clouded with tenderness.

It was good to be able to meet him by day. It put our relationship on a more secure basis. There were still the thrilling nights, when I got up at three or four in the morning to go out to the Marquis of Membury's Garden in search of him, but it was pleasant to be able to broaden our acquaintance by slipping into the trees on the way back from a lecture, or after one of Dr Gray's tutorials. He couldn't always be there, but I would often find him waiting for me, patiently, beneath a leafless tree. He didn't look out of place there, even though he always wore his black cloak.

I knew by virtue of its texture that Maldureve's cloak must be very warm and cosy, but he never huddled within it, or shivered when he threw back its folds to take me in his arms, the way Gil would have done. Cold was nothing to Maldureve, and he didn't mind at all when I wanted to part the cloak in order to put my hand inside, over his beating heart. The suit he wore underneath was quite modern and perfectly ordinary; I could easily have believed it if I'd found a St Michael label inside it. He never wore a waistcoat, only a cotton shirt.

'I need blood,' I told him, half proudly and half apologetically. 'I'm becoming like you. I have to take blood from someone, and I need you to tell me how.'

He looked down at me, and I could see the sadness in his eyes. He knew that it would soon be over between us, that he'd have to move on. I hoped he wouldn't pick on anyone I knew, but I couldn't make up my mind whether it would be better for him to go away or stay on campus. In some ways, I knew, a clean break might be better. On the other hand, it would be nice to see him again sometimes, to be able to talk to him as one vampire to another, even though we couldn't *do it* any more. In fact, it would be necessary as well as nice; there was still so much I needed to learn about the borderlands, about the mysterious owls, about the prospect of immortality. He could teach me; he was the only tutor available. I needed more from him now than words of love.

'I've shown you how,' he said. His voice was no longer as eerie as it had once been. Now that he was solid, it emerged from his mouth like anyone else's; it didn't have to sound so strangely inside my ear.

'But I don't know how you make the flesh change,' I said plaintively. 'I don't want to start sucking Gil's neck, expecting it to become fluid, and find that all I'm doing is sucking the sweat off his skin. I need to know how to do the magic.'

'It isn't magic,' he told me. 'It's our nature. *Ours*, my beautiful Anne – not just mine any longer. You feel the hunger, don't you? Your heart aches for the blood of others?'

'I feel it,' I confessed. 'But I'm not sure how to answer it, how to serve its need. Does my body *know*? Will it do it of its own accord?'

'Not quite,' he said, touching his hand to my cheek, very gently. His fingers were long and very smooth. His were the sort of hands of which Dad would have said, half enviously, that they'd 'never done a day's work in their lives'. Which, of course, they hadn't.

'You have to want it, beloved,' Maldureve continued. 'You have to want the blood very much indeed. The hunger isn't enough, on its own. You have to have the determination as well as the desire. If you doubt yourself, or if you can't bring yourself to do it, you'll fail – and the hunger will eat *you* instead.'

'I want it,' I said, intensely. 'I want it more than I ever imagined it was possible to want anything.'

The sadness came back into his face, and a shadow darkened his gaze. I knew that it wasn't just regret. I'd seen that look before – that slightly haunted look.

'You mustn't think, beloved, that ours is an easy existence,' he said, as though it pained him to tell me, although he felt duty bound to do it.

'You will easily discover, if you have truly accepted your new nature, how to take blood. If doubt prevents you, simply think of me. Imagine yourself as a phantom of the shadows, and remember the joy that I have brought you. Only remember what I am to you, and you will quickly master the art of feeding. But you'll discover, too, that not all the things which you see with your enhanced senses are beautiful. The art of the invisible carries its own penalties. You'll learn to love the shadows, as I do, and to fuse your being with theirs, but you'll also catch sight of the things that hide in light: creatures with staring eyes and avid claws. You must learn to flee as well as to feed; your nature knows how, but for that too you must find the determination. If you doubt, or hesitate, the owls will seize you and drag you screaming into their region of the borderlands, where you would come to know the savage pain which is counterpart to the refined joy that I have shown you. I beg you, beloved, *remember me*. When you see the owls, think of me and what I was before you brought me forth into the world with your keen and needful vision. Flee from the owls; learn to hide from their angry sight.'

'Wouldn't you come and rescue me,' I asked, 'if I fell victim to the owls?' It was, I suppose, a teasing question, intended to imply that he was, after all, my hero. He had rescued me once already from a fate worse than death.

'I could not come to you in *their* realm,' he said, very soberly. The sadness of his tone felt suddenly desolate and chilly. 'My trade is joy and inner strength; you have made me firm and let me walk in the gentle light of cloudy days, but the owls can't be wrestled or broken or torn. They are the predators, not you and I. We drink the sweet and heady blood of men, while they know no hunger at all, but theirs are the claws which rend and tear. The owls cage their victims in light, and ply them with such torments that their hearts break and their minds are lost. Never look into the heart of light, beloved. Once you have seen the owls, you give them power over you. They will reach out for you, if you consent to their solidity.'

'But I can avoid them, can't I?' I said, anxiously. '*You* avoid them, don't you?'

'It's possible,' he assured me. 'Be on your guard, and you will learn the skills of evasion. Cleave to the darkest shadows, and their blinding light will never sear your eyes. Flee their touch, and their claws will never lacerate your flesh.'

I did wonder, as I left the wood, whether it was still possible to change my mind, but it was a purely hypothetical question. I had the determination to complement my hunger; my body had chosen life, and my mind was too reasonable to deny its choice. I wasn't really scared of the owls – how could I be, never having glimpsed them, not knowing what they were? I knew that Maldureve intended his warning to be taken seriously, but I also knew that he didn't want me to fail and die. He wanted me to succeed; he wanted me to be like him. Even though my blood would become useless to him, he wanted me to succeed, to become a companion instead of a lover.

Maldureve could have left me, of course. He could have stopped feeding on my blood, and let me use the iron tablets to build my red count back to normal levels. He could have found someone else whose blood he could drink while the hunger died away inside me and the fugitive pink gleam came back to my cheeks. He could have come back to me, after sufficient time had elapsed, for a brief reunion. It was still possible, at that point in time, for me to have the cake and eat it too, provided that I only had one slice at a time, at widely spaced intervals. I could have lived an almost normal life, trysting with my vampire lover once a year or so, for a few nights of delirious excitement, while he kept a troop of similar concubines for all the times in between. That way, we could have preserved our relationship over time, and kept it as it was. But that wasn't what either of us wanted. I didn't want a lover who'd visit me for a month or two every winter. I wanted something permanent, something that would transform me, something that would make me stronger. I didn't want to be forever becalmed in my thin, fearful, baby-Anne self. He wanted the same, because he had my best interests at heart. We were true lovers, who could be content with nothing less than excess.

Or so I thought at the time.

I don't regret my mistake; it was natural enough. I had to go through that phase, en route to maturity. It was only young blood: young and sweet and foolish blood.

The meal I cooked for Gil was a triumph. He gorged himself on the lamb, and so did I. The red wine was smooth and dry and gently intoxicating. Gil was excited, too, because of some minor breakthrough in his research. I couldn't concentrate on the details of it, but he didn't feel let down by my lack of understanding.

'Don't you ever worry about being infected by one of these viruses?' I asked him, in the hope of putting up some show of intelligent interest.

'There's always a danger,' he said, 'but it's very small. Most viruses can't survive outside living cells for long – a matter of minutes, usually – and they're very vulnerable. My sterile technique is good; I'm never careless. Viners and Teresa are old hands at the game, so there's infinitely less chance of picking up a virus in the lab than there is in the dining room of one of the Halls, or a Union disco. Even if I did get infected, I probably wouldn't show any symptoms at all, except maybe a headache or a mild high, before my immune system got to grips with the invader and knocked it out. At the worst, I might have bad dreams, or mild and temporary sensory derangement – and what a golden opportunity for clinical observation that would be!'

'Knowing as much as you do about psychotropics must make

you a bit sensitive,' I said, contemplatively. 'Every time you wake up with a hangover, do you have to ask yourself whether it was just the booze or a slip of the test tube? And then do you have to start taking notes, just in case?'

He laughed. 'I'm reasonably robust,' he assured me. 'I never get headaches, except on long plane journeys. My immune system is in ace condition and my brain chemistry is in perfect working order. Knowledge is great armour against over-reaction.'

Pride, I thought, goeth before destruction, and haughty manner before a fall. It was Dad's favourite proverb; he loved quoting it to the TV set, when someone he didn't approve of was holding forth to camera. There were a lot of people he didn't approve of. I wondered whether he'd approve of Gil, when the time came for introductions. Probably not – he and Mum would think Gil was too old for me, only after one thing, using me. Little did they know.

We were still pleasantly tipsy when we went to bed. We didn't bother to switch out the bedside light. I was a little self-conscious about that, but it was better than usual – the ordinary sex, I mean. I thought it was only fair to let him do his thing before I did mine, and he always stayed inside me for a little while afterwards, relaxing. I knew that would be the best time.

When the moment came for me to do what I had to do, I was very nervous. The hunger seemed to grow as the appointed time approached, and I could feel it taking hold of me, not painfully, but urgently and irresistibly. I did what Maldureve had suggested, and thought of him. I thought of the way it felt when he pressed his lips to my neck, and how my flesh felt while it was consumed by that unique, indescribable pleasure. I put myself in his place, trying to imagine what it might be like to give that pleasure instead of receiving it.

It didn't matter that I was underneath instead of on top; it didn't matter that Gil wasn't even paying attention, that he was lost in the borderlands of sleep, doubly drunk with wine and contentment.

He didn't start with alarm when it began to happen to him, when his flesh became fluid and his blood began to ooze into my mouth. I was certain that he felt the same kind of joy I had, the same unprecedented thrill, but he didn't seem to feel it consciously. He stirred and shifted, quite gently, as if he were trying to thrust himself further into me – his neck, I mean, not his prick – and I knew that his body was absolutely loving it, wherever his mind had wandered off to.

He let out a little gasp at one point, full of surprise and luxurious delight, and that gave me a thrill because I'd never known him do anything but grunt even while he was coming. And the blood! The blood cascading in my throat was so very thick and *rich*, and not at all sickly, as I'd feared it might be.

I didn't feel the same kind of lift that I got from letting Maldureve feed off me. I didn't scale the heights of ecstasy. I was surprisingly calm, considering what I was doing, what I was becoming. If I was intoxicated at all it was the aftereffects of the wine, not the blood. And yet, the experience was superb, after its own fashion – so very smooth, so very *satisfying*. It was beautiful and orderly, and I knew exactly when to stop and let Gil's flesh begin to change back again.

By morning, I knew, there'd be nothing left except a mark like a mottled lovebite, not so very different from any other purple badge of passion. He'd seen the one Maldureve left on me, but he thought it was something I did myself, with a fidgeting fingernail. I'd let him believe that, even though it wasn't very flattering to be thought of as a nervous wreck.

I'd shut my eyes while I was feeding, but I opened them again afterwards. Gil seemed to be asleep on top of me, but I didn't feel in the least sleepy. I'd never felt more awake in all my life.

I looked around, although there wasn't much to see. Even the cracks in the ill-plastered ceiling suddenly seemed to be worthy of attention. There was a pleasure in the faculty of sight itself that I'd never felt before, and I longed for something beautiful to look at.

Gil was too close, and not quite beautiful enough. It would have been perfect had Maldureve been there, standing beside the bed, looking down at me with a proud parental smile on his face, but he wasn't. I looked instead at the patterned blue lampshade masking the bedside light. It was translucent, in a papery sort of way, and I could see the glare of the electric bulb that burned inside, like a sun half hidden by a cloudy sky.

The glare seemed very bright, and I wondered whether Gil had mistakenly fitted a hundred-watt bulb where a sixty-watt would have been far more appropriate, maybe because they didn't label bulbs the same way in America, where the mains voltage was probably different. The brightness hurt my eyes but nevertheless held them captive, and the glare seemed to overwhelm the receptors in my retina, the way it sometimes does, so that everything dissolved into an expanding blur of dazzlement.

And then, realizing my mistake too late, I saw the owls.

I couldn't see them clearly, because they were hiding in the light, and I couldn't make out any authentic shapes or colours in the dazzle, but I saw them. I saw their staring eyes, incredibly full of wrath, *and I saw their eyes catch sight of me, and flare with anger and enmity.* I saw their beaks and claws, incredibly sharp, *and I saw their talons reach out towards me, avid to slash and scar.*

I screamed.

I shut my eyes as tightly as I possibly could, but of course it did no good, because when your eyes are dazzled like that the retinal cells continue to sizzle and flash at your poor befuddled brain, and you can't get away from the glare.

You can't get away from the glare, or whatever is hiding within it. You can't ever get away from the owls as easily as that.

10

The owls were inside my head, and I screamed. I tried to strangle the scream, but I couldn't, any more than I could banish the owls by closing my eyes.

Gil woke up, ripping himself out of me convulsively, thrashing about in communicated panic – but only for a moment. It was more startlement than fear, and I was quick to grab him and hold him and hug him. The owls were already receding, fading away. Their talons were groping impotently in the gathering darkness; their glaring eyes were confused by crowded shadows.

The phosphenes were insufficient to give them true life or real power. I knew, after the first horrid flash of panic, that I would be okay, that I was safe.

'It's all right,' I said, urgently, with my eyes still firmly shut. 'I'm sorry. It's all right!'

'Jesus,' he said, complainingly. 'You scared the shit out of me. What the hell was it?'

'A dream,' I lied. 'Only a dream.'

I opened my eyes again, careful not to look at the shaded bulb. The afterglow had almost faded away, and with it went the staring eyes of the owls. All they had done was stare – that was all. Reaching out with their talons had just been a tease, just a gesture to let me know that they had seen me and knew that I had seen them. They were just introducing themselves, offering ironic confirmation of Maldureve's warnings. They knew that they couldn't get to me yet. Like Maldureve at the very beginning of our acquaintance, they were quite insubstantial. They were too far out in their own borderland realm, and I knew that I'd have to see them much more clearly than *that* before I conceded them the power to cut and slash at me with their claws. As yet, they couldn't hurt me. I still had time to learn how to avoid them, how to keep out of their way.

I carefully eased myself away from Gil's sprawling body. I got out of bed and began to get dressed. Gil didn't want to get up. He felt weak, and I knew why.

'It's okay,' I told him, soothingly. 'It's fine. Don't get up. It's not late. I'll be all right.'

'Stay,' he said. 'You don't have to go.' His voice was slightly slurred, and he was obviously surprised by his own lassitude. He tried to sit up, but the effort was too much for him. He put his hand to his head. So much for his pride in the strength of his constitution. The tougher they are, the further they collapse when their egos are punctured.

'I didn't bring my things,' I said, being deliberately vague. 'I have to get back. Stay there – there's no need for you to get up.'

He didn't take much persuading. His eyelids were heavy, and his movements were sluggish. He made one more half-hearted attempt to get out of bed, but I pushed him back, and he consented to be pushed.

'Hell and damnation,' he said. 'I don't know what's the matter with me.'

'Too much excitement,' I told him. 'Go to sleep – get some rest.'

A little later, just before I left, I kissed him on the forehead. He was already asleep. The mark on his neck was still livid and raw, but it was fading. I couldn't tell exactly how much blood I'd taken, but I knew it wasn't too much. He'd be okay. He was strong. I knew it would be easier next time. I'd weakened his resistance. His flesh would get the habit, even if his mind remained in ignorance. Soon, I'd be able to explain it to him. Not yet, but soon. I'd be able to show him what was happening, and he'd have to accept it. He'd have to admit it into his scheme of things. And afterwards, he'd have to face the same decision I had. I was confident that he'd decide to live, and feed his hunger. I was sure that once he could get his head around the idea, he'd want to be a vampire too. After all, he did love me, in his own way.

For the time being, though, it was better to let him sleep. Maybe, I thought, he would dream of the velvet shadows and the things which hid there, of the infinite possibilities which lay beyond the glare of laboratory lights, beyond the chemical fantasies of tawdry viruses. Maybe, when he woke up, he would make notes on what he'd glimpsed.

There were plenty of people about on the campus, but it wasn't difficult to avoid them. It was easy to dawdle on the bridge, listening to the rustling stream, until I was quite alone, and Maldureve could come to me from the shadows.

He seemed a little less substantial than he had before.

'This is the beginning of the end, isn't it?' I said, realizing that I'd avoided saying it out loud before. 'Soon, you won't be able to come to me again – not to drink.' I felt slightly sick and a little forlorn. I had been so excited about what was happening with Gil that I had set aside the question of my own loss, and what it would be like to have known that special ecstasy, and never to know it again. Feeding had been different; pleasant, but different. There was a very special joy in being a victim, in submitting, which I'd have to surrender. I wondered if Maldureve understood that. Had he been human once? Had he been some innocent child of time, before he succumbed to the caresses of some svelte lamia? Did he still remember the glory of her glamour – or had it happened too long ago, if it had happened at all?

One day, I thought, he will tell me everything. One day, he will bare his soul to me, and tell me the inmost secrets of his heart.

'It isn't the end,' he whispered, taking me in his arms to comfort me. 'It isn't even the beginning of the end. It's just the beginning. I will always be here for you – always. There is much for us yet to share, and even if circumstances were to part us, still you would have the most valuable gift that is mine to bestow. All that has gone before has been a shadow and a sham; your true life, beloved, is only now beginning.'

He was right, of course. But sometimes beginnings aren't all they're cracked up to be.

According to Plato, the unborn soul has perfect knowledge, but when it becomes embodied it forgets everything, and has to go through the painful and laborious business of learning in order to catch what feeble glimpses of remembrance it can. No matter how wise a man becomes, Plato thought, he can never recover more than a tiny fraction of the enlightenment his soul once had, and the knowledge of his failure – which is, after all, a significant part of his wisdom – is a kind of tragedy. Plato, of course, was talking through his arsehole, but as Drs Gray and Chapman are fond of pointing out, the fact that he turned out in the end to be wrong about almost everything doesn't mean that he wasn't a great pioneer in the difficult business of thinking.

'I saw the owls,' I told Maldureve.

'I know,' he said. 'You must be strong and clever, if you are to resist and evade them – but you *can* be strong, beloved. I know you can be strong, and I know that you can be clever. The owls are dangerous, but we can escape them.'

'Thanks,' I said. 'Thanks for everything. I can come to you again, can't I? I can come, whenever I need to see you?'

'Always,' he assured me.

'You'll help me, won't you? You'll help me to be strong and clever?'

'To the limit of my ability,' he promised. He said it so firmly, so confidently, that I had every confidence in him. He wasn't like Gil, possessed by the kind of shallow pride that went before a fall.

He was older by far, and had all the wealth of vast experience at his fingertips. I trusted him, completely.

I trusted him absolutely, even though I really knew nothing at all about him. That's what love does to you. It makes you blind to evil possibilities. It makes you think you're safe when you're not, when you can't be. It wasn't really his fault for promising more than he could deliver; it was mine, for thinking that the limits of his ability were boundless.

I went back to my room feeling fine, certain in spite of my brief encounter with the owls that everything was right with the world. I could still feel the hunger, but it wasn't acute. I could still feel a little of the fear which the sight of the owls had awakened in me, but that wasn't acute either. I slept well, and woke up thoroughly refreshed, ready to do battle with Dr Gray and the whole world.

Our tutorial that day was about sex – or rather, it was about why sex didn't need to be dealt with, philosophically speaking, as a topic in itself. Sex, you see, raises no special moral issues. That was one of the first things they told us in the introductory lectures. I suppose it's obvious when you think about it, but it hadn't been obvious to me before. Like everyone else, I'd thought that what people meant when they talked about 'morality' was whether it was okay to screw around or not. By the time we had to thrash it out with Dr Gray, though, I'd learned better. I understood that moral problems were really much deeper matters, to do with causing harm to people, and that sexual behaviour had to be assessed by exactly the same standards as any other kind of behaviour.

I felt quite ready for Dr Gray – much readier, I think, than Daniel or Cynthia. Cynthia, in fact, was all fired up to take the opposite side of the case.

'It's all very well for *you*,' she said to Dr Gray, 'to sit their smugly and say that sex raises no special moral issues. It's not so easy for me.'

Dr Gray sighed. I could see that he wasn't looking forward to this particular wrangle. He was listless and bored. He was cruising on autopilot. For Cynthia, I think, that added insult to injury.

'There's a difference,' Dr Gray pointed out, 'between moral

problems and practical problems. Your particular sexual preferences may make things more difficult for you than the preferences
which are more generally sanctioned, but the morality of your sexual
behaviour still has to be settled according to the same criteria which
determine whether all your other actions are moral or not.'

'*You* think that,' Cynthia said, 'because you're a liberal. Other
people aren't liberal, and they think that certain kinds of sexual
behaviour are wrong in themselves. In the real world, criteria
don't get a look-in.'

'Cynthia's right,' said Daniel. 'It's all very well for philosophers
to say that there's some abstract realm of argument where sex is
just one more thing people do, when all the *Sun* readers in the
world just take it for granted that it's what you tell dirty jokes
about. It's like saying that from a philosopher's point of view, all
men are equal, when it's patently obvious that in the real world,
they aren't.'

'I think that the philosopher whose point of view you're trying
to distort might really have been arguing about matters of justice
and the law,' said Dr Gray. 'It's unfortunately the case that
attitudes in what you are determined to label the "real world"
are not always coherent or consistent; that's why the real world
needs philosophers, more desperately than it would ever dream
of admitting.'

That was just the beginning. The argument went on and on.
Cynthia not only wouldn't back down, but remained convinced
to the bitter end that she was winning – a view which Daniel
continued to support even when the hour had passed and we were
all released into the bracing cold. In fact, Daniel expanded even
more on the subject once he was free of Dr Gray's intimidating
presence, and he invited us both back to his room in Fremantle
Hall so that we could lament the unworldliness of philosophers
at our leisure.

I went along. It seemed only polite, even though I knew that
there was a danger that it might become a ritual, so that they
would expect me to play hostess in my turn, and even though
I thought they were both dead wrong. I was prepared to keep
discreetly quiet about it, but I was one hundred per cent behind
Dr Gray. Sex doesn't raise any special moral issues. I was glad

that I'd found that out, and that my tutorial partners had pushed Dr Gray into making it so abundantly clear. I was glad because I could see that the argument applied to other things too. I was glad because it reassured me that vampirism raised no special moral issues either. Thanks to Dr Gray, I thought I could see perfectly clearly that being a vampire couldn't be deemed wrong *in itself*, and that the behaviour of a vampire is subject to exactly the same standards as any other kind of behaviour. It didn't matter whether vampirism was 'natural' or not – Dr Gray was always very firm about the abuse done to the word 'natural' and very scathing indeed about the commonplace assumption that what is 'natural' is automatically good.

While Daniel and Cynthia raged against the awful ways of the world, lamenting its petty bigotry and its oppressive intolerance, especially as manifested in the tabloid press – much as Mum and Dad would have done, with slightly different targets in mind – I followed my own private lines of reasoning. I knew how inept I still was as a philosopher, but I really thought I was beginning to get the hang of things.

There was nothing innately evil in taking blood from a human donor – how could there be, when hospitals do it all the time? As long as the donor was willing, I figured, it was perfectly okay. As long as nobody got hurt. In fact, I decided, it wasn't just okay; it was desirable. After all, a vampire needed blood to survive, or at least – so it seemed at the time – to maintain solidity, to emerge from the metaphysical borderlands into authentic physical existence. The person who gave a vampire blood was performing a noble act, all the more noble for the slight self-sacrifice involved. Surely I was a better person, from a moral point of view, when I let Maldureve suck my blood than when I let Gil screw me? And when I took Gil's blood, in my turn, I wasn't doing anything so very terrible, even if I had to conceal the truth from him until he could understand it better. I was giving him pleasure, and I was giving him the opportunity to increase his knowledge and his powers of perception.

What greater gift could anyone possibly offer to a scientist?

I was quite clear in my own mind that I'd done nothing wrong, and that I was perfectly entitled to go on from the beginning I'd made. In fact, I figured that I not only had the *right* to go on, but a positive duty. I had a duty to myself, to Maldureve and to Gil. Any harm which was being done by anyone to anyone was so trivial as to be negligible, and against it one had to set a treasure trove of enlightenment and pleasure.

It was easy enough to reach that conclusion, once I'd set my mind to it. I knew that if I said it all out loud, Cynthia and Daniel wouldn't be in the least impressed, but what did they know? Weren't they just as narrow-minded as the people they were complaining about?

I thought I was right. I thought I had wisdom. A little knowledge is a dangerous thing.

When I went back to my room the arguments were still buzzing in my head, and I was winning them all. I had convinced myself, and then some. Vampirism wasn't *wrong* – not in itself. Bram Stoker couldn't have understood that, and generations of movie-addicts had never even taken the trouble to think about it, but it seemed indisputable to me. The people who were wrong were the people who thought that a vampire ought to be staked through the heart, or beheaded and burned, simply for being a vampire. I supposed that Dad, like his sixteenth-century namesake, would be perfectly happy to destroy a vampire, were he ever to be convinced that such things existed, just because it *was* a vampire – all the more so if he knew that it had sucked his daughter's blood – but I had no doubt at all he'd be wrong.

My own attitudes had always been different. Even before Dr Gray had made an effective beginning on the troublesome task of turning me into a real philosopher, I had felt differently about such things. Maybe, I thought, that's why Maldureve had come to me. (But I knew in my heart that it was every bit as much a freak of chance as Gil's zeroing in on me at the freshers' dance.) It was nice to think that there had been a good reason, that I'd been *chosen* because of what I was. And there *was* a sense in which, long before I knew what Maldureve was or what there was to want, I wanted him. But it was okay to have wanted him; it wasn't unnatural; it wasn't wrong. It was just a fact of life. I brought him out of the borderlands and made him something better than a shadow, and I wasn't mad, foolish or wicked to do it.

All of that, I decided. It all seemed perfectly clear.

The hunger of vampires posed no special moral issues – just the ordinary ones, which we all have to face every day of our lives, however dull those lives may be.

Just the ordinary ones!

11

I expected Gil to come round that evening, but he didn't. We hadn't actually arranged to meet – we'd been unable to agree anything when I left his flat because he'd been asleep – but I was a little bit hurt when he didn't show up, after we'd had such a special evening. I knew that he'd probably be busy in the lab, but I thought he might have spared half an hour at dinnertime to cross the campus and say hello. I didn't want to go up to the lab to peer at him as if he were something in an aquarium, beckoning him out for a quick embrace, so I watched TV in the Hall for a while and then made my duty call, using the new phonecard which Mum had thoughtfully enclosed with her most recent letter, to make sure I had no excuse for not phoning.

Mum was well; Dad was well; Sharon was well, except for the usual things. 'Why anyone with naturally fair hair should want to dye it black I'll never understand,' Mum complained, 'and she makes herself up to look like I-don't-know-what.' I knew what. I could still remember her former favourite tape, and hum the choruses of 'All Women Are Bad' and 'The Creature from the Black Leather Lagoon'.

'I'm well,' I assured her in my turn.

'No news?' she asked, obviously suspecting that there was something I wasn't telling her, though she'd never in a million years have guessed what.

'No news,' I assured her. 'Just the usual sort of thing.'

On the following day, after lunch, I got tired of waiting for Gil to appear, and I went to his department in search of him. He wasn't in the lab, and neither was Professor Viners, but Teresa was in there, idly watching over a huge basin of some kind of gel.

When I rapped on the window she put on a pained expression, but she strolled over to the double doors and unhurriedly let herself out.

'He's not in,' she said. 'He hasn't been in for two days.'

'Was he supposed to be?' I asked, slightly bewildered. She was looking at me as if she were thinking: What can he possibly see in her? Her face was no prettier than mine, but she had bigger tits and wider hips than I had. Voluptuous, I thought, remembering Bram Stoker's favourite adjective. Does he fancy her, I wondered? What did they talk about when they were working late together? Did they talk about me?

'I don't know,' she said. 'He'd just finished a series of experiments; I don't know when he planned to start another.'

'Did he phone in to say he was sick?' I asked.

She shrugged her shoulders. 'I don't think so,' she said. 'He doesn't have to report to me. Mike didn't say anything. Maybe he's writing up.'

I wondered if she called Profesor Viners 'Mike' to his face. She was putting on an act, making out that I was just an irrelevant nuisance, and that it wasn't worth her while to be out here talking to me. But she wasn't much older than I was, and she was only a lab assistant, even if she did work in a fancy goldfish bowl.

'Thanks,' I said. 'Sorry to drag you away from your animals.'

'You're welcome,' she said, with blatant insincerity.

I was a little bit reluctant to go round to Gil's flat. I suppose that was an echo of Mum's ghostly voice whispering in the back of my mind, telling me how undignified it was for a girl to go chasing after a boy. But I set the reluctance firmly aside. After all, it wasn't just a matter of boy-meets-girl with Gil and me, and I didn't see why I should take any notice of the usual etiquette. I wasn't desperate, but I was hungry. I could have enjoyed a session in bed – and I couldn't quite understand why he wasn't avid for one.

Was it possible, I wondered, that he'd slept right through the most wonderful experience of his life? Or did he think it was all some kind of dream conjured up by his own imagination, and nothing to do with me at all?

The most worrying possibility, it seemed to me then, was that he hadn't felt anything remotely like the pleasure I'd felt when

Maldureve fed off me. I didn't want him to be incapable of that kind of joy. I didn't want to be incapable of giving it.

When I knocked on the door of the flat there was no answer. I knocked again, and then I tried the handle. The door was locked, but somehow I couldn't be satisfied with that. I didn't think he could have gone away without telling me.

'Gil!' I called – not too loudly, but loudly enough to be heard. 'Gil, it's me. I know you're in there. What's the matter?'

I waited. Ten or fifteen seconds slipped by, but then I heard someone moving in the flat, and I knew he was coming to the other side of the door. Still he didn't say anything.

'Let me in, Gil,' I said, in a normal voice. 'I know you're there – why won't you let me in?'

'Sorry, Anne,' he said, finally. 'I can't let you in.'

'Why not?'

'I'm not well. It's nothing – just a cold – but I don't want you to catch it. I'll be okay in a day or two. I'll come see you as soon as I'm sure I'm okay. I'm sorry I couldn't get in touch.'

'You don't sound as if you have a cold,' I said. It was true. His voice was normal. His ns didn't sound like ds, and his ms didn't sound like bs.

'It's not that kind of cold,' he said. 'It's in my throat and on my chest.' He coughed, but it sounded like a forced cough to me, put in to add plausiblity to his claims.

'It doesn't matter what kind of cold it is,' I told him. 'I'm bound to catch it anyway, aren't I? I've probably got it already.'

'No point in taking the risk,' he said, but quickly added: '*Do* you have a cold? Have you a headache or a sore throat?'

'No,' I said. 'I feel fine.' *Just hungry*, I added, silently. *Lusting after your sweet red blood.* And then I remembered what I'd asked him before, and belatedly realized what he meant – what he must be thinking. He'd misunderstood completely what had happened after we made love. He'd misinterpreted the feelings he'd experienced while I sucked his blood. It seemed terribly unfair.

'You think you've been infected, don't you?' I said, faintly. 'You think you've picked up one of your psychotropic viruses.'

I wanted to tell him that it wasn't true, that what he'd felt when I sucked the blood out of him, and what he felt *now*, had nothing to do with his sliced brains and crazy rabbits, but I realized that he wouldn't believe me. He'd cling to his own interpretation no matter what I said now to try to persuade him that it was all very different, and not at all what he imagined.

'No,' he said. 'Hell, I knew we shouldn't have had that stupid conversation. Now, every time I sneeze you're going to think I've infected myself. It's all perfectly safe at the labs, Anne. We really are very careful. Nobody can get infected. It's just a cold: a perfectly ordinary cold. Hell, Anne, it's December and I'm in a foreign country – I don't have any stored-up immunity to your local bugs. All Americans get colds when they come to England in the winter.'

'If I'm immune,' I said, 'then there's no reason why you shouldn't let me in.'

'It's a senseless risk,' he said. 'Hell, Anne, I don't mean to be difficult, but I really don't feel very sociable right now. I hate being ill – it's so yucky. Let me get over it, please. I'll see you very soon. It'll be two days, three at the most. *Please*, Anne. I'm sorry.'

It was the *please* that did it. It made me feel that I had to go, no matter how unreasonable or hateful he was being. I felt hurt. Whatever the truth was, I thought, he shouldn't turn me away. He shouldn't shut me out. He had no right to do that, considering what we were to one another. Even if it had just been the sex, he shouldn't have shut me out. It wasn't nice. But he'd said please, and I went away.

I hadn't been particularly hungry before, but appetites always become fiercer when the thing you need is no longer within reach. I'd thought that I could have his blood any time, just by letting him screw me, and I'd taken it for granted that he always *would* want to screw me, maybe not every night but at least twice a week. I'd never thought that he might simply go off me – and if it had ever crossed my mind that there was any danger that he might eventually have had enough of me, I'd simply have assumed that the danger would evaporate once he was introduced to *real* pleasure, to true and unadulterated ecstasy.

As I walked numbly across campus, I began to wonder whether he'd even *liked* it. Maybe, I thought, it was different for men.

Maybe it was different for those who didn't go into it with open eyes – those who didn't *choose* to offer their blood to be drunk. I tried to remember the way he'd looked, and wondered whether I could possibly have made a mistake in reading his expression.

Without even meaning to, particularly, I wandered into the Marquis of Membury's Garden, and stood leaning against the trunk of a tree, waiting. It was only an oak tree, just like any other oak tree, nothing strange or tropical. The sky was a uniform grey, and I felt that the whole vast blanket of cloud was pressing down on me.

'Maldureve,' I said, softly. 'Where are you, Maldureve?'

There was no whispered answerer, no black-cloaked figure in the shadow of the evergreens.

I knew that I had to resist linking the two events. It was daylight, after all, and there were plenty of people on the path not thirty yards away. In any case, Maldureve must have a life of his own to lead – projects of his own to occupy his time. I knew that I mustn't start wondering if he'd deserted me, just as Gil had – because, after all, Gil hadn't . . . not really.

I stayed there until the cold began to seep through my anorak and my sweater, and made my blouse feel like a sheet of ice against my shoulder blades. By that time, the light had faded from battleship grey to the sombre colour of Dad's best suit. I resumed walking before the lamps lit up, knowing that I didn't want to have to look up at them when they came on pink and slowly brightened to orange. I knew that the owls would be lurking in the heart of every electric bulb, and I didn't even want to be on my own in my room, where the light was cleaner and more even and not threatening at all.

I had my evening meal, as usual, in the dining room, but I couldn't eat much and what I did eat didn't do anything at all to soothe my hunger. Afterwards, I went to the common room and watched TV, even though it was only soap-and-sitcom hour and I couldn't concentrate at all.

What will I do, I thought, if Gil doesn't want to see me any more? What will I do for blood?

When I really thought about it, though, I realized that it wasn't a problem at all. The campus was full of boys so desperate for a score that they'd screw anything with a wet slit between its legs, whether it was thin or fat, whether or not it would look better with a bag over its head, whether there was joy in it or whether it was just like eating a packet of crisps. I realized that I could feed to my heart's content on every blood group known to man, and that once the word got around that I was a slag who'd screw anything, they'd be queuing up outside my door.

I didn't need Gil; I didn't *need* anyone special at all, and if I didn't bother to have anyone special I didn't even need to confront anyone with the choice of living or dying. I could feed and feed to my heart's content, and nobody would get hurt. There'd be a minor epidemic of anemia, but iron tablets were cheap enough.

It's nice to have someone special, I thought, but you can live without niceness if you have to.

Even without niceness, I realized, it still wouldn't be *wrong*. They'd all be begging for it, and they'd all be grateful when they'd had it. They wouldn't know what it was, but they'd know that they liked it, and I wouldn't be doing them any harm – not really.

I didn't want it to be that way. I wanted to have Gil, not because I loved him – I didn't, much – but simply because I'd chosen him, or had been chosen by him. I had at least formed some bond with him, which made me want his blood rather than another's, and made me want to give joy to him rather than to another. We meant something to one another. But if I couldn't have Gil . . .

I could have anyone I wanted.

There was no shortage of young blood. Not here – not anywhere.

I sat in the darkened room, hiding in the shadows, watching the glimmering TV screen, and realized that there were potential victims to my left and to my right, in front of me and behind me. All I had to do was let one of them buy me a drink, and smile, and let him get deliriously high on the idea of taking me back to his room.

It would be easy.

After a while, I went back up to my room, on my own. The urgency had gone out of my hunger again, now that I knew how simple it would be to answer it. I could have done some work, but I didn't want to. I tried to read for a while – just an ordinary novel, nothing heavy – but it was flat and tasteless, and I couldn't help wondering whether Gil was lying on his bed, feeling bad. I couldn't help thinking about Maldureve, either, and how utterly good it would be to offer him my blood, to have him stroke me and liquefy my flesh and thrill my soul.

I went to bed earlier than usual, but it was difficult to sleep. There were too many other rooms above and below me, and a corridor outside my door along which people were for ever passing back and forth. I could hear Karen's excited voice echoing from the wall between our rooms. Although I had my curtains drawn, the coarse fabric was all aglow with the yellow light of the electric bulb that was no more than a dozen feet away from my window ledge.

At first I was careful to keep my eyes shut, so that they wouldn't be drawn to that glow, because I was afraid of what might be lurking within it, hiding there ready to pounce. Eventually, though, I opened my eyes and I deliberately looked at the curtain, curious to know what would happen. After all, I told myself, I could hardly avoid looking into the light for the rest of my life, and this was such a faint, diffuse light that it surely posed no threat. Could the owls really be so fearsome, I asked myself, given that they had so far done nothing but stare at me and tease me?

It wasn't particularly brave of me to look into the light, because it was a very dull, subdued light, and I wasn't particularly scared; in the space of four short weeks I had become a braver person, and a more curious one. So I looked at the glow behind the curtain, and didn't make any effort at all to prevent myself looking *through* the curtain, into the heart of the light. I remember telling myself, quite punctiliously, that if the worst did come to the worst, I could always practise the other skill which Maldureve had told me I would now be able to cultivate: the art of fading away into the shadows, of dissolving myself into darkness.

From the heart of the light, the mysterious eyes stared back at me.

I was alarmed, at first, by the penetration of their stare, and their apparent hostility. But then I began to wonder whether they were really as malevolent as they seemed, or whether it was just mere appearance. Given that they weren't human, why should

I assume that I could read their expressions accurately? There were the claws, to be sure, which seemed to be reaching for me just as they had done two nights before – but even that reaching out seemed less vindictive, less contemptuous, less threatening now.

'You can't touch me,' I whispered, not knowing whether they could hear me or whether I ought to hope that they couldn't. 'I'm invulnerable. I'm a vampire, and I can't be hurt. Not any more. I have everything I need, even if I can't have everything I want.'

The owls didn't reply. In fact, they faded away. They had no substance.

I felt a bubble of gas burst in my gut, and cursed the embarrassment it made me feel. The hunger was still there, constant and unsatisfied. It wasn't hurtful, just *there*. It didn't prevent me from drifting off to sleep in the end, but it sent me disturbing dreams.

I2

Although the dreams faded from my memory within minutes of waking, they left a sour legacy. I knew that they had not been true and terrifying nightmares, but they had been uncomfortable. I felt awkward and annoyed, because I was sure that they had been embarrassing in their surrealism, as lurid dreams so often are.

I woke up with a headache, which didn't go away as I washed, dressed and brushed my teeth. I went down to breakfast, but I couldn't eat anything except for cornflakes and cold milk.

It took a surprisingly long time for me to guess that I might have caught Gil's cold. Somehow, I had assumed that becoming a vampire would make me invulnerable to vulgar illnesses. Either the assumption was wrong or I was not yet vampire enough.

When I did realize what was wrong, my feelings were strangely mixed. Usually, I loathed having colds, because I could never seem to shake them off, and the misery sometimes extended itself over ten or twelve days; but the thought uppermost in my mind just then was that Gil would now have to let me in. Now that we were both infected there was no earthly reason for him to tell me to go away. Anyhow, it didn't seem to be a particularly bad cold.

The cold weather had abated, as the weather forecast I'd seen on TV the evening before had said it would. A ridge of high pressure was pushing up from the south behind a rapidly moving low, and the wind was dragging warm air from somewhere around the Canary Islands. There were still clouds about but they were white and fluffy, and the sky behind them was peacock-blue. I sweated in my coat as I crossed the campus, but I couldn't tell whether that was the effect of the unseasonal weather or of the virus I'd picked up. The streets seemed brighter than I'd ever seen them before.

I kept my eyes lowered; I didn't dare look at the sun.

I ran up the stairs and knocked on Gil's door, calling out: 'Gil, it's me. Let me in.' Then I listened, waiting for him to shuffle across the floor to stand on the other side. At first, there was that same silence born of indecision, while he wondered whether he should pretend not to be there – but he knew that I knew that he *was* there, and in the end he came to the door.

'I'm not better yet,' he called out.

'It doesn't matter,' I said. 'I've got it too.'

Again, there was silence, while he considered the implications of that reply. I knew that he was wondering whether I was just saying it in order to make him open up, and I was hurt by that. He ought to have trusted me, I thought. Given all that we were to one another, he ought to have trusted me not to tell him an outright lie.

'I've really got it,' I told him. 'Headache, sore throat. No sniffles yet, but I can sort of feel them building up. I don't think it's a local bug at all. Maybe you brought it with you, all the way from California. Maybe it'll run riot through the south of England.'

I was joking. I knew that viruses didn't lie dormant for that long. Not usually, at any rate.

He unlocked the door and let me in. I'd imagined that he'd be standing there in a dressing gown looking woeful, maybe even clutching a hot-water bottle, but he wasn't. He was fully dressed. He did look slightly off colour and his eyes were bloodshot, but his nose wasn't red.

'I'll make a cup of coffee,' he said, offhandedly. He didn't seem pleased to see me. He looked anxious and wary. I thought that he ought to have made more effort, however bad he felt. I was his lover, after all, and he hadn't seen me for two whole days.

When he came back from the kitchenette with the coffee, he said: 'Is there an epidemic on campus? Is everyone coming down with it?'

'Not as far as I know,' I said.

I could see that he had mixed feelings about the reply, as if it might be bad news or might be good. I'd worked out by then what it was all about. 'You *are* afraid that it's something from the labs, aren't you?' I said. 'You don't really believe it, but you decided to hole up just in case. Now I've got it too, you're worried in case it's escaped. You really think it might run riot, don't you?'

He shook his head. 'The fact that you've got it too makes it even more likely that it's just an ordinary bug. That's the overwhelming probability. I know it, intellectually, but . . .'

'I suppose men who work with dynamite jump out of their skins every time somebody pops a crisp packet,' I said, meaning to be comforting by making light of it all. But we both remembered how vehemently he'd denied that his work would make him sensitive. He was ashamed that he couldn't take his own advice, and couldn't quite live up to his own expectations.

'Even if it were one of ours,' Gil said, defensively, 'it's still just a virus. The worst that could happen would be a few bad dreams. Have you had any bad dreams, Anne?'

'No worse than I'd expect on the night I started coming down with a bug,' I told him. I didn't have a single pang of anxiety about Maldureve. I'd already done all my worrying about the possibility that he might only be a hallucination. He was solid enough, and he'd been around for far too long to be a product of some silly fever dream. I was more worried about the possibility that Gil had written off what had happened between us two nights ago as a symptom of his sickness. I wanted to show him that it wasn't, and I wanted his blood, too. But I knew that if I started on him now, he'd just be confirmed in his view that it was the virus that was responsible for his feelings, and not me at all.

As I sipped my coffee, though, I began to wonder whether that might be altogether a bad thing. Maybe, I thought, it would make it easier for him, in the short term. Maybe it was a way of getting him used to the truth while his guard was down, so that he'd find it easier in the long term to accept what was happening to him. I didn't want him to die, and I didn't want to have to desert him in order to go hunting other prey. I wanted him to choose to live, to choose to be a vampire, and I thought that it would be much easier for him to make that choice if he could be persuaded, one way or another, that vampires were real. While he was Gil the smart scientist, Gil the streetwise Californian, it wasn't going to be easy for Anne the wilted northern English rose to persuade him of that, and if there was any way that the common cold – or, more precisely, his anxieties regarding the possibility that his particular cold was by no means common – could be recruited to the cause, then I ought to do it.

'What if it is an epidemic?' I said, while I thought about it. 'What if something has escaped from your lab which will sweep across campus, and then across the world?'

'Even if it were something from the lab,' he said, 'which is a million-to-one shot in itself, the odds are still stacked against it doing any damage at all, even if it could spread – which it almost certainly couldn't. If it were something from the labs, it wouldn't be a common-cold virus, tailored by natural selection for maximum contagiousness, no matter what symptoms it produced. It'd be a weak and feeble thing, which probably couldn't pass from one person to another without *very* intimate contact. I haven't had intimate contact with anyone else but you. Not lately.'

He looked at me in what seemed to me to be a peculiar fashion, although it may have been just his bloodshot eyes. I could't help wondering whether he had his suspicions about my seeing someone else. I couldn't help wondering, either, whether Maldureve had any inbuilt resistance to the viruses of our world, or whether they might be as fatal to him as earthly bacteria had been to H. G. Wells' Martian invaders. It was an authentically horrible thought, in its way, but it was comical, too, because I couldn't believe it for an instant. I must have smiled very faintly, suppressing a giggle, because Gil didn't seem to think that my reaction to his provocative remark was all that could be desired.

'Hell, Anne,' he said, 'we shouldn't be doing this. We're just winding one another up. I thought I was all ready to go in at the deep end and work with these things, but maybe I need more practice controlling my anxieties. I didn't know it would hit me like this the first time I came down with a bug. God, I'm so stupid.'

'Maybe you'd better ring Professor Viners,' I said, 'and make sure that *he*'s feeling on top of the world.'

'No,' he said, positively. 'It has to stop right here, right now. We have to stop scaring ourselves with these macabre little jokes. Let's just see this thing through. Shouldn't you go home to bed?'

'It's not that bad,' I said. 'Don't you want me to stay?'

'I know it's a mite churlish,' he said, 'but when I'm not well, I really do prefer to be alone. If I could, I'd just crawl into a hole and zip it up behind me. It's not that I don't . . .'

He stopped before he said, 'love you'. He always did. I don't know why. It can't have been lack of practice in the gentle art of lying. He was five years and a few months older than me, and well-schooled in the theory that it's okay to say anything whatsoever to a girl if you have a chance of scoring with her. Why was he so reluctant to say that he loved me? I could have said it to him.

'I can make you feel better,' I told him.

'I really don't feel up to it,' he said.

'That's not what I mean,' I told him. I stood up and went over to his chair, and looked down at him. I was scared, because I wasn't entirely sure I could do it, but I knew I had to try. I had to think of Maldureve – put myself in his shoes – and believe with all my might that my eyes had magical hypnotic power. I had to choose to be able to do what I had to do.

I looked him straight in the eyes, and I said: 'Trust me, Gil. Don't do anything – just trust me.' I didn't pose it as a question, but as a command. I didn't want any evasions, any hesitations. I stared into his eyes, and I tried to be a true vampire: a gaudy lamia; a charismatic *femme fatale*. I tried to catch him and hold him, in spite of his sickness, in spite of his reluctance. I tried to reach out, to summon all his young blood from the depths of his being, to take full possession of whatever vestiges of lust were in him.

He looked up at me, frowning in puzzlement. But then the frown began to fade away, to be replaced by a different kind of uncertainty. He looked into my eyes with awe. He didn't know what he was seeing, but he knew that I wasn't just Anne any more. He knew that I was something more than that, and I was glad. I hadn't quite realized how desperately I needed someone else to be able to see me, and to know that I had undergone a miraculous metamorphosis.

When Gil looked up at me with awe in his eyes, I knew that everything would be all right.

Then I bent down to kiss his neck. The mark was still there, the size of a fifty-pee piece, blue turning to purple and yellow. It was beautiful and tender, and I could almost see the flesh softening in anticipation of my caress.

I kissed him, and held the kiss long enough to be sure that he wasn't resisting, and then, very gently, I began to drink. I didn't know whether it would conjure up all the good feelings of which he was capable, given that I had to go ahead without any significant foreplay, but I knew that he was wide awake, and I knew that he could tell himself, if it made it any easier for him, that it was only a delirious dream, only a hallucination, only some stray psychotropic protein making merry amid the synapses of his deluded brain.

For me, it was better than the first time. My hunger was no more avid, but this time I knew what to expect. The anticipation of the taste added to the pleasure of consummation. I was able to relax more, to revel in the glorious sensation of his blood flowing into my mouth, into my inner being.

I suppose we weren't ideally positioned, with me standing up and him sitting down, but it didn't matter. The sensations associated with the flow of the blood drove out all others, and sent me soaring as high as a kite. It was utterly beautiful, infinitely satisfying.

Perhaps I drank too deeply. When I stopped and discreetly withdrew, his bloodshot eyes were glazed. The wound on his neck was angry and ugly, glistening with unspilled blood. He sank back into the armchair like a discarded doll. His eyes were still open, but he wasn't wide awake any longer.

For one dreadful moment, I thought he might even be dead, but then he started breathing again, raggedly but forcefully. I could see the wound fading, as if it were folding in upon itself. It was as if the practised flesh knew better this time how to go about the work of healing itself, obliterating the record of what had been done to it.

I felt dizzy, intoxicated, *full*.

All my life, I'd had difficulty because of my inadequate appetite. I'd never wanted to eat as much as other people wanted me to, because I'd never really wanted to be full. Being full, in the ordinary stomach-loading sense, had never seemed to me to be a pleasurable sensation; it had always been a kind of discomfort. This was different.

This was *very* different.

'Gil,' I said, softly.

He heard me, but he didn't reply. His only response was to adjust his position slightly, to relax even further. He let his anxious, staring eyes fall thankfully shut. He looked as if he had drifted peacefully away to blissful sleep. There wasn't actually a smile on his face, but he was calm and serene. He had been possessed by pleasure; I had no doubt at all about that.

'I told you so,' I said, wondering whether the quietly spoken words would sound like a disembodied whisper in his ear, spilling into his peaceful dream from the borderlands of existence. 'I told you I could make you feel better. For now, you can think of it as a recurrent dream, if you want to. You can get to know it on those terms – learn to love it on those terms. Think of it as a lovely and precious hallucination, something better than vulgar reality could ever provide. When you've learned to love it on those terms, how very glad you'll be to find out that it's real after all! How immensely grateful you'll be to learn that there *are* more things in Heaven and Earth . . . and you won't be frightened by the owls, Gil. Not you. You'll be able to deal with *them*. We'll tackle them together. We're one and the same, now.'

Then I licked my lips and left him to recuperate. I felt absolutely fine. My headache was gone and my throat felt perfectly okay. The whole world was in sharper focus, and I was walking on air.

I realized that I hadn't had a virus at all – that all I'd had was a lurking anxiety, which had brought on withdrawal symptoms far earlier than was necessary. Perhaps vampiric invulnerability, I thought, was adequate after all to repel such vulgar ailments as the common cold. When Gil made his choice, as I was determined that he should, he too could stop worrying about million-to-one possibilities. He too could be strong, and happy, and *full*.

Even though the sun was still out, steering an unsteady course through the passing clouds, shining down as though it were June instead of December, I didn't feel that the eyes of the owls were upon me at that particular moment, or that their tiny claws had any power to prick my heart and lacerate my soul.

13

That afternoon we had a lecture on Descartes' first medita- tion. I expected it to be boring, and in a way it was, but I was taking such an interest in everything that I couldn't help getting involved in the argument. I suppose I was gradually turning into a philosopher, as a result of Dr Gray's incessant assaults on my stream of consciousness.

I couldn't believe that anyone could be so mind-bogglingly daft as Descartes, who had set out to doubt *everything* so successfully that he had reduced the realm of the indubitable to the mere fact of there being a doubting thought, and then had promptly put the whole damned universe back in place, as bonny and bright as ever, simply by jumping to the absurd conclusion that God wouldn't lie to him. Could this be the same God, I wondered, who ordered Abraham to sacrifice his son, and then said 'Sorry, Abe – only joking'? Was this the same God who slaughtered the first-born of Egypt, innocent or guilty, just to make a point that all his other plagues and pestilences had failed to make? Was this the same God who moved in such mysterious ways that all the philosophers and logicians in the world couldn't make head or tail of what he was supposed to be doing, or how, or why?

Dr Chapman, of course, tried to let Descartes off the hook. It was, he suggested, just a way of dramatizing the fact that there was a minimal act of faith involved in assuming that the world of appearances was intelligibly connected with things as they were. Descartes had to be diplomatic, Dr Chapman pointed out, given that he was living in a time when accusations of heresy could be dangerous to a man's health. I suppose Dr Chapman was right, but I wasn't in a compromising mood that day. I was full of myself, and full of Gil's blood. And I thought that I knew far more than Descartes or Dr Chapman about the reality behind the world of appearances, and what mighty follies might be concealed by little leaps of faith. Pride, as Dad would have reminded me, goeth before . . .

I'd never been able to believe in God, even though Mum and Dad – who weren't churchgoers themselves – had forced me to go to Sunday school until I was eleven. Sharon had just refused to go, but in my own more docile fashion I'd avoided the fuss, and simply refused to believe a single word I heard. I found it much easier to believe in that malevolent demon who might have designed the entire world as a crazy dream, just to fool poor old Descartes – and I couldn't find any sympathy in my heart for Descartes, who obviously hadn't felt the same.

Naturally enough, I didn't say anything to Dr Chapman. I might have made him lose his place in his yellowed notes, and he wouldn't have appreciated that.

In a way, I was still in Sunday school.

After the lecture I was buttonholed by Cynthia, who said that she wanted to ask me about the essay we were doing for Dr Gray's next tutorial. I suppose she did. She also, as it transpired, wanted to ask my opinion about all the lecturers, all the philosophers about whom the lecturers lectured, all the social problems currently afflicting the north of England, the south of England and the rest of the world, and anything else she could think of to keep the conversation going. She simply couldn't be shaken off. There was no way in the world I could avoid inviting her back to my room for a cup of coffee and a long conversation.

At first, I thought she might be trying to seduce me, and I wondered whether I ought to be amused, flattered or insulted, or a bit of all three – but I wasn't scared. Even though the possibility of being propositioned by lesbians had been too unthinkable to figure in the long catalogue of dire warnings which Mum and Dad had issued before they consented to wave goodbye to their darling daughter, I wasn't scared. I just wondered whether Cynthia's blood would taste much different from Gil's, and whether she might be a useful person to cultivate, given that Gil would one day turn into a vampire and become as useless to me as I was fast becoming – perhaps had already become – to Maldureve.

Eventually, though, I realized that she wasn't hellbent on going to bed with me at all. She was just lonely and uncertain. She just wanted someone to talk to, and be with. She was ten years older than I, but not that much different. Her self-assurance was as haphazard as the spare flesh which lay about her unslender person; it had simply grown there over the years, without any regard at all to whether it was attractive or useful or well designed. She felt out of her depth at the university. She was desperately afraid that she couldn't cope with the work, with the examinations which would one day loom up on the horizon, and with life itself.

I was astonished – not so much by the discovery that she was so screwed up, but by the fact that she'd come to me for reassurance and moral support. To *me*!

'You're clever,' she said, defeatedly, and perhaps not meaning it sincerely. 'I can see that. Cleverer than I am. When I was your age I was in a dead-end job and glad that I was six months pregnant, even though my boyfriend had disappeared, because it was a ticket out of the job. A ticket from the frying pan to the fire, as things turned out – not that I'd be without Janine now, you understand. She's all I've got, bless her. She doesn't mean to be awkward. It's just her age. It isn't easy being a single parent, and it didn't get any easier when I decided to stop pretending that I could form relationships with men and came out. I didn't realize how clever people were until I came here. Your essays are ten times better than mine, and Dr Gray doesn't begin to make a fool of you the way he makes a fool of me, week after week.'

I tried to make the right noises. I tried to tell her about all my own anxieties and feelings of inadequacy. For the first time in my life I felt a temptation to declare that I had anorexia nervosa, instead of just being thin, so that she'd remember that there was one problem in the world that she didn't have. She'd have liked it, I think, if I could have joined in with the long, miserable howl of anguish. That was what she was expecting of me.

I didn't do very well. I don't think I'd ever have done very well, but if she'd come to me four or five weeks earlier I'd at least have been able to make a reasonable confession of my own inadequacies. As things stood, it was too late for that. And as things stood, I knew that I was capable of doing far more than paying her in false coinage. I knew that I had the power to save her, the power to give her real joy and real strength. But I couldn't say so – not right away. I wasn't ready yet for further complications, when I still had Gil to deal with. So I tried, instead, to meet her expectations. I told her that I wasn't very clever really, and that I felt out of my depth too, and that I thought it was tremendously brave of her to try to do the course while she had a little girl still in primary school, and that I was sure that in the fullness of time everything would be okay. I just didn't make a very good job of it.

She thanked me when she left, said I'd made her feel better, apologized for having inflicted herself upon me, and asked if she could come again some time.

I said that was okay, and good, and it was no trouble, and yes of course.

It was all meaningless. It was all babble, all hypocrisy, all ritual. I could see that perfectly clearly. Dr Gray and Maldureve, between them, had enabled me to see all of that, and more.

Later, after dinner, I started work on my essay. I went to the library and sat at a desk there until it closed at nine o'clock. It was very peaceful. Peace and quiet always descended like a dark cloak upon the library, once the bars in the Halls and the Union were open. I liked sitting beside one of the big plate-glass windows on the second floor, looking out into the darkness, from which I could see the tops of the nearby trees, and all the lights blazing in various labs in the science blocks. But I didn't look directly at the lights that evening, because I didn't want to spoil my mood by seeing the owls staring back at me. I concentrated on my work for as long as I could, and when I looked up and out of the window I looked into the darkest shadows.

It was still warm when I set out to walk back across the campus; in fact, it felt just as warm as it had by day. It was easy to imagine that the scent of tropical flowers was still floating on the air which had been carried up from the Canaries by the not-so-gentle wind. Nobody was about, though. Everyone seemed to be indoors, imprisoned by force of habit and cages of electric light.

As I crossed the bridge, I realized that I desperately wanted to see Maldureve. It wasn't a physical desperation; it was an authentic longing. I wanted him to drink my blood, one last time, while my change was not yet quite complete. I wanted that last occasion to be special – to be a glorious celebration of all that had been and all that was yet to come. I wanted it to be slow, so that I could savour it. I wanted to be able to etch it on my memory so deeply that it could never be erased by mere forgetfulness, so that I'd have it for ever, to treasure.

I stopped by the wood and looked into the trees, into the intricate web of multitudinous shadows. I waited for a few seconds, then I stepped off the path and moved into their dark and fond embrace. I felt sure that Maldureve was there, waiting – waiting for me to come to him. I felt sure that he was as enthusiastic as I was to make our last encounter a memorable one, to build an emotional link which would bind us together eternally, as long as we both should live, no matter where we might roam in search of fresh blood to sustain our miraculous existence.

The shadows caressed me gently. I wondered whether he might be hiding, teasing me just a little.

Then, without warning, a gloved hand clamped itself over my mouth.

The glove was made of coarse wool, and it was moist and dirty. I could taste something earthy as the fingers tried to block my mouth and stifle my voice. There was a sudden stink in my nostrils – not just the reek of the glove but the foulness of bad breath. It was quite horrible. I wanted to scream, but I couldn't. It was as though the air had been knocked out of my lungs by the shock.

I felt another arm snake around me from behind, but this one didn't grab at me. The hand already had something in it, tightly gripped. I struggled, but the arm was strong, and the horrid smell was palpable.

'Shut up!' said a whispering voice, close to my ear, urgent with the panicky force of its command, although I hadn't managed to utter a sound. 'Keep quiet, or I'll cut you!'

I felt the tip of something sharp press against my neck, against the spot where Maldureve had so often kissed me, from which he drew my blood. I knew it was the inert steel blade of a knife, but it felt like a claw. It was like something living, viciously avid to slash, to hurt, to punish.

I closed my eyes, beset by horror, but it was no good. I could *feel* the eyes staring at me, accusing me, hating me. There's no escape from the owls, when they cease to hide in light and come out into the shadows – the warm, caressing shadows which feel so very safe, but aren't. The owls were there, and all they needed was a little light to make themselves seen and felt.

Silently, I screamed for Maldureve. The shadows were all around us: *his* shadows; *his* world. But he didn't come in answer to my plea. The shadows didn't move at all.

'Get down, you bitch!' The words hissed and buzzed in my ear. 'Get down, you filthy, fucking bitch.'

I hadn't forgotten what Maldureve had said – that he couldn't come to save me from the owls, if ever they should seize me – but I couldn't help it that I didn't believe him. I felt absolutely certain that he would come, as he had before, surging out of the shadows to save me. I thought I knew him better than he knew himself. I howled for him to come, in the silent recesses of my skull.

I got down, sinking so meekly that the man who held me thought he had me, thought that I was his, thought that he could do whatever he liked with me. He had a knife at my throat and he thought I'd given in, that I'd consented to be his victim.

He was wrong.

As soon as the grip of the wet, foul glove relaxed upon my mouth, I screamed out loud. I screamed with all my might. I screamed for help, and the three syllables of Maldureve's name split the darkness like great claws, tearing the shadows.

I screamed, as a demon might have screamed, with rage and fury as well as terror and the fear of pain.

I felt the pain which the shadow felt. I felt the blade of the knife prick me, groping for my soul. But it only pricked me, and my soul was far beyond its reach. It was a lighter touch by far than Maldureve's, and although it was all pain, all tearing, I knew that it was really nothing and less than nothing. I knew that mine was no ordinary flesh, that it could flow and mend itself, that it couldn't be destroyed.

It would have been all right, if the bite of the steel blade hadn't somehow filled my eyes with kinaesthetic light. It would have been all right, If I'd been able to fade into the shadows. But I saw the terrible eyes of the owls, and I knew that the blade was really a claw, and that the owls had come to claim me.

I would have laughed, but I was too busy screaming and fighting back. I grappled at the owl with my slender arms, and when that foul furry talon came back to try to clamp my mouth shut, I bit down on it as hard as I possibly could.

Even through the woollen glove, with its stinking burden of moisture and dirt, I could taste the blood. It wasn't sweet – not in that coarse bed of soiled and matted fibres – but it was good enough. With my own fingers splayed like claws on a talon I groped for his eyes, for those horrible staring eyes that I couldn't see. I wanted to tear the tearer, terrorize the terror . . . to spill blood, in whatever quantity I could. I wanted to hurt the thing that was hurting me, to show the monster that I was a monster too, a haunter of the dark, full of supernatural strength and vampiric power.

Then, all of a sudden, he was gone, fluttering away through the darkness, with his great wings battering the leafless branches as he fled. He was gone, and I had won.

I knew that I hadn't hurt him – not really. I hadn't drawn nearly as much blood from him as he'd drawn from me; that became obvious when I put my hands to my neck and felt the wound that the knife had made. Touching it increased the pain a hundredfold, but I didn't even flinch.

I could hear other people crashing through the wood by then, and I knew that they weren't owls or freaks or predators drawn as though by some mysterious magnet to the Marquis of

Membury's Garden. I knew they were coming in answer to my scream.

Maldureve hadn't come – Maldureve had told me the simple truth when he said that he couldn't come to my aid against the owls – but I still hoped that he *would* come, in his own time, so that he might soothe my wound with his gentle lips, and so that we could make our special kind of love for one last time: slowly, lovingly, languidly, carefully.

I still hoped, even then.

I knew that I was losing blood and losing consciousness, but I still hoped that I was going to be all right. I tried with all my might not to be scared. I told myself, as sternly as I could, that I wasn't frightened at all. I told myself that Maldureve had taught me not to be frightened – of the dark, of demons, of rape, of dying, of my own hunger.

I knew that I was losing blood, but I hoped as fervently as I could that it wouldn't matter. I thought, in my innocence, that hope might be enough to save my life. I didn't want to die, and I really thought that if I hoped with all my heart that I might live, then I *would* live, and never die.

I put my fingers to the gaping wound in my neck, but the nails felt like claws, eager to rip and rend. I only wanted to stop the cut, but the blazing touch of my own claws filled my head with white light, and in the heart of that light I saw the owls.

There were thousands of them, perhaps millions. Their eyes were vivid and fiery, and their feathers were like coloured flames. They filled me up, and they caught my soul, and bore it aloft into their realm of frightful light.

They took me, and caged me, and left me to wait – all alone – for the purifying fires of Hell to ignite inside my heart.

Secondary Phase:
Fever

I

I guess there are times in everybody's life when everything that previously seemed stable, settled and dependable suddenly becomes unstable, unsettled and unreliable. It's not such a big deal when something like that happens; you have to expect it once in a while. It's freaky, but it isn't so out of this world that it's unthinkable. Maybe it's happened to you some time. Maybe you can remember a day when the world changed gear, when you looked in a mirror and thought, 'Who am I, anyhow? *What* am I?' and found that you didn't exactly know.

We take ourselves so much for granted that we sometimes don't know how much we've changed since we last took stock. It's easier than you think to find, all of a sudden, that you've become a stranger to yourself. You don't have to be in a foreign land, cut off from your folks and your old friends and the California sun, though all that sure as hell helps. It could happen any time: today; tomorrow; next Friday night. It could happen without warning. You could just wake up and it could hit you, like a punch in the gut, that you aren't any longer the person you thought you were, and that when you get right down to it you just don't know who the hell you've become.

Sometimes, when I was alone, I used to say to myself, as if I were introducing myself to some stranger. 'I'm Gil Molari.' I used to do that quite a lot, as if I were trying it out for size – not the name, but the tone. I wasn't just saying it as a matter of information, I was saying it to make an impression. I was saying it so as to imply self-confidence and pride. I was saying something about the kind of Gil Molari I wanted to be: an all-right guy; a guy whose name *meant* something; a guy another guy might have heard of, and might be proud to become acquainted with. I always wanted to *be* somebody, to achieve something that would command respect. I knew I was smart enough, and I had the motivation. I knew I could make a name for myself, if only I could find the right arena, some up-and-coming field where there were names and reputations to be made.

But you can be wrong about who you are. Not about the name, but about what it means. You can be wrong about who and what you are, and not realize it for a long time, until it suddenly hits you that you've become someone and something different. Self-confidence can be misplaced, and pride – as the Bible says – can go before . . . well, anyway, you can be wrong.

I really was smart, though. I had lots of ideas, maybe more than I could handle. They'd hit me all the time while I was in the labs, during the boring intervals that all experiments have: the waiting times. Those were the best times for daydreaming, for wondering. I didn't have the same kind of daydreams and wonderings Teresa had . . . well, sometimes, maybe . . . but I had a whole lot of smarter dreams. I jotted them down in the margins of my lab book, the way great scientists are supposed to do, so that later – when I was somebody – that book would be a monument to the evolution of my genius. They were only daydreams; I didn't have any delusions of grandeur. We all have daydreams, don't we? And who among us settles for ordinary achievements, in the arena of our daydreams? Why should we? In our daydreams, we can be anything we want to be, and it doesn't do us any harm at all. It helps us, in fact, to keep the self-confidence and the pride in our voices when we say. 'I'm . . . whoever.'

Whoever.

And on those occasions when we surprise ourselves, when we suddenly discover that we're not the person we thought we were, we still have our daydreams to use as building blocks to reconstruct ourselves, to build ourselves up to something better than we ever were before, so that we can say again, 'I'm Gil Molari,' and mean it.

It could happen to anyone. It could happen to you.

I didn't realize at first, of course, that I'd been infected by an unusual virus. Maybe I struggled to resist the idea far too long. I wish now that I'd had the courage to admit it to myself much sooner. Other people, when they became aware of my unease, were unanimous in thinking that I overreacted and jumped to the wrong conclusion on the basis of inadequate evidence, and I could hardly blame them, because I'd tried as hard I could to sustain the same opinion. Alas, the real truth was that I didn't jump quickly enough; if I had, things might have worked out differently.

I didn't mean to infect Anne. I didn't mean to infect anyone. If I'd known – if I'd even suspected – I'd have done it all differently. But I didn't know. How could I? How could anyone?

Now, with the aid of hindsight, I can see the full significance of what happened the last time Anne and I had sex, after she came to the flat and cooked that special meal for us. At the time, I thought it was just a cruel trick of the imagination, but now I know that it wasn't. It was the first frantic outburst of the rogue virus which had established itself in the grey matter of my brain, spitting its toxins into the dark corners of my mind.

The sex was better than usual, and I suppose I have to consider the possibility that *that* was due to the virus, too, although I'd prefer to believe that it wasn't. I'd like to think that I had finally begun to break down the wall of anxiety with which Anne had somehow surrounded herself. The fact that she was willing to cook and eat the meal supports that view – I really was getting through to her, getting her to loosen up. No matter how often she denied it, I was utterly convinced that she was anorexic, and so her new interest in food seemed to me to be a hopeful sign that she might be pulling herself together. I knew well enough that she hadn't yet begun to enjoy sex – that it was something she did because she thought she ought to, or because she thought she had to do it in order to hang on to me, to keep me interested – but I had always thought that she'd learn to relax, in due time, and begin to take pleasure in it. That evening, she seemed to be on the very brink of doing that. She seemed more confident, more eager, more expectant.

I felt rather spaced out while I was moving back and forth inside her. At the time I put it down to the wine, but I really

hadn't drunk very much, and now I know that it was the virus
getting into gear. For me, sex has always been primarily a tactile
experience, so there was nothing unusual in the fact that I had my
eyes shut, but I'd never before felt so disconnected from anything
outside the immediate experience.

I don't usually fantasize much – not *that* much – but I
couldn't seem to help certain images floating into my mind;
I was powerless either to resist or to take hold of them. They
didn't make any sense: menacing shapes half formed and half
visible in pools of shadow; eyes and feathers all confused. There
was nothing explicitly sexual about them – not even, so far as
I could judge, in any Freudian-style symbolic fashion – and yet
they seemed to intensify my feelings and sharpen my sensations.
The touch of Anne's hands as they brushed lightly over my back
seemed impossibly soft and luxurious, and her skin, wherever it
was in contact with mine, felt strangely insubstantial.

The intoxication I felt when I came was unexpectedly vertiginous; I felt that I'd completely lost my sense of gravity. I lost that
sense of location which normally gave me a comfortable sense of
being behind my eyes and between my ears, and for a moment
or two I didn't seem to be inside myself at all, but somewhere
else entirely. I remember thinking, in a disappointingly academic
fashion, that it must be some similar sensation which convinces
certain gullible people that they can project their 'astral bodies'
out of their physical flesh, but I didn't seem to fly away. It was
more of an expansion than a displacement.

My eyes were still shut, but I experienced a weird kind of
quasi-visual hallucination. I 'saw' Anne tilt back her head,
opening her mouth as she did so, to take hold of my neck as
though to bite it – but I knew she didn't really do any such
thing, because I couldn't feel her lips or teeth at all when she
lifted herself slightly to make contact. Instead, I felt as if the side
of my throat were becoming numb, strange, molten. It felt as if
something were being drawn out of me, ever so gently: perhaps
blood, perhaps energy . . . or perhaps something else, something
unnameable, unimaginable.

I gasped in surprise, because the sudden awareness that the
horizons of my experience could still be stretched in that almost
magical way seemed to be a very significant discovery.

I felt dizzy, and then I felt tired, but the way the dizziness dissolved into tiredness was so very smooth and seemingly natural that I just went with it and didn't try to resist at all. I felt that I was falling, and I just let myself go, without any thought at all of what might happen when the fall was arrested. I think I would have fallen into a drugged sleep, if it hadn't been for Anne.

All of a sudden, Anne screamed.

It probably wasn't the virus which made her do it – I'm not certain that she'd already been infected at that point in time. I think it was probably me. She was probably relaxing, falling asleep herself, when I let my full weight down on her. I had always taken good care to support my weight on my elbows, but in the grip of that strange drunkenness I must have become a dead weight – and she must have suddenly become aware of me pressing down, seemingly threatening to crush and suffocate her. Maybe it recalled some secret fear of hers, or invoked one of those irrational phobias we all have.

Anyhow, she overreacted.

Her scream pulled me out of it, and I immediately caught myself up, pulled back from her. We came apart, and I tried to throw myself sideways, to set her free – but she caught me and tried to hold me. She was presumably ashamed of her overreaction, trying to take back the effect of her scream.

'It's all right,' she said. 'I'm sorry – it's all right.'

'Jesus,' I said weakly, not yet quite able to get my thoughts together sufficiently to make light of it. 'You scared the shit out of me. What the hell was it?'

It was a stupid question, but I was still befuddled.

'A dream,' she said quickly. 'Only a dream.'

When she let me go, I carried on falling, overtaken by an overwhelming lethargy. There was nowhere to fall *to*, but even when I was flat on my back I seemed to be falling still. I didn't know what was happening, and couldn't seem to pull myself together.

'It's okay,' she said, while she was putting her clothes on. 'It's fine. Don't get up. It's not late. I'll be all right.' Her voice was forced, but it was more embarrassment than fear. She was ashamed of herself for having upset the mood of the moment, and now she wanted to run away. She was often like that, and I had never figured out a good way to handle it. She was so nervous, sometimes, that she had to be allowed to run and hide; any attempt to make her stay would simply make her shrivel up with anxiety. Even so, I told her that she could stay, that she didn't have to go. She muttered something about not having brought her things, and I knew it was useless to press the point.

I was still falling. I felt as weak as a kitten. 'I don't know what's the matter with me,' I said, more truthfully than I knew.

'Too much excitement,' she said. 'Go to sleep – get some rest.' It was an embarrassment to her that I was still awake; she just wanted to get out. It was a pity, after we'd achieved so much earlier in the evening. I had to hope that we'd be able to pick up the pieces another time.

I let myself down on the pillow. I must have fallen asleep before she left the flat.

I woke up next morning knowing that I'd had a bad night, beset by delirious nightmares I couldn't quite remember. There must have been a few minutes in between sleep and wakefulness when the substance of those nightmares was still present to my awakening mind, but I lost my grip on them before I could collect myself and force myself to review them carefully and lucidly.

By the time I was fully conscious I could only remember that there had been predatory vampires in the dream, and that I had become obsessed – as I so often used to do in disturbed dreams – with the absolute necessity of carrying out some inherently absurd and appalling action. The details were soon lost, overwhelmed by the knowledge that I had a headache and a sore throat. The mere fact of becoming aware of these things seemed to make them instantly worse, and I knew that I had a cold coming on.

At first, when the thought that I might have picked up a virus at the lab came into my mind, I was inclined to dismiss it as the kind of anxious speculation which had to be scrupulously avoided by a person in my line of work – but then I began to remember what had happened before I went to sleep, and I began to wonder.

'No,' I said, in the end, speaking aloud for emphasis. 'Don't be paranoid. This is the first test, and you have to stick to your guns.

It's just some lousy British virus discovering American flesh for the first time.'

I tried to take things slowly. I got up, made myself a cup of coffee, and took two aspirins for the headache. I got dressed and forced myself to eat some cereal and toast for breakfast, thinking that I'd be able to get a proper grip on myself once I was in a fit state to face the day. It didn't work. I felt awful. I kept telling myself, over and over, that I only felt awful because I had a cold, and that it was only the slight fever associated with the cold that was filling my head with other fears. I wasn't convinced, but I tried to put *that* down to the cold, too. I was in such a state of confusion that I didn't dare go out of the flat, let alone go into the lab.

Eventually, I went back to bed. I switched the radio on and played with the dial until I found a station which hadn't been entirely taken over by moronic disc jockeys with verbal diarrhoea. I lay there, silently instructing myself to stop being silly, and to remember all my own good advice about it not mattering overmuch even if some chance-in-a-million slip in sterile technique did lead to my infecting myself, because the infection would only last a few days, and would be no more troublesome than any everyday cold virus.

This advice – sound or not – would probably have been sufficient to calm my anxieties for a while, had they not been complicated by thoughts of Teresa. Because I was alone, with time weighing heavily on my hands, I couldn't help my fears extending themselves. I couldn't avoid saying to myself: 'Suppose it wasn't a chance-in-a-million failure of my sterile technique; suppose the failure had already happened; suppose you caught it from Teresa.' Nor could I help saying to myself: 'That's only guilt talking; only your own inability to take what was offered as casually as it was offered; only . . .'

Ironically enough, I had also to wonder whether my very confusion, my inability to think straight, might be symptoms of a hypothetical psychotropic virus.

Once any such possibility is entertained, of course, anything and everything can become relevant evidence. Even the fact that I wasn't yet prepared to jump to any conclusion might be regarded as a symptom, or at least as something symptom-affected.

The opposite, I suppose, is also true and equally ironic. My eventual decision and firm conviction – my eventual absolute certainty that I had been infected, either by my own carelessness or by Teresa – might have owed more to the fact of the infection than to the incontrovertibility of rational argument. But none of that matters. The simple fact is that I *was* infected, and thereby doomed. From that very first moment, when I felt my flesh melt, impossibly, beneath the intangible pressure of Anne's hungry mouth, I was damned.

The moment I began that uncanny fall, my eventual fate was sealed and certain, written in the book of destiny in my own bright blood.

2

C oming to England wasn't such a big deal for me. I think it meant more to my dad. It's not that I wasn't ambitious, but I'd have been content to stay with the system I knew if the prospects had looked better. CalTech didn't seem so bad to me, and most people would consider it a better school than any in England, except maybe Oxford and Cambridge. But Dad always had this big thing about US insularity and the necessity of a cosmopolitan world-view – his words, of course. His own parents had come to the States as refugees, dispossessed of whatever heritage they'd had by the political chaos that followed the end of World War II. I don't know for sure what part of what country they came from, or even what language they spoke. Dad must have known a little of the old language when he was a kid, but his parents made a big thing out of speaking English at home, so that it would become his first language, and he dutifully forgot what he knew of the other, so that they could be proud of him. At a guess, where my grandparents came from was probably part of Yugoslavia when they left it, though it must have been some other country when they were born and it looks like being some other country again before much longer.

The world is less stable than it seems. Borders come and go. Names change. And all the while, blood is shed by those who seek to preserve or change them.

Dad's ideas of what Europe was like were all illusion, of course. Not that he hadn't been there, on business and as a tourist – it's just that he'd seen whatever he'd seen through the lenses of his illusions, and thus preserved them from any breakage. He really thought it was great when I got the chance to come here, even though England was only the home of his adopted language, not a place to which any of us could trace authentic roots.

Even psychotropic biology was a compromise between us. Dad had tried his damnedest to push me in the direction of commercial biotechnology since I was fifteen and first showed aptitude in the relevant sciences. I had tried my damnedest to stay out of it, but not for any good reason. I just wanted to be my own person, not something shaped by my dad out of his own frustrated ambitions. The net result of his shoving and my sidestepping was that I ended up in the borderlands between biology and psychology, neither one thing nor the other.

His grudging judgement, when we finally settled the matter in a slightly hot-tempered debate, was that my chosen field did seem to have potential, but that it was perilously close to the lunatic fringe. How right he was! How absolutely typical of him to be far more precise in his choice of words than he could possibly have imagined. But he really was trying to look out for me, trying to steer me right. He was no bully; he was just trying to lay the groundwork for a successful life. He always wanted me to be able to be proud of who and what I was. He wanted me to be a credit to the family name, and he wanted the family name to be a credit to me.

He pulled strings, in the end, to get me what I finally decided I wanted. He got money from the Foundation so that I could become a spy for American science in a half-forgotten corner of the great big world of scientific research.

He was pleased when I described what I was doing in my letters home. When I told him about the animals, he was reassured that it was real science – authentic hands-on stuff. He probably didn't know what chromatography and electrophoresis were, but when I sent him some colour slides I'd made of rabbit brain-tissue he was delighted. They didn't mean a damned thing in the context of my research but they were something he could shine on the wall instead of home movies. They were solid; they were *real*.

Everybody warned me that England would be cold and grey and dismal, but it wasn't as bad as I'd expected. There was no snow on the ground, even in December, and no sub-zero temperatures. It wasn't warm, but if God hadn't meant us to be able to live in cold climates he'd never have given us synthetic fur and central heating. As for being grey – well, I guess if you averaged out the days they'd have a pretty cloudy mean, but there was a lot more standard deviation about the weather in England than there ever had been back home. It was too interesting to be dismal. It wasn't quaint, although I'd half expected it to be, but it was different. There was always something to look at that wasn't the way it would have been back home, always something to overhear that was funny.

September was a good time to arrive, because it was the very end of summer; practically from the day I stepped off the plane the landscape began to slough its skin. The leaves started falling off the trees; the colours started changing. Every day, in every way, things were just a little bit different. The campus was a good place to see all that, because it was such a crazy patchwork. The university had just moved into this old park, colonizing it bit by bit, but you could still see traces of earlier inhabitants, and patches of wilderness which didn't really belong. Some of the old buildings tended to the grotesque, but that didn't matter; that was just *character*. It was a great place to be, especially in the first couple of weeks, before the undergraduate term started, when the serious scholars didn't have to lose themselves in crowds of kids.

If I wanted to be cruel, I could say that the most dismal thing about England turned out to be Professor Michael R. Viners, but that wouldn't be entirely fair. Maybe I was expecting too much of him, on the basis of the paper he'd given back home; like most people, he had a special conference persona quite distinct from the personality he wore when he was doing the day-by-day work. Conferences require performance and a bit of glitz, and you only have fifteen minutes at the podium to make your point. In the lab, you have to work the year round to produce the results that go into your fifteen-minute presentation, and you have to be patient, painstaking and methodical. You have to be dull, in fact.

If I'd thought about it sensibly, I'd have realized that Viners in his home environment would be cooler and greyer than the English weather. It was a mistake to assume, or even hope, that the world's leading man in a sexy subject like psychotropic genetics would be a bit of a wild man – an unorthodox, anti-Establishment genius. I should have known that when we renewed our brief acquaintance I'd find him prim and distant and utterly uptight. Not that he disapproved of me – quite the opposite. Thanks to Dad's good friends at the Foundation, I was the academic equivalent of a World War II food parcel, come to lend a little milk and honey to a resource-starved project. I was a gift-wrapped donation from the wonderful world of private enterprise, of a kind that the British government had apparently instructed all university departments to seek out, but that very few of them seemed to be able to find. In his own scrupulously polite and ever-so-slightly downcast fashion he made me very welcome.

'I can't promise you fame and fortune,' he told me. 'Nor can I promise you that the journals will be enthusiastic to publish the results of your research. Mere mention of the word "psychotropic" is enough to set all their alarm bells ringing, I'm afraid. I can't even guarantee you a safe and routine passage to your doctorate. All I can promise you is that you'll be involved in some genuine research, exploring uncharted territory.'

'That's what I want,' I assured him, sincerely enough.

'I hope that you don't find it too boring,' he went on. 'The actual work isn't nearly as way out as it sounds.'

'I know the score,' I told him. 'You have to get right down into the experimental gutter if you really want a clear sight of the theoretical stars.'

'Precisely,' he said, with a weak and watery grin.

Later, when I tried to picture Viners playing sex games with Teresa in the mid-range CT room, it seemed too absurd to be possible. But absurdity and impossibility are two very different things. I had to wonder whether, if I *had* caught the virus from Teresa, he might have caught it too, in exactly the same undignified fashion. I even wondered whether it might have been the other way around – whether he might have infected her. Later, though, I found it very difficult even to begin to imagine Viners being driven by the hunger. If he'd ever suffered any symptoms at all, I decided, when things first began to look really bad, he couldn't have looked at me the way he did when I confessed my fears to him. He *couldn't* have. He was far too straight to carry off that kind of lie. That was Viners. Not dismal, exactly, but straight.

Even without Anne, England would have been okay, but Anne added that special extra ingredient. Looking back, I suppose I have to be suspicious even of the attraction I felt for her, but at the time it seemed to be perfectly innocent, uniquely pleasant and wholly good, and it probably was. It was something about which I never had a qualm of conscience, because it felt so natural. I never wanted to hurt her – not for a moment. I only wanted to do her good, and I was utterly sincere in that intention. I won't call it love, and I certainly won't call it love at first sight, but it was never an act with Anne, the way it always had been with other girls. I really did feel protective towards her, and gentle. It wasn't just a plan of campaign to persuade her to put out. I know she didn't see it that way – not at first – but that was only to be expected. If there was one thing I wanted more than anything else it was to persuade her that my feelings were authentic, that my intentions were honourable.

That's why the insinuations of that slimy detective were so vilely insulting.

Okay, I will say it. Why shouldn't I? I loved Anne. Not at first. At first I just thought she looked cute: frail and lonely and helpless and luminously pretty. But in time, as I tried harder to draw her closer to me, to break down the wall of her anxiety and restore her wounded self-esteem, I began to love her. I never told her so, but that was because it was true, not because it wasn't. I could have said it easily enough if it had been a lie, a move, a stratagem, but it's not so easy to say something like that when you have to weigh the meaning very carefully, when you want to be absolutely accurate. Whether I said it or not, it was true. I loved Anne. Not at the beginning, but certainly in the end – before everything blew up in my face.

Our first meeting was an awkward one, pregnant with embarrassment on both sides. Our first conversation was almost monosyllabic – I think it took me nearly half an hour to wring a complete sentence out of her. I just couldn't find a way to get her involved, and I was so desperate that I made a couple of real foot-in-mouth blunders. I actually asked her whether she was anorexic, and had to watch her face set hard in response. Of course she was anorexic – it stuck out a mile – but the last thing I should have done was accuse her of it. It made it so much harder, later, to try to ease her out of it.

She was a little crazy, too. No, not crazy – just very, very nervous. That was only to be expected, I guess, given that she was away from home for the very first time, and given that her home seemed to have been a real oasis of calm in a troubled world – the kind of safe haven that a home is supposed to be and almost never is. From what she told me I gathered that her parents were every bit as ambitious for her as Dad was for me, but their tactics couldn't have been more different – layer upon layer of kid glove, and never a single lecture on how tough you have to be to get by in a tough world. Anne wasn't tough. Neither was I, really, but I was every bit as tough as Dad could make me. But Anne's wasn't just the ordinary, expectable nervousness. It cut deeper than that. Nor was her anorexia the only symptom.

How many neurotic habits and rituals she'd accumulated I couldn't really say, because she never let me close enough to observe them all, even after she let me into her bed. But there was one that was plain enough for all the world to see. She had this weird way of clutching at her own neck, worrying and scratching it with her fingernails. I'm not sure that she was even aware that she was doing it. Once or twice when I actually reached out and pulled her hand away she looked far more surprised than annoyed. She had a permanent mark on the side of her throat, which looked a little like a lovebite, though it obviously wasn't. Sometimes it faded a little, but she was always picking at it.

Once, I made her look at the mark in a mirror. 'You've got to let it heal, Anne,' I told her. 'Hell, it could get infected.'

'It's nothing,' she told me, flatly. 'Nothing at all.'

'People are going to think I did it,' I said, hoping that if I could make a joke out of it I might somehow crack the neurotic impulse behind it.

'So what?' she said. 'It's nothing. It doesn't hurt.'

She lived on the far side of the campus, in what I thought of as the old part, though the Hall she lived in was as modern as the others of its kind. Her department still retained certain traditional echoes of the theological college which was one of the ancestors of the modern university, and was housed in the worst building on campus – an ugly, dilapidated thing whose grounds were infested with rats. It was regarded with the kind of unquestioning reverence people usually give to things that are old, but in my opinion it was the kind of place which ought to have been pulled down so that something functional could be put up in its place.

Anne really liked the dump, although it took her some time to overcome her initial terror of the guy she had to see every week to talk about her paper. I could never understand why she liked it. There was a little bridge over a stream close to the building, and that's where I first kissed her; but while we were standing there I could hear the rats moving in the undergrowth, coming out of their hidey-holes on their nightly pilgrimage to the campus garbage dumps. I couldn't bring myself to feel any exaggerated sentimental attachment to the location.

'They should build a gym here,' I told her once. 'A real sports centre to replace that god-awful pavilion thing. They should rip out all those ragged trees and build a real stadium.'

'Secretly,' she said, 'you just want me to be a cheerleader. All the rest is just an excuse to get me leaping about in spangled boots and a miniskirt, waving pom-poms.'

I tried to make a joke about her having to eat more and build up her muscles, but she just switched off, the way she always did. I didn't push it, because I had this naive faith that a real relationship – not necessarily love, just a normal, healthy relationship – would cure her of everything. Eventually, I thought, she'd wind herself down and loosen up and just start eating. With a little ordinary care and attention, I figured, she'd stop mutilating herself. She'd lose her peculiar affection for all things dark and shadowy, and her antipathy for bright lights and slick design. Even though she had signed up to be a philosopher, to learn to worry about all the things the rest of us took for granted, I thought she'd straighten out. I thought that just being with me – me being, of course, a paragon of normality – would gradually shape her up into a sensible, laid-back, fun-loving person.

Evidently, I thought too highly of myself. Either that, or I seriously underestimated the extent of her hang-ups. One way or another, it didn't work. Every time that stupid mark on her neck faded and I'd start hoping for a breakthrough, back it came again, redder and bluer than ever.

If ever there was anyone who shouldn't have been infected by the thing that somehow got into me, it was Anne. She never stood a chance against it. She was wide open to its ravages. If someone like me couldn't cope – and I sure as hell failed in a big way – what possible chance had someone like her?

I did love her. It was because I loved her, in a way, that I accidentally gave her the virus. If I hadn't loved her she wouldn't have been condemned to lie so long in her unnatural coma, beset by frightful dreams. Sometimes, you just have to pause and ask: what kind of world do we live in, where such things as that can happen?

It was really no big deal, of course, compared to what happened to me, but I was a volunteer. Even though I had no real idea what the risks were, I went into Mike Viners' lab knowing that there were things in it which might really screw me up if I got careless. Even in my wildest dreams, I'd never have guessed how completely screwed up I could become, but I knew that I was taking on something new, something unknown, something with *potential*. That was why I came to England in the first place.

If you wanted to be really cruel, you could say that I got what I deserved. Anne didn't. Anne deserved the best.

I wish I could have given it to her.

B y the time Anne came looking for me I was in a reasonably level-headed frame of mind. I thought I knew what I had to do. It still seemed to me that the odds were stacked against my having picked up one of Viners' viruses, but I felt that I ought to cover all the angles. If I'd been infected by one of the laboratory specimens – and at that point I was still thinking very much in terms of *if* – then my obligation as a scientist was to make the most of the opportunity for scientific observation. I had to stay calm, stay indoors and make notes.

I'd long ago realized, of course, that the kind of work we were doing in the lab was working blindfold. The animal operations gave us a chance to observe behaviour, after a fashion, but you can't see into an animal's mind. You don't really have any idea what it's experiencing. The rest of the stuff, with the brain tissue, was just cookery. I knew – and I knew that Mike Viners knew – that trying to study psychotropics without access to real conscious minds was at best only half a research programme. There was no way that sectioning brains and mapping the brain proteins by chromatography and electrophoresis could ever approach the real questions: those big, deep questions which fascinated me. I also knew that in the golden years before there were such things as ethics committees and the Food and Drug Administration it was standard practice for scientists to be their own experimental guinea pigs.

For a few paranoid seconds I even entertained the fancy that maybe Viners had arranged for me to be infected – that maybe he'd brought me all the way from California so that he wouldn't have to try it out on someone close to home – but I soon let go of that one. I knew I had to avoid paranoia, and pay more scrupulous attention to matters of fact.

Even so, I had to consider the alternatives thrown up by the elementary calculus of probability.

If I really had picked up a virus, then the probability was that I'd already passed it on to Anne. Should I warn her? The answer, I quickly decided, had to be 'no', or at least 'not yet'. There was no point in worrying her unnecessarily, and there was every reason to assume, given her tendency to anxiety, that she'd react badly to any such suggestion. Better to keep insisting that I couldn't have caught anything, and that even if I had, and even if she were to catch it from me, its effects would be entirely innocuous. At that point in time I'd had no recurrence of the spaced-out feeling that had affected me the night before; I had every reason to think that it *would* be innocuous.

Having settled that, I quickly moved on. The only other people I might have infected were Viners and Teresa, who were also the prime candidates for consideration if I had been infected by someone else. It wasn't easy to judge how many other people either of them might have infected in their turn. I knew that Viners was married and that Teresa lived with her parents, so the probability was that it wouldn't stop with them if they did have anything. Then again, if it took really intimate contact to pass this kind of virus on, Teresa's parents would be safe. She and I didn't talk all that much, and I could never have plucked up the courage to ask point-blank how many other people she played games with. I suspected Viners – I could hardly help suspecting Viners – but even that possibility seemed so bizarre that there was no way to attach an estimated probability to it. What she did off campus, I had no idea. I hadn't a clue whether or not she had a steady boyfriend, or whether she spent every night putting herself about.

In the end, I decided that there wasn't much point worrying about a possible epidemic. If Teresa had given it to me, I reasoned, she must have gone through the whole cycle already, and had obviously shown no lasting ill effects. The same was true if she'd given it to Viners, or he to her. If the bug had been going round for some time before catching up with me, then it was evidently harmless. On the other hand, if my infection were recent and original, it wasn't very likely that I'd passed it on to either of them. I hadn't been into the CT room with Teresa for at least two weeks.

I was tempted to let go of the epidemic question then, in order to focus on my mental condition, but I kept coming back to it. I knew that I had to consider the whole matter very carefully and objectively, lest I should ever have occasion to put it all on the record for the benefit of future generations of psychotropic geneticists, but it was difficult looking back on the Teresa situation with calm objectivity, and even harder to contemplate writing it all down one day in careful scientific language. Maybe I'd led a sheltered life, but to me it still seemed like the stuff of cheap pornographic fiction, the kind of thing which couldn't possibly be reported in a scientific paper.

I guess I was sweating out my guilt, maybe far too belatedly. No matter what the calculus of probability said, I couldn't help coming back again and again to the question of Teresa. Had I caught it from her? Had she caught it from me? And in either case, so what?

It all began to seem so weird, while I was going over it in my mind, that I began to wonder whether it had ever really happened. Perhaps, I remember thinking, that too was just a hallucination generated by some momentary outburst of a stray virus. Maybe it was just a sexual fantasy triggered by infection, given an altogether false gloss of perceived reality simply because my brain wasn't expecting to be hit by a dream from that direction. I tried hard to recall the exact circumstances of the first encounter, searching belatedly for some kind of clue which might serve to prove its reality or its falsehood.

We were working in the high-security lab, on separate experiments – she on one of Viners', me on one of my own. It wasn't that late, but it was already dark outside; it must have been the last week in September. Viners had gone home at the usual time, leaving us to it. He did his fair share of late-night stints; this one was just our turn on the rota. It had been a long afternoon, requiring steady if not intense concentration, but now we were just culling the results, recording at regular intervals. There were periods of half an hour when there was nothing to do. I was tired; she must have been utterly bored, letting her mind wander wherever the mood took it.

There were no conversational preliminaries; she just came over to where I was working, and said: 'I'll give you a blow job if you'll give me one.'

I had never been so shocked in all my life. At first, I thought I'd misheard her, but when I looked at her lopsided grin I saw that she'd known exactly what effect her words would have. She was playing with me; the blush must have been the first part of the payoff for her, the first tiny thrill. I can't imagine what the expression on my reddening face must have looked like, but I didn't have to ask her to repeat what she'd said, or what she meant. I didn't want her to think that I could be *that* slow on the uptake. After all, I was from California, not some shitty backwoods English village.

All I said, after what must have been a heavily pregnant pause, was: '*Here?*' I did my best to seem casual.

'The medium CT room's comfortable,' she said, laconically. 'Not too warm, not too wet.' The way she said it was calculated to imply that she'd done it before, many a time, but that may have been bluff. Perhaps she was covering up the outrageousness of her own action by trying to give the impression that it was no big deal, that it was her favourite sport. Perhaps she was deliberately trying to make me believe that it was a regular thing between her and Viners, when they were here after dark,

The lab had three constant temperature 'rooms' – no more than big closets, really. One was maintained at thirty-seven Celsius – blood heat – and had a high enough relative humidity to choke you; it was heaven for tissue cultures. One was kept at four Celsius and near-zero RH, and was good for keeping bacterial cultures and infected tissues in suspended animation. The medium room was twenty-four and thirty, supposedly the kind of external temperature at which infectious agents had to be equipped by natural selection to migrate with reasonable efficiency from one host to another, by means of touch or bodily fluids.

There was a certain irony in wondering whether it might have been in that CT room that the virus migrated from Teresa's body to mine, or vice versa.

She leaned against the soft plastic wall and shoved down her tights and knickers, leaving it to me to drag them further down. I was already kneeling down. She lifted up her skirt and spread her legs as far as the tights around her ankles would let her. When I looked up she had already leaned her head back against the wall and closed her eyes.

She was attractive enough, in her way, but I'd never really thought of making a move on her. I suppose that was strange, given that we spent so much time in high-security isolation. A lot of guys would have asked her out within the first week, or at least asked probing questions calculated to test her availability. I'd been there for three weeks, maybe four, and hadn't said a word out of place. Maybe it was just that I felt out of place myself, that I hadn't settled yet into England, or into the lab.

Even then, while we were playing the game, I didn't feel that it was the beginning of a relationship. Maybe it was too casual a leap from mere acquaintance to an exchange of orgasms; maybe that froze me a bit, made me wary of her. It was impersonal, trading rather than sharing. However crazy it sounds, it didn't really break the ice between us. Maybe it would have been different, given more time for a real relationship to develop, but that first time was just six days before I first met Anne, and on the other occasions – there were only three more – my relationship with Anne was in the way. I couldn't help comparing the two of them, and deciding that Anne was the one I liked best. Teresa had the fuller figure, the softer flesh, the casual self-confidence – but I could never have warmed to her the way I had warmed to Anne. In spite of what Teresa and I did – maybe because of it – I didn't want to get involved with her. I never wanted her to be *my girl*.

When Teresa was finished, we swapped places. She always went first, and then did me. It was quick, mechanical and curiously unsatisfying, as different as could be from making love to Anne, which happened when it eventually did happen in a more orthodox and infinitely more leisurely fashion. But Teresa did come, with an alacrity and an apparent satisfaction which suggested abundant practice, and Anne never could.

Afterwards, Teresa and I just went back to work. We tucked our things away and became scientists again.

If it had only happened the once, I think I might have given more time and attention to the theory that it was a phantom memory, a hallucinatory product of the virus; but it had happened four times, and I couldn't believe in a phantom memory which had that kind of redundancy built in. Could I have picked up the virus that way? If Teresa's sterile technique was as loose as her sexual habits, I thought, there might be every chance that I'd licked the virus right out of her, under optimum conditions for infection. And if, by chance, it had been me who'd got it first, I might have shot it straight into her avid mouth.

If I had it, I felt guiltily certain, then she must have it too – or must once have had it. And if she had it still, there was no way of knowing just how fast the epidemic was going to spread. But I had never heard her complain of any illness, had never seen her blow her nose or heard her cough. She certainly hadn't had a day off work in three months. All of which meant that if I had caught it from her, and she'd had it for some time, it hadn't caused her the least anxiety. If it had done anything at all to her, it had done it in her dreams, unless . . .

Unless what she'd done with me had been an effect of the virus. Unless she'd been driven to it by something freaky in her head.

I had to let that one go, too. I knew that if I began to follow lines of thought like that I could eventually have begun to wonder whether this still purely hypothetical virus might have been responsible for every crazy thing that had happened in the British Isles, Europe and the rest of the world since the decline and fall of the Roman Empire.

The thing to do, as I knew full well, was to begin monitoring my own state of consciousness, alert for any alteration – but not so enthusiastically that I started inducing odd states of mind by the very intensity of my introspection. I had to try to act naturally and behave normally.

It was easy enough to do that, in the beginning. When Anne knocked on the door, even when she accused me of thinking I'd been affected, it was perfectly plain what would qualify as a rational answer to every one of her questions and complaints. It wasn't quite so easy when she'd gone again, hurt and annoyed, leaving me to wonder what she might be going away *to*.

Even so, the day wore on without my experiencing anything that I couldn't have brought on myself just by looking for it, even without the aid of a slight cold in the head. I was restless, jittery, and slightly feverish, but I didn't hallucinate and I didn't feel stoned. I wasn't hungry, but I raided the refrigerator at irregular intervals and made half a dozen cups of coffee, just for something to do.

In the evening, I wished time and time again that I had a TV set, because I couldn't concentrate on reading and the radio couldn't provide anything like the level of stimulation which I needed. I went to bed ridiculously early, and tossed and turned for at least two hours, wondering whether I was going to lose myself in the most spectacular nightmares of my life. In one way, it was strangely exciting, but in another it was a real bummer.

In the end – in spite of the fact that I'd resolved not to take anything that might interfere with the experience – I got up and took a couple more aspirin to soothe my unsteady head. When I finally went to sleep, the time slipped by as staggeringly as time always does when you've got a feverish cold.

I dreamed. I know that I dreamed, endlessly and luridly. I think I remember telling myself over and over that I had to remember my dreams, and had to try to write them down, because they were of great significance – but somewhere en route I lost my way completely, and when I finally woke up, properly and fully, the next morning, the details leaked into the crevices of forgetfulness, and were gone before I could recover the intention to grab a pen and start recording their substance.

As I staggered out of bed, I felt far worse than I had done the previous day, but only physically. I didn't feel spaced out, high, or even hung over. My senses were behaving as well as could be expected, given that I was aching in my head and my limbs, and still slightly feverish. I felt a little better after a cup of coffee, and even better after two more aspirin, but I still felt bad.

On re-examining my situation from a scientific point of view, I concluded that I most certainly had a virus. I also concluded, yet again, that it could easily be any common or garden English virus, and that I'd probably spoken more truly than I intended when I had assured Anne that it was just the kind of cold that any visitor from foreign climes might be expected to pick up in the course of an English December.

Anne came much earlier that second day, and when she called out, 'Gil, it's me, let me in,' I really wanted to. I held out for a minute or two, telling her I wasn't better yet, but I couldn't have stalled her for long, even if she hadn't said: 'It doesn't matter – I've got it too.' I didn't open up immediately, but I gave in soon enough.

After I'd made her a cup of coffee, I said: 'Is there an epidemic on campus? Is everyone coming down with it?'

She half evaded the question, and I knew I'd have to talk it through with her, to soothe her fears. I had the arguments all ready, but I already knew they probably wouldn't work because I'd tried them all out on myself, and I knew they hadn't worked on me. I was worried that she might get really frightened, but she didn't. We talked about it at some length, and she didn't show any signs of alarm. In fact, she seemed even calmer and more controlled than usual, although the mark on her neck was still clearly visible, advertising the fact that she wasn't yet firmly set on the road to recovery.

I was really surprised when she suddenly said: 'I can make you feel better.'

I'd been trying to persuade her to leave, to let things rest until we were both feeling better. 'I really don't feel up to it,' I said, maybe a little too quickly.

'That's not what I mean,' she said, but not as if she blamed me for misunderstanding. It was as if she had expected to be misunderstood – as if she'd been teasing me. She stood up and came over to the chair where I was sitting, and looked down at me with her intense blue eyes.

'Trust me, Gil,' she said. 'Don't do anything – just trust me.'

And that was when the virus hit me. That was when it reached out from the depths of my brain, where it had been lurking for days, and hit me with everything it had.

Everything went haywire inside my head, and I simply lost it. I lost my grip. One moment I was okay, and the next I was out of it. Way out of it. The psychotropic samurai sword cut me clean in two.

I wish I knew what I said to Anne, or what I did. I'm almost sure that I didn't say anything at all, and didn't do anything either, but almost isn't quite enough, in the circumstances.

The next time I saw her – the next time I *remember* seeing her – she was lying in the intensive care unit of the county hospital, in a coma. And in spite of what I told the detective who questioned me, I couldn't be absolutely certain – not *absolutely* – that it wasn't me who had put her there.

4

I think Anne leaned forward, bending over me, but I don't know for sure. Maybe she kissed me, maybe not. I didn't immediately lose consciousness, but I was overtaken by an extraordinarily acute impression of falling, similar to that which I'd experienced after we'd last made love, but much more intense. It was as if my mind had been plucked out of my body by a force stronger by far than gravity, and dragged precipitously downwards. The fall seemed to last for seven or eight seconds, but how much time passed in objective terms I can't say.

At the end of it there was a kind of whirling effect, and suddenly I was back inside my head again, looking out. But I must have been looking out all the time, without being aware of it, because there was no sensation of light returning after a spell of darkness.

I felt drained of all my strength. I felt incredibly heavy, the way I sometimes did when I became half-conscious that I was dreaming, and tried unsuccessfully to move my dream-body in response to some impending threat. I tried to lever myself up with my arms, intending to stand up, but I couldn't even muster enough force to shift my position in the chair. I was pinned down there, unable to struggle effectively against the burden of my own weight.

More time passed. Maybe minutes, maybe hours. I closed my eyes for a while, but I didn't sleep. I couldn't.

When I was finally able to open my eyes again, Anne was gone.

I wasn't alone. Standing over me, where Anne had been, maybe only a few objective moments before, was something straight out of a lurid comic book. It was a man, but his thin, gaunt face was uncannily pale and weirdly contorted, and there were smudges of what looked like blood at the corners of his mouth. He was dressed in some kind of thick black cloak, which hid his arms and hands, so that the only part of his flesh that could be seen was his face. His eyes were bloodshot, and the irises were nearly as dark as the pupils. There was such an expression of malignity in his stare that I longed to be able to turn away, but I couldn't do it.

I couldn't turn my head, or move my eyes within their orbits. I met his gaze, helplessly, and felt as if my flesh were melting under the pressure of his hostility.

He leaned forward slightly, and said: 'You must live. You *must* live.'

I wanted to speak, if only to ask him who or what he was, but the effort I made to force air from my lungs was pathetically inadequate. No matter how I exerted myself, my intentions were quite impotent. It was as if my mind had been dislocated from my body, unable any longer to initiate signals in my nervous system.

As if he'd read my aborted intention, the comic-book vampire said: 'I am Maldureve.'

His voice was strange, almost as though he were speaking over a telephone link. He pronounced the name to rhyme with 'deceive', but I knew enough French to figure out that the virus was making play with the ideas in my head, pulling stupid puns out of the deep recesses of my consciousness.

Evil of the dream, indeed!

The realization that it was something in me that was projecting the image – that this perverse vaudevillian was a product of my own subconscious, kick-started into apparent existence by something too small to be seen without an electron microscope – made me feel better; but I still couldn't move.

'She loves you,' said the monster, earnestly, as though he thought that I could understand perfectly well what he meant. 'She doesn't want you to die. She wants you to live. She wants you to be *together*'.

His gaze flickered very briefly, as though his purpose had been momentarily clouded by uncertainty. He leaned even further forward, and his right hand emerged from the folds of his dark cloak. He laid it on top of my own right hand, which rested palm down on the arm of the chair. His fingers were unbelievably cold, and I felt the communicated chill travel along my nerves, striking rivulets of pain into the neighbouring tendons and veins.

'Feed the hunger,' he said, insistently. His weird voice had taken on a slightly higher pitch, as if he had now cottoned on to the fact that I didn't know what the hell he meant but was determined to make sure that I couldn't forget his words. 'When the hunger comes, *feed it*. I will come to you again. I will guide you until she returns. Trust me, and I will show you how to feed. I will show you what you must do.'

He stepped back, relieving the pain in my hand. Then he stepped further back, pivoting on his heel as he did so – and was suddenly gone. It was as if he had turned into a shadow, and vanished by means of some casual trick of the light.

At first, there was no change in my own condition, but after a pause of several minutes I began to feel lighter, and I felt the power of my will flow back into my body. At last I was able to clench the fingers of my paralysed hand, and shift myself within the armchair – but several more minutes passed before I had the strength to raise myself up, and when I had done that I still felt as weak as a kitten, hardly able to walk.

There was a pattern of bruises on the back of my hand where the apparition's fingertips had rested, which stubbornly refrained from fading with the last sensations of the hallucination. I had to admit, in the end, that I'd actually inflicted a psychosomatic injury upon myself, and I felt a thrill of fear as I wondered what else I might do if the virus took hold of me again. I understood that if and when more and worse nightmares were to come from the dark depths of my being, they might actually have the power to hurt me.

It was only with considerable effort that I made it to the bathroom, and as I leaned over the lavatory pan I had to support myself by placing the palm of my uninjured hand flat against the wall. I felt that I might faint at any moment, but I knew that I had to get back to the bed.

I made the journey three steps at a time, pausing twice to take a deep breath and gather my strength. When I finally got to the bed I just collapsed, falling asleep the moment I had drawn my legs up to lie down.

I must have slept for nearly twenty-four hours.

I was out cold. If I dreamed at all, the dreams fled far beyond the reach of memory before I began to wake.

The sound of knocking which eventually woke me seemed to be sounding in an infinite black vault, calling me back from oblivion.

It wasn't easy to wake up, and it was hard to get off the bed and stand up, but I managed it. I wasn't as weak as I'd been before. Once my head was reasonably clear, I managed to walk all the way to the door without stopping for a rest. By that time, the person knocking on the door must have beaten his impatient tattoo four or five times.

I opened the door, and leaned against the jamb. I found myself looking into the curious blue eyes of a thickset man with short-cropped hair. In spite of its shortness the hair had been greased with some sort of oil. He looked like a mobster or a con artist.

'Mr Molari?' he said.

'Yeah.' I was slightly surprised to discover that I was able to speak.

He produced some kind of card with his photograph on, and flashed it briefly before my eyes.

'I'm Detective Sergeant Miller, Thames Valley Police. I'm sorry if I . . . woke you up, sir. May I have a word?'

The calculated hesitation in the middle of the apology was a ritual signal of surprise, to tell me that he'd observed that although I appeared to have recently awakened I was fully dressed.

I moved aside so that he could come in.

'I'm sorry,' I murmured. 'The mess . . .' There wasn't that much mess, but there was enough to make me feel that the ritual apology might be called for.

'Perhaps you'd like to sit down, sir,' he said. His politeness seemed almost sneeringly insincere.

I sat down in the armchair where I'd had the hallucinatory interlude the day before. Because so little had happened in between, it seemed frighteningly recent, but I sat down in it reflexively. He sat down in the other one, about six feet away.

'I believe you know Anne Charet,' he said.

I nodded.

'May I ask when you last saw her?'

'Yesterday,' I said, slowly putting two and two together. 'Yesterday morning. Why – what's happened?'

He was studying me carefully, almost making a pantomime of it. 'Miss Charet's in the county hospital,' he said, blandly. 'She's not seriously hurt, so far as the doctor can tell, but she was still unconscious when I last saw her. She was attacked last night, on the campus. Her attacker ran off when she shouted for help, but he had a knife and he wounded her. She needed a blood transfusion and some stitches but she'll be all right.'

I felt suddenly sick. I couldn't help but wonder whether the virus had anything to do with what had happened. She had to be infected; she'd told me that she was feeling the other symptoms. I knew that I had to be careful what I said, until I'd thought the situation through – until I'd seen her and talked to her.

'I'd better go out there right away,' I said. 'Thanks for coming to tell me.' I knew it wouldn't be as simple as that, but the way he was playing his part somehow made me respond in kind. We were both pretending that everything was perfectly straightforward.

'There's no rush,' he said. 'How long have you known Miss Charet?'

'A little over two months. We met at the beginning of term. The first week in October.'

'Do you know her well?'

'Yes,' I said. 'Quite well.'

'Would that be an American quite, sir, or a British one?'

Clever bastard, I thought.

'She's my girlfriend,' I said. 'I know her well, okay?'

'I'm sorry, sir. I do have to ask you these questions. I'm investigating a serious crime. It's necessary. Please bear with me.'

I tried to meet his placid stare, wondering what an innocent party was supposed to look like in this alien land, and how I ought to behave in order to diffuse whatever suspicions he felt compelled to harbour. Can he really think I did it? I wondered. Would he like me to have done it?

'Yes,' I said, after a brief pause. 'I see that. But you don't think I did it, do you?'

He shook his head. 'We've no reason to think that, sir. Just for the record, where were you last night?'

'Here. In bed. Alone.'

'*All* night, sir?'

'Yes. I came down with a virus a couple of days ago. It knocked me out a bit. I don't have any immunity to your local bugs, you see. I'm from California. I haven't been out of the flat for three days.'

'You haven't seen a doctor?'

'No. Hell, it's only a heavy cold – maybe flu. It just knocked me out a bit. Anne came round yesterday – and the day before, though I wouldn't let her in then, because I didn't want her to catch it. Yesterday she told me she *had* caught it, so I let her in . . . but then I sent her home, to rest.'

'And that was in the morning, was it?'

'Yes. I don't know exactly what time. Ten, ten-thirty. That's the last time I saw anyone.' I was telling the truth. The comic-book count didn't count. He wasn't real. 'Other people must have seen Anne after that time,' I added.

'Oh, yes,' he confirmed, offhandedly. 'She had a tutorial in the afternoon, and she was working in the university library for most of the evening. It was while she was returning to her hall of residence that she was attacked. It wasn't very late – there were still people around. It's lucky there were, or the incident might have been even more serious. It's not the first time there's been an attempted rape at that particular spot. There ought at least to be railings round that little wood, and better lighting.'

'Yeah,' I said. 'It's too dangerous to let places like that run wild in the middle of a university campus.'

'Did you ever meet Miss Charet in that patch of woodland?'

'We walked past it dozens of times,' I told him. 'We never went into it.'

'You didn't ever meet her there, in the early hours of the morning?'

'Of course not. Why the hell would I?'

'One of Miss Charet's neighbours in the Hall told me that she'd seen Miss Charet leaving the Hall on more than one occasion, after midnight. She said she got the impression that Miss Charet was going in that direction. Perhaps she was on her way to some other meeting place?'

'I never met her after midnight,' I told him, with entirely unfeigned astonishment. 'Not in that lousy wood, nor anywhere else. I walked her back home plenty of times, and then I walked back that way, but the only time we were together near there later than midnight was the first time we met. Maybe I've left her room once or twice in the early hours – maybe it was me the neighbour saw.'

'The girl was quite certain,' he countered. 'I've no reason to doubt what she said.'

'I can't believe that she'd go out on her own at that sort of time,' I said firmly. 'She's nervous of the dark. I mean, she likes that damned ruin where she has her tutorials, but only by day. She's nervous walking there at night, even when I'm with her. At least . . .'

He let a few seconds go by before saying: 'At least what, sir?'

'At least, she used to be,' I said. 'Maybe lately . . . she'd got accustomed to it, I guess. It had become familiar. Too familiar, maybe, if she was willing to walk that way alone after dark. But it wasn't late, you say? There were people about.'

'One too many,' he observed dryly. 'Nobody saw him, I'm afraid – except Miss Charet, of course. With luck, she'll be able to give us some sort of description when she comes round. She may well have seen him by the light of the lamps beside the path, if he came out of hiding to drag her into the trees. With her help, we might well be able to clear this one up without too much difficulty. The doctor says that she'll come round any time now.'

There was a short pause after he stopped speaking, while I waited to see whether he had anything more to say. Then I said: 'Is that all? If it is, I'd like to go to the hospital to see her – if that's okay with you.'

'Certainly, sir,' he said. 'There's a policewoman with her, and we've already notified her parents – I expect they'll travel down this morning. She's in the intensive-care unit, but that's just a precaution. They'll probably move her when she wakes up. I'm not sure that they'll let you in to see her right away, but if you'd like to wait . . .'

He trailed off, putting his head slightly to one side as though listening to some invisible voice which was telling him what to do next. He stood up, and said: 'Do you mind if I have a look around, sir?'

'Why?' I retorted.

'Just to set my mind at rest, sir. So that I can say that I did it, if it should ever become relevant.'

I shrugged, not having to try too hard to seem insulted. 'The knives are in the kitchen drawer,' I said. 'They haven't left the flat either.' But even as I said it, I had a vision of him pulling open that drawer and finding a carving knife inside, still wet with Anne's blood. How could I be *sure* that there wasn't exactly such a spectacle awaiting discovery? How could I be absolutely sure?

There wasn't. He looked, and found nothing, and had the decency not to look too hard, once he was reasonably sure in his own mind that everything was normal.

'Sorry,' he said, for once not adding the half-insulting *sir*. 'I have to check everything, you see. She'll be okay – and we'll catch the bastard who did it.' For the first time, there was no trace of any implication in his voice that the bastard in question might be me. He believed me. Unfortunately, I was just starting to wonder how strange and nasty the effects of the virus I'd caught might be. After Maldureve, I could hardly doubt that it was one of ours, and no mere cold in the head. All possibilities seemed suddenly to be open, including the worst.

As the detective moved towards the door I was already asking myself whether I dared go out, fearing as I did that I might lapse into hallucination at any moment. I was guiltily aware that I had a secret that I must at all costs hide from Sergeant Miller and all his colleagues. If they found cause to doubt that I was in full control of my faculties, I'd certainly be back in place as a suspect.

I almost had the door closed behind him when he suddenly turned back. Maybe he'd been watching too much television, or maybe it really had just occurred to him on the spur of the moment.

'Sorry,' he said. 'Just one more thing. Miss Charet had a mark on her neck close to the wound. It wasn't inflicted by the knife.

It looked rather like a lovebite. I'm sorry to have to ask, but were *you* responsible for that?'

'No,' I said. 'She had this habit of rubbing and pinching a fold of skin, whenever she was nervous or concentrating hard. She did it herself. It was just a habit.'

He raised his eyebrows slightly. 'Do you have a similar habit, Mr Molari?' he asked.

'No,' I said. 'Why?'

He looked genuinely puzzled – not, I gathered, by the *no* but rather by the *why*. As soon as he'd turned away, I went to the bathroom to look into the mirror. Sure enough, there it was: a mark on my neck, a little like a lovebite, exactly like the one that Anne had.

I touched it gingerly. It felt sore.

As I drew my fingers away, I saw the marks on the back of my hand: the psychosomatic bruises which my body had produced in response to my vision of the comic-book vampire who'd laid his icy hand on mine. They looked sufficiently similar to convince me that the mark on my neck had exactly the same origin – but I couldn't for the life of me figure out what they signified.

5

I didn't go to the hospital immediately. When I'd washed and changed my clothes I felt a whole lot better, and not nearly as weak as when I answered the door, but I did feel ravenous. I hadn't eaten anything for more than twenty-four hours, and my body knew it.

I took the return of my appetite as a sign of returning health, and became convinced that once I'd filled my stomach the worst effects of the virus attack would be well and truly over. My throat still felt a little sore, but the rawness was fading, and I didn't need aspirin to soothe my head. I congratulated my immune system on the alacrity of its response, and even began to feel quite pleased with my flirtation with the escaped bug. One particularly vivid hallucination, experienced while I was literally incapable of taking any action, suddenly seemed to be something of interest, well worth the price of the minor symptoms and the momentary anxiety.

I resolved to write an exhaustive account of the entire episode when I had time, but it didn't seem urgent. However awful delirium seems at the time, it fades quickly from the memory once the system is up and running again. The better I became, the better able I felt to look back on my experience and laugh.

I ate a bowl of cereal, then finished off the rest of the fresh milk that had been delivered that morning, but I still felt hungry. I knew that there was a burger bar on the corner of St Saviour's Square which served 'all-day breakfasts', so I put my jacket on and went for it, full speed ahead. My step was still a mite leaden, but the thought of hot solid food pulled me through. It was an English imitation burger bar, not a real McDonald's, and it served a thoroughly English breakfast – thick sausages, greasy bacon, eggs sunny side up, glutinous fried bread and thin strings of black pudding – but the whole thing looked like the fruits of paradise to me. I washed it down with tea so strong that the metallic taste of tannin stung my tongue.

When I finished, I felt full – not entirely satisfied, but full. I leaned back in my chair, and remembered what the creepy guy in the old-fashioned cloak had said.

'When the hunger comes, *feed it.*'

'Right on,' I murmured. 'You got it, brother.'

A slight tingle ran up and down my spine, but it was just a momentary awkwardness kicked off by my deliberate dalliance with an uncomfortable memory. The guy with the eyes had promised me that he would be back, but I couldn't believe it.

'You're history, brother', I told him, silently. 'You got chewed up and spat out by Molari's Marauders, the greatest antibodies in the world.'

It was childish, but it served its purpose. No more shivers crawled along the length of my spine.

There was a post office next to the burger bar and I went in to buy a phonecard. I bought Mercury because the Mercury phones in the square hardly ever got a visit from the local vandals and there was never a queue to use them. I rang the department and got through to Viners.

'Professor Viners?' I said. 'This is Gil Molari. I thought I'd better ring to explain why I haven't been in for a couple of days. I picked up some kind of virus and it really laid me low. I don't have a phone in the flat and this is the first time I've been out in three days.'

'Did you have any experiments in progress?' he asked, as businesslike as ever. Not 'What kind of virus, Gil?' Not 'How are you feeling now?'

'No. I was going to set up another run on Wednesday, but it can wait. Look, Professor, I don't think I'll be in today either. My girlfriend was hurt last night. She's in the hospital. She was attacked in the wood near Wombwell House – maybe you heard about it?'

'I heard about the attack,' he said, in a markedly different tone. 'Was she badly hurt?'

'I don't know. The policeman who quizzed me about it said not. She got stabbed and lost some blood, but they gave her a transfusion and stitched her up. Apparently she's expected to come round any time. I ought to be there. Her parents live way up north and they probably won't be able to get here until this afternoon. Somebody ought to be there.'

'Of course. Is there anything at all that needs to be done here? Teresa can take care of it, if it's only routine.'

Teresa can take care of a lot of things, I thought, uncharitably.

'No, it's okay. I'll be in tomorrow to get things going again.'

The digital display on the phone was running through the units on the card with cruel precision, and it was hinting very strongly that I ought to ring off if I wanted to preserve its usefulness for another day. But Viners wasn't quite ready to say goodbye.

'There's no rush, Gil,' he said. 'I don't want you to come in until you're fully recovered. Given the kind of work we do, we can't afford to import infectious agents into the lab.'

It struck me as a peculiarly bizarre comment, though it shouldn't have. I wondered whether he was worried about our viruses catching something, but I knew even as I formed the thought that it wasn't what he meant. We had an awful lot of animals around, and tissue cultures specifically designed to play host to viruses. Sterile technique is supposed to work both ways, but it's easy to get careless with things that aren't part of your present experiment.

'I'm fine,' I assured him. 'It was just one of those short-lived things. Hasn't anyone else had it? These trivial things usually go round like wildfire.' I tried, perhaps too hard, to sound matter-of-fact.

'It's only natural to be anxious,' he said. I knew he was talking about my anxieties, not his. 'I've had half a dozen colds since I first brought the experimental bugs into the lab. I always start keeping track of my symptoms, studying my dreams. It wasn't easy training Teresa to cope with those kinds of fears, but I finally managed to persuade her that she was producing her own symptoms under the spur of her suspicions. I know what you've been thinking, Gil, and there's no need to be ashamed of it. You seem to have coped very well. Come in when you're sure you're one hundred per cent, and not before.'

He was being kind, and there wasn't the slightest reason to doubt his sincerity in spite of the colourlessness of his tone. Even so, my instinctive reaction was resentful. Clever bastard, I thought. But it was the resentment of a man who had an uncomfortable feeling that he'd been found out. An hour before, I'd been certain that I'd had a close encounter with an authentic psychotropic virus. Now, the doubts had come back. Maybe, I thought, I *had* manufactured my own symptoms. Maybe I'd seen the comic-book vampire because I'd expected to see something, and he had been all that my subconscious had been able to come up with on the spur of the moment.

'I'm okay,' I told him, dully. 'I have to go now, Professor. I have to go to the hospital.'

'Goodbye, Gil,' he said, as precisely as ever. 'Thanks for letting me know.'

It wasn't until I'd hung up and retrieved my card that I suddenly homed in on what he'd said about Teresa. I had a sudden vision – entirely the product of my own imagination – of Teresa sitting in Viners' office, tearfully telling him how convinced she was that she'd infected herself, and what terrible hallucinations she'd been having. It didn't take a genius to work out exactly how Viners would reply to her, and what tone of voice he'd use. It was a little more difficult, but only a little, to visualize Viners talking to himself, telling himself very precisely that whatever he'd experienced was only a dream, easily accountable in terms of self-induced fears.

I knew that the scenes would both have run in exactly the same way whether the two of them really had picked up one of the experimental viruses or not. They could have infected themselves without ever admitting it. Either or both of them.

It was a cold, sunny day and the square was crowded with shoppers. I was full to the brim with traditional English breakfast. Maldureve was fading fast into the uncertain mists of memory. It could happen to anyone, I thought. Anyhow, every damn virus has some psychotropic effects. Even if a virus did hook into my inner dream-machine to cook up something out of the ordinary, it doesn't prove that it was one from the labs. But then I touched my fingertips to my neck, and looked at the bruises on the back of my hand. The stigmata were still there.

There wasn't any way out of the maze of uncertainty, I realized. Psychosomatic bruises were no proof of alien intervention; nor was the clear sight and sound of a creature who was so obviously based in a camp fictional stereotype. No matter how hard I thought about it, I couldn't reach any kind of conclusion. The sensible thing was to stop and tell myself that it didn't really matter, at the end of the day, whether the virus I'd caught had been one of ours or not. Either way, it had to be something in my own psyche that had shaped the particular hallucination. The virus wasn't some kind of prerecorded videotape, and it had never read a comic book in its life. Maldureve had to be mine, no matter what had provoked his enigmatic appearance. If he were to be explained, he had to be explained in terms of what he symbolized and signified in the context of my memories and fears, not in terms of the origin of the DNA which had invaded my bloodstream and my brain chemistry.

I resolved to give the matter further consideration when I had time to do it.

I had to check the route map in the bus station to figure out how to get to the county hospital, but it wasn't far and the relevant bus didn't leave for a quarter of an hour. I set out to walk, figuring that the exercise would do me good. Maybe it did, but I didn't feel it. I got tired very quickly, and even though breakfast was still sitting on my stomach like a sack of beans I had also gotten hungry again with remarkable rapidity. By the time I arrived at reception to enquire where Anne was, I needed to sit down.

That was perhaps as well, because they told me unceremoniously that she hadn't come round yet, and that I couldn't go in to see her until she did.

I went where I was told to go, and ended up on a wooden bench, whose only other occupant was a very bored police-woman. At first she just glanced at me, but then she suddenly perked up.

'You're her boyfriend, aren't you?' she said. She didn't sound accusative – if anything, she sounded glad to have someone to talk to.

'Yes,' I said, shortly. I didn't want an action replay of what I'd been through with Detective Miller.

'She'll be okay. I saw the wound – it wasn't deep, just ragged. It's just a matter of waiting until she wakes up.'

'I know.'

'DS Miller's seen you?'

'That's right.'

'He had to question you,' she said defensively, having inferred from my tone that I hadn't much enjoyed making Miller's acquaintance. 'It's nothing personal. We're pretty sure that rape was the motive for the attack, and statistically speaking most victims of attempted rape know their attackers. Even though this one followed a classic pattern, we had to look at all the possibilities.'

'I realize that,' I admitted. I made an effort to relax. The policewoman seemed sincere enough.

'I'm WPC Linton,' she said. 'What's your name?'

'Gil. Gil Molari.'

'You're American.'

I was briefly tempted to be sarcastic and award her full marks for observation, but I bit it back, because she didn't deserve it, and just said: 'Yeah. I'm over here doing postgrad research.'

'She's a pretty girl,' said the policewoman, reflectively. 'Very frail, though. Must have taken guts to fight back against a man with a knife. The standard advice is not to fight, not to get hurt

– but getting raped *is* getting hurt, and letting it happen can get the hurt all confused with guilt and shame. I think she did the right thing. When she wakes up, you be sure to tell her what a brave girl she was. You make her feel good about herself, okay?'

'I'll do what I can,' I promised. 'I'd have been with her if it hadn't been for this damned virus I picked up. It should never have happened. I told her to stay home. She shouldn't have taken that path when she was on her own. Not at night.'

'Don't tell her that,' said the policewoman. 'Don't say anything that might make her blame herself. She'll need some help to get over this, and you mustn't make things more difficult than they are. I'll try to take things gently, but I have to get answers to some questions. It'll be up to you to make her feel better. Do you see what I'm saying?'

I did see. I could see perfectly clearly.

'How many of these guys do you actually catch?' I asked. My throat had gone dry, and the tiredness induced by the walk seemed to be spreading slowly through my body.

'It depends,' she said. 'This time, we have a good chance. The attacker must have got blood on his clothes, you see. There's every chance that someone saw him before he could change. And if we do find him, there'll be stains somewhere – something we can use for evidence. Are you all right, Gil?'

I wasn't. I'd lost track of what she was saying. I didn't want to listen to any more, but there was nowhere to go.

'Sorry,' I said, faintly. 'Aftereffects of the virus, I guess. I'll be okay in a minute.'

Embarrassed because I was under observation, I let out a deep breath, putting my tiredness on public display. Then I tilted my head back, looking up at the neon strip-light which lit the corridor. I didn't shut my eyes against its glare; I wanted to be dazzled. Miniature suns exploded in my eyes as the receptor cells in my retina were overloaded, blinding me. Then I looked away, knowing that the sunbursts would linger, blinding me for ten or twenty seconds.

Something suddenly came hurtling out of the clouds of light – something which couldn't possibly have been there. There were shapes made out of coloured light, flying things with flaming feathers and huge round staring eyes, things with claws which reached out for me avidly and angrily.

I shut my eyes, hard, but that had no effect at all. The things were already inside me, and it was all I could do not to gasp in terror.

The sunbursts were dying away, and the shapes died with them, but I couldn't suppress the feeling that they'd flown into the dark recesses of my mind, to hide from consciousness until the opportunity came for them to surge forth again to rend me and lacerate me with those claws.

'Are you sure you'll be okay?' asked WPC Linton.

'Sure,' I lied. 'Just a twinge.'

It wasn't until I'd said it that I realized that my hand, as if impelled by some unsuspected reflex, had gone to my neck, and that my fingers were plucking nervously at the mark which had somehow appeared there during the last few days, just as Anne's fingers had so often plucked at hers.

I snatched my fingers away, guiltily, but it was too late. The policewoman was studying me carefully, puzzlement giving birth to belated suspicion. She had me down as some kind of screwball.

'It'll be okay,' she said, possibly referring to Anne, possibly to me – or possibly meaning nothing at all.

'Yeah,' I said. 'I know. It's cool. All under control.'

She didn't believe me. Neither did I.

6

'Anne's told us a lot about you in her letters,' said Mrs Charet, by way of introduction.

It was the sort of announcement which always sounds ominous, and my heart sank as I faced the three of them.

'She told me a lot about you, too,' I said, defensively. A reply of some sort seemed to be obligatory, even though we all had one eye on the doctor, who'd come out to explain the situation as soon as Anne's parents had arrived.

Mrs Charet was an athletic, ruddy-faced woman who'd tinted her hair red to cover up the grey. She wasn't anything like Anne, so far as I could tell. She was very smartly dressed, as though she'd felt obliged to put on her Sunday best in order to race to her daughter's side. Mr Charet was less striking, and gave the impression that he was very easy-going when he wasn't worried. At present, he was worried. Anne's sister, Sharon, didn't look much like Anne's description of her, apart from the black-dyed hair. Her customary uniform and make-up had presumably been abandoned – or maybe banned – in honour of the occasion. Anne had told me that she looked much older than she was, but to me she was very obviously sixteen. She was worried, too. We all were. Even the doctor was perplexed.

'I'm not sure why she hasn't come round yet,' the doctor said, addressing himself to Mr Charet, 'but it's just a matter of time. She's fine.

'It's not a coma, is it?' Mr Charet said. 'There's no damage to her brain?'

'It's not what we'd normally think of as a coma,' the doctor replied, failing miserably to conceal the blatant circumlocution. 'There's no evidence of any head injury, and she didn't lose very much blood from the cut – but she was rather anemic, so it's possible that her brain was oxygen-depleted for a while. There's plenty of brain activity, and periodic rapid eye movements, so it's not a classic coma. In fact, she seems to be simply asleep – but we can't seem to wake her. She probably needs a little more time.'

'I've been worrying ever since she left,' Mrs Charet said to me, in the tone of one offering a serious confidence. 'You can't keep them at home all their lives, can you? But you can't help worrying when they go, either. I've always been scared that something like this would happen. Always. Every time you switch on the news there's something – rapes, murders. It's getting more like America every day. Nobody's safe. Why do people *do* this sort of thing?'

'I don't know,' I said truthfully, wondering whether I ought to reassure her that this wasn't exactly an everyday occurrence in small-town California. I felt trapped, smothered by her urgent concern.

I'd been in the hospital for four hours, waiting for Anne to recover consciousness, continually being assured that it couldn't possibly be much longer. But something was wrong – something the doctors hadn't figured on – and I was back to wondering about the mysterious virus and its occult powers, even though I knew how utterly futile it was to wonder.

I wanted to get out, to get some fresh air, but I daren't go. I felt that I couldn't go while WPC Linton was still there. The arrival of Anne's parents had only served to intensify my sense of imprisonment. I'd had three cups of coffee from the trolley which did the rounds of the wards, and two lots of sandwiches from the dispenser at the end of the corridor, but I still felt hungry and thirsty, and the unassuageable sensation of need was beginning to annoy me. Now that I had rested the tiredness had gone again, but I didn't feel *right*. The whole situation was out of kilter.

Mrs Charet turned her attention to the policewoman, and began the rush of hypothetical questions all over again. WPC Linton was much better at inserting the requisite nods and clucks of sympathy than I had been.

'If we can get a good description,' said the policewoman, 'there's every chance that we can catch the man. Every chance. Even if Anne didn't see him clearly, someone else will have seen the bloodstains.'

'There'll always be more,' said Mrs Charet, dolefully. 'It doesn't matter how many you lock away . . . there's no safety any more. You can't feel safe even in your own home.'

Sharon was looking me up and down, appraisingly. I felt uncomfortable under her inquisitive gaze. Her blue eyes were disconcertingly ill-matched to her black hair.

The doctor, having delivered his uncertain verdict, walked away. Mr Charet turned back to the rest of us. The way he looked at me suggested that he didn't like me much, but I knew it was nothing personal. He was the kind of man who'd look with disapproval at any and all his daughter's male friends, wishing all the while that she hadn't had to grown up, that she might somehow have remained a child for ever. Maybe he thought that I was too old for her, but that was just one extra item to be added to a long list.

'You'd better stay here,' he said to his wife. 'I'll go book into a hotel. Then I'll have to make a few calls. I have to phone the office, to let them know the score. I'll be back as soon as I can.'

Mrs Charet nodded meekly in reply. She looked as if she wanted to cry, but couldn't. The policewoman guided her to the bench and sat her down. I stayed where I was, standing up. I wanted to get away, but I didn't know how it would look, or how I could excuse myself. The black-haired girl went to sit beside her mother.

'She was usually so careful,' Mrs Charet said. 'She was such a sensible girl.'

Not according to the sergeant, I said to myself, silently. But even as I said it I knew that I would have made exactly the same judgement. Anne was very nervous, and precisely because of that she *was* careful; she *was* sensible. Could it possibly be true that she'd left the Hall before, in the early hours of the morning? And if it were true, what could it possibly signify?

The policewoman stood up again, and spoke to me in a low voice. 'I'm sorry, Gil,' she said, 'but now that Anne's parents have arrived, I think it might be better if you left. It seems that the doctor's estimate of when she might be expected to come round isn't entirely to be trusted, so we might be in for a long wait. Why don't you phone in tonight to ask whether she's conscious? If she is, you can come to see her then.'

I was grateful for the suggestion, but I didn't want to show it. I feigned reluctant compliance, trying to make her think that she'd persuaded me against my will. Once I was outside I walked back towards St Saviour's just as fast as I could go. I was still tired and weak, but I didn't want to wait for a bus. I just wanted to get away, to be on the move. I didn't want to have to face Anne's parents. In fact, I didn't want to face anyone. I wanted to be on my own.

I went to the supermarket to renew my depleted stores. While I walked around the aisles I kept looking round, searching the shelves for inspiration. I felt so hungry, but I couldn't see anything that I wanted to eat. Whatever I looked at, I just felt indifference, and it wasn't just because the supermarket didn't have the same range of goods as the ones back home. I could feel my hunger, like a physical ache in the pit of my stomach, and I couldn't shake off the idea that it wasn't a general hunger at all but a very specific one, which could only be answered by exactly the right food.

I could still remember my comic-book vampire saying: 'When the hunger comes, *feed it*.' But when I passed by the meat counters, surveying the bright red steaks and the packs of minced beef, I didn't feel any special attraction to them. I remembered vampires' minions in cornball films pouncing on spiders and flies, cackling all the while, but there didn't seem to be any connection between my unnatural appetite and theirs. I had no compulsion to go hunting live meat – the problem was that I didn't have any specific compulsion at all, just a desire which couldn't or wouldn't reveal itself fully. It was as if it were determined to drive me crazy by refusing to let me know how to answer it.

I bought the things I usually bought: easy things to prepare, ready meals for a lazy cook.

Under the bright neon strip-lights of the supermarket my headache was beginning to creep back, so I bought a pack of dispersable aspirin and a small bottle of scotch. If in doubt, I told myself, get drunk. I was uncomfortably aware of the fact that I'd been premature in thinking that I might have recovered, that I might have beaten off the virus. What had gone before had only been round one; there was obviously more to come.

It was only three-thirty when I got back to the flat, but I set about preparing a meal right away. I had a pizza which would cook in ten minutes once the oven was hot, and a pack of ready-mixed salad. I wanted to hit the hunger with *something*; I knew all along that it wasn't going to work, but I didn't know what else to do and I didn't want to do nothing.

The pizza was okay, and I ate the whole damn thing. It helped a little, and it filled me up, but it didn't entirely do the job. Something still felt wrong inside.

At four-thirty I went to the square again, and used up a couple more of the units on my phonecard ringing the hospital. Anne was 'stable and comfortable' but she hadn't woken up yet. I bought another card on the way home, figuring that I was going to need it.

The thought that Anne wasn't really comatose, just asleep

and dreaming, wasn't much of a comfort. Whether she was in the grip of a virus or not, there was no way of knowing what kind of dreams she might be having. I wondered briefly if it might be worth trying to suggest to the doctor that he do some tests, looking for abnormal brain chemistry, but I knew there'd be no point. Even if he could find something that dovetailed with the kind of lab experiments Viners and I had been running, how could it possibly help? What would we actually know about what was going on inside her head? It certainly wouldn't help her to wake up any sooner.

At five-thirty, I drew the curtains in the flat against the recently descended darkness and stretched myself out on the bed, intending to interrogate my state of body and state of mind as precisely as I could, in order to try to figure out just what the hunger might be that was still gnawing at my guts, and what my vision of the previous day might signify.

I was still trying to compose myself, planning how to carry out the task before me, when there was a knock on the door. I knew immediately that it wasn't the detective; it was a very different kind of knock, light and tentative.

I opened the door hesitantly, keeping it half-closed while I looked to see who it was.

Teresa was standing there, wrapped up warm against the chill of the premature night.

'Hi,' she said. 'Mike told me you weren't feeling well. I thought I'd call in on my way home.'

She had never been to the flat before, nor had she shown the slightest interest in continuing our relationship – such as it was – outside working hours. She must have got my address out of the files. I was suspicious, wondering whether it might have been a thirst for gossip about Anne that had brought her to my door.

'Aren't you going to let me in?' she asked, as I looked dumbly back at her, still holding the door half-shut. I stepped back, and let her through.

'It's just a cold,' I said, automatically.

She had thrown her shoulder bag down beside the leg of one of the armchairs, and was already unbuckling her belt. When she slipped the coat off she handed it to me, expectantly. She looked around the room, taking it all in during a single sweep of her gaze.

'I'd like a place like this,' she said. 'I'm pig sick of living at home. Would you believe that my mother takes twenty-five pounds a week out of my paypacket just for housekeeping? I'd rather pay real rent. I've been trying to save, but you know how it is.'

'Yeah,' I said, noncommittally

'It was your girlfriend who got attacked, wasn't it?' she said, unable to keep up the polite chatter any longer. 'Last night – out near that creepy old house.'

She sat down on the chair, shifting her bag slightly with a pointed shoe.

'Yes, it was,' I said, finally moving to hang the coat up on one of the hooks behind the door.

'Mike suggested that I might like to call,' she said. 'He'd have come himself, but he thought I might be better able to reassure you about the cold. I told him you wouldn't need it – that you're far too level-headed to start imagining things – but he said better be safe than sorry, so I thought I ought to. Haven't had any bad dreams, have you?'

I sat down on the other chair, where Maldureve had appeared to me the day before. 'One or two,' I admitted. 'How about you?'

'Not lately,' she said. 'I suppose I'll catch whatever you've got, if it's going round. On the other hand, I'll probably be all right this time. You get used to it, you see. It's like reading medical dictionaries – you always think you've got the symptoms of something absolutely horrible. Mike told me that everyone who works with pathogens starts wondering whether they've committed accidental suicide every time they get the sniffles. The more you try not to think about it the less you can help it. It's like being told not to think of a white horse, isn't it? So he asked me to drop in, just in case. *Have* you been winding yourself up?'

'I've been seeing things,' I admitted, cautiously. 'And I've got this funny feeling in my guts. Feels like hunger but won't go away when I eat.'

'I never had that,' she said. 'Just the bad dreams. What're yours about?'

'Vampires,' I said, trying to make it sound like a joke.

'With me,' she said, 'it's more *animals*. Hairy, sweaty, lots of teeth. Dogs, pigs, monkeys . . . Mike said not to worry, and not to bother with a therapist. He doesn't have a high opinion of therapists, the prof.'

'He wouldn't,' I commented. 'The theoretical basis of his research assumes that all mental phenomena have specific physical correlates. He's hardly likely to be a fan of Freud.'

'You should tell him about the vampires. He'd be interested. He won't tell me what he fantasizes about when he gets het up. He says he still worries, even after all this time, but not much. Honeymoon blues, he called it, when I first got convinced – and I was absolutely convinced – that I'd infected myself. Have you got a drink? It's been a long day – that solvent I've been using stinks to high heaven, and you can't even get a buzz out of it.'

'I've got some beer in the icebox,' I told her. I didn't mention the whisky. I thought I might need that later.

'That'll do.'

I fetched two cans and two glasses, but she put aside the glass I gave her. After popping the ring-pull she drank straight out of the can. I poured mine out, trying to control the head. I had to do the job in three stages, taking gulps in between. By the time the can was empty I wished I'd followed her example.

'How's your girlfriend doing?' she asked.

'Stable and comfortable,' I quoted. 'Fast asleep and showing no sign of waking up, but not technically comatose.'

'Can't see what you see in her,' she opined, licking froth from her lips. 'I suppose you know she's anorexic.'

'I'd noticed.'

'Do you like them like that? Pale and thin, like plastic dolls?' She grinned, as if challenging me to deny it. She was teasing; she was enjoying the fact that she'd been sent forth on an errand of mercy, to quieten my anxieties. She was waiting for me to proposition her, but she was determined to wait. She wanted to be asked. She wanted to be *desired*.

'What makes you think you were wrong?' I asked her.

She blinked, blank incomprehension on her face.

'About the virus,' I explained. 'When you were absolutely

convinced hat you'd infected yourself. What made you change your mind?'

'I got better,' she said, as though it were obvious.

'Even if it was one of the experimental viruses, you'd have got better,' I pointed out. 'That's exactly what we'd expect – symptoms not too different from a common cold, plus some mild psychotropic effects, then recovery. Maybe you did infect yourself. Maybe I have, too. Maybe you won't catch it from me because you've already had it. You might be immune by now.'

She looked at me suspiciously, not sure whether I was serious or just trying to wind her up.

'Either way,' she said, 'it's nothing to worry about. You'll get better. That's what the prof wanted me to tell you. Soothe your fears, that's how he put it. So I'm here to soothe your fears – as your regular soother can't be here.'

'That's a bitchy thing to say,' I pointed out.

'Sorry,' she said, unrepentantly. 'So you've got it all worked out, then? You've got it under control, vampires and all?'

'All except for the restlessness in my gut,' I told her.

'You're just thirsting for blood,' she told me. 'Maybe I'd better go.' But she didn't move an inch. She just waited. 'Or maybe it isn't blood you're thirsting for,' she added, after half a minute. 'Maybe it's something else.'

She was still waiting, still playing games. I took another mouthful of beer and weighed up my options. Then I shrugged my shoulders, thinking: What the hell?

'Maybe,' I admitted, cautiously.

7

I didn't really want to go to bed with Teresa, but the way she was teasing me I would have felt like a coward if I hadn't. I could have excused myself on the grounds that I wasn't feeling well, but it wouldn't have been entirely true, and she would have known it. In any case, there seemed to be a possibility that what she had said was true: that the insistent appetite that I kept calling 'hunger' for want of a better word might be a kind of disguised lust. It sounds improbable, put like that, but I had some reason to believe that my sensations might be distorted, and there did seem to be a real possibility that what I was feeling was sexual desire, subtly altered in such a way as to make it unrecognizable. The thought that I might be able to satisfy the hunger and calm the ache was attractive enough to license the gamble.

Or so it seemed at the time.

I'd never seen her with all her clothes off before, nor kissed her on the mouth, nor entwined my limbs with hers the way that lovers are supposed to do. Because of all that, it seemed like the first time. It was the first time, not just in terms of what we did but in terms of being *intimate* – except that we weren't really very intimate. She was silent, eyes closed, concentrating on her own sensations; I was even more self-enclosed than usual, lost in a confusing morass of sensation which became more and more chaotic by the minute.

Whatever excitement I'd started with soon ebbed away. I didn't cop out, but I began to feel that I was just going through the motions. The feel of her body was good, and I should have been building up some pressure, but I felt that the stream of my emotional energy was somehow being diverted.

The hunger didn't go away, and it came no nearer to revealing its true nature. It seemed perversely determined to prevent my knowing what I hungered for. Such sexual excitement as there was couldn't begin to displace it, and seemed instead to awaken painful echoes in my head and in my heart. Almost as soon as I'd started I knew that I wasn't enjoying it and wasn't going to enjoy it, but by then I couldn't bring myself to stop. It wasn't Teresa's fault; she was doing what she always did, and she felt fine – much softer than Anne, more voluptuous, reasonably enthusiastic in her introspective fashion. Another time, it might have been very good; this time, it wasn't.

This time, as I surely should have anticipated, it gradually turned into a nightmare.

Visions began to come into my head: not controllable fantasies, or memories, or any of the kinds of images that ordinarily came into my head while I was screwing. These were both vivid and sick, and I identified them immediately as products of the virus that was still inside me, fighting back against the antibodies I was forming against it.

The images were jumbled and fragmentary, like a series of jump cuts in a movie, played so fast as to be almost subliminal. It was impossible to make sense of them in terms of any kind of temporal sequence or alternation of scenes, and they resisted all the reflexive attempts of my mind to knit them together into any kind of coherency, but they did have a theme of sorts, and that theme was the consumption of human flesh.

Sometimes, I would seem to be a naked savage among others of my kind, tearing at the raw flesh of a dead companion – a woman or a child. My hands sometimes didn't seem to be hands at all, but clawed talons – and at other times, indeed, I seemed to be a vulture or a raven perched atop some putrescent corpse, dipping a greedy beak into the lacerations which my talons made. Sometimes it would not be a beak I was dipping, but a snout and a gaping mouth armed with huge canine teeth, or the multitudinous tiny teeth of a carnivorous fish.

More bizarre still were the moments when I seemed to be *inside* a human body, devouring from within, as though I were a hookworm clinging to the wall of the gut, or a burrowing tick. In these moments the sensations became entirely tactile, and yet they had strange visual illusions connected with them – illusions based on TV programmes I had seen in which tiny cameras were intruded into various parts of the body.

Sometimes, I seemed to be even smaller: to be virions spilling from a ruined cell into the busy bloodstream. Here too there were visual illusions, based in textbook diagrams and electron micrographs, eccentrically extrapolated into virtual reality.

There was nothing in these images to boost the level of my sexual excitement in the way that images of fetishistic cruelty might have done; nor was there anything in them to satisfy the awful cravings I felt, although I could only presume that it was those inner cravings that were conjuring them into being. All of it seemed to be happening deep inside me, having little or no connection with the rhythmic motions of my body. I felt no impulse or temptation to bite Teresa; it was not *her* flesh that I desired.

I came as quickly as I could, but it wasn't easy to get there, and it wasn't quick enough for me. Released from my observations by the belated orgasm, I immediately pulled away and rolled over on my back. I brought my hands up to cover my face and grip my pounding head, and I tried desperately to shut out all pain, all discomfort, all terror.

For a brief moment the flickering images held their inner ground, persisting in spite of my determination to be done with them and to be done with everything, but then they died. The colour went out of them, and all the energy. They faded away into one last monochrome slow-motion impression, in which I was a sleek black leech drawing warm blood from some vast hairy expanse of human skin.

Teresa grabbed one of my hands and yanked it down to her moist slit, unceremoniously demanding that I help her finish off. I began to move two fingers mechanically back and forth while she held on to the hand, adjusting its position. She came within a couple of minutes, and I drew my sticky fingers away with profound relief.

'Sorry,' I murmured. 'Not quite up to my best.'

'Not quite,' she agreed, ruefully but not brutally. 'But it helps, doesn't it? It takes your mind off what you think you've got.'

She really did think that she'd been offering therapy, doing me good. She thought that she'd been helping to soothe my irrational fears about what had got into me, even though that wasn't her main motive. But she hadn't. If anything, she had given me further evidence to support the hypothesis that alien psychotropic DNA was having a ball inside my brain. I couldn't believe that what I'd experienced could possibly be the result of some glitch in my own subconscious, taking advantage of my disconcertion to unbalance me.

Anyhow, I thought, if Mike Viners was right about all our dreams and neuroses being rooted in the activity of psychotropic DNA, domestic or alien or both in collaboration, what difference did it make where the ultimate source of my trouble lay? Whatever else might be in doubt, I was one hundred per cent certain that my head was far from straight. I was *sick*.

I didn't move when Teresa hauled herself up and clambered over me to get off the bed. I kept one hand over my eyes, protectively, while she went into the bathroom. When she came back and began putting on her clothes, I watched her through the gaps between my fingers. I didn't feel able to remove the hand altogether.

The light was still on – the main light, not just the bedside lamp – but there was something strange about the quality of its illumination. The room was the wrong colour, dimmer than it should have been. It was as if someone had surreptitiously removed the hundred-watt bulb and substituted a sixty, or maybe even a forty. I knew, of course, that it had to be my eyes and not the bulb at all, but I couldn't feel anything in my eyes to confirm the knowledge.

While I watched Teresa take down her coat, all the while continuing to shade and shield my eyes, the room seemed to grow even dimmer and more colourless, as if it were being invaded and gradually filled up by discreet shadows.

'You still look a little rough,' she observed, when she was all ready to go. 'Is my face okay?'

She meant her make-up, which she'd renewed while she was in the bathroom. It looked as okay as it ever did.

'Fine,' I said. 'Look, I'm sorry. I'll see you in the lab – probably Monday.'

'Take your time,' she told me. 'Invest in a few cloves of garlic to keep the vampires out.'

I remembered what she'd said about her own dreams featuring animals with lots of teeth. I wondered whether she'd diplomatically censored out any reference to what the animals were doing. But what could it prove, either way? I didn't ask.

'You'll be okay,' she told me. 'I was. I'd stay, but Mum's expecting me. She's bound to have heard about the attack. She worries when I'm working late. If I didn't have to spend money on those damned taxis I'd be better able to save – sometimes I could swear she makes me take them just to keep me at home. I have to get my own place soon. This is no way to run a sex life, is it?'

I didn't know how to reply to that, but it seemed to be a rhetorical question. She didn't come back to kiss me goodbye; she just gave me a wave from the doorway.

'Hang in there,' she said, grinning because she thought it was an authentic American goodbye. It could have been worse. She could have said 'Have a nice day.'

I intended to get up as soon as the door closed behind her. I intended to get dressed and make coffee. I intended to eat something, for want of any better response to the hunger which I still felt, and to take some aspirin for my bad head. I didn't do any of that, because the room wouldn't stop fading. It didn't become pitch dark, but it lost every vestige of its colour. It was as if I'd been suddenly stricken with partial blindness.

I finally took my hand away from my face, as if this were the moment I'd been waiting for all along.

I didn't see how Maldureve came in. Maybe he didn't come in at all; maybe he just coalesced out of the gloom. I wasn't surprised to see him, and I wasn't entirely displeased, either. The opportunity to confront some part of my recalcitrant nightmare face to face was perversely welcome.

'You don't exist,' I told him, assertively. 'You're just a phantom, born out of the interaction of my own powers of imagination with some stray DNA. You're damned. You'll burn to phantom ashes when my antibodies really get to work. From nothing you came, and to nothing you'll return, scattered by the bracing wind of rational thought.'

He smiled. He still had smudges of blood at the corners of his mouth, but I knew that they were fake. As special effects go, they were distinctly second-rate. His whole image was pathetic. He was strictly low-budget, more camp comedy than real horror.

'You might die,' he said, levelly. 'In the space of an hour, some time tonight, or the next night. They'd call it meningitis. It could ruin Professor Viners, if they tracked it to his laboratory. His whole career could be destroyed. Anne doesn't want you to die, and nor do I. Anne wants me to exist, to be real. She helped me to put on frail flesh and live. Anne was taken by the owls, but you might save her. I can't, but you might. Feed the hunger, Gil. Feed the hunger, and live.'

The pressure of his words built up as he talked. It was as if he were turning some kind of screw that bit deeper into my flesh with every twisting sentence, every revolutionary thought. I couldn't taunt him any longer; I didn't have the strength of will to deny him, to prophesy his extinction, to disqualify him from true existence as a mere thing of shadow. I couldn't even dismiss him as a silly caricature.

The stereotypes of comic-book fiction can become stereotypes only if they have something to refer to – something already inside us, about which we feel desperately uneasy. He was a joke, but he was a joke with all the underlying nastiness and savagery that underlies so many of our jokes. A sick joke; a black comedy. The fact that he seemed so ridiculous only reflected on me, not on him.

'I can fight this thing,' I whispered, more to myself than to him. 'It's not like HIV; it can't take up permanent residence. It's too weak.'

I wanted to believe all that, but I knew that I couldn't be sure. Some viruses can't ever be dislodged. Some viruses can even become integrated into a person's indigenous DNA. Mike Viners thought that some cases of chronic mental illness might be accountable in those terms. I'd formed wilder variants of the same hypothesis, and written them down in black and white in my lab book. I couldn't turn my back on my own ideas and deny that I'd ever had them.

There was a real possibility that I might be going mad.

If I did, there was a real possibility that I might never recover my sanity.

And if I couldn't get back to home base, to normality, I might have to live for ever in the world where vampires were, and where my hunger could never be satisfied.

'Do what you must,' said Maldureve, his staring bloodshot eyes contriving to seem baleful and pleading at the same time. 'There's no way back, but there *is* a way forward. If you can't become as we are, you'll die . . . and if you can't become as we are, the owls may do whatever they please with Anne.'

'What the fuck are the owls?' I demanded harshly, no longer content to lie there and let his nonsense spill over me. 'And what the holy fuck are *you?*'

'We're the creatures of the borderlands,' he told me, as though it were a serious answer to a serious question, and not mere obfuscation. 'We're those who lie beneath the cutting edge of evolving perception. We're the inheritors of the world, whose advent has been long foreseen. You must join us, if you have any ambition to belong to the future of the world. If you can't become as we are, you'll die. Few will have the choice, but you do.'

'Bullshit!' I said. 'Stupid fucking bullshit!'

'Feed the hunger,' he retorted, losing his smile as he did so. 'Feed the hunger, or cut your stupid fucking throat.' His mouth was twisted into a taunting sneer, as though he held me in utter contempt. I suddenly caught the stink of him, like a cellar filled with mould – but he was still in black and white, like something out of a very old movie. The obscenities sounded entirely out of character. It was as if the actor playing the vampire had suddenly spoken with his own voice, cutting through the script with cynical contempt.

I knew that I, and nobody else, was the actor, and the scriptwriter too. I was taunting and tormenting myself. The virus had turned me against my own flesh.

'Go away,' I said, softly. 'Just go, and leave me alone.'

He was already gone, like a shadow betrayed by a trick of the light.

I expected the colour to come flooding back into the room then. I expected the electric bulb to regain its normal power of illumination, and spread the healthy glow of normality over the carpet and the furniture, the bedclothes and my own naked flesh. I waited for it to happen, for ordinary experience to come creeping back.

It didn't.

Nothing changed. I was still peculiarly colour-blind, condemned to inhabit a world of gloomy shadows.

I suspected even then that there was going to be no way back for me, but I didn't want to believe it. I wanted to do everything I possibly could to avoid believing it. I was determined to avoid ever having to admit that it had all gone too far, and that whatever else Maldureve was lying about, he was telling the simple truth when he said that I might die.

I rubbed my eyes with my knuckles, but it did no good. It was as though I'd already slipped halfway out of the world, and half dissolved into shadow.

'Fight it,' I said, to my oh-so-heroic antibodies. 'Get in there, and blow the bastard virions to kingdom come. You can do it. Do it for me. Please.'

I hadn't expected an answer, and I didn't get one. They were too busy to come to the phone. They had a job to do. I had to let them get on with it.

There was no other way.

8

As soon as I'd had breakfast I phoned the hospital, but there was no news, and it didn't seem to me that this was one of those occasions when no news could be reckoned good news. Anne was still asleep, still in the coma which wasn't a normal coma. I wondered whether there was any colour in *her* world, to dazzle and amuse her rapid eye movements, or whether she too had been relegated to some half-world within which life looked like an ancient B-movie.

There might, I supposed, be compensations in being asleep while the virus made play with her imagination, if that was indeed what was happening to her. Being asleep in hospital might ensure that her body was safe, or as safe as it could be.

I still had bruises on the back of my hand, and the lovebite-like mark on my neck hadn't completely faded away. I didn't feel too bad. I had no headache, no sore throat, and I was growing accustomed to the hunger, which now felt muted, but there didn't yet seem to be any grounds for hoping that the worst was over. My eyes had forgotten how to see colour, and it seemed that they barely remembered how to react to light.

The new day was as crisp and bright as anyone except me could have wished, but for me the clear sky was black instead of blue, and the people who moved through the streets around St Saviour's were like the shades of the dead, clinging dumbly to their routines because they did not know yet that the grim reaper had scythed them down.

There was only one place I could go, so I went.

Professor Viners looked across his desk at me with faint disapproval. 'I advised you not to come in again until you were

better,' he said. *Advised*, not *told*. He was criticizing me for not
being sufficiently responsible to take advice, hinting that people
who couldn't take advice ended up having to take orders.

'I couldn't,' I told him. 'I need a . . . what do you call it here?
. . . a tutorial.'

He frowned. He didn't like to think that someone might be
mocking him. I wasn't. I had simply forgotten the word for a
moment. Aphasia or just a slip of the memory? Paranoia was so
easy, now I'd got the hang of it. Easy to do, difficult to resist –
like smoking.

'I'm sorry, Professor,' I said. 'I know that I'm not going to be
able to persuade you, but I'd like you to listen anyway. I'm not
saying that what I'm going through is caused by one of your little
pets, and I don't mind at all if you want to believe that it's all in
my mind, that it's something I'm doing to myself. I can accept
that. But even if that's so, it warrants description. It needs to be
recorded, for later reference. If I'm fit and well again by Monday
morning, I can ask you to forget the whole thing, but you need
to be told what's happening, whatever the outcome is. Will you
hear me out?'

The frown was still there, but now it was only puzzlement and
apprehension, not annoyance.

'Of course,' he said, as if there could never have been any
doubt about the matter. He was an Englishman, after all.

'I've gone colour-blind, and my eyes have lost most of their
light-sensitivity.' I said. 'It may be psychosomatic, I guess, but the
symptoms are real. I have this strange feeling – I keep thinking
of it as a hunger, but that's only for want of a more accurate
word – which won't go away. It's a dull, fierce need. It's a little
quieter now than it has been, but it's driving me crazy because
it stubbornly refuses to let me know what I'm hungering *for*.
That's the physical side of things. I'm also hallucinating: I've
been visited twice by a schlock-horror vampire in a cloak who
keeps telling me things that don't make any sense but somehow
feel as if they ought to. I don't want to be humoured and I don't
want to be reassured. I want to be taken seriously. I want to hear
some hypotheses – not about what might be happening, because
we both know all the alternatives – but how and why I'm being
affected *this way*.'

Viners leaned back in his chair and put his hands together, palms apart but fingers touching, each one lightly pressed against its counterpart.

'You were right to come to see me,' he said, neutrally. He gave the impression of a man who was thinking hard.

'We can treat the question as hypothetically as you like,' I said. 'We can look at it from both sides, one by one. But I need to know how this thing is going to develop. I need to know whether to get myself admitted to a hospital. I'm scared of doing that, not only because of what I'd be admitting to myself, but also because it might make Detective Sergeant Miller think again about appointing me suspect number one in his investigation – which he might well do anyway, given that his chances of getting a statement from Anne aren't looking too good right now. If I am infected, by the way, I think she must be too.'

'I think you ought to be aware,' said Viners, 'that I've never suffered effects of the kind you describe. Vivid dreams, yes – but never physical symptoms like those you mentioned.'

'Perhaps you only *thought* you might have picked up one of the experimental viruses,' I suggested. 'Perhaps I'm the first person actually to do so.'

'I can assure you that's not so,' he retorted.

I hadn't expected that he'd have any surprises for me tucked up his sleeve, and it was quite a shock to realize what he meant.

'You've infected yourself?' I said, feeling the need to make sure. 'Deliberately?'

'Of course. These viruses do occur in nature, you know. They weren't cooked up in the laboratory by some Frankensteinian madman. They're out there in the world. Animals and people catch them all the time. The ones I've isolated for investigation in the lab aren't endemic to Britain, nor to California, but they can be imported just like influenza viruses and common colds. Exploring the chemistry is all very well, but how could I hope to begin explaining anything if I didn't know anything at all about the psychological correlates?'

I stared at his grey, shadowed face. He didn't much resemble the Professor Viners I was used to seeing, so it was less astonishing than it might have been to hear that he was a wild man after all, a swashbuckling cut-the-crap kick-it-and-see-what-happens merchant.

'Why didn't you tell me this before?' I asked.

'It wouldn't have been fair. It might have seemed that I was urging you to try a similar experiment. Actually, I had another reason, too. I presumed that the idea would occur to you in time, and I didn't want to discuss my symptoms in case foreknowledge affected your own. I assume, however, that this infection – if it *is* an infection by one of the experimental viruses – was quite accidental?'

'Damn right,' I murmured. 'What about Teresa? Has she played guinea pig too'

'She hasn't volunteered,' he said. 'I'd never have infected her deliberately without her informed consent. Any symptoms she's had were presumably imaginary, unless she got careless and infected herself by mistake. I hope you haven't been thinking that I might have used *you* as an unsuspecting guinea pig. I certainly didn't slip something into your lunch box while you weren't looking. To tell you the truth, I've always had high hopes that you would one day decide to get properly involved. I suppose we tend to have a rather glamourized view of Californian daring in these strait-laced isles. But I really do think that your present symptoms must be psychosomatic.'

I swallowed the swearwords which sprang to my tongue, and substituted sarcasm. 'I suppose it didn't occur to you,' I said, 'when you tried the virus on yourself that the damn things might take up permanent residence in your body – that you might become a walking incubator. You might be infectious, damn it! You might have passed viruses on to Teresa in a perfectly ordinary way – and she could have passed them on to me.'

'As I've already pointed out,' he said, gently, 'these viruses are out there in the world. They infect thousands of people every day, and they're not killers. People suffer a slight fever, mild delirium, and then recover. They're not anywhere near as contagious as the most effective cold viruses, and certainly no more dangerous. When I conducted my experiments I did so in private, and I made sure that I was clear of any symptoms before I renewed contact with my wife, my children or Teresa. I have no reason to think that anyone else has been infected.'

'Then what the fuck is happening to me?'

He winced at the obscenity, but he didn't complain. He just looked at me from the depths of his dark-grey eyes and said: 'I don't know, Gil. That's what we have to try to work out.'

'If it's a mutant,' I said, 'we're in trouble. All of us.' I suddenly thought about what I'd done with Teresa the previous evening. Maybe it had all been her imagination before, or maybe she'd only had the harmless strains. But now . . . could she possibly have antibodies that would still protect her, the way antibodies to cowpox could protect against smallpox? I hoped so.

'It could be a mutant,' the professor admitted. 'And if it is, there could indeed be further problems. Quarantine might be in order.'

'Isn't it a bit late for that?'

'I don't know. Have you had sexual relations with anyone else recently, apart from Anne Charet and Teresa?' He asked the question in an apologetic manner, as though half fearful of giving offence. There was no point in having an argument about the way he'd jumped to the conclusion, given that he was right on the nail.

'No,' I said.

'I presume that Miss Charet is still in the intensive-care unit, isolated as long as she remains there by the procedures intended to keep *her* safe from infection. It only remains to make sure that Teresa doesn't pass anything on. I think she's been here long enough to take a precautionary warning in the right spirit, especially if we stress that it's to ensure *your* peace of mind.'

I couldn't quite decide whether he was being thoroughly sensible and level-headed, or criminally irresponsible. I knew that he didn't believe there was any danger. He didn't think that I had picked up any new mutant. He was just humouring me. But he had a duty to think about all the possibilities, didn't he? I reminded myself that I was the one with defective vision and an incomprehensible ache in my gut. He couldn't know how desperate my situation felt – and I was, after all, sitting in his office discussing the matter. I had nothing external to show for my travails except a few faded bruises.

'Professor Viners,' I said, trying to make him understand how bad things were, 'I might be going blind. *I can't see properly.*'

'I understand that,' he said. 'I might need outside help to carry out a full physical examination, but that won't be a problem if and when we decide that it's necessary. I can certainly find out right here whether you've been exposed to any of the experimental viruses, and whether there's any abnormality in your brain chemistry. I can't tell you not to worry until we have a better idea what's going on, but it's far too soon to decide that the trouble can't be fixed, let alone that the world might be swept by some terrible epidemic. If you come through this unscathed – and I have no reason at all to believe that you won't – you might have the makings of a very interesting thesis.'

The last remark sounded uncomfortably like a sick joke, but I could see that he was serious. He was half hoping, in a way, that I did have something strange and interesting.

'Anne's in some kind of coma,' I reminded him. 'She's dreaming, and can't wake up. I can't help suspecting that she is *not* having a nice time. Nobody saw her attacker – nobody is absolutely sure that there really was an attacker. I have a psychosomatic bruise on my neck, and I can't discount the possibility that the cut on her neck was psychosomatically inflicted, too. If we're victims of the same virus, I think we have to be prepared to concede that it's the kind of bug that can really screw people up, don't you?'

'It's possible,' he agreed, but he was still humouring me. He was too much of a scientist to jump to those kinds of conclusions, even if he was wild man enough to test-drive his own diseases. He was still telling himself that no one had died yet, that no one could even be proven to be seriously ill.

I felt a sudden impulse to throttle him, to try to shake a proper sense of hazard into him. It started out as one of those impulses which you feel but would never put into practice in a million years – more a sort of self-indulgent fantasy than an authentic intention. Even as I pictured myself taking him by the throat – and it wasn't a particularly vivid fantasy – I was passing on to the next thought, planning the next sentence, bending under the pressure of the next anxiety. Suddenly, though, the idea seemed to catch hold of something inside me, as though it were a hook unexpectedly seized by a too-powerful fish. Suddenly, it didn't seem to be my impulse any more, but something independent of me: a compulsion urging me to act, screaming at me to hurl myself forward and *do it*.

I stopped myself. It wouldn't have mattered if it had been an utterly trivial impulse, to pick my nose or say 'Fuck you, Viners'; the mere fact that it had abruptly transformed itself from an unintended whimsy into an awful command was enough to make me resist it with all my might. But all my might seemed as it if might not be enough – my hands started shaking violently, as though they longed to become talons, and the fingers claws.

'Holy shit!' I said, as I watched them, pale and white among the shadows, dancing and shivering in midair, as though caught up by a dozen violently shaken puppet-strings.

I was possessed by a dreadful desire to get to my feet and hurl myself upon Professor Viners, to grab him and squeeze him and show him that the world wasn't the bright and orderly place he thought it was, but a dark and hellish realm where nothing could be relied upon and where violence lurked in every beating heart. I wanted to do it, but the want didn't seem to be mine – not really. It was just a *want*, with no subject of its own, which happened to have burst forth inside me.

I moved forward, impelled by some force which was within me but not part of me, and might have gone further but for the fact that I came up against the desk, and was in any case off balance. The shock of the impact on my knee knocked me back, and I was able to snatch my hands back too, suppressing that hideous quivering.

I saw Viners looking up at me, his white face seeming suddenly tiny in an infinite wilderness of shadows that was no longer confined by the walls of the room.

He was scared. He was very frightened. As well, I thought, he might be. As well he ought to be.

'Gil,' he said faintly, as though he were a million miles away. 'Gil, what is it?'

'Fuck you, Viners,' I said, my voice hissing as though I were speaking over a bad telephone line. 'Do you have any idea what you've done to me?'

I turned and ran, as fast as my feet could carry me. I barged through the door which connected Viners' office to the corridor, and I raced to the stairs that would take me down to the ground floor and out of the building.

The people on the stairs took evasive action to let me through, and they must have looked after me in open astonishment, but I didn't pause. I didn't know whether it was really me that was doing the running, or whether I was simply capitulating to something that wanted to run me, but whichever it was, my body was desperate to flee, desperate to race away from what had suddenly become an incredibly awkward confrontation, towards . . .

But I had no idea what I was running towards.

No idea at all.

9

Viners didn't try to follow me out of his office, let alone out of the building. I didn't go past the isolation lab, so Teresa never saw me. I passed more people on the pavement when I got out into the cold, clean air, but they moved out of my way easily enough. I was just a person in a hurry, no big deal.

I could have slowed down once I was away from the building. The urgency had gone out of my flight, but I didn't try to stop until I was a couple of hundred yards away, away from the looming black towers.

It was still a clear, bright morning but to me it was grey and dark and full of grotesque shadows. The sky was sullen and the sun, which ought to have been a blaze of white light, was like a dark pit sucking the light and colour out of the world. Nothing made sense; although I knew that it was me who was out of sensory step, I couldn't help feeling that it was the world around me which had changed and become alien.

I continued moving, but only at walking pace. I didn't go towards the road and the town but in the opposite direction, towards the wilderness which lay at the heart of the campus.

I slowed down again as I approached the bridge over the

stream, and finally stopped there to catch my breath. My heart was hammering and it was difficult to suck air into my lungs. I had a pain in my side which folded me over, but it didn't last long.

As soon as I felt able to do so, I walked on, past Wombwell House. There were students passing in and out, laughing and gossiping. I went past the main door. My hands and feet seemed to belong entirely to me again – I was back in control. My eyes wouldn't see straight, and the hunger was still stirring inside me, but the fit of pure madness that had seized hold of me in Viners' office had subsided. I'd run it off. I stopped again, to lean against one of the ancient lampposts on the path which ran alongside the stand of trees where Anne had been attacked.

To me, the woodland was lightless and sinister, every bit as menacing as it must have seemed to Anne as she'd tried to walk past it on her way home. To everyone else it, it must have seemed to be at its mildest and most ordinary.

I stared into the unnatural darkness, at the black, leafless branches. They captured and held my gaze. Somehow, they seemed pregnant with life, as though half-formed shapes were stirring in every problematic shadow, trying to capture my attention.

Here, I thought, here are monsters.

'You're Gil Molari, aren't you?'

I started, and turned abruptly to see who had spoken.

It was a woman in her early thirties, wearing a shapeless sweater – apparently grey, although it probably didn't look that way to her – and baggy black slacks which presumably were black in actuality. She had a child with her, a girl perhaps ten or eleven years old, much thinner and paler than her mother.

The woman blinked uncomfortably, taken slightly aback by the way she'd made me jump. The little girl looked bored and deliberately uninterested, as if she'd rather be anywhere else in the world than where she was.

'Sorry,' said the woman. 'I'm Cynthia Leigh – I'm in Anne's tutorial group. I've seen you with her. I just wondered if you knew how she is.'

I couldn't find the words for an immediate reply, and she continued nervously.

'It's just . . . at first we heard that she wasn't badly hurt, but since then . . . well, you know how rumours are. Do you know if she's recovered consciousness yet?'

'I phoned this morning,' I said. 'An hour ago – slightly more. They said there's been no change. She's still unconscious, or was then. They expect her to wake up any time.'

'Oh,' she said, unhappily. She cast about for something else to say. 'This is my daughter Janine. She has a dentist's appointment at twelve-thirty, so she didn't go to school, but I have a lecture first, so she came with me.'

'Hi, Janine,' I said, automatically. The little girl seemed surprised that I'd bothered, and looked at me a little more intently. To me, her eyes were dark and her hair nondescript, but she might have looked pretty if I'd been able to see the colour in her face. She had neat features, and she had already learned to look up from beneath her eyebrows in a slightly coquettish fashion.

'It happened in there,' said Cynthia, nodding in the direction of the shadow-crazed wood, which must have looked quite innocent to her in the bright light which I couldn't perceive. 'It's not safe at night, this path. It could have been –'

She stopped, and looked away in discomfort. She had been about to say that it might have been anyone, implying that it might have been her, but she hadn't dared to complete the sentence – in case it had made me say silently to myself that it *wouldn't* have been her, because she was too old, too plain. I wouldn't have thought any such thing, because I knew full well that rapists are unselective. They only want someone to hurt and humiliate and terrorize, and don't care at all about sexual attractiveness. Not that there was anything especially unprepossessing about Cynthia Leigh – she was just fleshy and faded and dispirited. When she'd been younger, she must have looked more like her daughter, and more like Anne. There was nothing wrong with her looks that a touch of anorexia and a little coquettishness couldn't have cured.

'Dr Gray was very upset,' said Cynthia, changing the subject to cover her confusion. 'He likes Anne. We all do. It's a terrible shame.'

'I should have been with her,' I said bleakly, trying to halve the burden of her sorrow by sharing it. 'I had a cold, and stayed at home with it. Just a cold.'

The words rang unexpectedly hollow as I stared at her colourless form.

'Will she be all right?' the woman asked, looking for further reassurance.

'I think so,' I said. 'It's not a real coma. There's no possibility of brain damage, the doctor says. She'll wake up when she's ready. It's just a matter of time.'

I hoped that I was telling the truth. I hoped that it was all a matter of time, and that the world would put itself to rights if only I waited long enough. I wanted the coloured world back again, and I wanted Anne back too. I wanted it all to be over, and no harm done to anyone.

'She wasn't a strong girl,' said Cynthia Leigh. 'It was the stress of being away from home, I think. I should have done more, taken her under my wing a bit. I should have made more effort. Someone said that she often went out at night, late – was that true? Do you know why?'

'I don't know,' I answered. 'The policeman who came to tell me what had happened said that a girl on Anne's corridor had told them that, but it was news to me. Perhaps it's a mistake. Even if it's not, *often* is probably an exaggeration.'

She nodded, wanting to believe that it wasn't important, that it meant nothing. I was astonished by my own capacity for common sense.

'Has it always been like this?' she said, tiredly. 'The world. Was it always this bad, or is it getting worse?'

For just a moment I set the words in the context of my own perceptions: the colour-blindness, the hunger. But she knew nothing about that. She only meant what Anne's mother had meant; it was the same sense of disappointment with the failure of other people to do unto her as she was disposed to do unto them. She yearned for a harmless, polite society of nice people. And why shouldn't she? Why shouldn't she want the kind of world in which she could live the kind of life she wanted to live, and bring up her daughter in safety?

I didn't answer the question. What was there to say?

'I have to go,' she said. 'Thanks for telling me the news. If you see Anne, tell her I sent my best wishes. Dr Gray's and Daniel's too. Tell her . . . well, you know. Say goodbye, Janine.'

'Goodbye,' said Janine, and flashed me a tiny smile as if to say that she meant it, in spite of having no choice but to say it.

'Bye, Janine,' I said. 'Best of luck with the dentist.'

When they'd gone, I relaxed again, although I hadn't been aware of becoming tenser. The ordinariness of the conversation had brought me back from the depths of my desperation, but the show of politeness I'd put on had been an effort. I wondered how long I'd have to continue doing that – passing for human when in fact I was beset by all kinds of bizarrely dehumanizing circumstances.

I lifted my hand to stare at the palm, hoping to reassure myself that I was fully in control.

I wasn't. The hand was shaking. I was unaware of any alien intention with which my own will was in conflict, but I daren't dismiss the tremor as some random trick of the nerves, significant of nothing.

I'm possessed, I thought. The virus is like some medieval demon, tormenting me and trying to make me do things I don't want to do. Maybe Viners is right. Maybe all abnormal mental states are down to infections like these. Maybe there was a time when anyone could be possessed, as easily as they could contract smallpox. Maybe natural selection picked out those who were immune – except that there are always freaks, always throwbacks. Maybe it isn't the virus that's mutated. Maybe I'm just one of the unlucky ones, who get hit much harder than the rest. Maybe I'm carrying some recessive gene which lets delirium run wild in me.

I didn't scare myself. In fact, it was the other way around. My capacity to think about it in those terms, to draw up a new hypothesis and confront it squarely, seemed to be an invaluable proof of the continuing power of my reason, and the authority of my logic.

Possession isn't permanent, I told myself. This thing can be exorcized with the aid of patience, calmness and ruthless self-discipline. I'm a grown man and a scientist. This is the twentieth century, nearly the twenty-first. I can beat it. It can blind me to the beauty of the world, and turn the sun inside out, and fill me with unanswerable appetites, but it can be exorcized if only I don't weaken. My immune system is churning out vast armies of antibodies: hosts of avenging angels to slay the demonic virions in open combat. All I have to do is keep body and soul together, get my head behind my heart . . . think, think, think.

My hand stopped shaking, and I turned back to look at the weird wood, determined to stare it down.

Maldureve was standing among the trees, looking back at me. As usual, there was nothing visible of his flesh but his head. Everything else was enveloped by that thick black cloak which melted into the shadows. His face was stark white – far whiter than anything else I could see – but his lips were black and the pupils of his eyes were pits of darkness rimmed with swollen blood vessels like thin ebony dendrites.

'We are always self-possessed,' he said. He didn't move his lips, and the words seemed to arrive inside my head without disturbing my ears en route. 'We are possessed in turn by all those who have intimate knowledge of us. Small wonder, then, that we are possessed by demons too. They are born in us and they live in us and they do not flee from our flesh until we die. Theirs is a restless and malevolent host which will not readily yield to the empire of reason.

'Our possessors move us and curse us. We struggle to make them captive by naming them and taming them, but they constantly evade our traps of meaning and our tricks of education. Who lays envy to rest by counting blessings? Who conquers wrath by placing it in the service of righteousness? Who slays lust by disguising it with the decorations of love?

'Everyone – and no one.

'Our inner demons possess our dreams and our desires. Our inmost souls are castles we cannot defend, no matter how sternly we set the features which we display to the world. We are *possessed*, and there is no limit to the number of our possessors.

'We are bought and bartered a thousand times a day, seized as trophies and discarded as broken wrecks. We are precious and worthless, instrumental and detrimental, used and abused. We are without help and without hope. We are all *possessed*, every minute of every day, and there is no release from such slavery as this. This is the heritage of man.'

'You bastard,' I said. 'Leave me *alone!*'

I would have seemed insane to anyone who passed me on the path just then, but it was three or four minutes past the eleventh hour, and the students had vanished as though by magic, called to whatever appointments their timetables designated. All those bound for Wombwell House had been swallowed up by it; all those emitted by the edifice had passed on. I was alone, except for this perverse phantom of my imagination, who was trying to turn my ideas back upon myself, trying to twist my rational hypothesis into all kinds of knots, trying to make my attempts at self-discipline seem absurd.

I was determined to stop him, to fight him.

'Listen to me,' he said, almost pleadingly. 'We are all possessed, and it could not be otherwise. Our thoughts, our dreams, every facet of our existence is determined by our possessors. No one can resist or escape, unless by way of death. Feed the hunger, Gil. Live!'

'You're just a bad dream,' I told him, speaking out loud. 'Bad in both senses. You're an incompetent dream: a shallow cliché. Vampires don't terrify us any more – they amuse us. We laugh at them. We make jokes of our ancient superstitions, and conquer them with laughter. You're a joke, Maldureve.'

He looked back at me with open contempt, as though I didn't deserve an answer. He thought that he didn't need to answer, that my argument would simply run out of steam, and thus expose its own frailty.

It worked. I hesitated. I faltered. I couldn't suppress the fear that was building inside me. No matter how hard I fought, *I couldn't suppress the fear*. Again, I felt that I was possessed, that some raging demon inside of me was wrestling for control of my body and my mind. I was in turmoil, and I hated it.

'I won't do it,' I said, though something in me turned my words upside down inside my mind even as I spoke them, mocking my inability to make them true. 'I won't become like you. You can't make me do it.'

'Feed the hunger, Gil,' he whispered. The whisper sounded loud and clear inside my head in spite of the fact that he was thirty feet away. 'Anne loves you. She wants you to live. She wants you to be together. She'll never wake up if you can't wake

her. That hunger inside you is hers, and it has to be fed. Feed
the hunger, and save your life. Feed the hunger, and save *her*.'

'Fuck you,' I said, in a shout no louder than a whisper. 'Fuck
you, Viners, and all your malign viruses.'

'It's time,' said Maldureve. 'It's time for you to feed.'

'On what?' I said, helplessly. Immediately, I felt a rush of
shame, an acute awareness of disgusting cowardice and failure.
I didn't want an answer; I wanted to be rid of him. In response
to the emotional surge which flooded my body I ran full tilt at
the dark-clad figure, lifting my hands high as though to rake
his face with claw-like fingers, as though to tear him into rags
and tatters.

It was no good. Just as I came close to him and reached out to
hurt him, he melted into the shadows with astonishing ease and
appalling grace. He didn't have to fade away by slow degrees;
he was a master of the art. The shadows were his natural home,
his world.

Even as he departed, his final words echoed in my besieged
consciousness. It was the answer that I didn't want to hear.

'Blood,' he said, in a voice that was hoarse with unholy avidity
and lust. '*Young blood!*'

10

Frustrated by the vampire's disappearance, I lashed out at
the wizened trunk of the nearest tree, but I did far more
damage to my hand than to the unexpectedly sturdy tree. The
pain which ran up my arm helped to clear my head and restore
my equilibrium, and I turned around so that I could lean my
spine against the uninjured trunk.

It was a quarter after eleven in the morning, but as far as I
was concerned it was more like midnight beneath the spreading
branches. I could feel the spirit stirring inside me – the greedy
spirit which I'd earlier called a hunger, but which now seemed
like an indwelling demon that had dispossessed my soul. I felt

it move within me, and credited it in my imagination with a vague semblance of human form and human personality. It was somehow easier to see it in these terms, no matter how unscientific they might be. It was easy to imagine its glowing eyes and its rubbery, drooling lips.

I told myself that its hunger was not *my* hunger, and that was why I had been unable to assuage it or even figure out what its object was. But once I'd conceded that, I couldn't help remembering what Maldureve had said – that its hunger was Anne's hunger, mysteriously displaced from her sleeping body into mine, as though injected into me by her loving kiss.

I confronted and was carried away by the notion that what possessed me was some fragment of Anne, encapsulating the shadow of her being: her love, her lust, her hope, her hunger. It had darkened my sight, but not for ever . . . if its needs could only be answered, Anne would awake, and the glory of light and colour would be restored to the world . . .

'Stop it!' I said aloud, desperately trying to stem the flow of madness. I tried with all my might to reimpose the authority of my sceptical intelligence, the empire of my scientific training.

'These are nothing but my elemental fears,' I told myself sternly, not speaking aloud but forming my silent words very deliberately, moving my tongue and my lips as though to whisper them. 'These are primitive terrors, bursting free from that stratum of subconsciousness to which mental discipline long ago confined them. The virus is unbalancing me, bringing the maleficent chaos of dreams into my waking life, but it has no intelligence of its own, no will of its own, no purpose of its own. This dark caricature which appears before me in order to haunt and torment me is nothing but a doppelgänger – the antithetical echo of my own reason. It can tell me nothing but lies, and the truth will help me be free of it, if only I can cling to the truth. I am my own master.'

But the light didn't come flooding back; colour was still banished from the world's false night. No matter how hard I insisted that I was in control, the world refused to yield.

'Are you all right?'

The words cut through my introspective fugue like a scalpel. I tried not to jump with alarm, and I tried not to scare the person who had spoken as I turned to look at her. I was afraid that I might suddenly have acquired the petrifying power of a gorgon.

It was Cynthia Leigh's daughter Janine.

'What are you doing here?' I whispered, trying with all my might not to sound angry or threatening.

'I didn't want to go to Mummy's lecture,' the child explained, painstakingly. 'She said that I could stay with the secretary, but the secretary was typing and talking on the phone, both at the same time. It was boring, so I came out. I saw you run into the trees.'

'You shouldn't wander off on your own like that,' I said. 'Not here, of all places. You'll make your mommy very anxious. One of her friends was hurt, right about here. You mustn't do things like this.'

'I'm not on my own,' said the girl. 'You're here.'

I looked at her helplessly, wondering how I could possibly explain the awful folly of what she was doing without frightening her. But I could see that she was old enough to understand, old enough to know better than to do what she had done. She had done it deliberately, almost provocatively.

'I'm all right,' I told her. 'I'm not feeling very well, but I'm all right. I've got a cold, and it gives me a headache. You'd better go back. I don't want you to catch the cold.'

'I get colds all the time,' said Janine dolefully. 'Mummy thinks I do it on purpose, but I don't. She thinks I don't like going to school because I don't have a daddy, but that's not why. I don't like the dentist either. I don't like the way he pokes things into my mouth, trying to find soft bits in my teeth. His breath smells, and when he tries to see right inside my mouth it makes me want to throw up.'

She was looking up at me from underneath her eyebrows, putting her head on one side in a slightly teasing fashion. She *was* teasing. She knew how pretty she was, how cute; she knew what effect she could have on people if she tried – especially men. It was utterly innocent – just something she had learned by trial and error, as a means of making people like her – but it was nevertheless a sly appeal to sexual attraction. She was flirting, as only a ten-year-old could flirt.

My mouth was dry. I was uncomfortably aware of how it might look if we were found here together.

'We have to go back,' I told her. I wanted to reach out and offer to take her by the hand, but I didn't dare. I wanted her to go away, but she showed no sign of doing so.

'I don't want to,' she said, pouting. The thought of a trip to the dentist was making her irresponsible; suppressed fear was making her reckless. She was trying to enlist me to her cause, knowing it couldn't work but not really caring.

She suddenly seemed very like Anne, and I realized that it was not so much because she looked like Anne as because Anne's behaviour sometimes seemed just as innocently provocative, just as defiantly helpless. Their faces would not have been so similar but for the fact that Anne didn't eat; their figures would not have been so similar but for the fact that Anne was trying with all her might not to grow up, subconsciously insisting on remaining a little girl, eligible for protection.

I couldn't help finding the little girl attractive, not just because of her amateurish flirtatiousness, but also because of what she was. I was attracted by her bony features, by her slim body. There wasn't anything sinister in the attraction, or anything abnormal. She was attractive – a creature capable of awakening lust no matter how inappropriate an object of lust she might be. Youth is itself attractive; so is innocence; so is helplessness.

I wanted to help her. *I wanted to help her.*

'Please,' I said, plaintively. 'You have to go back to Wombwell House. Your mommy would be very upset if she thought you'd come into the woods. Just because your mommy spoke to me, it doesn't mean I'm not a stranger. You shouldn't have followed me. You shouldn't have come after me the way you did. You have to be more careful, Janine, for your mommy's sake as well as your own.'

'Mummy's a lesbian,' she said, as if the revelation were somehow relevant. I remembered that I knew it already. Anne had told me about Cynthia in slightly hushed and nervous tones, determined not to seem judgemental.

'You shouldn't be talking to me like this,' I told her, fighting to keep my voice steady. 'It was kind of you to worry about me,

but these woods really aren't safe. Your mommy's friend was
hurt right about here.'

'That was at night,' Janine pointed out. 'It's the middle of the
day now.'

Not for me, I found myself thinking. I've been banished from
the light of day, sentenced to live in eternal night until . . .

I cast aside the train of thought, fearful of where it might
lead.

I tried hard to suppress the lust that was infecting my gaze as I
looked at the child – not because it was cruel lust, unleavened by
authentic affection, but because any kind of lust was dangerous,
so unendurable that it had to be repressed. I couldn't do it.
There was too much virus in me, lending support to the dark
doppelgänger. I wasn't sufficiently self-controlled, not entirely
self-possessed. I couldn't help but look at her with longing, with
excitement, with desire.

I wanted to run, but I couldn't move. Now, when I most
needed the motive force of panic, panic wouldn't come.

'I'm sorry,' I told her. 'I'm not well. You mustn't come any
closer, or you might catch it.'

'I don't mind,' she said, coming one step closer. 'I get colds
all the time. I don't mind.'

She reached out her hand, generously and tenderly. There
was a curious expression on her face, as though she sensed that
she was somehow in control of the situation, although she didn't
know quite how or why. She liked the sensation. She couldn't
even begin to understand how foolhardy she was, what terrible
danger she was in. I wasn't myself. I was possessed.

She held out her hand towards me, submissively inviting
me to take it in order to lead her back to Wombwell House.
She wanted to be led; she wanted to go back with me. She
wanted me to be involved, to be on her side. She didn't know,
and couldn't begin to imagine, what I was feeling. She was
innocent, unknowing, blind to the true nature of the world
of human thought and desire. She could see the colour and
the brightness in the world, and was blind to its darkness. She
had no idea what kind of world I was living in, or what kind
of forces were moving in me, unvanquished as yet by my inner
legions.

Something in me reached out and took her hand. That shadowy demon, the Anne-thing, reached out to its tiny counterpart, and took her by the hand. Then it bent down and opened its arms wide in an invitation to embrace ... and the little girl accepted the invitation, gladly. She liked me. She was attracted to me, although she didn't know the true nature of her immature, submerged attraction.

The touch of her hand and the warmth of her body triggered some reaction which drove me back from the heartland of my own being, dispatching my true will into the mysterious borderlands of my soul, where it was withered by cold and rendered impotent by darkness.

The doppelgänger which took possession of my body – so very smoothly, as though equipped to do so by long and manifold experience – picked the little girl up and lifted her until her face was level with mine. From a great distance, I looked deep into the jet-black pupils of her eyes, rimmed with misty grey, and I saw myself reflected there: smiling, loving, animated by amusement.

I felt the pressure of the kiss which the doppelgänger visited upon her lips: the tender, gentle kiss which she welcomed and returned, hopelessly unaware of the significance of her own nascent and precocious desire.

I felt my body hug her to me, and the pressure of her frail arms against the back of my neck. I felt my face nestle into the corner between her shoulder and her cheek, felt my lips seek out the pale white skin to the left of her throat, where the excited pulse of the carotid artery was perceptible. All of this was as sharp and clear to me as if I had been in full possession of my faculties. There was no colour in it at all, but it was as sharp and clear as a photograph.

Then things fell apart, and chaos came again.

I felt my lips press themselves greedily to her neck, and I felt her flesh shift and flow under the pressure, becoming soft and almost liquid. I felt something drawn into my mouth: a sudden cascade of blood, which tasted unbelievably sweet.

I felt, absurdly, as if my rebel soul fused with that of the little girl, so that our sensations were joined. I knew that she felt no pain, but only joy. Whatever possessed me possessed her also, and dragged us both down into a whirlpool of orgasmic luxury. Neither of us had ever known or suspected that such extreme sensual pleasure could exist.

There was no sound at all, and no light. My eyes were shut now, and I was alone with the splendour of my sensations – *our* sensations. My other self, my demon anima, drank the child's blood, and drank the child's soul. There was no element of caricature in it, no horror-film cliché, no comic-book parody. Any ability to laugh and sneer at vampires which my true self might have had was banished now; here there was only lovely lust and sybaritic satisfaction. Here there was only delirium, of a kind which made mockery of all the rewards accessible to sane, staid consciousness. Here there was only ecstatic madness, drowning mere reason with its purity and fury.

To say that the alien hunger which had plagued me was answered would be a ludicrous understatement. All its discomfort, unease and pain was converted by that sustaining flood into its opposite, and the fulfilment was incredibly luxurious.

From the borderlands of my being, my true self might have raised a cry of protest – but the cry, and the reason which formed it, were lost in the silence of infinity.

If only my reason might have remained lost, never to return . . .

But it did return. It had to return. It wasn't permitted to hide itself away, to deny what had happened.

In being answered, the hunger died. The glorious explosion of sensation dispersed the hunger and the pain and the anguish, to leave a black void in my heart, into which my reason was helplessly drawn and compelled to fill. My doppelgänger vanished into shadow, as he had been bound to do, and contemptuously restored me to myself.

I set the little girl down, as gently and as reverently as I could. She was very light, far too thin for her height and age. She was limp and lifeless, and I knew already that this was no mere sleep or coma. I knew how deeply I had drunk of her blood and her being, and it did no good at all to cry out in the dark night of my frightened mind that I had intended no harm, that everything I had done I had done for love, for innocence, for life.

In the side of her neck there was a great jagged wound: a huge rip which looked as if it were the work of an enormous claw. It was black and sticky, like a great gaping vagina, but no liquid blood fountained from it. Her heart had ceased to beat, and there was no pressure in the artery to force out whatever blood might still remain within her slender body.

The black blood which stood upon the edges of the wound didn't look real. It didn't look like human blood at all. It was all just a movie, just an ancient black-and-white movie. I wasn't really there and neither was she. It was all just make-believe.

Her black eyes were open and sightless, staring blindly into nowhere. Her mouth hung open too, and I could see her tongue within, quivering reflexively.

I knelt over the body, tears welling up in my eyes as I saw what had been done to that lovely, precious child. I felt sick with horror and despair. I knew that in some sense, I had died with her – the explosion of sensation which had consumed her had consumed me too, but had left the mere shell of me ironically unscathed. I knew that I was dead, that I was no longer myself, that I was just a ghost. I knew that everything I had been before was obliterated from the record of real time, leaving only the monster which had possessed and dispossessed me, discarding me as casually as if I were a rag doll.

I could run, now. But there was nowhere I could possibly run to, nowhere I could possibly hide. Wherever I went, people would know me. They would know me for what I had become.

The police would come after me, now. There was no escape. They would call me mad, but they would never, ever forgive me.

How could they? I was damned.

How could I ever forgive myself? Ghost or not, how could I possibly live with the memory of what I had done?

II

Now that the hunger was finally gone I felt much calmer inside. In fact, I was unnaturally calm. I felt that my body and its actions had become mechanical: robotic, inorganic, dead. There was no blood on my hands or around my mouth, and none on my clothing. As soon as I had turned my back on the dead girl I was able to put the awareness of what I had done to the back of my mind, secreting it away. I ceased actively to think about her, lest the horror of it overwhelm me. I gave no thought to the possibility of trying to conceal what I had done. I accepted that I couldn't escape the consequences of the act, and shouldn't even try. My aim now was to take control of those consequences, to make sure that everything was done neatly.

I had to put my affairs in order.

I retraced my steps, passing the doors of Wombwell House and the bridge over the stream. There was no one about. No one saw me emerge from the wood, unless someone happened to be looking down from the upper windows of the house. I walked unhurriedly, with a precisely measured stride. I felt empty and deserted; the doppelgänger which had haunted me was no longer in evidence, inside or out. It had vanished, or become one with me.

The world was still black and white, without any vestige of colour, but the sun was no longer a black pit sucking up the light from the sky; it was too white to look at, shooting forth its pallid rays in profusion, although there was no warmth in it at all.

There were lights on inside the science buildings, even though it was as bright outside as it ever was in December. The biochemistry and physiology departments shone like beacons; psychology was more discreet, but gave forth radiance nevertheless. There were always lights on in the buildings on that part of campus; their labs and lecture rooms harboured many inquisitive souls who could never be satiated by natural enlightenment, who needed more precisely controllable conditions in order to run their experiments and their lives.

No one gave me a second glance as I went up the stairs to Professor Viners' lair. I was in my natural element, entirely at home in the environment. There was no blood on my hands, and my movements were meticulous. The fact that I was now a murderer and a madman did not show at all in my face or my bearing. The mark of Cain was inside me, secret and invisible. I was a monster in mechanical disguise.

I went into the high-security lab before I returned to Viners' office. Teresa looked up as I came in, and said: 'Hi! Feeling better?' But she looked at me oddly. I knew that Viners must have said something to her after I ran from his office – something enigmatic and uncommunicative, no doubt, but *something*.

'The symptoms have just about cleared up,' I told her, matter-of-factly. 'I think I'm coming to the end of it. But I only came in to pick something up. I'm not staying.'

She didn't say anything else, but she looked at me expectantly. I didn't know what she wanted me to tell her. She might only have wanted me to explain what it was that I had come to collect, but she might have been fishing for something more. Perhaps, now that she'd deigned to visit me at home, she was expecting an invitation, or at least an acknowledgement that there now existed a relationship which she had not permitted before. Perhaps she wanted to move in with me. She was as unfathomable as she was unpredictable. I'd never known anyone who could switch herself on and off the way she did. And she did it all by herself, without a demon or a doppelgänger to help her.

I went to the instrument cabinet and unlocked it. Then I pulled out one of the shallow drawers and inspected an array of stainless-steel scalpels. I selected one with an evenly curved, sharply pointed blade. I put a plastic sheath over the business end, and placed the instrument in the pocket of my flying jacket.

Teresa could not have seen what I'd taken, but she could see which drawer I had opened. She raised a dark eyebrow, but all she said was: 'You'd better bring it back when you've finished with it. I'm responsible for all that equipment.'

'It's okay,' I assured her. 'Everything is under control.' I picked up my lab book from the bench and weighed it in my hand, but it was too big to go into my pocket. Anyhow, I decided, it would be better left where it was, as a record of my discoveries and my adventures in ideas. Viners might need it one day.

'Gil?' said Teresa, uncertainly. But she didn't know what to say next.

'Sorry,' I said. I left it there. Sorry is a word that has to carry an intolerable burden, but you have to have a word like that, where the buck stops.

I went through the first of the two doors which connected the lab to Viners' office, and knocked on the second. He seemed surprised to see me when I walked in; he must have assumed that it was Teresa.

'Gil!' he said, hitting the EXIT button on his keyboard. 'Are you all right? What happened?'

All he'd seen, I remembered, was that I'd gotten a fit of the shakes. He might not even have heard the curse that had escaped from my lips before I left.

'A new symptom,' I told him. I sat down, uninvited, and he sat down too, slowly and slightly warily. 'Cold shivers and ants in my pants. I had to get out. I'm all right now. But there's something we have to clear up before I go home.'

'I've been thinking about what you said,' he told me. 'I think we do have to assume that you've picked up one of the experimental viruses, and that it's hit you rather badly. Viruses are tricky – they don't take everyone the same way.'

I didn't feel the slightest impulse to laugh at the margin of understatement.

'What we have to do now,' he continued, after a pause, 'is to work out how best to handle the problem.'

'I think I know how to handle *my* problem,' I told him, drily. 'But there are wider implications. If anyone outside figures out that your experimental material has run out of control, even in a single instance, the vice chancellor will put a stop to the entire operation. They'll send in men in diving suits to sterilize every inch of the lab. If they discover that the escaped material is dangerous, your whole subject area is likely to be taken over by . . . what do you call the local equivalent of the Pentagon?'

'The Ministry of Defence,' he said, mechanically. 'But I doubt if any of my infective agents are dangerous enough to interest *them*, given that they're having so much fun with HIV and anthrax and Rocky Mountain spotted fever. You're right about the VC, though. He's very conscious of public relations difficulties. What exactly are you trying to say, Gil?'

'What you're doing is important,' I told him. 'I wouldn't be here if I didn't think so. The biochemistry of mental aberration is something we need to know far more about, and the fact that its exploration raises practical and ethical problems of a particularly thorny kind shouldn't be allowed to kill off research – especially research like ours, which the Establishment regards as highly speculative. You and I both know that in a field like this, only the highly speculative research is likely to turn up anything valuable or exciting. Only men with guts and imagination have a chance of making a real breakthrough.'

They might have been his own words echoing. Most of them were. He nodded, still waiting for me to tell him what I was leading up to.

'I'm probably an unusually vulnerable individual,' I said. 'It was probably just a freak of chance which made me react so badly to infection. Like you say, that's always a problem with medical research – different subjects react differently to the same treatment. But in future, Professor Viners, you're going to have to be more careful. The ability to induce spectacular insanity in previously normal people would certainly prove your pet hypothesis about the possibility of there being causal links between viral infection and mental illness, but it's a very costly proof.'

'If I thought that there had been any possibility . . .' he began. Then he stopped, and began again. 'Let's not overreact, Gil. I don't know how you became infected, but it was an accident. We'll tighten up our sterile procedures, and I'll do those tests I mentioned before. You'll recover, Gil – please don't doubt that.'

'That's not a problem,' I assured him. 'The question that disturbs me is whether *you* made a full recovery from the infections to which you exposed yourself.'

He looked pained. 'Don't make this into a cheap melodrama, Gil,' he begged. 'We're involved in serious scientific research, not a remake of *Dr Jekyll and Mr Hyde*. I suffered mild delirium, not a personality change. Of course there's a possibility that the viruses I've isolated affect some people far more profoundly than others, but epidemics of wholesale insanity are a mercifully rare phenomenon. Even if you've been very unlucky, there's every reason to think that you'll be perfectly all right in two or three days' time. Let's not get sidetracked. Let's not make up our minds about what's happened to you until we've got some hard data.'

'I'm not jumping to any premature conclusions, Professor Viners,' I assured him. 'And I'm honestly not worrying about myself. First and last, I'm a scientist. I'm worrying about the wider implications. That's why I wanted to come work here – because I'm fascinated by the wider implications of the work you're doing. I found it very exciting to think that I might be working in an area like this, where all kinds of wild and crazy ideas have a chance of turning out to be true: the possibility that our dreams – our routine, every-night dreams – may be the product of stray DNA and not our own brains; the possibility that certain kinds of insanity might be literally infectious; the possibility that the creative imagination of some artists might be affected by resident viruses. I always knew better than to *believe* those kinds of ideas in advance of any real evidence, but the mere possibility that they might be true, and that I might be in on the work which proved them true, was enough to bring me halfway across the world. There were wilder ones, too – ones so wild I never told them to anybody. You can read about them in my lab book, if you can decipher my handwriting.

'Don't get me wrong – I knew what the actual work would be like. The tissue cultures, the cats and the rats and the rabbits, the endless chromatographic and electrophoretic analyses. I knew that it would be like trying to do a jigsaw puzzle with ninety-nine out of a hundred pieces missing. I knew it would be hard and frustrating work. But the sense of being connected, however weakly, with big ideas, big theories, big possibilities – that was what made it all worthwhile, for me. I would have volunteered to be a guinea pig, you know, if there seemed to be a real need, and a real possibility of a breakthrough. I'm not blaming you for what's happened. I'm not here to accuse you of anything. I'm here to forewarn you, to give you advance notice that you can expect a sudden and confusing proliferation of data in the near future. You'll probably be the only person who can begin to understand what's happening, and you may have to make some hard decisions about whether or not to go public with what you know.'

'It's the girl in the hospital that you're worried about, isn't it?' he said, uneasily. Conclusion-jumping wasn't his forte, but he was no fool.

'Among other things,' I agreed. 'If she has been infected, and I think she has, she may need expert help to understand and to sort herself out. She knows what line of research I'm in, and the fact that she doesn't understand the chemistry won't prevent her suspecting that these labs are the source of the infection, so she might try to blow the whistle on you. There are going to be problems, Professor, and you have to be ready to meet them, or everything you've ever done will simply go to waste.'

'I see,' he said, although, like the proverbial blind man, he really couldn't see at all. Not even in black and white.

'We can never know for sure,' I told him, carefully, 'what proportion of all the ghosts and demons which have ever haunted the human imagination have been the products of psychotropic DNA. It would be too convenient by far to discover that they all were. It's likely that by far the greater number originate inside of us, born of entirely natural fears and anxieties, incarnate in all the impulses which we have to repress in order to live in a semicivilized society. But it's also likely that those ghosts and demons can be fed and nourished by the kinds of DNA you're interested in, amplified by infection to the point where they can literally possess us and take us over. Most of us are strong enough to throw off the infections before they reach that stage, but some aren't. Most of us will never be conquered by our nightmares, but some can only succumb. You have one of the keys to the mystery of mental aberration, Professor; it needs to be studied and understood to the best of our ability. I know that, and I care about it. That's why I came back. I had to warn you. There'll be some real heavy stuff coming down during the next few weeks, Professor, but if you can survive it, and come out wiser, it won't all have been for nothing.'

'Is that what you feel, Gil?' he asked, full of genuine concern – for me, not for himself. 'Do you feel that you can't cope? Is that what you mean by being possessed?'

'That's what I feel,' I agreed. 'That's what I mean.'

'It's only an illusion,' he said, insistently. 'It won't last for ever.'

'I know it won't,' I assured him. I was still thinking with artificial precision. My mind was running like a well-oiled machine. The inside of my head felt as smooth as silk. Everything seemed to be *in place*. I wasn't scared. I knew what the situation was, and how it would develop. I had the ample foresight of the good scientist, dealing with a problem where all the variables were known and quantified. Events would unfold with the perfect orderliness of a set of calculations. For me, there was no uncertainty left. For Viners, though, things would be different. For him, everything would be clouded with confusion, mystery and heartache.

'Maybe I should call the hospital,' he said. 'Admit you, just as a precaution. I have friends there, among the consultants – Hodgson and Maclaine. I can tell them what's happened, without any fear that they'll over react. They can do a full range of tests there, and keep a close eye of your condition. Perhaps that would be best.'

'No,' I said, flatly. 'No hospital. You can take blood from me now – as much as you want – to do your own tests. Then I'm going home. Don't worry about me. I'll take care of myself. The worst of it is over now. I'm one hundred per cent sure of that.'

He hesitated for a moment, and then said: 'I'm sorry, Gil.'

'It's not your fault,' I told him. 'If anyone was careless, it was me. Neither of us could possibly guess that I'd react so badly. The important thing is not to be sorry, but to take the opportunity we have to learn from what's happened. You have to be on your guard now. You have to look out for yourself, for Teresa and for Anne, in case it's not over. What's done is done, but we have a responsibility to learn from it, to increase our understanding of what makes people tick and what makes people sick.'

I stood up, and began to roll up my sleeve. He stared at me for a few seconds, then he got up too. He left the room, to fetch a hypodermic in which to collect the blood that I'd offered him. He returned a few minutes later. The needle was packed in plastic, sterility guaranteed. He broke the pack carefully.

His was a practised hand, but for once he was a little clumsy. His fingers trembled. I didn't mind the pain of the insertion at all; it was dull and faint, almost as if it were happening to somebody else.

'Not much of a vampire, are you?' I said, drily.

Neither of us laughed.

In my own eyes, my blood was jet black. In his, no doubt, it looked as red and healthy as ever.

When his analysis was complete, I figured, he'd know different. He'd know the extent to which my inner being had been polluted, and he'd know what that pollution had driven me to. I wished that I could make him a gift of my brain, so that he could track the corruption through all its phases, but I couldn't. He'd have to make do with the pieces of the jigsaw he already had, and those which time and circumstance would make abundantly clear.

12

Maldureve was waiting for me when I got back to the flat. He was sitting in the armchair, far more solid and substantial than he'd ever been before. He wasn't wearing his cloak, and for the first time I could see what shape he was. He wasn't much taller than me, but he was built differently – lean but muscular. His hands were pale and gnarled, much older than his face. He wore a black suit, cut in a modern style. He might have been an undertaker or an insurance salesman. There was no blood at the corners of his mouth, and his eyes looked normal. He'd shed the caricature aspect of his personality; now he simply seemed businesslike.

I wasn't afraid of him. I knew what he was and how to deal with him. I put down the can that I'd bought at the gas station on the corner, and put the bottle of bourbon that I'd bought at the liquor store on the table. Then I took off my coat, and hung it up on the hook on the back of the door.

'Don't do this,' he said to me. 'It's not necessary. You're one of us now. You don't need all this any more. You can live in the borderlands.' His elegantly withered hand waved negligently as he said 'all this'. He didn't just mean the flat and its furnishings. He meant *all* of it. He meant normality and humanity and colour and brightness and flesh and blood. He was offering me shadows instead. He was offering me the half-life of the undead. He was offering me old movies and outmoded ways of thought. He was offering me the opportunity to become the Typhoid Mary of infectious madness.

Some career move, I thought.

I didn't sit down. I stood opposite him and looked down at him. It felt safer, being able to look down. Position implies moral authority. 'I can't help being sick,' I told him, 'but I don't have to capitulate with my sickness. Just because you were born from the swampy depths of my own subconscious doesn't mean that I have to like you. When a man discovers that he has gangrene in his soul, he has to destroy it. He has to cut it out and cauterize it, or it spreads and spreads and spreads until it consumes everything. I'm not afraid. I'm a scientist. I understand the logic of surgery. I understand the necessity of intervention, the folly of letting nature take its course.'

'That's not the voice of reason talking,' he told me. 'You haven't recovered your sanity – far from it. Your state of mind is more unnatural at this moment than it was before. You mustn't refuse to recognize the actuality of the situation.'

'It's a straightforward matter of black and white,' I told him. 'You can't control me. Whatever you do, you can't control me.'

The flat was becoming darker by the minute. There were shadows everywhere, all around us. The whole world was turning to shadows, like an infinite mist of cobwebs. The light was dying, and the darkness was haunted by the scuttling ghosts of things that had once been bright and full of life. Maldureve was trying to fix me with his eyes, which were slightly luminous with wan white light. He was trying to make me concentrate, and make me forget.

'Anne loves you,' he said. 'She wants you to live. You can be together.'

'She's got an infectious disease,' I told him. 'It's screwed up her head. She doesn't know what she wants, if she's in any condition to want anything at all. But you can't get to her while she's asleep, can you? Unconsciousness is part of the body's defence mechanism. The odds are in her favour. It's a hundred to one that her immune system will fight off the virus, obliterate it from her system. In the meantime, she's safely immobilized.

She has the good fortune to be a masochist. She automatically turned her delirium and her derangement against herself. She's safe now. She isn't going to hurt anybody. When she wakes up, she'll be better. It will all fade into a vague memory, the way everyday nightmares do. You'll lose her the way you lost Viners and Teresa. She's fighting free.'

'She'd rather find you waiting for her,' he said. 'She'd rather wake up to find that you and she can be together.'

'That's not possible,' I said, flatly. 'Not any more. I was too confident and too weak. I let it all get on top of me, and now there's only one thing left to do, for my own sake as well as anyone else I might turn on.'

'You've got it all wrong,' he said. 'You haven't been listening to me. You think you understand, but you're perverting everything to fit what you want to believe. It's your belief that's destructive, Gil, not the hunger. You think that you're an imaginative person, daring to think things which have never been thought before, but you're not. You're trapped in the morass of your convictions, imprisoned by the straitjacket of your assumptions. You haven't even begun to consider the real possibilities. Give yourself time, Gil. You can be free, if only you'll consent to learn the art of the invisible, if only you'll embrace the shadows. Possess *yourself*, Gil.'

'You're just some dissociated fragment of my personality,' I reminded him. 'You're just some nightmarish rag doll, avid to take over from the real me. Well, you can't. I'm in control now, and there isn't time for the hunger to grow again. For at least a little while, terror and confusion can't muster the force to enslave me or tip me over the edge. Neither threats nor persuasion can weaken that control, and by the time the hunger grows again, it'll be too late.'

'Wait for the result of Viners' blood test,' he said quickly.

'Why?'

'It's clear. No antibodies at all. You haven't been infected by any of the experimental viruses. Viners was right all along.'

'Bullshit.'

'It's true. Teresa didn't infect you, and you didn't infect yourself. You didn't infect Anne. *She* passed the hunger on to *you* – the hunger she accepted from me. Accepted, Gil. She chose it, embraced it willingly. She wanted to be what she is – what we all are.'

'Vampires?'

'That's right. Vampires.'

'And who made *you?*'

'I came from the borderlands. Anne helped me. She *saw* me. She gave me substance by the force of her perception, and then she fed me, to make me independent of her sight and touch. That's why I can come to you now. I'm not an illusion, Gil. I'm real. I am what I appear to be.'

'If I prick you, will you bleed?' I said, sarcastically. I reached into my pocket and pulled out the scalpel I'd brought from the lab. I stripped away the plastic sheath to expose the curved blade.

'I won't let you prick me,' he said, shaking his head slowly. 'I can't afford to bleed. The owls are hunting me across the borderlands, and I have to keep close company with the darkest shadows. I can't let you hurt me, just for the sake of proving what I say. You have to believe me, without that kind of proof.'

'What other kind have you got to offer?'

'You have to wait. Anne may wake up at any time. She really was attacked and traumatized, but she will wake up. The hunger will wake her, if nothing else does. She has to feed, Gil, and she may need help. Only wait to hear what she has to say, and she'll confirm everything. She *knows*, Gil. She knows what's really happening.'

'Bullshit,' I said, again. I didn't doubt for an instant that I was right. It was all as plain as day to me; there was no lingering uncertainty to haunt and harass me. My mind was crystal clear, and my thoughts were in perfect order and delicate balance, like some intricately wrought watch mechanism.

'Listen to me, Gil,' he said. 'You think you're being clever, being rational, being scientific – but you're not. You think that this can all be translated back to biochemistry, but it can't. Science is fine, when all it has to deal with is the world of dead objects and forces, where everything is measurable and all transactions can be represented by equations which proceed with mathematical relentlessness. The world of the mind isn't like that, Gil, and the psychologist's hope that the world of thought and emotion can ever be reduced to simple biochemistry is just a delusion. The world of the mind is frankly and essentially mysterious; it evades all attempts to make models of it, to build theories about its workings. Science can never account for dreams, Gil, no matter how hard it tries. It's pure folly to think that dreams and mental aberrations can be explained simply by inventing hypothetical viruses. The world of the mind is magical – literally magical – and in the borderlands where mind and matter meet there's a vast well of potential. Those borderlands can be crossed, Gil. People who have the talent, or the strength of will, can draw entities out of the borderlands, or learn to enter the borderlands themselves. There are people who can master the art of *becoming*, who can make a gift of that art to those whom they love. Anne has that gift, Gil. She wants to make a gift of that art to you, because she loves you. If only you can wait until she wakes up, you and she can explore the art together. You can be and become anything you want to be: vampires, magicians, gods.'

'Murderers,' I said. 'Monsters.'

'Only in the eyes of the human herd,' he said. 'Those who cannot be anything other than they are will always fear those who can *become*. Those who have no magic will always strive to destroy those who have, out of envy and out of the fear of being superseded. You're no longer of their kind, Gil. You owe them no more than they owe their cattle; your loyalty now is to a very different community. You have the potential in you to become powerful, to be something more and better than human. You drank more deeply than you needed to from the little girl, but you had let the hunger go unanswered for too long. You must learn to live with your hunger, Gil. You must learn to be its master and not its slave. Anne will teach you, when she wakes. Anne has the gift, the talent, the artistry. I will do whatever I can to help you both. Together, we three will be immensely stronger than any one of us could ever be alone. Together, we might even resist the predations of the owls.'

'It's no use,' I told him, patiently. 'I know what you are. More to the point, I know what *I* am. I couldn't help myself, but I know how feeble an excuse that is. People ought to be able to help themselves. They have to be able to help themselves, if they're to live together in civilized society. I'm not prepared to become a creature of the borderlands, nursing and nurturing my madness like some deformed but perversely loved child. I won't do that. It's not just the hunger. I really believe that I could cope with that. It's also the fact that I might infect other people – other people as vulnerable as me. I'm dangerous, and the fact that it's no fault of my own doesn't really enter into the equation. I have to be destroyed. You must see that.

'*I'm a fucking vampire, for fucking Christ's sake!*'

I hadn't meant to shout. I had intended to demonstrate that I could be calm and perfectly logical, in spite of everything. I had intended to keep my voice perfectly level, my manner perfectly reasonable. No hysteria. I wanted everything to be done properly. I wanted to be in control. I *was* in control, even though I was a vampire.

'Yes, you are,' said Maldureve, stubbornly trying to fight calmness with calmness, true sanity with the appearance of reason. 'You're already becoming detached from the world, already edging into the borderlands. My hope is that you won't really be able to stab yourself with that ridiculous little knife, any more than you could drive a wooden stake through your own heart. My hope is that your flesh will simply fade into the shadows, as mine would – and perhaps will – were you to try to destroy me. If you have any gift at all, that may well happen. You may not be able to kill yourself. But if you haven't even talent enough to protect yourself from your own rebel conscience, perhaps you aren't worth having. Perhaps Anne and I will be better off without you. There will always be others, you see. There's never any shortage of young blood. Whatever you do, it can't make any real difference to the rest of us, or to the world at large.'

'You're wrong,' I told him, confidently. 'You're just a doppel-gänger. When I go, you go with me. I know you can't admit that. Maybe, if you have any independent existence in the bottomless pit of my mind, you don't even know that it's true. Maybe you think you do exist. But this is the boss speaking. This is the voice of *consciousness*. This is the real me, the guy who has to take responsibility for everything . . . even for shit like you. You're dead, Maldureve. You're history.'

'You can't kill a vampire that way,' he assured me, silkily. 'Anne and I will go on, whatever happens to you. We were lovers, you know. That's why she went down to the garden at night – to meet me. She gave me substance in order that I could become her lover, and I was a better lover by far than you could ever be.'

'Was,' I said, seizing upon the operative word.

'Was,' he agreed. 'We don't need that any more. We've passed on. Our relationship has entered a new phase. We still love one another, but we're more like brother and sister now. One for all and all for one.'

'Just good friends,' I said. 'Vampires together, cruising the shadows in search of prey.'

'It's you who keep trying to turn me into a caricature,' he said. 'It's you who keep trying to pretend that I'm only a joke, unworthy of belief. If you could only allow yourself to see clearly, to admit the truth . . . but you insist on hiding behind that shield of false belief, that absurd idea that I'm just a hallucination brought on by a fever. You're your own worst enemy, Gil. If you weren't, you wouldn't be so determined to kill yourself. If you were really in control, you'd understand that.

'Please, Gil, think about this. At least consider the possibility that what you now think of as control is actually the opposite. You're being controlled, Gil. You've made yourself into some kind of clockwork toy, because you think it's the only way of keeping doubt and confusion at bay. At what cost, Gil? Doubt is healthy. Confusion is simply a recognition of the fact that the real world has borderlands, that there are more things in Heaven and Earth than are dreamed of in Professor Viners' philosophy. Accept what you are, Gil, and accept the legacy of what you might in time become.'

'You're just a cold in the head,' I told him. 'You're just a fever dream, which has to be disposed of. You don't exist, and you don't *deserve* to exist. I'm going to X you out of existence, cut you out of my soul. You can fade into the shadows if I lash out at you, but you can't escape if I turn the knife on myself and let my own blood flow. When I drain my own veins, vampire-fashion, you drain away too.'

'That's not true,' he said, as if he felt truly sorry for me. 'You can't get rid of me that way. The only person you can hurt is yourself. It's pointless, Gil. You'll realize that, afterwards. I only wish I could make you understand how pointless it is.'

'You're history,' I told him again.

'Of course I'm history,' he said. 'I'm history and myth and nightmare. I'm the wickedness of the dream, Gil. I can't be banished, destroyed or forgotten. Nobody can control their dreams. The most that anyone can hope for is that their dreams will consent to leave them unharmed. Everyone knows, deep down, that their dreams have the power to disturb and distort and distress them, and to tear their fugitive self-confidence to shreds. We're all possessed, Gil – it's just that some of us have absentee landlords and quiet tenants.'

'We?' I echoed. 'Are you one of us now?'

'We have dreams too, Gil,' he said. 'You have no idea what nightmares possess *our* kind. But you soon will. Believe me, Gil, you don't want to find out. Not until you're ready for it.'

I picked up the can which I'd earlier put down, holding the handle in the same hand as the scalpel. I used my other hand to unscrew the cap. The odour seemed to fill the room, driving away the noisome odour of the grave which Maldureve exuded.

'Petrol,' he said.

'Gasoline,' I corrected him. He had no right to use the English word. He was an American hallucination.

I jerked the can in his direction, trying to drench him in the stuff. As the jet of liquid spewed out, he dissolved into the darkness which was crowding us both around, ever more insistently. I'd assumed that he would. I knew that he wouldn't stick around to the bitter end. He didn't have the courage to do that.

I knew that vampires were mortally afraid of fire. After all, I was one of them myself.

I locked the door to the flat, and wedged one of the dining chairs under the old-fashioned handle. I didn't want anyone bursting in. I knew that the fire station was less than half a mile away, and the windows of the flat were easily visible from the end of the street. It was only a short walk from there to the telephone boxes on the edge of St Saviour's Square. It wasn't that I was worried about being saved – I expected to be well beyond help by the time a concerned citizen could dial 999 – but I didn't want anyone else getting hurt unnecessarily. I wanted the heroes of the fire brigade to be absolutely certain, when they arrived, that there was no earthly point in rushing in where angels feared to tread.

There were other preparations to be made.

First of all, I put the screw cap back on the can of gasoline. I'd let enough out while casually dismissing Maldureve to make the place stink, but I didn't want to soak the furniture just yet. That had to be done carefully. I didn't intend to burn to death; the real purpose of the petrol was to ensure that I was thoroughly cremated. I couldn't tell how dangerous I'd become, and I felt obliged to be as tidy as possible. There was Anne, of course, and Teresa, and the body of the little girl . . . but Professor Viners knew the score now. He would be able to judge, once he'd investigated the generous donation of blood I'd made, whether any further precautions were necessary – and, if so, how best to proceed with them.

There was no point in leaving a note. I could make sure it didn't burn in any one of half a dozen ways – simply throwing it out of the window would have sufficed – but there was nothing I could usefully say. The truth would seem like madness to any potential reader, even Mike Viners. I had already told Viners enough; to tell him more would have been at best superfluous, at worst confusing. Once he heard the news about poor Janine

Leigh, he'd know at once how seriously to take the matter; nothing I could possibly have said to him could have achieved as much as that simple revelation. The blood he'd taken from my veins was worth infinitely more than any amount of verbal explanation.

Blood can't hallucinate, or make mistakes, or lie.

It would have been nice, in a way, to have been able to communicate with Anne, but I knew that anything I wrote now, whatever means I might use to direct it to its intended recipient, would become public property. I didn't want the issue clouded. The necessary information was in the right hands; matters merely sentimental had to go by the board.

I went into the kitchen. I cut some bread from the rump of a loaf I'd bought that morning and half consumed at breakfast. I knew that I had to eat something. If I drank the scotch and the bourbon straight they were likely to make me sick before I was properly drunk. I needed to be thoroughly drunk – I was that much of a coward, in spite of the apparent reduction in my sensibility – but I wanted to approach drunkenness in a measured and sensible way. I needed to know what was happening. I needed to ease my way into the appropriate state, and to judge its imminence accurately.

I didn't bother to butter the bread. I just wolfed it down.

After the first couple of mouthfuls my supplies of saliva became inadequate, and I had to wash it down. I uncapped the scotch I'd bought the day before, which was still in the kitchen, and used it to help the rest of the bread down. I didn't use much to begin with, but I increased the dose bit by bit. It was cheap whisky – sheer force of habit had prevented my buying better quality – and it was a little raw, but I didn't mind. In a way, it was useful to feel that slight cutting edge, that marginal abuse of sensation. I didn't want it to be too much of a shock when I got to work with the scalpel. It was only a small bottle, and I finished it pretty quickly. I was still clear-headed, but that didn't matter. I still had the bourbon.

My motives were still clear in my mind and I went over them one by one, ritually and mechanically.

Destroying a possible centre of dangerous infection wasn't foremost among them, although there was certainly a chance that what Viners might find when he analysed my blood was that something in me had helped to turn a previously harmless virus into a vicious psychotropic plague. I couldn't overlook the possibility that I was as yet the sole carrier of a dangerous mutant which had only undergone its crucial transmutation within the last few days, after I'd infected Anne, perhaps even after I'd last screwed Teresa.

Nor was it a sense of justice that impelled me, although I'd always held hard to the opinion that the notions of retribution and punishment ought to be taken far more seriously than stupidly over-optimistic crap about rehabilitation. I'd always believed that an eye for an eye wasn't a bad principle to employ. I was the kind of person who felt a duty to stand by his beliefs and I was fully prepared to accept that I deserved to die for what I had done, not only to protect innocent people from my next bout of homicidal insanity but simply because I had killed an innocent person and in doing so had forfeited my own moral right to life.

My real reason for deciding to die – and perhaps it was a less worthy reason than either of the others – was that the alternative seemed worse.

I wasn't afraid of Hell, in the sense of an eternal afterlife. Never for one instant had I been able to believe in the existence of the kind of soul which could go on to eternal punishment or eternal reward, and all Maldureve's crazy talk about the borderlands of existence had not shaken that item of faith. I had no doubt whatsoever that my soul – my consciousness, my psyche, my intelligence, my persona – would die with my body, and utterly cease to be. The only hells which had ever existed, I was morally certain, existed on Earth: man-made, man-administered hells. In torture chambers, in concentration camps, in trenches dug for the conduct of war, there were real and actual and loathsome hells, as there were in the worst kinds of housing projects, the worst kinds of sweatshops, the worst kinds of ghettos, the worst kinds of prisons and the worst kinds of insane asylums. I could tolerate the idea of death, which held no threat over someone like me save the threat of oblivion, but I couldn't tolerate the idea of being condemned to a living hell, which would certainly have been my fate had I cared to wait for Detective Sergeant Miller and his colleagues to seek me out and charge me with what I had done.

Such, at least, was the theory on which I based my plans.

Putting the theory into practice was not quite as easy as this uncompromising summary might suggest.

As I worked my way slowly down the bourbon bottle, I wished with all my heart that I was at home. At home there was a gun in my father's desk, and another in his bedroom cabinet and a third in my mother's purse. Even the least of them – even the small Saturday-night special my mother carried in stark defiance of the law whenever she went out alone – would have been adequate to blow my brains out through the top of my skull in response to one convulsive jerk of a trigger. That kind of instantaneous and merciful release seemed to me now to be the one thing left in life that was worth desiring: the only happiness, the only heaven. Had I not been a stranger in a strange land, lonely and afraid in a world I never made, I might have had some similar recourse. Shotguns, I had heard it rumoured, were available in all the very best houses in England. Alas, I had no means of access to any such house. The only thing I could lay my hands on was a scalpel.

I had never understood why so many suicides used poisons, and unreliable poisons at that. Pills would have been particularly inappropriate to my case, but I couldn't see any justification for their use in *any* case, if the practicalities of self-murder were what counted. Even in gun-free England there are railway stations through which fast trains rush like raging juggernauts, and subterranean London is honeycombed with subways wired to deliver a fatal jolt to anyone who cares to leap down from the platform. Instant annihilation is available to all who seek it. I wondered, as I drank my last supper, what the attraction of pills was to those who were drawn to that particular method of self-exorcism. Was it the gambling element – the sense of placing one's personal fate in the hands of some grander unpredictability? Was it a calculated dissociation of act and consequence, as if by separating them in time one could reduce one's moral responsibility? Or was it the fact that some peculiar bond of intimacy already existed between pill-poppers and their chosen instruments, just as there did between many gun-eaters and theirs?

I was attracted, inevitably, to the last hypothesis. This was only natural, given that I could more easily draw a parallel with myself. The scalpel on the table was not mine, and I had no way of knowing whether I had ever used that particular tool before in performing elementary brain surgery on a rabbit or a cat, but there was a propriety in my relationship with it. I was a scientist, and a scalpel was a scientist's implement. I hoped that I would be able to wield it with scientific precision and objectivity.

I hoped. I dared not take it for granted. Had I not been a coward, I would not have needed the scotch, let alone the bourbon. Had I not been a coward, I wouldn't have been so terrified by the contemplation of a living hell.

By the time I'd finished the bourbon, its effects were taking a powerful hold. I'd never in my life drunk so much in so short a period of time. Thanks to the bread in my stomach, however, which was holding the liquor like a sponge, my spiritual ascent into intoxication was relatively graceful, like a Boeing 767 taking off: power and discretion in perfect combination. I stood up immediately and unscrewed the cap of what I now perversely decided to call, in belated recognition of local etiquette, my petrol can.

I spread the precious liquid very carefully, laying down a spiral trail so that the flames would march in military order throughout the room. The gallon didn't go quite as far as I had planned, and there was barely enough left at the end to fill the empty bourbon bottle. I placed the bottle precisely in the centre of the table, and made a wick out of three clean handkerchiefs which I had taken from the chest of drawers and neatly entwined.

I brought the matches from the kitchen and set them down beside the whisky bottle. I took a single match out of the box and placed it neatly on top.

Having no particular expertise in the making of Molotov cocktails, I couldn't make an expert guess at how long it would take for the wick, once lit, to ignite the gas – the petrol – in the body of the bottle, or how soon after that the spreading lake of burning fuel would turn the room into a blazing inferno. I knew that scenes I had witnessed in the movies would not be reliable, given that directors and special-effects men paid such close attention to the melodramatic potential of gaudy explosions. In the movies, you always see fiery explosions three times, from three different camera angles. I knew that I wouldn't have that luxury in real time. I didn't know for sure whether I would have ten seconds or two minutes to do what I had to do, which was to let enough blood out of my body to fall gently unconscious.

There was once, I vaguely remembered, a famous British military man who had been enjoying an amiable conversation at his home with a couple of friends when he suddenly asked to be excused, went directly to his bathroom, and there took up the razor which he used for shaving, and efficiently cut his throat from ear to ear, presumably while observing himself in the mirror. Not having majored in history, I was uncertain of his name – it might have been Clive of India, or General Wolfe, but not Gordon of Khartoum, whom I had seen done to death in quite a different fashion in the movie starring Charlton Heston. I desperately wanted to do likewise, but I wasn't certain that I could, even without the mirror to inhibit me. I knew that I could find the carotid arteries readily enough, but severing them both with a single sweep would require considerable force, given that they were protected by surrounding muscles. I wasn't sure that I could dig that deep – or, even if I could do it, that I could get from one to the other in one unrelenting sweep.

I considered the other alternatives. Slitting my wrists, of course, was quite out of the question. I knew well enough that one had to cut lengthwise along the forearm rather than across the wrist, and that the artery would not be difficult to locate or to reach, but I also knew how impossible it would be to transfer the scalpel from hand to hand with the job half done.

I gave more serious consideration to the heart, but I knew how deceptive the gaps between the ribs could be, and how difficult it might be to drive a blade through the intercostal tissues, even if it had a sharp point. The scalpel I had borrowed was designed for cutting, not for stabbing. I didn't want the instrument getting stuck with the job undone. Above all else, I didn't want that.

I also considered the femoral arteries as a possible target. It would be an unusual method, I knew, and one suited only to expert anatomists. They were deep-set, but if each could be severed with a well-aimed stab, no sweeping would be necessary. Again, it was the design of the scalpel that forced me to reject the possibility.

It had to be the carotids. In spite of the problem of getting from ear to ear, it had to be done that way. That was what the scalpel was designed to do. My chosen weapon determined my method.

I undressed, but only partly. I removed my trainers and socks, my trousers and shorts. And then I paused, trying to come to terms with my cowardice.

I told myself that I had not quite reached the appropriate point of alcoholic anaesthesia, but I knew that I was lying. Fear was beginning to take hold as the moment of truth approached. I was possessed now by a new and more subtle demon, which was extending its horrid grip throughout my being, insinuating its deadening presence into my limbs, trying to deny my rational will the power to institute the actions which I had so carefully programmed.

I took up the match and the box, and made as if to strike, but my hand froze. The intention was there, but the response was not. I ordered the hand to move, but it had acquired an alien will of its own – a demonic will, supernaturally opposed to that which was native and natural and rightly sovereign.

There was a knock on the door: a sharp, imperious rapping.

I recognized the knock. I knew at once that it was Detective Sergeant Miller, come to play Nemesis, probably with half a dozen uniformed officers to back him up.

I tried with all my might to strike the match, but I couldn't do it.

'Mr Molari! Are you there, Mr Molari?' It was Miller's voice.

I tried with all my might to move my rigid fingers, but they wouldn't obey me.

I heard Miller try the door. I saw the handle turn, and heard the straining of the lock. The lock was flimsy, but the chair set beneath the handle was an extra line of defence. I knew that if they tried to break the door down the chair would ultimately make no difference, because the set-up was simply too frail to withstand the kind of pressure the policemen could put on. But they could only use shoulder-charges or kicks; they surely hadn't come equipped with a sledgehammer.

'Mr Molari,' said Detective Sergeant Miller's voice, still coolly reasonable. 'I need to talk to you. I know you're in there. Please open the door.'

I exerted the full force of my will, feeling that if reason could not triumph over demons and blind fear then the whole world was lost and damned.

The match struck, as if by its own volition. I touched the light to the sodden wick descending from the lip of the whisky bottle. Then I took up the scalpel, holding it in my fist as though it were a dagger, and I set the blade beneath my left ear. I cut into my flesh, towards the throbbing artery.

Once the initial cut was made, it all became easier. Once that first hurdle was overcome, and I realized how little pain there was, it wasn't dificult at all to draw the keen blade across, in a long slow arc. I felt it sever the left jugular, the windpipe, the right jugular.

It was such a beautiful arc, so stylish, so uncompromising, that it brought tears to my eyes. Nothing could interrupt or retard it, not even the cartilaginous reinforcements about the trachea.

When I reached the right carotid, not without a certain awkwardness because of the kind of grip I'd taken, I felt a blissful tide of relief sweep through me.

I had done it. I was dead. I had cheated Maldureve. I had cheated Hell itself.

I saw one of the door panels splinter and burst inwards. I had not realized that the structure itself was so flimsy. I saw the detective peeping through the gap. He had caught the smell of gasoline, and had taken action because of it. He was alone. I wished that he had not been able to do what he had done, thus exposing himself to unnecessary danger. I didn't want him to be hurt, to be burned. But he could only look. He couldn't get through the door, to do anything foolish

'Oh, shit,' said Detective Sergeant Miller. His voice carried to me as though delivered by a telephone link, from a vast distance.

'Watch this,' I said, triumphantly – or perhaps would have said, had there been any breath to say it with. I knew that I could now do anything I wanted to, and that all the demons in Hell could not contrive to stay my hand.

I plunged the point of the scalpel into my right eye, which had given me more than enough offence.

The operation, astonishingly, was a success. My left eye recovered its sight. The darkness which had beset me for so long was dispelled as the room burst forth into a riot of vivid yellow fire, and I saw the colour of my own blood, flooding out of me.

My blood was red: beautifully, gorgeously, youthfully red.

I knew that I would be able to appreciate the sight for less than a second, so I tried as hard as I could to draw a full measure of appreciation from it. The pain made it difficult. The pain had come back too, along with my power of sight.

When merciful unconsciousness swept down upon me, I assumed that I reached the end. I still felt triumphant, as if that single moment of bright-lit time was compensation for all that had happened to me, and all that might have happened. I was in great pain, but I felt that I had won, and that my victory was a victory for reason and sanity over unnatural hunger and foul disease.

It should have been the end.

If the world had only been the kind of world it ought to have been – the kind of world I had always believed in; the kind of world all men of wisdom believe in – it *would* have been the end.

But it wasn't.

Unfortunately – not to mention comically, tragically and astonishingly – it wasn't the end at all.

Tertiary Phase:
Derangement

I

I woke up to the sound of Doktor Avalanche pounding away, and the whole group joining in with Andrew Eldritch to sing the chorus of 'More'. I was singing along with it in my head and I knew that I must have been singing along, subliminally, for quite some time. I must have sung along all the way through 'Dr Jeep' and, before that, 'I Don't Exist When You Don't See Me'.

I opened my eyes, but at first I couldn't see anything. It was as dark as the dead of night. Part of me was still in the borderlands, bathing in the glory of the light. Part of me was clinging to the owls, reluctant to come back to the dull, cold world. But I could hear quite clearly, and what I heard beyond the insistent pounding of the music was the voice of my sister Sharon, screeching: 'It worked! I *knew* it would work!'

After that, the voices became confused. People were moving about, calling in the distance. The music was too loud; I couldn't make out what was being said or by whom.

I kept my eyes open and slowly let the real light in. It was bright enough, I suppose, but it seemed weak and ochreous by comparison with the light which had caged me for so long, in the world of the owls.

Sharon was there, bending over me, trying to remove the Walkman from my ears. In the end, she succeeded. The urgent clamour of the Sisters of Mercy died away to that tinny pulsebeat which always leaks annoyingly out of other people's personal stereos.

I knew that Sharon had stolen the idea from something we'd

seen on TV. She had put the earpieces of her Walkman to my ears, loaded with the tape which would be most familiar to me – the tape which was most certain to remind me of home, of her, of the great wide world. She'd fastened on the idea that people in comas could be coaxed out them by familiar sounds, and the doctor – figuring, no doubt, that it couldn't possibly do any harm – had given her the go-ahead. And who could ever say, now, that it hadn't worked? Who could ever convince her that my recovery at that particular moment had had nothing to do with the music? Why should anyone even want to?

Sharon was trying to kiss me, and Mum was trying to pull her away. I turned my head in bewilderment, not knowing which of them to look at. I saw Sharon's eyes fill with tears. Then, it seemed, pandemonium broke loose. The moment of clarity was lost in utter confusion.

It isn't easy to return to the world after being apart from it for so long. It's hard to turn the tap which stems the flood tides of sensation and memory, to get everything under control. It's even harder when those about you, heedless of the good advice of Kipling's celebrated poem, are busily losing their heads and clamouring for attention.

Everybody wanted to be the first to welcome me, first to talk to me, first to ask me questions. The nurse, being on her home ground, came in first by a short head. She shooed my oversolicitous relatives away, begging them to wait for someone called Dr Fellowes, who was supposedly 'on his way down'. Mum consented to be shooed as far as the wall, but continued babbling all the while.

When the doctor arrived, he completed the expulsion so that he and the nurse could perform whatever arcane rituals they considered necessary. They took my pulse and peered into my eyes and asked me elementary questions in words of one syllable to see whether I could understand and talk to them. They did some other things, too, with the contraptions that had been stuck into me and the various recording devices I'd been hooked up to. It was all rather undignified, and more than a little painful. It seemed to take a ridiculously long time, too, but I guess doctors have to be seen to be doing something when patients come out of comas, or people would begin to suspect that they aren't really in control.

'I'm okay,' I told them, when they'd finished. 'I feel fine.' I didn't know what all the fuss was about. Somehow, I'd assumed that all the time I'd spent in the world of the owls had been merely subjective. I had no idea at all how long I'd been asleep.

Mum and Sharon were allowed back in when Dr Fellowes had gone through the motions, but they'd hardly had time to tell me how worried they'd been, and to explain that Dad had driven home so that he could go back to work, before the shooing started all over again.

This time, it was the police who took over. Theirs was, after all, the most serious business requiring my urgent attention.

There were two of them: a plain-clothes detective sergeant named Miller, and a uniformed WPC named Linton. They seemed irredeemably dull and ordinary, although they were both a little flushed. They must have rushed from the station at top speed.

'I'm sorry to bother you when the doctor probably needs to take a closer look at you, and when your family wants to be with you,' said Miller, 'but it's vitally important that you tell us everything you can about what happened to you. Do you understand that, Anne?'

'Yes,' I said. My voice sounded strange. I hadn't quite got the hang of speaking yet.

'Do you remember what happened to you?'

Oddly enough, I hadn't remembered, until he asked. I knew that there was a reason why the police wanted to see me, but I hadn't actually reminded myself what it was. Now, though, I remembered.

Maldureve had let me down. He hadn't come to save me.

'I was attacked,' I said. 'In the Marquis of Membury's Garden.'

The detective let out a sigh of relief, as if he'd been more than half convinced that I wouldn't remember anything at all.

'Did you see the man who attacked you, Anne?' he said, urgently. 'Can you describe him?'

I had heard so many stories about people blanking such things out, and losing all consciousness of them, that I was mildly astonished by how easily the memory came floating back into my head. I had been on a long journey, and yet it was all still there, as fresh as if it had happened moments before. All that was missing was the fear. The memory was crystal clear, but it was like a movie I'd seen, not something that had actually happened to *me*. I could remember everything, quite dispassionately.

The young WPC reached out and took my hand, squeezing it reassuringly.

'I'm sorry, Anne,' said Miller, insincerely. The urgency that was in him drowned out any possibility of sorrow; he had a hunger for answers which had to be appeased. 'We have to know, and there isn't any time to waste. Did you see the man who cut you? Can you tell us who it was?'

'No,' I said, faintly. 'It was too dark. He grabbed me from behind. I didn't see his face.'

'Are you *sure*?' said Miller, intently. 'Are you sure you didn't know him?'

'No,' I said, before realizing that it would sound ambiguous. 'I mean, of course I didn't know him. I didn't see him, either. He spoke to me, but I didn't recognize his voice.'

'What did he say?' the detective asked. 'Exactly, if you can.'

I could. I paused a for a few seconds, to make perfectly certain, and then I told him. 'He said: "Shut up! Keep quiet or I'll cut you." Then, he said: "Get down, you bitch. Get down, you filthy, fucking bitch!" Exactly. That's exactly what he said. If I ever hear his voice again, I'll know him. I think I'd know him again. I'm sure of it.'

I couldn't understand why DS Miller looked annoyed. I couldn't understand why he looked at me as if he were half convinced that I was lying.

'What else do you remember, Anne?' said the policewoman gently. 'What else can you tell us about him?'

I hesitated again, and then spoke slowly, trying all the while to remember every last detail. I wanted to make certain that what I said was the truth, the whole truth and nothing but the truth.

'He wore gloves,' I said. 'Thick woollen gloves. They were dirty – soiled. I could smell and taste the soil when he put his hand over my mouth. He had bad breath. His body was solid and hard. Muscular. But he wasn't tall. Not for a man. He was bigger than me, but not much. He had a knife. It wasn't long, but it had a sharp edge. A "kitchen devil", I think. He cut me. Here.'

As I spoke the last few words I put my hand up to my neck to feel the wound. I no longer expected it to be painful. If it had had stitches put in it, the stitches had been removed or had dissolved. The wound was healing well. What I could feel was just a scar.

'It's okay, Anne,' said WPC Linton. 'It'll show, but it isn't bad. You needed a blood transfusion, but you're fine. You should have recovered consciousness a week ago, the day after the operation, but maybe your body felt that it needed time.'

Had I really been unconscious for a whole week? Longer than that, apparently.

The detective thought all this was a waste of time. 'Miss Charet,' he said, in a tone that was almost stern enough to be accusative, 'I'm sorry, but I have to be quite clear about this. Is there any possibility that the man who attacked you was Gil Molari?'

I stared at him, and the stare made him move back slightly.

'Gil?' I said. 'No, it certainly wasn't Gil. Why would he?'

'Are you absolutely certain?' said Miller, apparently hoping against hope that I wasn't.

'Yes,' I said. 'It didn't sound like Gil and it didn't feel like Gil. Everything was wrong: his height, the texture of his body. Everything. Gil was home in bed, with a bad cold. Why on earth should you think it might have been Gil?'

It was their turn to hesitate. The policewoman semed disapproving of Miller's tactlessness, but there was something conspiratorial in their exchange of glances, affirming that they both knew something I didn't, and that neither of them wanted to be the one to tell me.

'Anne,' said Miller, much more softly, 'you aren't the only one who was attacked. Two days later, a little girl was found dead less than ten yards from the spot where you were attacked. I think you knew her mother, Mrs Leigh. Cynthia Leigh.'

I was still staring. 'Janine?' I said, hesitantly. 'Janine Leigh is dead?'

'Gil Molari is dead too,' said Detective Sergeant Miller, with a curiously flat and weary inflection. 'He committed suicide, the same day the girl was murdered. He cut his throat. He'd soaked his flat in petrol, and he set fire to it just before he did it.'

I wanted to go on staring, to remain absolutely stock-still, as if by refusing to move I could freeze time in its tracks. I couldn't do it. Tears filled my eyes, and I suddenly felt desperately weak. I ought to have wondered whether I might still be unconscious and dreaming, but the reality of the world was sharply obvious to me, and I couldn't muster the least defiant doubt to combat what the detective was saying.

In the end, I whispered: 'You can't possibly think that Gil killed Janine.'

'We're not saying that he did,' said Miller, awkwardly. 'He spoke to the girl and her mother outside Wombwell House, but we don't know his movements for about three-quarters of an hour after that, until he turned up again at the laboratory where he worked.'

'We think he might have been the last person to see her,' WPC Linton put in. 'If he was still around when she came out of the building. But there's no real evidence to link him with the murder. None at all.'

The detective sergeant didn't seem to approve of this intervention, but he let it pass.

'I'm a policeman,' he said. 'I have to ask these questions, and I can't ask Gil Molari anything. He spoke to you on the day you were attacked; he spoke to the little girl not thirty minutes before she was killed. He may have been the last person to see her alive, and he did a very thorough job of killing himself within a couple of hours of her murder. I have to investigate all the possibilities. If Gil Molari didn't do it – if this man who attacked you also killed the little girl – then we still have a very dangerous and violent person running around, who might very well kill again. You see why I have to be sure?'

I could see that he had hoped that it was Gil, so that he could close both cases. But it hadn't been Gil who attacked me. I knew that, beyond the shadow of a doubt.

'We haven't found a murder weapon,' said the policewoman, who was still trying to soften the blow for me. 'We don't even know what kind of weapon we're looking for. According to the postmortem, the little girl lost a lot of blood, but it wasn't on the ground where she was found, so we're not even sure where she was killed, let alone by whom. We've been hoping that you might be able to help us. We desperately need any information that you can give us'

I shook my head, slowly. 'That's all the description I can give you,' I said.

'You see,' Miller went on, 'there's so much about this entire affair which seems to make no sense at all. All three of you – you, Molari and the little girl – ended up with cut throats. Both you and Gil had some weird kind of bruising to the throat even before you were cut. Gil told me that you have a nervous habit of picking at your throat, and that was what raised your bruise, but he couldn't explain his own. He didn't even seem to know that he had it. Can you explain that?'

'No,' I said. It was the first lie I'd told, but I told it without hesitation. 'That is . . . I suppose I used to pick at my throat, when I was fidgety. Gil told me to stop doing it half a dozen times. He didn't do anything of that kind, though.'

Miller was still staring at me, accusatively. 'This is all very weird, Anne,' he said. 'Very weird indeed. Do you have any idea why Gil Molari would want to kill himself, if he didn't kill the little girl?'

'No,' I said. He wasn't satisfied with that, but there seemed little point in my insisting that Gil hadn't a care in the world, if he really was dead. 'Perhaps it was an accident,' I added, lamely.

'I watched him do it,' said Miller, in a curiously aggressive tone. 'It was no accident.' After a pause, he went on: 'I also talked to his supervisor. He said that Gil believed that he'd picked up some sort of virus in the lab where he worked – and that Gil was extremely disturbed by that belief. But the professor swears that he *hadn't* picked up any such virus, and that even if he had, it would only have given him a cold in the head. He did have a cold in the head, didn't he?'

'Yes,' I said.

'I talked on the phone to his father and mother in California, and spoke to them face to face yesterday, when they arrived here to fly the body home. This is one hell of a mess, Anne. I just don't know what the hell is happening here. The newspapers are already talking about some kind of Jack the Ripper character

– they seem to have taken it for granted that the guy who cut you also killed the girl. If that's so, he must be a real screwball to go back so soon to a spot where he'd already carried out one attack. The papers seem to feel that it was our fault . . . that careless policing let it happen a second time. But I had just smashed through the door of your boyfriend's flat when he struck that match, Miss Charet, and I'll never forget what I saw in those few seconds. Something very strange is happening here, and I don't know what it is. I want you to help me, Anne. I want you to help me figure out why one person is in the hospital and two are dead.'

'I don't know,' I said, faintly.

Detective Sergeant Miller looked as if he were about to contradict me. He looked almost as if he would have liked to charge me with having murdered both of them.

'She doesn't know, Derek,' said WPC Linton, becoming anxious about his state of disturbance. 'She really doesn't.'

The detective's pent-up anger seemed to ebb away. 'I'm sorry, Anne,' he said, eventually. 'I was hoping that you'd be able to give us a little more, but I guess we have to be grateful for what we've got. If there's any other detail, however trivial, that comes back to you, you have to let us know. If the man who attacked you is still out there, with one attempted rape and a murder already on his charge sheet, there's no knowing what he might do next.'

'No,' I said, dutifully.

'Whatever impression you pick up from the papers,' said the policewoman, still trying to be gentle with me, 'this isn't the kind of thing that happens every day. It's a once-in-a-lifetime thing for all of us. We were really hoping that you could help us . . . and you have. It's not much of a description, but it's something. It gives us something to go on. We'll do our level best to catch him, Anne.'

'Yes,' I said.

They got up from the bed as Dr Fellowes came back into the room. He looked at them as if to say that they'd had more than their ration of time. The policewoman let go of my hand, after one last reassuring squeeze. She really did care; I had the impression that she daren't let it show how much she felt for me.

She thought that she understood how I must feel, to wake up to news like this.

'The inspector will probably want a word,' said Miller. 'And someone will be in to take a formal statement. I want you to think very hard, Anne. Anything else you remember . . . anything at all.'

'It's important,' WPC Linton added, for the sake of having the last word. 'Take your time.'

When they had gone, I looked up at the doctor.

'Take it easy,' he advised. 'You may have been asleep for a very long time, but that doesn't mean you can't be tired. You'll have to stay in for a few days, while we see how you are. Just for observation, you understand. You're getting better, but it must have been a very nasty experience. You need time to get over it.'

He didn't know what he was talking about. He was just waffling away, for want of something better to say or do. I suppose that he'd been practising that kind of hopeful non-activity all his life, in between those brief occasions when actual treatment was being administered. He took my pulse again and looked into my eyes: more medical rituals, for the sake of reassurance. Then he went to the door and told Mum and Sharon that their turn had come around again, and that the field was entirely clear for their equally meaningless rituals of rejoicing.

I couldn't take part, even though they expected it of me. I couldn't think of anything except the fact that Gil was dead. I didn't know why, but I knew that I must have had something to do with it. Somehow, it was my fault. I'd never explained to him what I had done, or why. Somehow, it had all gone wrong, and now he was dead. So was Cynthia's daughter. What must poor Cynthia be feeling?

It was all Maldureve's fault, I thought, savagely. If he hadn't abandoned me – if he had only come to save me from the man with the filthy gloves, it would all have been all right. But if he had, I probably wouldn't ever have found out the truth about him, about the owls and about myself.

I closed my eyes, wishing that I could see the light again, wishing that the eyes of the owls were still upon me. There was nothing but the darkness; nothing but the empty, lonely darkness.

Mum's hand was on my shoulder.

'It'll be all right, darling,' she said. 'It'll all be all right, now.'

But she didn't know. She couldn't even begin to suspect. It wasn't all right at all; it was all wrong. It had to be *put* right, if only I could find the strength.

If only.

2

At first, being with the owls was all pain, all fear. At first, it was the ultimate horror. But that was because I didn't understand. How could I? How could I even begin to understand, when everything Maldureve had told me had been so cryptic, so evasive?

He'd intended me to be terrified of the owls. He wanted me to try with all my might to resist them. Because I loved him, I did try. Even though he'd failed to come to my aid, even though he'd let the owls seize me and imprison me, I still loved him. I was still his creature, as terrified as he'd intended, as determinedly resistant as he wanted me to be.

But he'd lied.

He'd lied about the owls. He'd lied about what they were and what they represented. Not that I believed them when they first told me that. I wasn't easy to persuade. No one is, when they're locked into a cage of blinding light, fighting the hunger.

At first, they were every bit as cruel and fearsome as he'd said. They subjected me to the torture of withdrawal. They denied me the blood for which I hungered. I hated them then, every bit as fiercely as Maldureve hated them.

Even when the pain eased, when the hunger gradually died inside me and left me exhausted, I wouldn't listen to them. Their voices were just noise. They could never have persuaded me with their voices alone. They had to prove to me that they were what they said they were, that theirs was the better way, the only true way. They had to show me.

When they showed me, I understood what it had all been about. I even understood why they had saved the ultimate experience for the end, for the climax. Afterwards, my re-education really was complete.

It was as far from what I'd experienced with Maldureve as what I'd experienced with Maldureve had been from my first awkward and embarrassing time with Gil. I'd say that it was perfect, except that I'm more careful about such things now than I once was. Everything is really only one more step on the way; there are always further heights to be scaled, further limitations to be exceeded. Just because something is unimaginable doesn't mean to say that it's unreal. Our powers of imagination are very primitive, and our powers of perception are almost blind. We should beware of the awful stupidity which tells us that what our senses perceive is all there is, just as we should beware of the ridiculous pride which says that all we need to fill in that awful void beyond the reach of our perceptions is faith in the visions of prophets.

There are no words to describe the ecstasy of the owls. How could there be? There aren't even any words to describe the common or garden kinds of sexual thrill. We have words which we use when we try to talk about such things, in our awkward, fumbling fashion. We have a few more which we recruit to help us think about such things in the privacy of our own minds. But they're all just fudge-words, groping for hidden and unreachable meanings in the Stygian darkness. We're a mystery to ourselves. We haven't got the proper tools to get to grips with the simplest of experiences. That's what pornography makes clear to us: that when we try to render the most fundamental of experiences into words, it turns into something absurdly vulgar and coarse.

There's nothing coarse about intercourse with the owls, nothing pornographic. But it *is* sexual, and unbelievably intimate. It is lust, as well as love.

The bodies of the owls are both unbearably soft and unbearably sharp. Their feathers are like silken cloth or like keen razors, depending on the way that you stroke them – or depending upon the way they stroke you. They tantalize and they cut, they thrill and they wound, but the experience is all one and seamless.

The distinction between pain and pleasure simply disappears, and there's only intensity.

When you eventually come it's like the moment of a violent death, with the feathers scything through every last fibre of your being, and soothing all the while, but it's like an infinite journey to the centre of sensation, a fall into the abyss of extremes. To get there . . . well, you have to fly, and you *can* fly, even though your body is perfectly still, perfectly balanced.

I don't mean to imply that you can leave your body behind, to become some sort of disincarnate astral entity. That's nonsense. Pleasure is a function of the body. It's born in the brain in response to signals transmitted by the nerves. It's a combination of electrical circuits and chemical states; it's *real*. I was never out of my body, nor was my body ever anywhere else than lying on the bed in the county hospital. What I mean by 'flying' is a state of mind, a sensation.

But the sensations are only a part of it, just as the feathers are only part of an owl. Pleasure is also consciousness: stimulus and response, mediated by intelligence.

Owls have huge round eyes, which stare with such awesome concentration, and owls have minds behind their eyes. Owls have consciousness; owls have wisdom.

So it wasn't just a matter of down-and-blade feathers, stroking and striking into me; it wasn't just a matter of feeling. People who say that when you come you turn into an animal, experiencing pure intoxication without the mediation of consciousness, as an animal supposedly does, are dead wrong. They have no idea what it is to be truly unconscious, because unconsciousness is by definition incapable of representation by ideas; one of the things consciousness can never have any intelligence of is its own absence. When you come, you come consciously; what happens to you then is something known as well as felt; something which you observe, in yourself, and to which you respond, with whatever intelligence you can muster. The higher the intelligence, the greater the wisdom, the better it is.

Believe me. I've been there. I know whereof I speak.

When I flew with the owls – when they brought me to the ecstatic moment of imagined annihilation – the whole of my existence was filled with light, and it seemed that the walls of the universe were made of huge and staring eyes.

I was frightened by those eyes at first, taken to the very limits of terror by their unrelenting gaze. Even the fugitive glimpses I'd caught of those eyes, before the owls came out of the borderlands and seized me in their cruel claws, had filled me with an unreasoning fear which struck directly at my heart. Actually to be with the owls in the borderlands, to live beneath the scrutiny of those focused, all-seeing eyes, was worse by far. But fear too resolves itself in the end to pure intensity. True ecstasy can no more exclude fear than it can exclude pain; true ecstasy isn't just pleasure magnified. The terror of those eyes, the terror of having them look at me – knowing that everything I was could be seen and examined, that nothing could be hidden – was all part of it.

Now, in a sense, those eyes are my eyes. I can see at least a little of what they see. The world outside, in which I move, is as full of shadows and lies and mysteries and uncertainties as ever it was, but I see myself with different eyes, different powers of perception. That's one of the ways in which the ultimate ecstasy transforms us. And it isn't just seeing. It isn't just staring and finding light where there was no light before. It's understanding, too.

We think of knowledge in terms of facts and skills; we think of wisdom in terms of adapting one's hopes, fears and expectations to the limits of possibility and plausibility; and we're right to do so. Wisdom is knowing how to *be in the world* in a balanced and rewarding way. It's the end of self-evolution. Wisdom is a reconciliation of intellect and emotion, the forging of a whole way of being out of the uncomfortable fragments of experience. Not many people have it, even in a primitive form. Maldureve and his kind don't have it either, and probably can't ever attain it, by virtue of their nature. The owls are very different. By virtue of *their* nature, the owls have all the wisdom they need, and that's perhaps the most important aspect of their enduring ecstasy.

The fact that I couldn't wholly share the experience with which the owls completed my initiation into their mysteries was due far more to the limitation of my wisdom than to anything else. In another era, bringing different resources from my experiences in the everyday world to the task of trying to understand, I suppose I would have imagined that I saw God, talked with an angel or penetrated the veil of the world-illusion to see the rooms of Paradise, but along with all the philosophy which I had absorbed in my half-baked fashion I had at least imbibed a healthy measure of doubt. The true wealth of wisdom was out of my reach, but I think . . . I believe . . . that I avoided the mistake of seizing upon some tawdry counterfeit coin.

Maybe, if I had been able to acquire true wisdom along with everything else which the owls donated to me, what happened wouldn't have seemed like a kind of lovemaking at all. But it *was* sexual, even if it was so much more as well. It was the same kind of thrill which sex is supposed to deliver but never really can: the ultimate, stark-naked reward of an electric explosion in the pleasure centres of the brain. It was connection with something not me, being to being, flesh to flesh.

It was love; deep-down true love.

It sounds perverse to say it like that. It sounds, I guess, like a crazy kind of masturbation. After all, I was in my hospital bed, fast asleep, and dreaming. But I wasn't really alone.

I wasn't really alone.

With the owls, I truly found that state of mind of whose possibility I'd had my first inkling when I let Maldureve suck my blood. I became the molten lava of steely flesh, the pure flux of hot young blood, and I glowed with incandescent fire. Their feathers smoothed me to polished chrome with their infinite softness, cut me to silken ribbons with their edges, pulled me apart with their barbs. And all the while, the eyes watched, infinite in number and infinitely dark: the eyes watched, and saw, and *understood*. The pain forbade screaming, the fear forbade flight, and the pleasure forbade intoxication . . .

Into the owls' world, I *came*.

After I woke up again, I kept repeating to myself, from time to time: 'I'm here still. Although I'm awake, returned to consciousness and active life, I'm here still.' Whenever I had time, and leisure, I'd add more, just for the pleasure of hearing the facts asserted. 'I'm beginning to understand,' I'd say to myself. 'I haven't yet acquired wisdom, but its seed has been planted, and one day soon, I'll find the words which will let me begin to know what I really am, and what I'm still in the process of becoming . . .'

It was comforting. It was necessary. The cold, bleak world didn't seem very welcoming, once I'd learned to love the owls. I needed the strength that the owls had given me, and I needed to remember where it had come from, what it was worth. I was afraid of forgetting, or perhaps being beguiled again by Maldureve and by the shadows from which he came. Once you've caught a glimpse of Paradise, you can't ever really be satisfied with anything less, and wherever you go you have to carry with you the horrible thought that perhaps you'll never get back.

I always knew that the owls were close at hand, that the borderlands were everywhere and anywhere, but sometimes – whenever the shadows drew in around me – I had to tell myself over and over again that I was still in *their* world, still in *their* safe hands, no matter where my body was or what I had to do. That was just the way of things.

In spite of everything, it still is, and probably always will be.

3

When I first woke up I was in a room of my own, but I was moved next morning to a ward. I was being kept in for 'observation' and didn't warrant special treatment any more.

The ward was awful. It was mostly populated by old ladies in for hip replacements and middle-aged ones for hysterectomies. It might have been a little bit interesting if there'd been some authentic human tragedy on display, but there wasn't. The prevailing mood was one of grumpy resentment; they felt that their bodies had let them down by failing to stand up to the pressures of everyday life, and they had all spent so long in queues waiting for vacancies at the repair shop that whatever patience they'd ever had was quite gone. Not one of them seemed relieved that it was going to be over at last; all their fear of the scalpel was diverted into streams of bitter misery. They took in one another's emotional laundry with evident relish, each one pandering to the paranoia of the next and all joining in together for the hymns of complaint. They envied me for having healed up already, and were not reluctant to make pointed comments about the unlucky person who was presumed to be waiting in line for my bed, plunged into abysmal depths of misery by fibroids or a dodgy pelvis. I hadn't even been properly raped.

I'd only been there half a day before I was longing to get out. I wanted to discharge myself, but Mum sided with the doctor in saying that I'd be a very silly girl if I did, given that I'd been unconscious for so long. Dr Fellowes didn't know why I hadn't woken up much earlier, and neither did Dr Hodgson, the consultant; they hadn't even got a theory to work on. They only wanted to keep me in so that they could pretend to be taking all possible precautions, but I had to let them. At least the hospital staff kept the reporters out – three or four of them tried to talk to me, but I only had to tell the nurses that I didn't want to. The nurses liked having an excuse to be firm with outsiders; it gave them a rare opportunity to vent their pent-up aggressions safely.

Dad drove all the way back for one day, just to see how I was, but he went home again in the evening so that he could go to work next day. He wanted to take Sharon with him, so that she could go back to school, but she stubbornly refused to go, saying that it was hardly worth it for half a week, and she'd come back at the weekend. Actually, there was no particular reason for Mum or Sharon to hang on, now that I was better, but Mum wouldn't have felt that she was doing her duty if she wasn't at my bedside every minute the hospital would allow.

It was difficult to believe that I'd only been away from home for less than a dozen weeks, and that Mum, Dad and Sharon had until recently been almost the whole of the society in which I lived. In the hospital, of course, Mum and Dad were out of their natural environment and out of their depth, but they seemed so very strange and alien that it was no longer possible for me to comprehend how I had let them shape and define my life and my identity for so long. They seemed ridiculously ineffectual as they racked their brains to try to think of new things to say and good advice to give.

They were just as uncomfortable, in their own way. Back home, when we were all together, they'd never had any reason to doubt that they knew best – that whatever situation I found myself in, they'd have the answers and the explanations, the essential wisdom to pass on. Whether it was falling down and gashing my knee when I was four, or seeing some freak expose himself when I was eight, or becoming infatuated with some boy at school when I was ten, or being mocked and harassed by the big kids at my new school when I was eleven, or starting my periods when I was thirteen, or doing GCSEs when I was sixteen, or leaving home when I was eighteen, they were always the experts. They had always been there. Even if they couldn't tell me exactly what to do – and they were sometimes scrupulous about letting me make my own decisions – they were perfectly certain that they knew how to go about weighing pros and cons.

They had convinced themselves, and me, that they knew how to live and how to teach others to live. They seemed able to take anything in their stride, even Sharon's crude and half-hearted attempts to go against the grain. Jet-black hair, studded jackets and the fervent idolization of the Sisters of Mercy weren't nearly enough to faze or frighten them. But once a façade like that cracks, it shatters. They were finished now, and useless. I knew it and they knew it, although they didn't quite understand why. They had no idea how far things had gone. They still thought I was human.

I knew how much Mum hated being away from home, and that she hated it three times as much now Dad wasn't there to share the burden, but I knew too that she couldn't have torn herself away from me without falling prey to agonizing guilt and anxiety. The pressure of absolute necessity forced her to go on being useless and miserable. I couldn't help but feel that she was the patient and I was the moral support. It all seemed rather unfair, somehow.

'I don't see why they can't transfer you to a hospital back home,' Mum said, in the faintly fretful voice which she always used when the world wasn't living up to her expectations and she couldn't quite figure out why it had to be so intractably perverse. 'Then Daddy could come to see you every evening, and Sharon would be prepared to go back to school.' Sharon evaded the critical sideways glance which accompanied this statement with a casual expertise born of long practice.

'I can't come back yet,' I told her. 'There's still a whole week of term left, and I'm way behind in my work. They can't keep me in much longer. There's no need for me to be here at all.'

'Daddy could come down in the car and pick us up,' she said, as if I hadn't said a word. 'He could drive you to the local hospital himself. We could all go back together. They wouldn't mind, at the university. We spoke to a Dr Gray – *he* said that you didn't have to go back, when Daddy asked about it. You could catch up at home, and have a nice long rest. A good Christmas is what we all need.'

'It's not as easy as that,' I told her. 'I need the library. Anyway, there are other things I have to do.'

'What other things?'

'I have to see Cynthia.'

'I don't see why.'

'And I have to go back to my room. I have to live in my room. I have to walk back and forth to Wombwell House, past the Marquis of Membury's Garden. I have to be able to do that.'

'They've put up a fence,' Sharon interjected. 'As soon as the police finished, the workmen started.'

'Locking the stable door, as usual,' Mum said.

'It's like one of those fences they put round electricity substations,' Sharon went on. 'Eight-foot metal struts, curled round at the top. It's incredibly ugly.'

'It's not supposed to be pretty,' Mum said critically. 'It'll do the job it's supposed to do. They're putting in extra lights, too. You won't recognize it – it's quite different. You'll feel perfectly safe walking there, now. You should come home.'

'I can't. Not yet.'

She tried the delayed-shock argument, the not-looking-after-yourself argument and the not-realizing-how-much-she'd-worry argument, but I stood them all off. Sharon helped, not because she didn't want me home but because the laws of sisterly loyalty demanded that she take my side against the common adversary.

I meant what I said. I *couldn't* go home. Maybe for Christmas, for a few days of pretending, but not for any length of time. I didn't live there any more. I wasn't the same person who had left, no matter how little time had elapsed. And I did have work to do, I had a mission to undertake. I had a monster to hunt down.

The one advantage in having Mum hovering around was that it helped to keep other people at bay. Her presence was a deterrent to the other patients, the doctors and the police. While she was listening in, they all had to stick to the rules. She even talked to a couple of the reporters, telling them that there was no point in talking to me, and giving them something they could print instead. Given a freer rein, I think, the curiosity of the patients and the police might have become more general, more intrusive and more problematic. Of course, she also inhibited people I'd rather have been able to talk to a little less self-consciously, like Dr Gray, who came to see me once, and Gil's father, whose embarrassment was quite bad enough without Mum's help. I was as kind as I could be, and I insisted that Gil couldn't have killed Janine Leigh even though I didn't have any real reason to be sure. At the end of the day, though, there's nothing at all you can say to a man whose son has cut his own throat and set himself on fire.

Cynthia didn't come to see me, although I thought she might have done. Neither did Professor Viners, although he probably wanted to. He got Dr Hodgson to give me a note – which he passed to me almost furtively on one of the quiet occasions when Mum wasn't around. *Dear Miss Charet*, the note said, *I would be greatly obliged if you could come to see me when you are able.*

'What's this about?' I asked Dr Hodgson.

'Mike and I go back a long way,' the consultant told me, irrelevantly. 'He's a good man. He's more than a little worried about all of this. Rumours are creeping round the campus, about viruses escaping from his lab. He asked me to run extra tests while you were unconscious, to make sure that you hadn't picked up any infection via your boyfriend. Apparently, he took blood from Gil Molari too, when the boy became convinced that he'd been infected. Nothing showed up – nothing at all. You can't blame Mike for being anxious. If he's shut down, it could wreck his career. People from the tabloids are fishing around, and they don't need much to set them off. We can keep them away from you while you're in here, but you won't be able to avoid them so easily once you're out. I think Mike just wants to ask you to be careful, to explain what it might mean if you were somehow to give them a hook to hang a scare story on. The ripper-on-the-loose story has already gone stale, and it only needs a spark to send them all haring off down some other melodramatic blind alley. Mike doesn't deserve that. Whatever happened to Gil Molari, it wasn't Mike's fault. All the tests were clear.'

I wasn't in the least surprised that the tests had shown nothing. I knew that whatever had happened to Gil was *my* fault. It was my fault for feeding on his blood, even though I'd done it out of love. It was my fault for having delayed making my explanations until he'd be unable to deny them. I knew now that I ought to have told him what was happening, even though he'd have thought I was mad. That way, he wouldn't have been so ready to believe that *he* was going mad when the hunger grew in him. It was my fault, because I was the vampire and he was the victim. It was my fault, because I hadn't done enough to stop him believing that he was diseased and delirious.

When I got out, I knew, I was going to have to make amends for that. I was going to have to make amends for everything, if I could. With the aid of what the owls had taught me – their powers, and above all their wisdom – I thought that I could do it.

At least, I intended to try.

'I'd really like to get out,' I told Dr Hodgson, in as sweetly reasonable a fashion as I could contrive. 'I feel fine, and I don't see that this observation business is achieving anything. If nothing showed up on my tests, surely there's no reason for me to be here.'

'It isn't quite like that,' the consultant said. 'It's *because* nothing showed up on your tests that I'm wary. You shouldn't have been unconscious for so long. It wasn't really a coma, though we call it that for convenience. Maybe narcolepsy would be a better word, but giving a thing a name doesn't mean we understand it. Something might still show up. I'm afraid that if you leave, you might just slip back into unconsciousness – and if you did that after I'd discharged you, your mother and the tabloids would be after *me*. You wouldn't want me to get into any trouble, would you?'

There was no point in telling him that I understood perfectly well why I'd been unconscious for so long. Coma and narcolepsy might be just fudge-words, but they were respectable fudge-words. Re-education by the owls was beyond the limits of the medical imagination.

'You know, Anne,' said Dr Hodgson, sitting down on the bed, 'I think your weight problem may have had something to do with your being unconscious for so long. I know you're not anorexic, and I'm not accusing you of consciously dieting too hard, but it really doesn't do any good to be too thin. Your thyroid isn't hyperactive, but you have a pretty fast-paced metabolism. Every model in the world would love it, but you're not a model and you haven't quite stopped growing yet. Try to make sure that you get lots of protein. It's not easy to eat well on a student grant, I know, and I suppose the Hall food is mostly stodge, but do what you can, okay? I wouldn't prescribe bacon-and-egg breakfasts to everyone, but in your case . . .'

'I feel fine,' I told him. 'I eat enough. I'm just naturally thin.' There didn't seem to be any point in observing that the hospital food was worse than the food in Hall, and that I certainly hadn't put on any weight while they'd been feeding me by intravenous drip and draining my waste fluids by catheter. I hadn't any complaints to make about that. I didn't feel hungry.

I didn't feel hungry at all.

Mum, of course, agreed with the doctor. 'If you came home,' she said, 'I could make sure you got whatever you need. It'd be the best thing all round.'

There was no effective defence but simple stubbornness. 'I can't,' I said, over and over again. 'I have work to do. I daren't get too far behind, or I'll never catch up. If I run home because of what happened, he really will have hurt me. He'll have wrecked things for me. I have to carry on as if nothing happened. It's the only way to win.'

Even Sharon, when she got a chance to be alone with me, wasn't so certain that I was right.

'You could ease up on yourself a bit,' she said. 'It doesn't hurt to take time-out when the going gets rough.'

'You've been watching Channel 4 sport again,' I said. 'This is England. You don't have time-outs in netball.'

'You haven't played netball since you were in primary school,' she pointed out. 'You're in the big league now. You have to be tough, but not that tough. You nearly got your throat cut, your boyfriend is dead and your friend's daughter was murdered. That's a lot of grief. It's not like falling off a horse and having to get right back up again.'

'You never rode a horse in your life,' I said. 'Or any of the rest of it. I've got to get out of this place, and I couldn't stand convalescing at home, with all the fuss. Anyway, I told the police I'd recognize the man's voice. They'll need me, if they catch somebody.'

'There are trains,' she pointed out. She was only putting up a show. She knew it was all decided, and that I'd have my own way. Only their little sisters know how stubborn people can be, when they really decide to dig in. She knew I'd win in the end.

'I did it, though, didn't I?' she said. 'I woke you up. I knew it would work. Detonation Boulevard – bang bang.'

'You did it,' I agreed, not really thinking that she had. 'You brought me back to the land of the living. I'll be sure to remember you in my will. Let me know what tape you want for Christmas. Something loud and dark and gothic, just like the world.'

4

When the man with the knife attacked me, I desperately wanted Maldureve to come. I wanted him to save me. I knew that our relationship had changed when I decided to live, and that once I became a fully-fledged vampire he would no longer be my lover and protector in the way that he had been before, but I hadn't yet got through the phase of wanting him and needing him and looking to him for succour and support. When he didn't come, I felt betrayed.

In fact, it was far worse than that. While I was fighting the man with the dirty gloves, and most especially when the blade of his knife cut into my neck, I was sick with anger because Maldureve wasn't already there. It wasn't just that he didn't come when I needed him; the Marquis of Membury's Garden was his place, and he should have been there already, lying in wait for the stupid predator who had borrowed *his* shadows for a hiding place.

It shouldn't have been me who was attacked at all; it should have been the monster, the vile thing who was lying in wait. Maldureve should have been there to sweep the thing into the folds of his cloak and rip its throat out. Why else had I granted him the gift of solidity? Why else had I made the supreme effort to see him, to help him emerge fom the borderlands, to bring him into the narrow, ordinary, everyday world? Why should anyone welcome a vampire to existence, unless the vampire is prepared to play the hero's role, to be the ultimate lover in every respect?

Maldureve let me down. He let me down badly.

It was bad enough that the owls came hurtling out of the borderlands in a cataract of light. It was bad enough that they seized me with their wrathful claws and seared me with their awful vision. It was bad enough that they bore me away to the cage of light, to imprison me with my awful hunger, to break me of my addiction to young blood. It was all quite bad enough without the sensation of having been abandoned and betrayed, sold down the river, left to rot.

I knew that Maldureve was scared of the owls, although I didn't understand why, but I hadn't expected him to be a coward. No matter how scared he was, I thought, he should have come to help me. No matter what danger he himself was in, he should have been brave. He owed me that much. You have to have more from a lover than sexual thrills, or he isn't really a lover at all.

It was because of that betrayal, more than anything else, that the cage of light was the abyss of Hell so far as I was concerned. After the initial shock, the claws didn't hurt. However bad the hunger became, it would have been bearable if only I hadn't known that it was Maldureve's hunger, given to me by him so that I might suffer in his place, as he would surely have suffered, in the confines of that dreadful cage.

In a way, though, the pain of that betrayal might have helped me. It made me bitter and it made me angry, and it hurt me, but it helped me to be even more determined not to die, not to fade away into the light until there was nothing left of me but a faint flickering shadow. When you're undead, you can't just let go of life. You fight.

If that creature of wool and slime and muscle had grabbed me six weeks earlier, before I first encountered Maldureve, I think he would have killed me. At the very least he would have raped me. I think I would have let him. I wouldn't have been able to fight back, and I would have been so utterly humiliated that I wouldn't have been able to resist the temptation to die. I don't know what *he* would have done – whether he'd just have raped me and run away, or whether he'd have panicked and stabbed me in the heart – but I would have wanted to die. I would have been so utterly sick about myself, so sick about the world and its treatment of me, that I would have wanted to die.

I would have died, for want of any substantial will to live. My strength would have drained away; my heart would have stopped. I would have made a tragic, beautiful corpse, all the more tragic and beautiful for having been spoiled and crushed and violated by that animal. That, after all, is how voyeurs see rape: as a tragedy of beauty and innocence despoiled – and before I met Maldureve, I too was just a voyeur, a spectator of my own life, a keening mourner at my own slow funeral.

Because I'd met Maldureve, and because he'd let me down, I couldn't be content to die. I had to continue to live, even when I found myself in Hell. I'd supped enough young blood to make me truly young, and truly sanguine.

I thought, for a while, that I went to Hell when the owls took me. I thought that I went to a place of punishment with no hope of redemption. I thought that their cage of light, which held me immobile and burned me with its intensity, was dreadful beyond my wildest imaginings. But I was being stupid and childish. It wasn't like that at all. The cage of light ceased to be Hell within hours, maybe within minutes, and became life. Just *life*.

I knew that I was in the borderlands, lost in the interstices of everyday experience, out of touch with the world of objects and sensory stimuli, but it was just a matter of *being there*, of getting by. There was a lot to learn, but I had my mind and my intelligence.

I wasn't dead. I wasn't defeated.

I wasn't, in fact, in Hell at all.

I got used to the eyes. It isn't so bad to be stared at, once all the suspense is exhausted. It isn't so bad, even when you know that the eyes which are staring at you can look into your heart and your mind, because your flesh and bones aren't mask enough to keep them out. It all becomes quite tolerable, once you understand that you have something to say about it, and that you can get answers in return to your questions.

A stare can't be menacing for ever, and once it isn't voiceless any more, its power to make you paranoid is much reduced.

The hunger wasn't so easy, because it was inside and not outside. But there comes a point where hunger can't get any worse, and after that it begins – slowly – to get better. Even real hunger is like that; even pain is like that. A vampire's hunger for blood is, in the end, only another kind of addiction. It doesn't have to drive you crazy, if you don't let it.

I was in pain with the hunger, sick with the hunger, desperate with the hunger . . . but I outlasted it, as the owls knew I could, as the owls knew I would. And when I'd done that, there was only the betrayal left to hurt me.

That was the hardest thing of all to come to terms with, although it wasn't nearly as painful as the hunger, nor as intimidating as the eyes. To master the memory of betrayal, I needed the owls. To get past that desolate sense of disappointment, I needed re-education. To learn to trust myself again, I needed my extended remand to the prison of light.

'You should not have brought Maldureve out of the shadows,' the owls told me, in their softly sincere voices. 'His kind is dangerous.'

'I needed him,' I told them, truthfully enough. 'I needed to be loved. I needed to be brought out of myself. I needed a better reason than I had to perform the empty rituals of everyday life. I needed excitement. I even needed the horror of him, the darkness, the threat. I needed the *unease*. I needed a vampire, and nothing less would do.'

'And he needed you,' they reminded me. 'The meeting of mutual needs is one of the fundamental processes of evolution: symbiosis is the beginning of integration, the first vital step in the quest for adaptation. But the coincidence of needs is never simple, never symmetrical. You have other needs, which Maldureve cannot meet; he has other needs, for which you are inadequate. The meeting of your needs has consequences for others, as does the meeting of his. You met your need by bringing the vampire from the borderlands, but now he is free and not all his victims will thrive on his attentions as you did. His freedom has consequences for our kind, too, for we are competitors, his kind and ours. That is the other fundamental process of evolution: competition and selection; the survival of the fittest. Love is as much a weapon in that war as hate. Love is a fallible yardstick, Anne: nothing is right because it *feels* right; nothing is true because it is beautiful.'

'I am one with him now,' I told them. 'I am of his kind. My commitment is made.' *But he let me down*!

'All your choices remain to be made,' they told me. 'You can be mistress of the blood without becoming slave to the blood. You have not sold your soul, and you owe him no debts. He needed you as much as you needed him, and now you are both different, both transformed. Sometimes, Anne, we must slay what we have summoned. Sometimes, we must take arms even against our own bodies and our own minds, when they threaten to destroy us. Although our appetites would let us starve, still we must eat. If a limb becomes gangrenous, it must be severed. If we have given solidity to that which is dangerous, and have thereby loosed evil upon the world, we must repair what we have done.

'Maldureve must be dissolved again into the shadows. Either his too solid heart must be staked, or his too sturdy flesh put to the torch. He must be made captive, Anne. Only you can do that. Only you can send him back across the borderlands, confine him once again to the realm of unbeing. Would that you could send him back to the land of never was, for his evil is spreading like a cancer, and more will die if he is not stopped.'

'He loved me!' I whispered. I wanted to say 'loves' instead of 'loved', but *he had let me down*!

'You made him love you, Anne. You imbued him with that love while you imbued him with solidity. You brought him out of the shadows as a demon lover, an answer to a perverse prayer. But you could not make him love your lover, or your's lover's lover. His love is exclusive to you, Anne, but his hatred knows no bounds. You can summon spirits from the vast deep, Anne, and bind them to your whim, but you cannot reserve them to yourself, or forbid their true nature. Maldureve is a killer, Anne

– a plague and a pestilence. Maldureve must be returned whence he came, or the world will be the worse for it. What the world needs is wisdom, Anne; what the world needs is enlightenment; what the world needs, in spite of their disquieting eyes, in spite of their sharp claws, is the owls.'

'I wanted him.' I told them. 'I wanted him so much. If he's evil, so am I. If he's a destroyer, so am I. I wanted him and I want him still. I crave his love, his touch, his glamour. If he were only here, I would cleave to him and beg him to destroy you all. I am his mirror, reflecting his soul in mine. Were I to turn against him, I would be turning against myself.' And yet, I remembered, when I required as much from him *he let me down*!

'Desire springs from the shadows,' the owls told me, gently and without anger. 'Sometimes half-formed, sometimes fully formed, sometimes fine and sometimes monstrous. You need not be ashamed of misshapen desires, Anne. But desire is only desire, and cannot compel action unless the will capitulates. You must be the mistress of desire, Anne, and not its slave. Although you want Maldureve, still you must return him to his own place. All appetites require restraint, Anne, lest they make us bloated and surfeit-sick. To turn against an appetite which, if left unchecked, would bring you to disaster, is not to turn against yourself: it is merely to protect yourself. You must defend yourself against Maldureve, Anne, else he will destroy you, and much else besides. You must hunt down the vampire in his lair, Anne, else he will spill and spoil more innocent blood, and unleash more monsters on the helpless world.'

'How can I believe you?' I complained. 'How do I know that what you tell me is true?'

'We wear no cloak of darkness,' they replied. 'We live in clarity; we are the light. You may grant solidity to us as easily as you gave solidity to Maldureve; you may be our reflection as easily as you have been his. He is a dark idol, which forbids you sight and light. Cast him down! We are the emblems of the light, whose honesty is plain to see. Deliver him to us, that we may turn his evil into good. Only love us, Anne, as you have loved Maldureve, and we will fly with you to the true heights of ecstasy and show you the true blaze of glory. Only consent to love us, dear Anne, as you have loved the darkness of misshapen desire, and we will teach you *wisdom*: wisdom alloyed with ecstasy.'

'I didn't do anything wrong,' I complained. 'I didn't deserve what happened. *I didn't do anything wrong.*'

'The past is the past,' they told me. 'The future is still to be made. It always remains to make a new beginning. The light is always there, Anne; there to be seen and there to be chosen. There are those who hide in the shadows, afraid of the light, and there are those who open their eyes, to behold the glory. Choose the light, Anne. Choose wisdom. Deny Maldureve, the betrayer. Only learn to love the light, and the shadows can never claim you.'

It was all rhetoric, of course. I couldn't figure out what it was supposed to mean. But locked in a cage of light as I was, it wasn't easy to oppose the flood of words, the entreaties, the power of the staring eyes. In the end, it simply wasn't possible. And they did begin, in their own bewildering way, to teach me the beginnings of wisdom.

They made good their initial promises, of course, just as Maldureve had made good on his. They loved me, and made me delirious with love of them. They flew me to the promised heights of ecstasy, bathed me in the promised blaze of glory.

I loved it. I even managed to convince myself that I understood. Pleasure is a powerful agent of persuasion, perhaps more powerful than pain. The owls had command of both, while I was in their world. What alternative did I have but to yield to their demands and their seductions, and to hope that when the time came, they wouldn't let me down?

One question remained unresolved, as it had to. One question couldn't be answered, or put to the test, until I was returned to the world of objects and sensory perception. One question remained, upon which everything would ultimately hang.

When it came to a matter of life and death, *could* the owls come to my aid, as Maldureve had failed to do? If and when I came under dire threat, would they do their utmost to save me? Would they serve me to the very limits of their courage and ability? Or would they, in the end, leave me to my own resources?

I didn't know. I told myself it didn't matter, that I would be no worse off even if they failed me, as the powers of darkness already had. But I desperately wanted to believe that they wouldn't, that there was *something* I could rely on, something that would never let me down. Maybe it was a weakness in me, but I needed something.

I needed hope – and hope, for me, was what the owls became.

5

The ward was never quiet, even at night. There was always someone moving or sniffing, always the sound of people shuffling back and forth. I could always hear the muffled footfalls of the people in the ward above, and porters shoving trolleys about the corridors. There was always something to be a nuisance, to prevent the ultimate fall of silence.

I found, unfortunately, that in the matter of sleep I had gone from one extreme to the other. For days no one had been able to wake me, no matter how they tried; now, by contrast, I found it impossible to surrender my grip on wakefulness. At first I took the pills the ward sister offered me, but they only seemed to make me drowsy and restless; they didn't actually knock me out. I didn't like feeling that my head was full of cotton wool and that my legs wouldn't be comfortable no matter how I arranged them, so I eventually decided to let nature take its course and try not to worry about the insomnia. After all, I thought, what's so bad about being alert? Why not just lie patiently awake, appreciating the relative peace and absence of pressure?

I'd never been the kind of person to be easily bored; I was always good at thinking about things, always an expert daydreamer. Anyhow, I had plans to make.

The ward's indigenous shadows had a meeting place in the corner where my bed was. The nurse on night duty had her station at the far end of the ward, and the light on her desk was carefully hooded so that it wouldn't annoy anyone else. At first, when the other lights were switched out, the darkness around me would seem profound and absolute, but it didn't take long for the subtler shades to come creeping in, dividing the not-quite-darkness into an awesomely complex pattern.

All through the first night of my voluntary insomnia, as I lay patiently awake, I kept wondering whether Maldureve would come, rising up from the shadow webs like a silent spider. I thought he might want to see me. I thought he *ought* to want to see me. When he didn't come, I wondered what his absence signified. Had he simply moved on to some other lover, some rich and untapped source of rich, sweet blood? Was he ashamed of the fact that he hadn't come to help me when I needed him so desperately? Did he know that the owls would have done their utmost to convert me to their cause and turn me against him? And did he know, if so, that they had succeeded? Did he lack the courage to plead his own case, to try to change my mind yet again? Or was he afraid that I'd leap up from my hospital bed, clad only in a white nightie, with a sharpened stake ready in my hand?

It was all pure speculation. He didn't come. I didn't know whether I should be disappointed or glad. I didn't know whether I was disappointed or glad.

Again, on the second of my lie-awake nights, I half expected something to happen. It didn't. On the third, I expected nothing; such is the determined perversity of circumstance that I was wrong again.

At first, when the shadows stirred, I assumed that it was Maldureve, and made the effort to be ready to face him. I simply took it for granted that anything trying to emerge from the darkness of the borderlands in my vicinity had to be my very own demon lover.

I didn't try to help him. I just watched the shadows shifting, trying to become something more than shadows, trying to acquire mass and form. I figured that Maldureve deserved to struggle a little, to feel the drag of my indifference, to know that his welcome was withdrawn. I didn't suppose that it would stop him, because I knew full well that I couldn't take back the consent I'd already given him, the power I'd already lent to him, the blood with which I'd fed him. I knew that he didn't need me in order to be real; I just hoped that without me, he'd find it a little less easy, a little less comfortable.

But I saw, in the end, that it wasn't Maldureve at all.

'Anne!' said a thin voice, which seemed to be borne on a slow and bitter wind from a very long way away. 'Anne! For the love of God, Anne, help me!'

For the love of God? It seemed like an odd reason, a remarkably careless figure of speech. According to my understanding, the lovers of God are supposed to turn their backs on voices like that, refusing to hear them. The lovers of God are not supposed to play necromancer. I was a witch and a vampire, albeit one who had allied herself with the owls. A more rational plea would surely have been in order.

I didn't recognize the voice – not at first.

I was a little bit afraid, but in a peculiar sort of way. It wasn't like the first time I'd heard Maldureve, when momentary fear had transformed itself by magic into something warm yet secretly sinister, but it was just as strange and unexpected. I was afraid, because something was trying to come to me out of the dark borderlands: something kin to Maldureve and not to the owls; something which might easily reckon me an enemy and want to do me harm. But I also felt a surge of triumphant self-esteem, to hear it calling to me, begging me for help. I knew that it needed me in order to take shape, in order to put on substance, in order really to *be*. I knew that the plaintive voice might only be a means of seduction, or a shabby trick, but still I had to help it. It needed me.

'Anne! Please! You have to help me, Anne! I can't exist without you, Anne! I love you, Anne! *I love you!*'

The voice was so faint, so very near to the threshold of audibility, that there was no hope at all of recognizing it, but the words told me who it was. He couldn't even give himself a name without my warrant, but he could identify himself by means of his feeling: the emotional core of his being.

'Gil?' I asked, very softly. I spoke the name aloud, but in the merest of whispers. There were others in the ward whose stertorous breathing was louder by far. No one standing at the foot of the bed could have heard me, but Gil was much closer than that, for all that he seemed so very far away.

'Please, Anne! Please, please, please!' No longer 'for the love of God', not even as a figure of speech. For love of Gil, and that alone.

'You're dead, Gil,' I whispered. 'They told me that you're dead.' But I wasn't denying his existence. I wasn't trying to make the shadows be still by exorcizing the spirit which was moving within them. I wasn't rejecting him at all. I was simply wondering. For those who have accepted the reality of vampires, the possible existence of ghosts can be taken for granted – and yet, I knew how empty of ghosts the world and its borderlands seemed to be. Even if one in seven of all the people who have ever lived are alive today, that implies that the spirits of the dead should vastly outnumber the living – but I had gone into the Marquis of Membury's Garden at dead of night a dozen times and more, to be partner to the creature of the shadows, and I had never seen the dead, or any evidence that their echoes still wandered the Earth. From the very beginning, I knew that if Gil was now a ghost, he was exceptional. His phantom state of being was not the common heritage of all the dead.

'Help me, Anne!' he begged.

In life, he had been so confident, so strong, so casually dominant. All the advantages had been his: age, size, sex, even nationality. Everything about his living being had made him master over mine. It didn't matter that he was just a young man, uncertain, unwise and inexperienced. He was still so much greater and more competent than I. Living, he had been entitled to determine the form of our relationship, to steer it, to take command . . .

Now that he was dead, it was a very different matter.

I was alive, possessed of solidity by right; he was merely a shade, who came to plead for the thinnest, weakest semblance of solidity as a gift. More than that: I was a creature of the light, entitled to walk in brightness; he was a thing of darkness, a haunter of the night. I had learned not merely to live in light, but to glory in the sublimity of brightness. I was now a daughter of the owls. What was he, by comparison?

'What do you want, Gil?' I asked him. It was not as ungracious a question as it might have seemed. Of course I was glad to hear his voice, flattered to think that he had returned even from beyond the grave to see me and hear my voice. He had been called back from the infinite abyss by love, and that was a marvel in itself. I could understand well enough how mourning lovers, desperate with loneliness, might be entirely willing to grope about in the shadows which surrounded them, desperate for one last scarcely audible word or one last scarcely tangible touch, deeply grateful for the experience, not able to care whether it might be evidence of their supreme sensitivity or their incipient insanity. I was not ungrateful for Gil's attempt to manifest himself, nor scornful of the effort which it represented . . . but I still needed to ask. I needed to know why he had come, and why he wanted me to grant him *presence*.

'I have to tell you,' he said, his voice half strangled by effort. 'I have to tell you about the girl . . . about Maldureve . . .'

What better reason could there be? I thought.

I tried with all my might to see him. I stared into the uncertain shadows with all the intensity I could muster, trying to perceive his shape, trying to find him and bring him forth from dreary obscurity. I wanted him to feel the warmth of his own dear flesh about him; I wanted him to be sensible of the beating of his poor ghostly heart.

With my help, he was eventually able to come and stand beside me.

I could understand why people who have seen ghosts – actual or imaginary – are commonly frightened by them. It is not that they wear the image of something terrible, but that they defy the most basic suppositions which we have about the order of things. They are here *and* gone; dead *and* alive; present *and* absent. They are insults to the principle of the excluded middle. They are more difficult to believe in than vampires, which merely have to be added on to the world we know, at its mysterious fringe. Ghosts violate our most fundamental frameworks of understanding; they are implicitly terrifying. Even to suspect their existence is to entertain a uniquely deep anxiety, a profound sense of the world's malaise.

I was afraid, but I was also proud. I smiled.

'You love me,' I said to him. I was no more sure of that, really, than most people are about the protestations of their living lovers, but I felt fully entitled to say it, to make my claim.

'I killed her, Anne,' he said, evidently under some pressure of urgency. 'I killed that child. *I couldn't help myself!*'

He killed her, but he couldn't help himself. That's what they all say, of course. The rapist with the knife and the filthy gloves might well have said the same thing. How can we ever tell which ones, if any, are telling the truth, and which ones are simply cynical, or desperate?

'You have to understand,' he said, in a voice which was still as thin as the susurrus which always surrounds us when there are others sharing the same space as ourselves: the ever-present susurrus which screens out the beating of our own hearts and the babbling of the blood in our veins. '*I want you to understand.*'

'I do understand,' I told him. I thought I did. I knew that it must have been the hunger. I hadn't been there to help him. I should have explained, even though I knew that he wouldn't believe me at first. I should have been there to guide him, to help him to be a loving vampire, to teach him to drink with care and consideration and maybe even love. How could he help but become a slave to his exotic passion, when he didn't *know*?

'It was the virus,' he told me. 'I think I understand what happened now. It was weirder than even I could imagine, at first, but I think I understand. My immune system didn't form any antibodies. The virus became integrated into my own DNA. It didn't act like a virus at all; it just took up residence, probably in the brain tissue. It's like a jigsaw; you have to have the slot which fits the projection, the curve which matches the curve, but if you have, you can just incorporate the viral DNA. It replicates, but it replicates under control. It doesn't destroy the cells. Teresa's probably just a carrier ... maybe Viners too. You have to tell Viners, Anne. You have to make him understand. But above all else, you have to protect yourself. I don't know whether it can incorporate in you, or what it will do to you if it can, but you have it too.'

'Never mind all that,' I said, as gently as I could. 'Tell me about Maldureve.'

'He's a product of the virus, Anne. He's the way my mind conceptualized the virus ... symbolized it. You can't sense a virus directly. You can't see or feel it, but you can translate its presence, its action, into images. That's what delirium is ... maybe that's what all dreams are. It's all part of the underlying chemistry of consciousness. You have to tell Viners what's happening. You have to make him understand. The virus he and Teresa are carrying is dangerous. It needed a lock to fit its key, but when it found one, it began to create monsters. I don't know what the odds were against the viral DNA finding the appropriate matrix, but once the key was in the lock, the whole thing became a different ballgame. For the love of God, Anne, you have to explain to him what happened. It made me kill the little girl. It made me kill myself. He's got to destroy it, wipe it out. First, you've got to make him understand. He's got to know what's happening here. I thought it would be enough to give him the blood, but he only looked for the antibodies. He thinks we're both clear, but we're not. Anne, we have to fight it. We have to make Viners understand.'

'I know you're dead,' I whispered lovingly, 'but we can still be together. It doesn't matter about the little girl – I understand, I really do. I know you didn't mean to do it. I've been with the owls, Gil. I can take care of Maldureve. You can help me. You can help me destroy him, and then the owls will begin to teach you wisdom. They'll teach you everything they taught me, and more. Don't be afraid, Gil. Don't be afraid of anything – not even of being dead. We can still be together. We can still love one another.'

'Anne,' he said, plaintively, 'you don't understand . . .'

'I *do* understand,' I insisted. 'I'm the one who does understand, because I'm the one who's been with the owls. I didn't understand before, when I helped Maldureve come out of the borderlands, but I understand now. First, I have to destroy Maldureve, if I can. Then it'll be just you and me. Just you and me, Gil, for ever and ever. You won't have to live in the shadows for ever, Gil. The owls can teach you how to live in the light. Don't be afraid, Gil. You don't ever have to be afraid again.'

'It's in the lab book,' he said, anxiously. 'There's a lot of other stuff in there with it, but the truth's there, if only he'll look at it with an open mind. You have to persuade him to take it seriously, Anne. You can do it, if you try. I'll help you. I'll tell you what to say, how to hook him. You can do it, if you go about it in the right way. You need his help, Anne. You really do.'

'Don't be afraid, Gil,' I told him. 'I've been with the owls. They can do anything. They can help you. I'll do what I can to bring you out of the borderlands. I did it with Maldureve, and I can do it with you. It's not the end, Gil. It's not even the beginning of the end. It's just the beginning.'

The shadows stirred in agitation. They moved behind and around and within him, reaching out to claim him again. He was fading into them, but I didn't try to hold on to him. I knew well enough that these things take time. I knew that this was just the first phase. I knew that I could give him substance and solidity. One day soon, he'd be able to make love to me again, and it would be better than before.

It would be *far* better than before.

'Anne,' he said, desperately, 'you're not listening to me . . .'

'I'm listening,' I crooned, as gently as if he were a babe in arms. 'I'm listening. I understand. Don't be afraid. Don't be afraid . . .'

I kept repeating it, like a mantra, while he dissolved into the tumultuous darkness, losing his all too fragile grasp on presence. He was just a phantom; there was no matter in him at all. I felt a slight prick of sorrow when he disappeared, but I knew that it didn't matter. I knew that I'd see him again. I knew that I could help him come out of the shadows again and again and again, just as I had once helped Maldureve. This time, it would be the right thing to do. This time, it would all work out for the best.

This time, I was in control.

6

In the end, the doctors had to let me discharge myself, because they needed the bed and they couldn't find anything sufficiently wrong with me to justify keeping me in. It felt wonderful to be out of hospital again: to be free; to be myself. It had been hot in the ward – far too hot – and the slow, cold December wind bit deliciously into my flesh, and made me feel more alive than I'd ever felt before.

There were two reporters waiting outside when the three of us left, but Mum went to talk to them. She told them what

I thought and felt with a calm authority and total conviction born of years of practice. She was unexpectedly good at seeming friendly and open but actually saying next to nothing – another skill, I supposed, cultivated over the long, laborious years and made into a habit.

Mum and Sharon came back with me to Brennan Hall to help me 'settle in', but there really wasn't much settling to be done and the actual effect of their presence was all in the other direction. I'd worked hard and long at the task of persuading them that I'd be all right, and that I had to restore my routines before running for the cover of my old home; they were both ready to accept it. It helped that they were homesick themselves. They didn't have any other routines.

Later, I went to the station with them. I had dutifully made all the ritual promises. Yes, Mum, I'll phone every night; yes, Mum, I'll be careful; yes, Mum, I'll make sure I get plenty to eat; yes, Mum, I'll wrap up warm; no, Sharon, I won't let the bastards grind me down. While we waited for the train to come in Mum kept looking around at all the people on the platform, as if she were searching for a pair of dirty woollen gloves. She couldn't quite get it out of her mind that the man who had attacked me was still loose. It didn't matter how improbable it was that he'd start following me around, waiting for a chance to finish what he'd started; she couldn't shake the fear.

'I wish you'd come home with us,' she said, one more time. She said it forlornly, almost as if she were the child/victim and I the parent/reassurer.

'I have to carry on with my life,' I told her. 'If I don't do that, I will have been raped, in a way.' It was a terrible cliché, but I meant it. If I'd gone scurrying home, I would have been violated. The man with the gloves had cut me, but I couldn't let him sever the thread of my ambition, the emerging skein of my destiny.

'It's a terrible world,' she said, with a sigh. 'Sometimes, I think I was wrong to bring children into it.'

'It's okay, Mum,' I said. 'Everything's going to be okay. I'll see you in ten days' time. I'll be home for Christmas. We'll all be together then.'

What present would she buy me, I wondered? What do you give a girl who's grown up in the space of a single autumn, changed into something you hardly recognize? She didn't ask me what I wanted. She never did. Sharon always told everybody what *she* wanted, and everybody knew that there'd be hell to pay if she didn't get it, but I never had. Even if someone did ask, I always said that I didn't mind, that I liked surprises. I didn't really like surprises, because they were never as pleasant as I hoped they might be, but I always said it anyway, innocently gambling on the possibility that some day . . .

This year, like Scrooge, I'd probably be visited by ghosts. One ghost, at least.

I waited on the platform while the train pulled out, so that I could wave to them until they were lost to sight. It was expected of me. Afterwards, I walked back to the bus stop. The world seemed to be in unusually sharp focus. The December sunlight was pale but bright. I felt fine. I was still full of energy and the excitement of simply being alive. The owls had done that for me. They'd taught me how to feel the fundamental excitement of being. I felt hungry, but not for blood. I felt hungry, and I was glad to be hungry, although I'd never been a hungry person before.

I got back to Hall just in time for lunch. When I walked into the dining room everyone looked up. There was one of those strange momentary silences when all conversations are briefly suspended. People I knew by sight and people I hardly knew at all looked at me, and asked me how I was.

I felt uncomfortable, not because I'd become a celebrity but because I'd become a celebrity for such a bad reason. There's something slightly off-colour about becoming famous because you've been attacked, because you've had your throat half cut. I'd walked into that dining room more than a hundred times without attracting more than the slightest flicker of recognition, and had almost always been allowed to take my tray to an empty table, or to the furthest corner of a partly occupied table, so that I could eat alone. This time, people came to join me, to crowd around me. They were people I knew – mostly girls from my corridor – who naturally felt entitled to reckon themselves my acquaintances. Their motives were impeccable. They really were concerned for me, and they really wanted to gather round and pledge their moral support, because they knew that it might have been any of them.

They wanted to be my friends, now – and they wanted to pool their horror over what had happened to Cynthia's daughter, to close ranks in the face of something monstrous and ugly. No one mentioned Gil. Perhaps they thought that their lamentations should be kept within reasonable bounds. Perhaps they thought that one and a half cut throats equalled a tragedy, but that throwing in a suicide as well would make me out to be a real bird of ill omen, deadly dangerous to know.

'If you need anything,' said Karen, the girl who lived next door to me, 'I'm only next door. Come round any time.'

'Thanks,' I said.

After lunch, I walked the familiar path to Wombwell House.

The new fence was absolutely hideous. It was made out of some kind of powder-grey metal alloy, each strut folded sideways to a near-right angle and curled over at the top like the frond of a fern. It was, as Sharon had said, exactly the kind of fence that local councils or British Rail set around dangerous installations, to keep trespassers at bay, lest vandals should wreak havoc or little children electrocute themselves. I hated it. It didn't make me feel any safer; it just made the little wood seem desolate and forlorn.

Dr Gray was in his office, reading a book. He seemed as world-weary as ever, but distinctly ill at ease. In all his years at the university he'd probably never had a tutee who'd been attacked, and he'd certainly never had a tutee whose daughter had been murdered. He must have felt that the flow of everyday circumstance had abruptly turned against him, malevolently determined to disturb his languid boredom and subvert his fanciful play with abstract ideas.

'I want to catch up as soon as possible,' I told him. 'I want to make up all the work I've missed. I might stay on after the end of term to do the essays – I can't do them at home during the vac because I don't have access to a proper library. It'd just be for a few days. I don't want to leave it until next term because I'd always be one step behind, always struggling. I like philosophy, but I don't find it easy. I'm not very good at it, as yet.'

'You're better than most,' he assured me, with a sigh which signified that the remark was a condemnation of the rest rather than a compliment to me. 'I could lend you some books, if you like. It seems a pity to stay behind, when everyone else has gone.'

'I'm not afraid,' I said, baldly. 'I'm going to be here for three years. I have to get used to walking around the campus without being petrified with fear by the thought that someone might grab me from behind. Even when it's dark. Even when it's deserted.'

'They should have done something about that wood a long time ago,' he said.

'It's a very ugly fence,' I said flippantly.

'I talked to your parents,' he said. 'I told them you were doing well – that you were genuinely interested.'

'Mum told me.'

'I'm sorry all this had to happen. What happened to you would be quite bad enough in isolation. To have something worse happen to Cynthia's daughter, and then to have that young man kill himself so . . . well, it takes things far beyond the ordinary limits of misfortune. In a way, I might feel more reassured if you seemed to be more frightened. It's paradoxical, I know, but the better you seem to be taking it, the more people will worry about the possibility of a delayed reaction. It's pointless to keep asking you whether you're sure you're all right, but people will. Even me.'

'It's all over,' I told him, although it was a plain, straightforward lie. I couldn't resist adding, for a joke: 'They say these things always come in threes, don't they? Nothing else can possibly happen now.'

He knew it was a joke, but he didn't smile. 'I'll do what I can to help,' he said. 'I'm always here anyway, so it wouldn't be any trouble to do a couple of extra tutorials. I feel more at home here than I do at home, and you know how much I like the sound of my own voice.'

'Do you live on your own?' I asked, because I was interested.

'Yes,' he said, and added, almost absent-mindedly: 'I was married once.' He didn't go on to say 'but it didn't work out', the way a lot of people would have done. He disapproved of meaningless formulas like that, and avoided them when he could.

'What's Monday's topic?' I asked him. 'I'll try to get an essay done over the weekend.'

'The emotions,' he said. 'There's a reading list on the handout you got at the beginning of term.' Still in his faintly confidential mood, he added, with another sigh: 'I'm not looking forward to it.'

For a moment, I thought that there was something about the topic that he found depressing, but then I realized that he meant something else.

'Will Cynthia be there?' I asked, already having guessed that she would be.

He nodded. 'She phoned in,' he said. 'She's as determined as you are to get on with things. I know that it's the fashionable view these days – if you fall off your horse, get straight back on again, otherwise you'll be a pedestrian for life – but sometimes I wonder whether it's asking a bit too much. It's perfectly all right to take time to recover. Will you be seeing her, do you think?'

'I thought I'd go round this afternoon,' I told him. 'I thought I ought to.'

'Tell her that she doesn't have to come in, if she finds when the time comes that it's too difficult. Tell her that she can have all the time she needs. Tell her that.'

He was trying his hardest to persuade me that it was only concern for Cynthia's welfare that moved him, but I knew there was a little bit of cowardice in there. He was frightened of having to face her, of having to face us both. The thought of having to talk to us clinically and sceptically about emotions was intimidating him, in a macabre sort of way. He was scared that there might be too much emotion pouring out over his eccentrically carpeted office floor.

'I'll tell her,' I assured him before I left.

As things turned out, though, I didn't tell her. I didn't say a word about the impending tutorial. The opening simply never arrived, and there were far more important things for her to worry about than Dr Gray's anxieties.

Cynthia lived in a tower block – one of the ones they always put on the front page of the *Guardian*'s 'Society' supplement to symbolize urban decay and deprivation. There was the usual graffiti in the lift and the corridors, and the usual gangs of children hanging around looking as if they were plotting to go out and mug somebody in order to buy their daily ration of glue. It was all illusion, really – just the way I'd been taught to decode the images.

Cynthia seemed both pathetically pleased and desperately alarmed to see me. 'The place is a god-awful mess,' she told me. 'I'm such a slut, sometimes. I just haven't . . .' She didn't bother to enumerate the things she hadn't, or the reasons why.

The social preliminaries were as awkward as I'd expected, but I got her through them. She made us a pot of tea before getting down to the serious business of self-criticism.

'I meant to come to see you in the hospital,' she said. 'I really did. I just couldn't face it. It was so terrible, what happened to you, but I just couldn't think about it after . . . it was my fault, you know. I should never have left her alone like that. It wasn't the secretary's job to look after her . . . but I hadn't the slightest notion that it could happen again, so soon, in broad daylight. Lightning isn't supposed to strike twice like that, not in the same place . . . but it does, of course. That's why there are lightning conductors. They wanted me to go on TV, you know, to make an appeal. They say it helps to encourage informers to come forward. I did it . . . of course I did it. How could I not do it? I was awful. I knew what people would think. Single mother – single *lesbian* mother – letting the child run loose in a place where somebody had been attacked and nearly killed less than a week before. God . . . and then your boyfriend doing that, so that the police began to think it was *him* who'd done it all . . . the questions, the reporters, the suspicions . . . I always wondered, you know, almost in a fascinated way, how mothers felt when something like this happened. You can't help it, when you've got a kid of your own. You always see them on the TV, don't you? And you can't help but wonder, what if it were me? What would I feel? You try to imagine feeling as terrible as it's possible to feel, but you know you can't really imagine it, because you know that if it really were you, feeling it for real, it would be far more terrifying than anything you can imagine.

'Actually, the most terrible thing of all is that when it is you, you *don't* feel like that, because you don't know *how* to feel like that, because you haven't ever been able to imagine feeling like that, and you just feel so horribly numb and empty, as if you're not able to feel anything at all . . . and you think you're going crazy. You *know* you're going crazy, because otherwise you'd feel something different, something worse, something with all the right kinds of pain in it ... but you can't and you don't, because you don't know how, and you wish it was you, you wish it was you that was lying in the hospital or the mortuary, you that had your throat cut, because then at least you'd know what to feel ... not because it would make Janine be alive again, but simply because it would let you – off the hook. This isn't making any sense, is it?'

She was weeping, but not sobbing.

What could I say? How could I say 'I know how you feel' when that would be an absurd contradiction of everything she'd just said? How could I say 'It's all right' when it patently wasn't? How could I say 'It isn't your fault, it's mine', even though that was the truth of it? I brought Maldureve out of the borderlands; I willingly became a vampire; I made Gil into a vampire too, and didn't tell him what his hunger was. How could I say 'I am the Frankenstein who made the monster which murdered your child in the throes of its terrible confusion. I did it. It's my fault'? I couldn't say it; she'd have thought I was mad, madder even than she.

Nor could I say 'Don't despair, it's not the end'. I couldn't tell her that it was possible to live after death, and that the dead could sometimes come back, into and through the borderlands, and that I had the power to help them through.

I couldn't say any of it, even though it was all true.

'I didn't love her enough,' said Cynthia, wiping away a few of the tears without stemming their flood. 'I didn't care enough. I wanted to do things for myself. I didn't want her to get in my way. I'm not sorry enough now that she's dead. I don't feel enough. I'm dead inside.'

'That's not true,' I said, finding my voice at last. 'None of this is your fault. You did everything you could. You're doing everything you can. You're not to blame.'

That was what I'd come to say. That was what she'd let me in to say. For the moment, the function of her friends and neighbours and everyone else in the world was simply to assure her over and over again that it wasn't her fault, that she shouldn't blame herself. It was the only way that the world could be made bearable for her.

I owed her that much, at least.

I let her put her arms around me and literally cry on my

shoulder. I held her fleshy body in my skinny arms and hugged her like a mother, as guilt and sentiment obliged me to do. And in the end, she allowed herself to be soothed, to be convinced – as she had secretly been all along – that it really wasn't her fault, and that everybody realized the fact, and that it was okay to go on living, breathing and maybe even hoping.

7

It had grown dark by the time I got back to the campus, but the science buildings were all ablaze with light, as they invariably were. The corridors weren't very crowded, because the staff and students were already trickling off home, but the double-doored lab where Gil had been doing his experiments was still lit up. Through the observation window I could see Professor Viners' research assistant, Teresa, washing apparatus at the sink. Her dark hair looked untidy, and she seemed more than a little impatient to be gone. She looked up briefly and saw me, but she wouldn't meet my eyes, or give any sign of recognition. She just turned back to her work. I could see my own reflection in the glass; it was as though I were standing inside the room looking back at myself. I seemed uncommonly relaxed, almost as though I belonged there.

I went to the door of Profesor Viners' office, and knocked.

He seemed pleased enough to see me – rather less uncomfortable, in fact, than Dr Gray had been. He got up when I came in, and gestured politely to the armchair on the near side of his cluttered desk.

'Thank you for coming to see me, Miss Charet,' he said. 'It's very good of you to spare the time.'

He waited until I'd sat down before resuming his own seat. 'How are you now?' he asked, but didn't wait for an answer. 'I know some of the people at the hospital quite well, including Maurice Hodgson; he told me you'd been released. He probably told you that he did some extra blood tests because I asked him to, and that there's nothing at all to worry about. I thought I'd better reassure you of that myself. I don't know what Gil told you, that day you were attacked, but I know that he thought, even then, that he'd been infected by something he picked up in the lab, and I assume he'd already told you a good deal about the kind of work he was doing here. I just wanted to make sure that you understood that there's no possibility at all that you've been infected by any of the viruses I've been working on. Have the reporters been on to you yet?'

I shook my head. 'There were a couple at the hospital, but I didn't talk to them.' I said. 'I don't think they'll bother with me any more.'

'I'd like to think that were true, but it isn't,' the professor assured me, dolefully. 'They'll be around for some time yet. I don't want to instruct you in what to say or what not to say when they do start asking awkward questions, but I do want to explain the situation here. My work is under threat, you see, and I want to make sure that you know what's at stake.'

'I understand,' I said. Not unnaturally, he couldn't be content with that.

'Gil came to see me the day he killed himself,' he said, awkwardly. 'He was very distressed – though I didn't, of course, realize quite how distressed – and he told me that he was worried about you. He was worried about the fact that you hadn't regained consciousness after the blood transfusion. I took some blood from him to test it for antibodies to the experimental viruses. We can do that, you see – if anyone does beome infected by any of our viruses, we can find out. Each antibody is quite specific; it always migrates to a particular spot on the relevant chromatogram. Do you know what I'm talking about? Never mind, if not. Just take it from me that if Gil had been exposed to any of the experimental viruses, the blood test would have shown it up. His blood was perfectly normal, Anne – just like yours. It was all in his mind.'

I remembered what Gil's ghost had told me in the hospital. He'd accused me of not listening, but I had been listening, and even though I didn't understand completely, I knew vaguely what he'd been trying to say.

'Your tests only showed that we hadn't produced antibodies,'

I said, to prove to him that I was no fool, that he couldn't just overwhelm me with the authority of his expertise. 'Isn't it possible that Gil's immune system simply didn't react? He said something to me once about the possibility of viruses not being recognized as invaders by the body – about their becoming integrated with the host DNA. Isn't there some theory which suggests that spontaneous integration of new DNA is an important aspect of the process of evolution?'

I watched a frown settle slowly upon Professor Viners' brow. It was a frown of uncertainty as well as anxiety. He had been hoping that it would all be easier than this.

'It's an unorthodox theory,' he said, blandly.

'Gil was always bragging about the unorthodoxy of his theories. He told me that some of your own ideas were considered way out.'

The professor took up a black notebook from the pile of debris beside his PC. 'I've been reading Gil's lab notes,' he said. 'He jotted down some fanciful hypotheses in the margins. I can't decipher them all, but one or two of them are more than a little wild. If the press got hold of it, or if someone else were to give them an account of Gil's ideas – even an ungarbled one – we could easily be made to look like a couple of mad scientists. Yes, you're right – even I'm considered way out by some of my colleagues. That makes it hard to get funding for my research. The dean of the faculty is always reminding me how publicity-conscious the university has to be nowadays, and how we might have to alter our research priorities and become "more practical", in order to attract money from industry. He'd far rather I were testing newly fashionable drugs on old-fashioned rats for the ever-fashionable drug companies. If Gil was infected by one of our viruses without forming antibodies, Miss Charet, it was a chance in a million. And no matter how badly it affected him, he shouldn't have done what he did. All he had to do was go into the hospital. That's what I told him to do, when I saw how worried he was. The police tried to pin the murder of that little girl on him – I suppose they were very disappointed when you told them that he wasn't the person who attacked you. I can't believe that he did something like that, no matter how deranged he might have been, for whatever cause. Can you?'

'No,' I lied. He relaxed a little when I said that.

'I won't try to pretend to you that my work is absolutely vital to the future of humankind,' he said, spreading his hands in an awkwardly pleading gesture. 'I can't even tell you what it is we'll eventually have discovered, if anything, when the series of experiments I've planned is complete. I know that they tell you over in the philosophy department that the purpose of experiments is to subject concisely framed hypotheses to rigorous tests, but that's too neat and too narrow. A lot of experiments are just exploratory, to see what might turn up.

'What I'm trying to do is explore the links between DNA, brain chemistry and certain psychological phenomena, like dreams and delusions. We can study the dreams of animals, you know – there's a body at the base of the brain called the pons, and if you remove it surgically you take away the off switch which normally prevents signals being relayed to the motor nerves during dreaming. Cats and rats and rabbits can be forced to act out their dreams. We can only watch what they do, of course; we have no idea what they *see*, but it's something – a baseline to work from. So we can observe, in a vague sort of way, how the dreams of our experimental animals are affected when they're infected by the viruses – if they're affected at all. We get a lot of negative results, because viruses which affect humans often don't affect animals at all, or affect them in a different way. We also do a lot of tissue-culture experiments, which allow us to study the fine biochemistry of infection.

'I've infected myself with some of the experimental viruses, at various times – I'll admit that to you, as I admitted it to Gil. They're *not dangerous*, Miss Charet. They all come from the general population to begin with; they're all ordinary products of nature. We don't do any genetic engineering here, and if we're secretive about what we actually do it's mostly because we don't want to attract the attention of those idiots who think that people who experiment on animals ought to be firebombed into seeing the light. It's true that viruses don't affect everybody the same way, and that certain particular individuals may react very badly to a virus which other people never even notice. If that's what happened to Gil, I'm very sorry – but if that *is* what happened, it may not have been one of my viruses at all. It could be any old virus that he happened upon for the first time, far from home in cold-ridden England. He could have caught it from anyone, Miss Charet – even you. Even so, I'd still have to ask you to be very careful what you say to the press. The *Sun* or the *Star* could close me down with one casual scare-story, and I don't want that to happen. Do you?'

'No,' I said, truthfully. I knew that what had happened to Gil was my fault, not Professor Viners'. I didn't want to blight his career.

'Thank you,' he said, warily. He didn't think he was out of the wood yet.

'Tell me about Gil's wild ideas,' I said, because I was genuinely curious. 'He used to tease me a bit, boasting about how way out they were, without ever spelling them out.'

He looked dubious. He was scared that I didn't mean what I said – that I might repeat anything he told me to other people, including the creepy-crawlies of the gutter press.

'This idea that our dreams might be caused by stray DNA, for instance,' I said. 'That's very intriguing, isn't it? I mean, I know that we have bacteria inside us all the time, and all kinds of other tiny parasites. One of the teachers at school once told my class that if everything in the world were invisible except for nematode worms, you could still see all the trees and buildings and people as faint white clouds of nematode parasites. I know that our blood and our brains are full of microscopic passengers, which mostly don't do any harm and sometimes do us some good, helping us to digest our food and the like, but nobody ever said at school that those invisible passengers might affect our *minds*. I suppose it's obvious, when you think about the way that flu or meningitis can make you delirious, but Gil thought it might go far beyond dreams, didn't he? Even you think psychotropic DNA might be involved in certain kinds of mental abnormality, don't you? Gil told me that.'

'It's a natural line of speculation to follow,' Professor Viners admitted. 'It's very difficult to figure out how certain disruptions of brain chemistry can be translated into highly specific delusions or patterns of behaviour. For the most part, I think, we manufacture our own dreams and our own delusions – and in spite of the sterling efforts of Dr Freud I think much of what occurs to us in our dreams is mere random noise. But there *are* patterns in dreams and delusions; there are even patterns in delirium. Of course I'm interested in the biochemical bases of abnormal psychology and of so-called religious experiences. It's only natural that I should be. The links between brain chemistry and particular mental events may be tortuous and tenuous, but they do exist. Our DNA does influence, in some way, the capacity we have for experience.'

'What about people who see ghosts? What about people who believe in vampires and werewolves? Do our genes affect those kinds of things?'

'It's easy to involve those kinds of things in the argument,' the professor hedged. 'But it's all just science fiction at present. We have to do the experiments, you see. We have to start from the bottom, with the things we can observe. I can't get seriously involved with speculations like these until I've done much more elaborate groundwork. I think Gil was a little overoptimistic about what our lab work might ultimately achieve – but in a way, it's good to be able to see the further horizons, to be able to take inspiration from the big ideas.'

'You haven't told me yet,' I pointed out, 'exactly what Gil's big and wild ideas were.'

'I only have his jottings to go on,' he said. 'But if I'm taking the right inference from them, he seems to have been wondering whether our minds are entirely – how shall I put it? – our *own*. He seems to have toyed with the idea that consciousness itself might be a collaborative endeavour, in which the part played by the DNA of our own genes interacts with the DNA of what you call our "passengers". As you may know, lots of the DNA in the nuclei of our cells doesn't appear to be active in making proteins. Most people think it's just redundant junk which gets copied along with the functional genes, but some – Gil included, I suppose – take pleasure in trying to figure out roles it might play. Some people think that viruses can become integrated into the chromosomes by inserting themselves in the non-functional DNA. That way, their selfish genes attain the end of reproduction without destroying the cells of their host. Gil wondered whether some of that apparently spare DNA might be involved in fundamental

mental phenomena. Not just dreams and delusions, but the basic properties of mind: thought, emotion, even self-consciousness. It's all pure speculation – not a shred of evidence in sight. Just game-playing.'

'You mean,' I said, trying to prove that I was on the ball, 'that consciousness – or some of its attributes – might be a kind of universal disease?'

'Not exactly a disease,' he corrected me. 'Gil wasn't quite that cynical – I think he'd have regarded any fundamental contribution made to human consciousness by non-human DNA as a matter of symbiosis rather than disease, although the notion of mental illness would then come to be seen in a different light. And if, as you suggest, Gil was sufficiently entranced by Hoyle and Wickramasinghe's ideas about evolution occurring by means of the continual co-option into existing genomes of DNA falling from the sky, he would presumably have envisaged that symbiosis is a preliminary stage in the process of absorption and incorporation. It's an idea for philosophers to kick around rather than serious-minded biochemists – perhaps you can have some fun with it in your department.'

He'd changed tack while he was speaking. He was challenging me now, deliberately becoming more abstruse in the hope that I wouldn't be able to follow the argument but would be too proud to ask for further clarification. And he was teasing me too, being condescending towards philosophers and their supposed unworldliness, as practical scientists so often are. But I'd learned enough from Gil to be familiar with most of the words, and I thought I saw what he was getting at.

No wonder Gil still thought, even after finding himself alive after death as a phantom inhabitant of the borderlands, that it was all down to some virus.

I could see too that if Gil were right about the virus, then what Professor Viners had said earlier might be true. Gil hadn't picked it up in the lab at all: he'd picked it up from me. I was the carrier, the centre of infection. I was the one whose consciousness had first been supplemented and gradually transformed. I was the one who might start an epidemic. Not Viners, his lab or his assistant: only me.

'It's all very interesting,' I told Professor Viners. 'I wish I understood it better. But I see what you mean, now, about the possibility that the press might get hold of the wrong end of the stick. It wouldn't be too difficult to make a real horror story out of it all. And scare-stories sell papers, don't they?'

'But you're an intelligent girl,' he told me. If all else fails, try flattery. It'll get you almost anywhere. 'You know what damage silly scare-stories can do. You're a philosopher – you know what follies sloppy argument can lead to.'

'You have to make Viners understand,' Gil had said. 'You have to persuade him to take it seriously.' But it wasn't that easy. Even if I had wanted to, I didn't have the power to make Professor Viners see what he was determined not to see. Even if I had told him everything – about me, about Maldureve, about what had become of Gil – it wouldn't have had the desired effect. If I convinced him that I really had been infected by something nasty, I'd also convince him that I was deranged. He wouldn't be able to take what I said seriously. Anyway, I didn't want to tell him, because I thought I understood what was happening better than any of them. I had been with the owls, and had begun to learn wisdom.

'I'll be very careful,' I promised. 'I won't speak out of turn to anyone, least of all the press.'

'Thank you,' said Professor Viners. He wasn't about to heave any tremendous sighs of relief just yet, but I could tell that he liked me and thought that he could trust me.

It had been an interesting meeting. I felt that I'd learned something. But I knew that Gil's theories didn't really matter. They didn't really change anything, even if they were true. It didn't matter whether or not the owls were really images born of stray DNA, because I already knew that thinking of them as 'owls' was just a matter of convenience. It was just a fudge-word. What mattered was not what they were but what they could do, what *difference* they could make to me and to the world. It didn't matter if everything was just a kind of delusion or disease; what mattered was finding a good way of life, a good way of being, a good way of operating in the real world. If it really was a virus that had provided the key to liberate my locked-up soul, the last thing I wanted was to be cured. I was more than willing to welcome it, to let it be part of me. I'd made some bad mistakes, but now I was better placed, better prepared and better able to do what had to be done.

I was the one who understood. I was the *only* one who understood. It was up to me to determine what needed to be done.

8

I walked back to Brennan Hall along the usual path. It wasn't late, and the path was by no means deserted. I didn't bother to fall into step with some other group, or dog their footsteps. I walked by myself, at my own pace.

I wasn't unafraid, even when I started out from the haven of light which the cluster of science buildings created. As I walked towards the gathering shadows, my heart began to beat a little faster, and when I came to the bridge it was pounding. The bridge itself was still dark, but the area beyond it had changed out of all recognition. The new lights which had been installed on top of the old Victorian lamp-posts blazed so fiercely that every inch of the path was clearly visible: every rut and ridge, every loose stone, every tiny lake of dust. It was like a model of the lunar landscape, drawn out into a great ribbon.

The ragged grass which grew on its left-hand side didn't reflect the light nearly as brightly as the path, but there was light enough to show it for exactly what it was: a patch of waste ground, its vegetation already withered and wasted in anticipation of the winter snows to come. But even the path didn't reflect the harsh and brutal light as brightly as the fence which had been erected to enclose the Marquis of Membury's Garden. In daylight, the fence had been a very dull grey, and its patina of oxides had seemed a mere sprinkling of quintessentially uninteresting powder. Now, the fence stood out starkly and defiantly from its background, proudly radiant with borrowed fire. The tiny particles of oxide shone like white ash in the heart of a log fire, incandescent with their delight in the forces of entropy and decay whose vanguard they were.

Once, the trees at the edge of the stand had been filled with uncertain shadows by the coloured sodium lights, every branch and leaf ambitious to trail a deceptive net of darkness as it swayed in the wind. Now, they were condemned to the ebony uniformity of Stygian gloom, confined as though to a punishment cell by the sleek, stiff spears which stood to attention before them.

I stopped beside the fence to peer through its interstices, into the abyss beyond. I imagined that Maldureve was there, as completely concealed from my eyes as he was from all others, hiding from me as he hid from the world. I didn't think of him as being trapped – I knew that no *cordon sanitaire* could contain him, and that no phalanx of curved swords could repel him – but I did imagine him enclosed and concealed. The shadows were his sanctuary now.

I stared into the caged darkness, trying to see him, although I knew full well that I wouldn't be able to. The whited bars were too powerful. I strained my ears to hear him, but there was only the continual rustling of tiny creatures in the undergrowth: furtive mice and huge black beetles, going about their business under cover of the night, or hurrying to their refuges before the cold clamped down upon them.

'Anne! Are you all right?'

The question made me start with alarm.

It was Karen, on her way back to the hall with two of her friends. The friends were both boys.

'Yes,' I said. 'Yes, of course.'

'You shouldn't be out here on your own,' she told me. 'I know it's early, but after what happened . . .'

'I'm all right,' I said. 'Nothing can happen now.'

'Don't you believe it,' said one of Karen's friends. 'You can't solve a problem like this with cages. You can keep the freaks out of the trees, but you can't keep them out of the world.'

'You should make sure you're *with* somebody,' Karen said. 'If you hadn't . . .'

She trailed off again, but this time it was diplomacy and not the desire to make the most of the dark implications of the unsaid. *If I hadn't been so fond of going out by myself at the dead of night . . .*

She knew that I had gone out, more than once, before the night I was attacked. She'd told the police about it. She couldn't know that I had gone to meet Maldureve, but she knew there had been something strange going on. She didn't dare say out loud that I had virtually gone out looking to be attacked, but in her private thoughts she must have wondered why it seemed that I had.

When the three of them resumed walking, obviously expecting me to walk with them, I obediently fell into step. But I didn't say anything more, and they accepted my compliance as a sufficient indication of my safety and my sanity. The four of us were still together when we reached the corridor where Karen and I lived, and when I saw the two people waiting by my door I became glad, at last, of the others' companionship and protectiveness.

'Miss Charet,' said one of the waiting men. 'Could we possibly have a word?' The words were polite, but they were hurried, rehearsed and overeager.

'No,' I said immediately, as fiercely as I could. 'No, you can't.'

The reporter looked genuinely surprised, as though he couldn't see why anyone who wasn't a corrupt politician, a crooked businessman or a naughty vicar would refuse to talk to him. 'We only –' he began.

'I don't want to talk to you,' I told him, flatly. 'I've nothing to tell you.' I shrank back, bumping into the boy who was behind me. He wasn't very big – certainly not a prop forward or a weight-lifter – but he knew when his moment had arrived. He knew that there was glory without risk in a golden opportunity to tell the gentlemen of the press to go fuck themselves.

'Please, Miss Charet,' said the second reporter, his tone hovering between plaintiveness and wheedling. 'We don't mean you any harm.'

'She said no,' said the boy, moving to stand shoulder to shoulder with me.

'We understand –' the first reporter began.

I didn't want to be told how understanding he was. 'You shouldn't be here,' I told him. 'You're trespassing. I want to go into my room. I don't want you here. I want you to go away and leave me alone.'

The first reporter's eyes flickered back and forth as he sized up the situation. If I had been on my own, outnumbered, I'm certain that they would have continued to pressure me, manoeuvring to cut me off and corner me, subtly trapping me so that they could blackmail me into saying something as the price of my release. But four was a crowd, and a hostile crowd at that. They didn't want a shouting match.

'Tomorrow,' said the second reporter quickly. 'An appointment. Anywhere you like. Please.'

'No,' I said. 'Nothing to say. Not now. Not ever. I want you to go away and leave me alone.' I wondered if it would help if I became hysterical or tearful.

'You bastards,' said the boy who had cast himself as my white knight. 'She's only just come out of hospital, for fuck's sake. Can't you see she's frightened? Why can't you miserable fuckers just *leave people alone?*'

The first reporter opened his mouth, probably to say that he was only doing his job, but the other put a hand on his arm. 'We're sorry,' he said. 'We didn't mean to scare you. When you're feeling better – ring us.' He extended a card towards me. I thought that the boy was going to take it and rip it up, but when we both reached out the reporter deftly delivered it into my hand rather than my protector's. The two men were already moving away down the corridor, backing off.

'When you're ready, Miss Charet,' the first one called, presumably trying to set things to rights, to demonstrate their essential reasonableness. 'When you're ready – please!'

I didn't look at the card, but I held on to it until they had gone.

'It's okay now,' the boy pointed out, unnecessarily. There was self-satisfaction in his voice, but he wasn't actually crowing. Not yet.

'Thanks,' I said, sincerely. Then I went into my room and closed the door.

I was nervous about going down to dinner, but I was too hungry to skip it. I sat with Karen and the boy and their other friends, and talked about what bastards reporters were, and how they were almost worse than freaks and rapists and lager louts. Afterwards, they all hung around while I phoned home to tell Mum and Dad that everything was okay, that there was no need to worry about anything at all, that everything was under control. I didn't tell Mum that I had a posse standing guard on the phone box, ready to fight to the death for my honour if anyone with a miniature tape recorder happened to come into view. It didn't seem necessary. Karen and the boy walked me back to my room again once I'd done my duty, but that wasn't necessary either. The reporters had gone, for the time being. Karen invited me into her room for coffee and chat, but I told her that I was tired and needed to lie down.

'I couldn't sleep properly on the ward,' I told her, by way of explanation. 'It was too noisy.'

'We'll keep the music down,' she promised. 'No heavy metal.'

It wouldn't have mattered; I had no intention of going directly to sleep. I switched out the light and lay down on the bed, but I didn't bother to close my eyes, even for a moment. I left the curtains half drawn, so that the yellow light creeping up from beneath the sill cast complicated coloured shadows on the white walls and the ceiling tiles. I needed those shadows.

The summoning wasn't easy; I was still relatively unpractised, and I think he had a long way to come, figuratively speaking. Even the combination of our efforts didn't make the matter simple. The path of true love never does run smooth, as Mum was fond of quoting, though it had never been entirely clear to me why it shouldn't. The path of her marriage to Dad had always seemed to run smoothly enough, from where we children stood. But my own paths had been extremely tortuous by comparison, and now that Gil was dead I couldn't honestly expect things to get easier. As complicating factors went, death was no minor hitch.

But he came when I called. From beyond the borderlands he came, brought forth by my eyes and my steadfast heart. He was wearing his stupid flying jacket, the way he always used to. I wondered whether the Californian borderlands were as cold and bleak as those which gave an edge to dreary Britain, or whether the ghosts which might be summoned from their depths would emerge wearing nothing but swimming trunks, with surfboards under their arms.

'Did you tell Viners?' he whispered. His voice was stronger now, and I could see he contours of his face quite clearly. He was all appearance and no substance, but his presence was reasonably well accomplished. I knew that I could give him substance and strength; that wasn't a problem – but could I give him peace of mind?

'He wouldn't understand, Gil,' I told him. 'He's reached his limits and he can't go beyond them . . . not yet. We have to handle this by ourselves. No one will help us. No one on this side, anyhow. They don't have the right mental equipment. Seeing is believing, and they can't see, so they can't believe. Even the ones who say that they believe in ghosts and vampires – their belief isn't of a kind that would be any use to us. I can't tell anybody. Nobody at all. We're on our own Gil: you and me. But we don't need anybody else. We can do what needs to be done.'

'No, Anne,' he said, tiredly. 'You have to make him understand how dangerous the virus is. You have to tell him about yourself. You have to tell him that it wasn't just me. You have to tell him that this thing is active, that the antibodies don't destroy it, that it hangs around, lying dormant, until it finds the lock it can open up. If you told him – if you told him *everything* . . .'

'He'd think I'm mad,' I said, a little less tolerantly. 'It's no good. We're on our own.'

I'd got through to him at last. He shifted awkwardly, putting his hand up to his throat as if to test its wholeness. His eyes, faintly luminescent, were doubtful. I wondered whether ghosts could weep.

While he studied me, I carefully took off my jeans and my socks, and then my blouse. I threw them over the back of the chair any old how, because I didn't want to have to stand up. Then I threw my bra and knickers after them. I settled back down again, wondering how pale my skin might seem to a dweller in the shadows, wondering whether my flesh would seem to possess the texture of marble when he touched me with his spectral hand.

'I love you, Anne,' he whispered, when he had found his voice again. It was what I'd been waiting to hear. I put my arms out to welcome him, and he drifted down into my embrace, as gently as an autumn leaf.

'It's okay,' I told him. 'This is the right way. I'm certain of it. Come inside me. All you have to do is come inside me.'

I wasn't sure, at first, that we could do it. I wasn't sure that there was enough *of* him. After all, I hadn't been able to do anything with Maldureve at first, until he had put on substance, and what I did with Maldureve didn't involve any actual penetration. I was afraid that making love to Gil's ghost might be like trying to catch the wind, and in a way, it was; but it was everything I could have hoped for, everything I could have desired.

He settled over me like a great cloak, unbelievably soft. The pressure of his body on mine was so very light, so nearly insubstantial, that it had a delicacy of effect I'd never thought possible. Always before, when he'd been a thing of crude flesh and blood, it had been uncomfortable and oppressive to have him settle down on me, no matter how carefully he balanced himself. I'd always felt restricted, nervous of being trapped and crushed. It was different now.

Now that his presence was almost without mass it was exciting without being punishing, erotic without being lumpen. There was no longer any hint of excess in his caresses or his kisses.

I'd thought that Maldureve was as much of an improvement on a human lover that I could ever expect to find, but the owls had taught me different. Now I learned that there were other possibilities too, that I'd hardly begun to explore the full spectrum of possibility.

I learned that there's no lover better suited to a frail girl than a male ghost. Penetration can still be achieved, by slow and patient insinuation, and the shaft of darkness easing its way into me felt infinitely smoother and more persuasive than Gil's actual prick, grotesquely bloated by the blood within, had ever felt before.

With Maldureve, that first time, I had felt as if I were on fire, bathed in supernatural heat which I could not help but liken in my innocent, inexperienced mind to Hell's imaginary fires. The pleasure which had swept over me had been tidal, surging through me in languorous waves and then ebbing by suspensefully slow degrees. With Gil's ghost, everything was overturned. The coolness of him was delicious, just cold enough to startle my nipples and the little hairs all over my arms and neck, but not cold enough to chill. The coolness was uplifting, refreshing, not so much beautiful as *sublime*. Nor did the pleasure come in great lazy waves. Instead, it was like a cool, swirling current from the ocean depths which caught me up as though

I were a floating diatom and danced with me, drowning me in sensation.

I came; for the first time, with Gil, I came. I lost myself in the shivering of my nerves, the spasming of my muscles. But he couldn't reciprocate. He had no such resources. There was nothing left in his phantasmal form which was capable of climax. There was only one thing he could do, and even that he could not impose, could not demand. Nor could he have begged such a favour from anyone but me, for only I knew what to do and how to do it. None but I had the power of the gift, let alone the inclination to offer it.

I thrust my naked neck into the shadow-maw of his ghostly face, and made my flesh flow, opening a fissure where even a thing of such slight presence as he might suck and drink.

I gave him blood to drink, knowing that I was binding him to be my familiar spirit, knowing that I was leading him substance, to help him come from the borderlands more expeditiously and more effectively.

I fed him with my own substance, made manna of my own mass, and shared communion with him while I dwelt in ecstasy, floating in the afterthrill of my orgasm.

He bent his dark, wanton head and drank. He took what I offered, gladly and with love. That night, we became one, united for ever.

Isn't that the way it's supposed to be? Isn't that the one and only real happy ending? Isn't that the finest of all possibilities, which even coarse creatures of everyday flesh and blood have glimpsed in their most secret, most sacred dreams?

'This is love,' I told him. 'This is what we are, and will be, always and for ever.'

9

When I got up the next morning, one of the two reporters who'd been lying in ambush the night before was waiting outside my room. It was the younger one, the one who'd given me his card. I know I blushed deep red, because I was still in my dressing gown. I ran into the loo and locked the door, but knowing that he was outside, able to hear me, was horribly embarrassing.

When I unlocked the door again and peeped out, the corridor was empty, but I knew that he hadn't gone. I knew that he had simply taken advantage of the situation to walk into my unlocked room and sit down on my warm and unmade bed. It seemed like a dreadful violation of my privacy, all the more dreadful because there was nothing I could do about it. He wasn't a rapist who could be fought and bitten and kicked; I couldn't yell for help and expect people to come and grab him, handcuff him and throw him in jail. What he was doing was wrong, but the fact that he was a reporter made it understandable, a necessary evil. He didn't care that people thought he was the scum of the earth; he was probably proud of it, in his own perverse fashion.

'Please go away,' I said, holding the door open for him.

'I know it's a nuisance,' he said. 'But don't you think it might be better to get it over with? Why don't I go outside while you have a wash, get dressed, brush your teeth and put your make-up on? Then you can invite me back in when you're good and ready, and I'll sit on the chair and ask my questions quietly, in a perfectly civilized fashion. I'm John Mackenzie, by the way. You can call me John if I can call you Anne.'

He didn't mind that I was still in my dressing gown. It gave him a sort of advantage, a little extra power of intimidation. He wanted to use that advantage to get my assent to his proposition.

'I don't have anything to tell you,' I said.

'That's not good enough,' he said. 'What happened to you is news. What happened to your friend's little girl is news. What happened to your boyfriend is news. Any connections between the three events, however tenuous or hypothetical, are news.'

'Is yours the kind of paper which prints words like "tenuous" and "hypothetical"?' I asked.

He grinned; he didn't mind the sarcasm at all. He was pleased to get a reaction of any kind. He stayed where he was, perched on the edge of my bed, usurping my personal space. It was all a

game to him, and he honestly expected me to play. He thought that everybody knew and respected the rules, and that my trying to get rid of him was just part of the ritual. He thought that I would follow the script in his head and give in, no matter how crass, stupid and intrusive he was.

'It's not news,' I said. 'The civil war in Azerbaijan is news. The European elections are news. The territorial disputes in Croatia are news. Even the prime minister's photo opportunities are news of a sort. ATTEMPTED RAPE VICTIM'S TORMENT isn't.'

'News is whatever the people who pay for papers want to read,' he told me glibly. 'I don't say that two point two million people can't be wrong, but as long as they pay for the privilege they can have all the human interest they want. Nobody gives a tinker's fuck about Azeris kicking seven kinds of shit out of Armenians, and nobody cares which particular bunch of pigs gets their noses into the Brussels trough, but they really would appreciate being told why your boyfriend topped himself so messily, or what it feels like to be a couple of millimetres away from death at the point of a rapist's carving knife. That's the way of the world.'

I realized, then, that what I'd told Gil wasn't entirely true. If I told John Mackenzie what Gil had pleaded with me to tell Professor Viners, he'd probably print it. He wouldn't believe it, and he'd almost certainly think that I was completely off my rocker, just as Viners would have done, but he'd probably print it. Even the ravings of a mentally unbalanced girl were news, provided that she was reasonably nice-looking and had nearly been raped. Once it was in black and white, even in the kind of paper that wouldn't print words like 'tenuous' and 'hypothetical' – perhaps especially in the kind of paper that wouldn't print words like 'tenuous' and 'hypothetical' – some people would believe it. Every word of it.

'Go away, Mr Mackenzie,' I said.

He sighed. 'It's not just me,' he said, shrugging his shoulders. 'It's all the others. It won't make much difference whether you say anything or not. Some of those guys are perfectly prepared to make it all up. Wherever you go today there'll be photographers waiting, and they'll need text to go with the pictures. Talk to me, and you have a chance to determine what gets printed.'

He wasn't even trying to sound convincing. He knew that I

knew that whatever I said could be adapted and twisted to suit whatever angle he decided to use. He knew that everyone knew that the whole enterprise was utterly and completely cynical. But he still expected me to play the game. This was where the prompter was supposed to urge me to say: 'Okay. What do you want to know?'

'Please go away, Mr Mackenzie,' I said again. 'I haven't anything to add to what my mother told your colleagues yesterday. That's all there is.'

He frowned. 'Hell's bells, Anne,' he complained. 'It's not as if we're out to make you look bad. We're on your side, remember – you're an innocent victim of misfortune and viciousness. Our readers want to sympathize with you, to feel sorry for you, to feel outrage on your behalf. Why did your boyfriend kill himself, Anne? Just tell me that. Just tell me why Gil Molari turned his flat into a crematorium. It doesn't have to be true – just tell me what you think. People want to know what you think, Anne. They want to know how you feel.'

'You don't seem to understand, Mr Mackenzie,' I said, trying to keep the tremor out of my voice. 'I want you to go. I want you to go now, and I don't want you to come back. The only thing I have to tell the other reporters is how *you* forced yourself into my bedroom, and how frightened I was, and what terrible memories it brought back of my other ordeal, and how very similar it was in every way. And I can quote you, Mr Mackenzie. I can remember every word you said – more or less. Anyway, what does accuracy matter if I get the gist of it? You like juicy quotes, don't you – you and your mates?'

He laughed, but he wasn't entirely sure of himself. He wasn't entirely sure that there was sufficient honour, or even discretion, left in his profession to make his opposite numbers refrain from printing that kind of story.

He got up, shrugged his shoulders again and left. I closed the door behind him and locked it. By the time I went down to breakfast, he had gone away.

He was lying about the photographers. They had better things to do with a Saturday than lie in wait outside Brennan Hall, in case some skinny girl who'd once been attacked came out. As news went, I wasn't really hot enough. I'd been in my false coma for too long, and out of it too long. I had cooled off, and unless I reignited the whole affair with some careless spark – some careless word about Viners' viruses, or vampires, or the equivalent thereof – it would fade out completely. There were too many attempted rapes nowadays, too many murdered kids, too many suicides. Serial killers seemed to be loose in half the cities in England and all the cities in America. I wasn't news unless I took the trouble to advertise myself, and I seemed to have convinced John Mackenzie, finally, that I wasn't going to do that. Maybe he'd even taken the trouble to convince his adversaries that it was no good, just in case I followed through with my threat, and just in case they decided to play along.

I went to the library and borrowed some books which had chapters on the emotions. They weren't on the official reading list, but I'd long since given up trying to find any of those. The competition was always too intense.

It was mid-afternoon before I was interrupted again by a knock on my door. I opened it by the merest crack, intending to slam it instantly if I saw John Mackenzie or anyone like him. When I saw that it was WPC Linton, I didn't feel relieved, but I didn't think that I could shut the door in her face either. I let her in and offered her the chair by the desk. She sat down, and I perched on the edge of the bed.

'Sorry,' I said. 'I thought you might be a reporter.'

'Have they been bothering you?' she asked, sounding neither surprised nor overly concerned.

'I don't have any answers to the questions they want to ask,' I told her, 'but I'm afraid of what they might make of my don't-knows.'

'I know the feeling,' she said. 'How are you, otherwise?'

'Okay.'

She nodded. It was the answer she'd expected. 'I've got some news,' she said. 'We arrested a man this morning. He's confessed to the attack on you. He hadn't really much option. We have the weapon and the bloodstained clothing.'

'How did you catch him?' I asked.

'His wife turned him in, indirectly. She couldn't quite bring herself to share her suspicions with us, so she eventually solved the conflict of loyalties by confiding in her mother. The mother had no compunction at all. We turned up the evidence easily enough once we knew where to search. He's confessed to three other rapes, one unreported. The other two were burglary-rapes, so we didn't immediately connect them with the attack on you. He knew we'd get him for them. We got semen specimens, and he'll match the genetic fingerprint. They're doing the tests now, but it's open and shut. He isn't going to retract. He'll plead guilty, but not to attempted murder. The CPS won't let us press that one, because we'd never prove it. He'll probably get seven years, maybe ten, and he'll serve five, maybe seven. I'm sorry it won't be more, but that's the going rate.'

'But what about Janine?' I said.

'That one he didn't do,' said the policewoman, regretfully. 'He was at work, with two dozen witnesses to prove it.'

'Oh,' I said. I didn't know exactly how I felt. Not relieved, certainly, even though I wouldn't have to try to identify his voice, and probably wouldn't even have to give evidence.

'I'm sorry,' said the policewoman, 'but I have to ask you this. Is there anything else you've thought of – anything else at all – which might have a bearing on the matter that's still unresolved: the murder?'

'How could I?' I said. 'I was in the hospital, fast asleep. Wasn't I?'

'Yes,' she said, uncomfortably. 'But . . .'

'You still think Gil might have done it, don't you? You want him to be guilty, so that you can close all your cases? What do you expect me to say? What could I possibly say that would be any help at all?'

'I'm sorry,' she said, with apparent sincerity. 'It's not like that. I talked to Gil Molari, you know, when he visited the hospital – while you were still unconscious. He was very worried about you. He was wobbly, though. He was definitely on edge. Sergeant Miller wondered about that mark on his neck. Yours was gone last time I saw you, but I see that it's back now.'

I put my hand up to the place where I'd allowed Gil to feed. It was slightly painful, but not raw. 'I'm sorry,' I said. 'It's a nervous habit I have, when I'm concentrating. I don't even know that I'm doing it. But it's not important.'

'No, it isn't,' the WPC agreed. 'I understand you went to see Professor Viners last night.'

A couple of seconds passed before I realized that this was just the next phase in the line of enquiry. Like the reporters, the police were still looking for more connections which would help them make sense of three incidents which were too closely associated with one another for them readily to believe that there was nothing linking them but coincidence. She was trying to find out more about Gil's state of mind.

'Yes,' I said. 'He asked me to. He sent me a note while I was in hospital.'

'Do you mind telling me what he said to you?'

'He asked me not to say anything to the reporters which might be misconstrued. He told me that his tests had confirmed that the virus which Gil caught definitely wasn't from his laboratory.'

'But it must have been an unusual virus,' said the policewoman, 'if it frightened him so badly that he killed himself.'

'He must have been upset because of what happened to me,' I said. 'If the virus prevented him from thinking straight, even for a day or so, it could all have got out of hand. Perhaps he blamed himself, because he thought he ought to have been with me.'

'He said that,' the policewoman admitted. After a pause, she went on: 'I'm sorry, but Sergeant Miller asked me to follow this up. I don't mean to distress you. The man who killed the little girl was probably just a copycat who read about the attack on you. That happens sometimes. But it's an awkward case. We don't have a weapon, you see – we don't even know what kind of a weapon was used, although the pathologist says that it definitely wasn't the scalpel that Gil used to cut his own throat. And then there's the matter of the blood she lost. There's something very weird about all this, you know. If it didn't sound so crazy, I'd wonder whether we're looking for some kind of vampire. Not the kind with fangs, you understand; just some freak with twisted ideas. Killers these days seem to do it for kicks, and some of them seem to be competing with one another to be the most disgusting, the most perverse, the most obscene . . . I can't understand why. It's beyond me.'

'Me too,' I said. It seemed to be called for.

The WPC was in full flow by now, and she wasn't content

with that. 'All this stuff about urban blight and the cycle of deprivation, video nasties and ritual child abuse ... none of it makes sense. I just can't imagine what gets into people. It's like a disease. Whatever Professor Viners has in his labs, it's probably nothing to what's out there. I'm sorry to keep coming back with more questions. You've been through enough already. But we have to keep asking, until we find out what did happen. You do understand that, don't you?'

'I'm sorry,' I said. 'I wish I could help you, but I can't. I honestly don't believe that Professor Viners' viruses have anything to do with this, and I really am certain that the man who killed Janine wasn't Gil. I know I was in hospital, unconscious, but I knew him well enough to be certain that he couldn't have done anything like that. If I could think of anything else to add to my statement, I'd tell you, but I can't. I just want to get back to everyday life. I just want to put everything back together again, so that I can carry on. I just want to be left alone. Please.'

She nodded sympathetically. Just like the newspaper readers John Mackenzie had cited, she was on my side. She felt sorry for me. She felt outrage on my behalf. She wanted to be able to protect people like me from people like my attacker. She wanted to put the world back together again, although she couldn't figure out how it had ever come to be so badly broken, so sadly in need of repair. She really hadn't come to harass me; in her own way, she was simply looking for reassurance – reassurance of the fact that sometimes the innocent did win through. I wanted to help her sustain that illusion.

'I'm all right,' I told her. 'Thanks for coming to tell me the news. I really do appreciate it. I don't mean to be rude. I just want to be on my own.'

She got up, nodding profusely.

'You were very brave,' she said. 'Fighting back the way you did. I just wanted to tell you that. No matter what they say about it being better not to resist, I'd have done the same. You were brave, and right to be brave – don't let anybody tell you different.'

'No,' I said, 'I won't.' I knew, far better than she did, that she was right.

That night, I went alone into the borderlands for the first time. Nor was I bound for the realm of light, into which the owls had carried me when they came to save and imprison me. I had to seek out and explore a place which was darker by far, into which the owls couldn't accompany me. It required courage to set forth on that journey, but I was braver than I had ever been, and I understood the pressure of necessity. To rid myself of Maldureve, I would have to go into the world that was his own. If I were eventually to banish him, I would first have to make sure that I could find him, and that I could face him.

The owls had told me a great deal about the borderlands, and the manner in which their tortured topology extended itself into an elaborate symbolic geography. They'd armed me with a vocabulary of empty names with which to begin the task of comprehension, and they'd taught me something of the secret language, too: the language of hidden meanings, by means of which everything that exists, inside and outside the world, may ultimately be connected. They'd described to me the most familiar large-scale features of the borderlands: the Sea of Sleep and the Plain of Silence. They'd warned me not only against the terrors of the Empire of Fear, but also against the seductions of the Wilderness of If.

My business, for the time being, was entirely to do with a certain house whose walls and battlements were but one-sixth of the whole; whose submerged cellars and dungeons were unfortunately dank and cold and labyrinthine. There, the owls told me, I could be sure of finding the vampire. It was there that his coffin lay, where he was obliged by the laws of his secret nature to sleep while the red sun poured down its baleful light from the star-filled sky. In the long night of the borderlands, the owls explained, I could never find or catch the vampire, because he could run with the wolves or fly with the bats or dissipate himself among the foetid mists which rose from the marshes of the vast demesne whose overlord he was; but by day – not the earthly day, but the dimmer day of the world beyond the world – it was possible to discover and trap him.

I knew, therefore, where I had to go. I knew what I had to do. I wasn't afraid. I started out from my room in Brennan Hall, whose shadows were so familiar to me. The borderlands are everywhere and they can be entered at any point, but the artistry of dissolving your everyday body into shadow isn't easily cultivated by beings who have lived their entire lives weighed down by matter. It's better by far to embrace shadows with which you're intimately familiar, like those that enshroud you whenever you lay down your head to sleep. It wasn't easy, even then, but the owls had schooled me well.

I took a heavy torch, which I'd bought at Halford's. It had a square-sectioned body moulded in black rubber, and a hand-grip and yellow push-button controls. I also had a spool of supposedly unbreakable thread, which I'd bought at BHS. I didn't take a sharpened stake; this particular journey was strictly exploratory.

'Should I also take a sharp-bladed knife?' I had asked the owls, but they had advised me against such unnecessary clutter. Sharp-bladed knives, they had explained to me, were symptoms and symbols of an outward defiance which merely masked an inner insecurity and a fundamental inadequacy. In the borderlands, they told me, surgery had no power to heal.

When undertaking journeys into the borderlands, it's a great advantage to have been a habitual lucid dreamer. Nothing we do in our waking lives prepares us for odysseys into the worlds beyond the world; if anything, the adaptations we make in bowing down to the crushing tyranny of the everyday, injures our capacity for such work by sapping our essential vitality, shrinking the horizons of the imaginable and withering the youth of the soul. If humans were not dreamers, we might easily find it impossible to confront the borderlands; but we *are* dreamers, and in our dreams we know what it is to be in a world where the rules of chance and determinism no longer apply. Because we're dreamers, we know how to float and fly. Because we're dreamers we know how to confront monsters; not without fear, but at least without mental catastrophe. Because we're dreamers, we know what it is not to be swaddled and choked by a surfeit of normality. Nevertheless, you always have to remember, when you take your first faltering steps into the actual borderlands, that you're not a dreamer any longer, and that you can't escape any threats which you face simply by wishing yourself awake. When we dare to cross the actual borderlands of experience, we make ourselves horribly vulnerable.

It's a vertiginous experience to come out of the shadows on the other side, to find yourself in a different world: to stare upwards, for the first time, into the starry vault of heaven which arches aloft the world beyond the world, and to see the stars in all the glory of their true hugeness, too bright by far to be eclipsed by the meagre sun. Not that the otherworldly sun is lacking in majesty, despite its relative modesty. The earthly sun is always at its best when it hangs above the western horizon, seemingly bloated, reddened by a moist and dust-laden atmosphere; at times like that, you can stare at it without fear of being blinded, and study it as a mere object, rather than an unbearable cataract of light. The sun of the borderlands is always crimson in colour, and it doesn't have the force to make us turn away lest we should be injured by its contemplation, but its essential authority isn't compromised.

In the borderlands, you can stand face to face with the engine of life, and look creation in its bleary eye. In the borderlands, you can see the universe behind the sun, and know that what we think of as creation is only the tiniest fragment of infinite possibility: lately born; ephemeral; fully ripe for growth, improvement and evolution.

I came directly to the threshold of the house which I had to explore; the borderlands are everywhere, and those who know how can step into them at will. Those who have been educated by the owls have no need of extended odysseys in exotica, which are the curse of the lost and the damned, and various other playthings of fate.

Before entering the house, though, I paused to look around at the marvellous landscape which stretched away to the mountainous horizon. It was very beautiful in its desolation.

The desert sands were silver, but while the sun stood high in the sky its rays painted the dunes and wind-stirred waves with scarlet fire. The distant hills were verdant, but in this light the foliage of the evergreen trees was tinted purple and blue. The great fissures which streaked the escarpments of bleak rock were jet black even at noon, their empty depths quite unilluminable.

I looked for the creatures which the owls had mentioned to me, and against which they'd warned me. Beware, they'd said, of the ancient idols; of the Hoggish Beasts; of the Destroyers of Souls – but know that you can tame them and defeat them, if only you can look them in the face, and know what they are.

The owls were right. I found faces in the patterns which the red fire made upon the silver sands; in the uncertain slopes of the distant hills; in the dark fissures which descended to the heart of the world beyond he world. They were vile faces: cruel, bestial, lustful for violence instead of gentle love; but they were faces which could be faced, terrors which could be confronted, conditions of existence which need not make existence unbearable.

I looked about for several minutes, and then I went into the house, easily parting the ragged strands of the ancient portcullis that had outlasted the rotted door.

It was cold inside the vestibule, and seemingly hostile. The corridors were narrow, their imperfectly whited walls stained by patient fungus and by swirling trails of limescale left by the creeping damp. The windows which let in the light of the blood-red sun were little more than narrow slits. No army had ever laid siege to the house, and no archer had ever stood sentry by any of its windows, but the design of the house reflected nevertheless a defensive caution near to paranoia.

I hesitated before setting forth to explore the corridors, knowing that I wouldn't have the advantage of the narrow windows for long. My path was a downward one, and I would soon be forced to depend on another kind of illumination, which I hoped would prove more prolific and more powerful. I carefully fastened the end of my silken thread to the doorway – not to one of the trailing strands of the broken portcullis, but to a huge iron plate from which the remains of an ancient rusted hinge still dangled uselessly. Then, steeling myself as best I could, I went on.

As I passed downwards into the darkness, unreeling the fine thread, I switched on the torch. Its light was white and dazzling. The walls around me, which had seemed to press in on me threateningly, were ruthlessly exposed as the poor, dead things they were, every flaw and blemish of their surfaces starkly outlined. But I knew better than to feel unduly exultant. I knew, for I had been forewarned, how extensive and how treacherous the labyrinth might be, and how very difficult it might be to find my way to the centre. I knew, too, that the silken thread was of finite length, and that the white light of the torch would gradually fade to a dull yellow as the battery slowly exhausted its potential energy. I knew, because the wisdom which the owls had imparted to me was coldly honest, that there was danger in what I was doing. There was a possibility that I would go into the deepest parts of the house only to find that my thread would stretch no further and that my light might not last until I had retraced my steps.

'Don't lose yourself in the darkness of the maze,' the owls had told me. 'From there, as from everywhere else, the earth is merely a single step away, but it's a step so difficult as to constitute an impossible stride. She who is abruptly wrenched from the heart of the maze instead of the threshold of the house risks madness, if not death itself; and she who remains, in darkness, holding the useless end of a broken thread, is at the mercy of the vampire's kin, who are rarely as inclined to be loving and gentle as he – in his uncertainly romantic fashion – sometimes is.'

The owls might easily have left me this instruction as an arbitrary imposition, of the same vexatious kind as the instructions which countless heroes and heroines of legend and fairy tale had been given by their supernatural helpers. But they knew well enough that someone like me couldn't begin to believe in any wisdom that was couched in aphorisms and commandments, without reasons and explanations, and so they told me what patterns of correspondence and representation underlay my mission and its milieu.

'The house is your own being,' they told me, patiently and lovingly. 'It's a kind of shadow, conceived as a structure because there isn't any easier way to conceptualize yourself. Your descent will be a descent into the hidden conduits of your own intelligence. The borderlands, you see, are the meeting place of the inner and outer worlds of your perception, where inner space is figuratively but accurately mapped. Maldureve is inside you, like a worm in the bud of your soul, and his power must be neutralized if you are ever to flourish and reach your full potential. If you are ever to come into your true inheritance, unfolding your inner being to meet the nourishing light of the crimson sun, you have to eliminate the cancer in your soul. This can only be done in the arena of allegory, according to the logic of dreaming. But you mustn't let yourself imagine that this decoding devalues what you must do. It's no mere story, no mere illusion, no mere adventure of the imagination. The inner world of thought and emotion, idea and imagination, is as real a dwelling place as the outer world of active objects and human community. It's every bit as actual, every bit as substantial, every bit as potentially hurtful and destructive as the world of blood and blades.'

I understood that, or thought I did. I had the beginnings of wisdom, or thought I had. I knew that facing Maldureve, and his malevolent kin, wouldn't be easy. If things went awry, I could be destroyed. If things went badly, the blood of my being might be drained away, warm liquor for the absolute intoxication of evil.

Bravely, though, I descended into the labyrinth, turning corner after corner, always unreeling the thread behind me. I heard creatures scuttling in the darkness beyond the light of my torch, fleeing from its illumination. Some scurried on four legs, others on six or eight, some perhaps on dozens or hundreds, but all of them were stricken by fear, forced to retreat before my steadfast tread. Sometimes, the white light was reflected redly back from tiny eyes nested in the darkness of cracks and coverts, but nothing came to menace me. At first I didn't bother to ask myself why not; I was content with the state of affairs, and eager to believe that it could be maintained.

I walked for hours, but didn't easily become impatient; I was understandably apprehensive about the end of the journey, and I wasn't in a hurry. While I was still in transit, I seemed safe; there was a certain comfort to be gained from the fact that the moment of my destiny was not yet come. I knew that time was by no means on my side, and yet I was able to let it drain peacefully away. We're all well practised in that kind of self-deception, we human creatures.

I did become very tired; my feet ached and my body was inceasingly racked by that aggregation of petty complaints which is the inevitable legacy of restless exertion; but I knew that I mustn't stop. It was one thing to find an understandable contentment in the fact that the climax hadn't yet come; it would have been quite another to cause a deliberate and dangerous delay.

I went down and around and around and down, never resting, not even for a moment. I understood, in a cerebral way, why a journey to the limits of my own being had inevitably to be long and arduous, but understanding didn't help to alleviate the pain of it. There was more irony than ignominy in the revelation that I could not plumb the depths of my own soul without my feet becoming blistered, but it seemed an unjust and irrational imposition.

More than once I heard footsteps behind me, as if I were being followed. The first time, I quickened my pace, but the pursuer only quickened hers.

'It's only an echo,' I told myself, sternly. But if it was an echo, why did it fade and come again?

The second time, I turned and shone my torch back, but when I stopped to turn the other footfalls paused too, and there was nothing there.

'It *is* only an echo,' I insisted. 'It's not an actual doppelgänger.' But as soon as I said it, I remembered something I'd heard quoted many years before, long before I ever suspected the existence of vampires: 'He who sees his "going-double" must go himself.' I knew then that I'd been lucky, and that if I'd seen the person who was following me – the other Anne – I'd have become like her, a mere follower.

The third time I heard the footsteps behind me, I didn't turn round. I knew they'd never catch me up.

Even so, I realized then that I was hiding something from myself. I realized that the emptiness of the corridors and the length of the journey were just evasions. I realized that I wasn't being wholehearted in my exploration, that there were things inside myself that I was still incapable of facing. I realized that there were nasty surprises lurking behind the corners of the labyrinth, awful spectres sealed in by the walls. I realized how necessary it was that I should now prepare the way for my second journey: a journey which would be more difficult and more dangerous. I realized that I'd have to arm myself with something more than a wooden stake. For the time being, I was only pretending to be brave. I wasn't quite ready yet to look myself in the eye and see into my heart.

In the end, though, I came to the heart of the maze. I'd always felt morally certain that I could and would, in spite of my failings. I knew that I could come to the threshold of my fears, and get a clearer sight of them. That, for the time being, would have to be enough.

Like the first doorway, this one had no door in it, but there was still a barrier separating me from the chamber where Maldureve – and perhaps many others – lay asleep. There was a multilayered curtain, made of half a hundred cobwebs strung from jamb to jamb and from lintel to floor.

And within the folds of that complex curtain, huge spiders lurked.

Only one or two were moving, with painstaking slowness, across the delicate bridges they had spun. The rest waited patiently in the shadowy corners. They weren't as monstrous as they might have been. Not one that I could see was more than a handspan across in the body, and their hairy, many-jointed feet weren't much longer than pencils or kitchen knives. They were large by the standards of spider-kind, but only by those standards. It semed that the constraints of nature applied here as they applied on Earth, save for the fact that such webs as these could serve no ordinary predatory purpose. These webs were not cast to catch unwary flies or beetles; these webs existed in order to form a maze within the greater maze, all the more treacherous for being more delicate.

I didn't doubt for a moment that the spiders could bite, and that their bite would be poisonous. Nor did I doubt that the moment I touched one of the dust-sprinkled webs, however lightly, the spinner of that particular web would come hurtling from its station, eager to claim its prize.

I had the same fear of spiders which most people have: an anxiety leavened by repulsion, unreasoning and yet profound. I wasn't hysterically arachnophobic; the spiders hadn't any *particular* terror for me. But that didn't mean that I could simply take myself in hand and walk towards the doorway. No one could have done that, except perhaps for a professional arachnologist who hadn't merely taken the trouble to desensitize herself by constantly handling such creatures, but had also learned to hold them in that purified, academic affection which is reserved for the platonic affairs of the wisest among us.

Perversely, I'd expected to find something worse. I'd expected something much more particular to my own anxieties, much more precisely geared to my own individuality: an Orwellian Room 101, whose contents would affirm by terrorism the uniqueness of my most intimate soul. This was almost an insult, almost a joke. But I had the beginnings of the wisdom of the owls, and I could recognize in the legend 101 a mere symbol of the female genitalia – labia and vagina – and I had the common sense to recognize that even in our most intimate souls we're not, after all, so very different from one another. We're more alike than we sometimes like to pretend.

Anyone would have had difficulty in going through that doorway. Anyone, no matter what courage they carried with them, or what foolhardiness, would have hesitated. Anyone could have found themselves rooted to the spot, unable to proceed.

Anyone at all.

I was brave; I knew that. But I couldn't step into that arched doorway. Maldureve didn't need anything extra-special, anything so very extraordinary, to keep me at bay. He only needed to play, casually, upon a commonplace fear that everyone has. Perhaps the most difficult thing of all to imagine, and to accept, is that when we come to the innermost core of our being, we will find nothing but a cliché.

I didn't despair. I knew what I had to do. I had at least to *look* through the doorway into the shadows beyond. I had to stand still and familiarize myself with it. I had to fix it in my mind, so that when I came back into the waking world I'd be able to remember it, think about it and come to terms with it. I had to work out a strategy for getting through it. I had to work out a plan. It didn't matter if the task proved difficult, because I could come back. I could come back time and time again, if I had to, until the time came when I could do what I had to do.

So I looked into the darkness. I looked through the maze of spider webs, into the core of my being, the secret fundament of my soul. I looked, trying my hardest to see, to be brave and to understand. I looked, knowing how useless it was to ask 'Who am I?' or even '*What* am I?' and expect an easy answer. I was still in the process of becoming, still en route towards the enlightenment of the owls. Maldureve was in there somewhere, but he was in hiding, like so much else.

'You can't win,' I said to him, very softly. 'This is *my* house, and no one can live in it, except on my terms. You tried to make me into a seed of evil, a monster and maker of monsters, but I'm going my own way now. I don't want to be your instrument, I want to be me. I will be me. I can do it. Even my own anxieties can't stop me. They're not strong enough. They're just ordinary, everyday fears. I can face them. And in the end, the house will be mine again – entirely mine. I'll build it better than it ever was before. I'll make it into a palace. I'm a Charet: a witch-finder and demon-hunter. I'm Anne Charet, and I don't need a disguise to walk about in my own world. All kinds of things can hurt me, injure me, destroy me – but you aren't one of them. I have the beginnings of the wisdom of the owls, and I'm in charge of my own destiny. It doesn't matter what you do or where you hide; *you can't win*. I'm going now, but I'll be back.

'Depend on it, Maldureve: *I'll be back.*'

I I

I was hard at work when Cynthia knocked at my door. There were open books all over my desk and half a dozen odd bits of paper on which I'd scribbled notes scattered hither and yon; but the sheet on which I intended to start my essay was still virgin, because the issues and the arguments hadn't yet coalesced into a proper beginning. I wasn't pleased to be interrupted, because it was already late afternoon and the December twilight had begun to fade. I knew only too well that I didn't really have enough time to get the essay done, but there was nothing I could do. Cynthia was far too obviously in distress to be turned away.

'Have you heard?' she said, throwing herself down on the bed.

'They've arrested someone – it was on the TV, in the local bit after the main news. There's nothing in the papers – not the *Observer*, anyway – but the newsreader said that he'd been in custody since yesterday. They've charged him with attacking you, and there was something vague about the possibility of further charges.'

'I know,' I said. 'A policewoman came round yesterday.'

'What? They didn't send anyone round to see me, the bastards. I don't count, I suppose. I'm only a lesbian mother.'

'It's not like that,' I said, slightly surprised by her vehemence. 'They told me that he didn't kill Janine – that he had an unbreakable alibi. He confessed to the attack on me, but he was at work when Janine was killed. The other charges are for other rapes. The policewoman said they were still waiting for the genetic fingerprint evidence to be checked. They probably didn't send anyone to see you because the arrest wasn't relevant to you – or only relevant in the sense that it proved the lack of connection between the two cases.'

'Oh!' she said, startled. 'I just assumed . . . you mean it was all just a coincidence?' The thought evidently seemed quite horrible to her. I guessed that the horror of it was not simply her inference that there was still a murderer on the loose, but rather that the idea of a complex coincidence of evils seemed intrinsically macabre and sinister: incontrovertible testimony to the implacable malignity of the universe. Like my mum and dad, Cynthia would doubtless have preferred to think that all the things which went dreadfully wrong with the world were the acts of a few insane individuals, who only had to be caught and contained. I could see their point of view.

She leaped up again, as abruptly as she had thrown herself down, and scanned the papers on my desk.

'Oh, God!' she said. 'You're working! How *can* you? Oh – I know it's the right thing to do, the only thing to do, that life has to go on and that it's far better to be doing something than moping around feeling dreadful, but I just don't see how people can. I wish I was half as clever and half as strong as you – then maybe I wouldn't just go to pieces. I don't think I can carry on, you know, quite honestly . . . I just don't think I can do it. I don't know that I can go back to Wombwell House. I'm frightened of it . . . I'm frightened of what just being there will do to me. I know that it isn't the least bit of good staying away, but I just can't cope. I just want to crawl into a hole and never come out again. I don't know how I'm going to go on *living*, let alone trying to take up where I left off. I don't think I can stay on the course . . . it's all too awful. I feel as if my entire existence has just run into a brick wall, and there's no way on earth to get to the other side, even if there's another side to get to . . .

'I know I'm just being a coward, and I know that *someone's* child dies every day of the week, including single mothers, and that they just have to carry on, and that they *do* carry on, somehow, but I don't know how . . .

'I mean, *how?*'

She collapsed on to the bed again, overdramatically. She started to cry.

I didn't know. I knew that she shouldn't be unloading it all on to me, given that I was ten years younger than she was and only just out of the parental nest myself, but I knew that she probably knew that too, and couldn't help herself. Anyhow, although she didn't know it, it was my fault, at least in part. I had a duty to her, a moral obligation to make some kind of reparation, however inadequate, if I possibly could.

I went to sit down beside her, and I put my thin arm around her shoulders. 'It's okay,' I said, hypocritically. 'Just let it all out.' I knew it was conventional advice. I knew it was what she was expecting. Personally, I'd always felt that the prejudice people had against bottling things up was stupidly mistaken. I didn't believe that 'letting things out' solved anything at all, or had the slightest cathartic effect. The idea was a hangover from the days when doctors used leeches to let the blood out of sick people: a useless superstition. But I had to play my part. I had created the monster which had killed her child; I was the source of the disease which had blighted her life. I had to do what was expected of me. It wouldn't have mattered even if I'd wanted to say: 'Die then! Don't try to cope! Kill yourself!' I could only say what I did say. It was all that the situation allowed.

Cynthia probably felt that she was entitled to do what she was doing, absurd as it might have seemed to someone looking in from the outside, because the circumstances were so extraordinary – but in fact, this was just a magnification of her customary craving for reassurance, her addictive dependence. I could see that now, because I could see how similar I'd been, all my life. Maldureve was even more inappropriate as someone for me turn to than I was as someone for her to turn to, but the principle was the same. I understood, now, how much supposed affection and how much supposed love must really be the demand for reassurance and the dutiful meeting of that demand.

'Well,' said Cynthia, when she finally found the strength to mop up the tears, 'at least I'm doing my practical homework, even though I'm not writing anything. What do you think Dr Gray would say if I volunteered to give a demonstration of the emotions in action, instead of an essay?'

'You have to give it time,' I told her, virtuously. 'Your wound isn't like mine – it can't just heal – but you have to live, day by day, until you learn to do it. Practice may not make perfect, but it makes possible. It's like a scientist who has to learn to handle viruses or tarantulas; no matter how hard it is to do, they just have to reach a point at which it becomes *possible*. Gil thought he could do that, but when he was tested . . . he went out of control. He didn't give himself time. He let himself become mad, and his madness made him kill Janine, and then he had to kill himself. You mustn't let yourself be destroyed. It would just be adding to the tragedy.'

She recoiled out of my embrace. 'You don't know that!' she said, profoundly shocked. 'You mustn't think that! It couldn't have been Gil!'

I did know it, but I knew that there was no way to explain it to her. I wondered if I had the power to bring Janine Leigh's ghost out of the borderlands, to let Cynthia see her; but I knew that no good result could possibly be achieved. Even if Cynthia could accept what she saw as real, even if everything were explained to her and made clear, it wouldn't make it any easier for her to begin to cope, to begin the painful work of reconstituting her life. Hers was not the kind of tragedy which knowledge could ameliorate.

'I don't know what to think,' I told her, falsely laying claim to some inner turmoil of my own, reminding her that she was not the only one to have suffered a loss. It was required of me:

Brian Stableford

I had to show solidarity, to imply as carefully as I could that my outward behaviour was only a mask hiding a dispiritedness and a despair at least comparable to her own.

'Why?' she whispered, playing the game. 'Why would he do such a thing?'

'He was very distressed,' I told her. 'He was scared that he'd caught some virus from the lab – scared for no good reason, but scared nevertheless. Then I was attacked . . . it must have made things much worse. He could have gone crazy. He could have gone completely crazy. That's what the detective sergeant thinks. It's possible. I don't know. We probably never will. If he did do it, they'll never be able to charge anyone. Nobody will ever know for sure.'

I knew for sure, but I had to pretend doubt. I simply had to, and that was all there was to it. There was nothing else I could do for her, except to play the part she expected. All she wanted for the time being was a straw to grasp, some phantom presence in her life which would allow her to think that she wasn't alone.

When she eventually went, she apologized profusely for having interrupted me, for having made such a display of herself and for having reawakened my own troubles. She seemed to me to be apologizing – at least by implication – for the state of the world at large, including the civil war in Azerbaijan and the eventual heat-death of the universe. I told her that it didn't matter, that none of it mattered, and that if ever she needed anything, she would always know where to find me.

It was all pretence, but it was true in a sense.

When I shut the door behind her, something made me reach out and turn out the light. I told myself as I did it that something must have afflicted my eyes, making me anxious for protective darkness – but that was a pretence, too. Inevitably, when I turned to face the window again, Maldureve was there.

I breathed out unsteadily, slightly disturbed even though I wasn't unduly alarmed. I had expected to see him again, at least once more, now that I had discovered and reached his resting place. I wondered, briefly, whether he had come to make threats or entreaties.

'I've missed you, Anne,' he whispered, after a long hesitation. 'You can't imagine how I've missed you.'

'The world,' I said, humourlessly, 'is full of blood. There's nothing very special about mine.'

I couldn't deny that I was a little bit afraid of him. He had substance and he had strength – gifts that I had given him and that now might be turned against me. It would have been easier to confront him on his own ground, where he was vulnerable, especially if he were quiescent in his coffin, as helpless as a baby.

'You can't hurt me,' I said to him, to bolster my own confidence. 'The owls will protect me. You told me that you couldn't and wouldn't protect me from them, but they're stronger. They can and will protect me from you.'

'I don't want to hurt you,' he said, reaching out with both arms to invite me into his embrace. 'I love you, and I always will. We've shared our blood and our being, you and I. How could you ever have thought that I would want to hurt you? I wanted you to be one with me and my kind. I wanted you to join me in the borderlands, to share the life of the shadows. We could have hunted and feasted together, . . . we still can, if only you'll dare to listen to your heart. The owls have lied to you, they've twisted your mind and turned you against yourself. You don't understand what they did to you. Do you think it was coincidence that the man with the knife attacked you? *They* sent him. They sent him to trap you, to deliver you into their care. It was no accident of happenstance, – it was a cruel act of malice. Why do you think I couldn't help you? Did you think I was simply frightened? How could I be frightened of some mere bag of blood wielding a knife? If that had been what he was, he would have been nothing to me – I could have torn him limb from limb and scattered his flesh to the winds. But he was bait in a trap, he was the instrument of the owls. I couldn't even warn you. But you don't have to be their creature. You have a choice. You can still listen to your heart. We can be together again, you and I. There's no true satisfaction for you, anywhere in the world, unless you have the hunger to be satisfied. I think you know that, in your heart. You knew it last night, didn't you, when you came to destroy me, and paused at the threshold? I knew then that the owls hadn't made you entirely their own. I didn't build that curtain of cobwebs – you did! You chose to awaken your own doubts, to play upon your own fears, because you *knew*, when you had descended to the real core of your being, that you and I are still the same: both of us creatures of the night; both of us hunters; both of us possessed of a hunger which nothing can satisfy but blood. I knew then that there was still hope. Here I am, Anne. Don't turn me away. Don't reject me. I love you. You can't imagine how much I love you. The owls don't love you – they're incapable of love as you and I know it. They have sex, after their own fashion, but they don't *love*, not with their hearts, not with every fibre of their being, the way you and I do. Have you forgotten what it was like? I don't believe that you have, or that you ever can. I was your first lover, and your only true lover. Let me love you, Anne. Come into the shadows, *for ever.*'

I was tempted. It was unexpected, and all the more powerful because of that. I could feel the force of his persuasion. I didn't know whether what he said was true or false – what do any of us know of those reasons which the heart is supposed to have but of which logic knows nothing? – but there was something in his voice which made me want to believe. His presence brought memories flooding back into my mind, filling my mind with a kind of turbulence I hadn't felt since the moment of my imprisonment in the owls' cage of light. And yet . . . how could I trust him?

'The owls are dangerous, Anne,' he told me. 'They're cruel; they have no feelings. They're utterly cynical. They pretend that they're teaching you wisdom, but they're only making you into their instrument. They're all mind and no heart, all thought and no emotion. They're beautiful, in their way, but they're robotic, inhuman, anti-life. If you do what they want you to do, you'll become more and more like them. You'll become a killer, Anne: a bright and vicious thing, all caustic fire and corrosive brilliance. You'll become a destroyer, a thing without a heart. You've been carried away by their kind of vivid ecstasy, but it's all just show. Our kind of love is better by far: softer, more gentle, deeper, more meaningful. You know that, really, if you'll only listen to your heart. If you'll only resist the glamour of the owls, you'll see what you really need, what you really desire, what you really are.'

I was tempted. It was all so very seductive, so very reassuring. But he no longer had the power to captivate me. I was no longer a ready-made victim. The iron had entered into my soul.

'You're a kind of disease, Maldureve,' I heard myself say, *in Gil's voice*! The vocal cords were mine, and I could feel the words forming in my throat, but the voice was definitely Gil's. 'You're an open wound in the soul, which has to be cauterized and sterilized.'

'You don't believe that, Anne,' he said, taking a step towards me. He was very substantial, very solid, for all that he was really made of shadows. I knew that if he were to seize me, catching me by the hair, and then yank my head back to expose my throat, he could drain all the blood from my body as easily as Gil had drained the blood from Janine's. I felt that I was in mortal danger, and that the only real recourse I had was to yield, to say: 'Yes, it's okay. Do it. Whether you love me or not, just get it over with.' I didn't have a crucifix to brandish in his face, or any faith that it would work if I did. I only had my strength and my wisdom, both fortified by the owls. With the enemy in front of me, looming over me like a great black spider, I didn't know if those resources would suffice. But I didn't give in. I didn't yield.

'You can't survive, Maldureve,' said Gil's ghost, from somewhere within my body, where I had granted it a place to reside. 'You can be absorbed, and integrated into the genome, on a purely somatic level; or you can be destroyed, crippled and ingested by the instruments of the immune system; but *you can't survive.*'

'I love you, Anne,' said Maldureve, mournfully. 'I don't want to be your enemy. I only want to love you, to be with you. What else matters, Anne? What else is there, if you don't have love?'

I looked up into his handsome, terrifying face. He was so seemingly powerful, and yet so rapturously infatuated. How could any face, I wondered – whether it belonged to an idol or a man – contain such contradictions? How could it be at once so loving and so utterly savage? And what was it in me which responded to that contradiction so yearningly, which desired to be crushed and broken and sucked dry? What was it in me which yearned for the oblivion which lay on the far side of his particular kind of ecstasy?

Perhaps, I thought, he was right; perhaps I did love him, and only him; perhaps we had been made for one another; perhaps the owls could not keep us apart, and should not ever have tried their treacheries upon the likes of us.

But Gil's voice couldn't be denied. It spoke again, triumphantly. 'You're just a disease, Maldureve. A fleeting venereal sickness. We know what you are, and we know how to destroy you.'

I watched him dissolve into the darkness, and heard him cry as he faded into the infinite reaches of the borderlands: 'I love you, Anne. *I love you!*'

It had to be a lie, hadn't it? What else could he do but pretend? What else was left to him?

It had to be a lie.

12

I was slightly surprised when Cynthia turned up for the tutorial on Monday. I told her I was glad, because she clearly expected some congratulatory gesture on my part. I think her real reason for appearing was that she thought it would win her a healthy measure of approval from all concerned. Daniel and Dr Gray were as gracious as anyone could reasonably expect of them.

I wasn't at all surprised when Dr Gray invited Daniel to read his essay. An invisible line had been tacitly drawn to separate those to whom circumstance had granted the gift of an undisturbed existence from the two madwomen who perversely insisted on getting their throats cut and their daughters murdered.

Daniel had obviously anticipated this honour – or had been terrified by the possibility of having to endure the tutorial alone – and had done his best to produce an essay of considerable breadth, if not depth. We were entertained to a brief history of the notion of the divided self, delivered at a gallop. It began, like most essays in philosophy, with Plato, who had supposed that the human soul must be purely rational, but that when it became embedded in its material shell it had perforce to be associated with irrational impulses. Daniel pointed out that in Plato's view this was not entirely unfortunate, for there were some impulses which were noble ones – ambition, the desire for power, righteous wrath – but the rest of these passionate forces were 'lower' in kind, to be feared, despised and disciplined. Daniel scrupulously noted that such base temptations ought, in Plato's view, to be subject to the ruthless tyranny of the intellect. From the ideal society outlined in the *Republic*, poets were to be cast out, because they 'nourished the well of the emotions' while the true aim of civilized society should be to dry it up.

Daniel observed that the more moderate views of Plato's successors were usually aligned on the same side. Aristotle felt that emotions could enrich experience, but also took care to draw a distinction between nobler emotions and the vulgar passions connected with basic bodily processes, which constituted the 'animal part' of man. The Stoics shared Plato's suspicions to the full, regarding the passions as perturbations of the mind, almost as a kind of mental disease. The Epicureans insisted on the naturalness of pleasure and preached a kind of hedonism, but there was no vulgarity in their pleasure-seeking; their search was for a purified, rather cerebral species of joy, fit for connoisseurs, and one of their mottoes was 'Nothing to Excess'.

It was obvious to me that Daniel did not much approve of the Stoics or the Epicureans, but he became even more contemptuous when he moved on to the Christian philosophers, for whom the passions were temptations of the devil, and giving way to them the very essence of sin. He noted that Descartes considered the passions to be excitations of the soul caused by the movement of 'animal spirits', and that Spinoza, in laying down the foundation stones of his quasi-Euclidean system of ethics, accepted it as axiomatic that human freedom was based in the rational power of the intellect, while the opposing power of the emotions must be reckoned a burdensome kind of servitude.

I observed while listening to this discourse that Daniel had already acquired the faintly condescending and contemptuous tone which philosophers sometimes have when discussing mere scientists. His account of nineteenth-century models of the conflict between reason and emotion dismissed the ideas of practical

men as mere parroting of ideas inherited from the great philosophers. Darwin, who considered our appetites and passions to
be part of our evolutionary heritage, operating independently of
the will as an 'undirected flow of nerve-force' was discarded in
almost the same breath as Freud, who contended that the human
ego must negotiate between, and if possible reconcile, two sets of
contradictory pressures: the anarchic and amoral bundle of appetites which is the id; and the censorious and orderly superego.
Daniel even took time out to put the boot into Havelock Ellis,
who had identified two 'great fundamental impulses' supplying
the 'dynamic energy' of all behaviour – hunger and sexual desire
– and had, like Freud, become preoccupied with the idea that
the latter might easily be transformed by 'sublimation' into other
kinds of creative endeavour.

Throughout the history of these dualistic acounts of human
being, Daniel maintained, only a handful of heroes had appointed
themselves champions of the passions. He spoke approvingly of
Rousseau, who firmly believed in the nobility of savagery and
became the father-figure of the cult of *sensibilité*; but he saved
his final accolade for the more fashionable figure of Jean-Paul
Sartre, whose theory of emotion refused to describe passion
in quasi-mechanical terms, urging that we should instead view
emotional experience as a kind of perception, characterized by a
'magical' world-view which contrasts with, but also complements,
the 'instrumental' world-view underlying our rational and scientific understanding.

'In this view,' Daniel's essay concluded, probably lifting the
quote lock, stock and barrel from whichever one of his sources
he liked best, 'we see the world in two ways, which overlap but
never quite come into perfect focus: we see a world of objects
to be manipulated, and a world of objects of desire. These two
worlds are differently conceptualized and differently evaluated,
and though we live simultaneously in both we can no more force
our experience into a repressive existential strait jacket which
recognizes only one form of perception than we can separate
ourselves into two distinct individuals. Our task instead is to
reach the most life-enhancing compromise we can.'

I quite liked the essay, but I assumed that Dr Gray wouldn't.
I knew that he thoroughly disapproved of Rousseau and that if

ever there was a man who wholeheartedly believed that the ideal state of mind must be subject to the uncompromising tyranny of reason, Dr Gray was he. For once, though, he didn't start chipping away at Daniel's argument with sly, loaded questions. Instead he chose to point out, rather laboriously, that Daniel had somehow failed to include the relevant ideas of Nietzsche, whose contrasting of the 'Apollonian' and 'Dionysian' elements of Greek tragedy had been borrowed by later writers to describe phases through which whole cultures might pass, in the one striving for the rule of calm reason, in the other for the wild abandonment of ecstasy. Nietzsche, Dr Gray scrupulously observed, had argued in his later work that the relationship between the two tendencies could be complementary rather than conflicting.

By this time, Cynthia was completely at sea, and even I – who had taken the trouble to read the relevant chapters of the books I'd borrowed from the library – felt that my resources were stretched to their limit. I hadn't managed to progress much further than the ideas of Spinoza, who seemed to me undeserving of Daniel's rapid dismissal as one more boring dualist. My own essay quoted Spinoza's disapproval of those who 'prefer rather to abuse and ridicule the emotions and actions of men than to understand them' and his determination to explore and explain 'those things which they cry out against as opposed to reason, as vain, absurd and disgusting'. My essay concluded with Spinoza's assertion of the essential naturalness of the emotions and his declaration that 'nothing happens in nature which can be attributed to a defect of it'. But that wasn't the direction in which Dr Gray chose to go.

'The idea of emotions,' he observed, 'is intricately tied up with questions of moral responsibility. We're sometimes ashamed of our desires and our actions, and we try to disown them. "I just couldn't help it" we say. "I was overcome. I was seized by blind rage; I fell in love; I was transfixed by fear". We conceive of our emotions as things which happen to us rather than as things we *do*, and so they become excuses for our failings.'

'But it's true,' said Cynthia, bitterly. 'These things do just happen to us. Some things do just well up inside us: anger, grief, fear. They're not things we choose. Even love isn't something we choose. Maybe we can control them to some extent, get a grip on them, act in spite of them, but that only proves that they're *there* – that it requires tremendous effort to suppress them.'

I could see Dr Gray's eyes shifting uneasily. He didn't want to put any pressure on Cynthia. He was afraid of the emotion pent up inside her – afraid that anything he might say might tip her over the edge into tears, hysterics or blind fury.

The situation was, to say the least, ironic.

His flickering gaze finally came to rest on me. It was neither commanding nor pleading – just hopeful. He wanted to be baled out. He wanted to pass the buck.

'I think,' I began, hesitating to give me time to make it true, 'that we need to ask where *there* is, exactly. Are our emotions part of us, or are they outside us, laying siege to the fortress of the mind? The answer to that depends on the definition we have of the self. What exactly do I mean by "I"? What does "I" include and what do I exclude from my concept of self? If I say that I'm just the reasoning part of my mind, which is constantly at war with the animal passions, aren't I making a rather primitive and probably unjustified distinction between my mind and my body? Plato and Descartes were happy to do that, imagining an immortal soul temporarily bound to a body, but I don't know . . .'

I stopped there. I knew I'd done enough. In philosophy, honest and articulate doubt is always respectable.

'That's right,' said Daniel. 'We have to get rid of that sort of stuff. We can't disown our feelings simply by defining ourselves so as to exclude them.'

'That's just confusing the issue,' Cynthia complained. 'What's disowning got to do with it? My anger is *my* anger, my grief is *my* grief, but they're things I can't help feeling. They're things nobody can help feeling, when the things which cause them happen. The best you can do – the very best – is to try to carry on in spite of them, and it isn't easy. Sometimes, it's just not possible . . .'

I could see that philosophy wasn't going to be much help to Cynthia. There was nothing Dr Gray could say that would make her feel better, and while he couldn't say anything that would make her feel better, whatever he did say was bound to seem irrelevant. She was too emotional to think rationally about her emotions. It was almost funny, in a way, but it was too serious to laugh at.

Dr Gray looked at me again, because I was up the same creek as Cynthia, but not quite without a paddle. I was the one who had the power to ease the situation down. I was the one who could speak without my words being construed as some kind of personal attack, intended to devalue and denigrate her experience. Effectively, I had both a licence and a responsibility to say whatever came into my head, to heal the yawning breach which had opened out between the four of us because philosophy, whatever its intellectual merits, was no cure for Cynthia's condition.

'The thing is,' I said, more vaguely than I might have hoped, 'that we have this idea of ourselves as coherent, organized wholes. Even if we accept the idea of conflict within ourselves, we want to see it in terms of a defined content of opposites, like a football match. Sometimes the emotions win three–nil, sometimes reason takes it into extra time and eventually wins on penalties. Maybe both ways of looking at it are too simple-minded. Maybe it isn't reason versus emotion, or superego versus id, or order versus chaos; after all, those ideas are all products of reason themselves – they're all biased, all circular. How can we describe ourselves, and see ourselves as we are, when we're all the time inside ourselves? How can we possibly step outside ourselves to see ourselves as objects?

'I talked to Professor Viners last week about something Gil wrote in his notebook. It's just science fiction, utterly unprovable, but it made me think. We think of ourselves – our conscious selves – as a natural and inevitable extension of our brains. We assume that our brains, unlike animal brains, are complicated enough to generate conscious minds, and that that's all there is to it. Suppose, though, that that's only partly true. Suppose that consciousness is a collaborative endeavour, something that arises in brains only because they're infected with outside agents: viruses, say, or bacteria, or other things which aren't just parts of our own brain cells defined by our own genes but are actually just parasites. Suppose consciousness, even at its most calm and philosophical, is much more like delirium than we ever imagined. What if mind itself is just a kind of infection, which our bodies can sometimes fight off, so that we become autistic or catatonic, but which can also sometimes be enhanced by new and further infections? What if our perception of the world – not just our notion of what things look like but our notion of what exists and what doesn't, and our notions of cause and effect – can be changed dramatically by alterations in the populations of infectious agents which swarm in our brains, engaged in a constant struggle for existence and thus in a process of natural selection, which inevitably produces mental evolution?'

'You mean that each emotion might just be a virus, like a cold in the head?' said Daniel, radiating contemptuous astonishment, and betraying his unfortunate inability to think in any but the crudest terms when he hadn't got a textbook to plagiarize.

'No, that's not what Anne means,' said Dr Gray, who was inevitably quicker on the uptake. 'What she actually said is rather more interesting than that. Every particular organ in our bodies is produced by the collaboration of thousands of genes; if what Anne suggests were true, then each identifiable emotion might be produced by the combined effect of many agents. That way, modification of any one of the agents might produce a modification of the emotion.' He didn't add anything else: no criticism; no objection. He was prepared to let the flight of fantasy run, for the sake of amusement, and for the sake of getting to the end of the allotted hour without anyone bursting into tears.

'Reason too,' I said. 'Maybe all the gods which people once took for granted were actually available to their consciousness as objects of perception. Maybe all the wars of religion were just contests between diseases of the brain. Maybe the world really was full of monsters once: ghosts and ghouls, vampires and werewolves. Maybe it will be again, if the cut and thrust of natural selection so decides. Maybe scepticism, atheism and rationalism are just temporary colds in the head, from which our poor brains will all recover in time – except for those of us who die of them. Maybe the questions of whether we can or can't control our emotions, or whether we should or shouldn't be able to, or to what extent they're things that happen to us as opposed to things we do, are just . . . symptoms. Maybe all our tutorials and all our dreams are just different reflections of the struggle for existence of our internal parasites. I think that's what Gil was trying to get at, in the notes he scribbled in his lab book.'

It was all wide open to wisecrack put-downs, but I wasn't particularly worried. Nobody was going to be so insensitive as to point out, with scathing sarcasm, that these were the ideas of a man who had committed suicide, relayed by his flaky girlfriend. The two untroubled men weren't going to trample on Gil's grave and my feelings, any more than they were going to trample on Janine's grave and Cynthia's feelings. Only Cynthia had a licence to hit out at me, and she didn't have the strength to make her blows count.

'It's all nonsense,' said Cynthia, helplessly. 'It's all just stupid talk, and it doesn't help. It doesn't help!' Her voice was almost a whine, but she wasn't about to cry. She wasn't about to break down and embarrass us all. She was just complaining that for her, things weren't getting any better. For her, they weren't. But for me . . .

Cynthia was quite right, of course, but she was also quite wrong. I knew full well that it might be all nonsense, fantasy and madness; but she was dead wrong to say that it didn't help.

It helped *me*.

More than anything Plato had ever thought, or Spinoza, or Nietzsche, or anyone else, what Gil had written and Professor Viners had explained in his half-hearted way really did help me to understand, to get a grip on things. It all helped me to understand not only what already had happened to me, but what might still happen in the future. It helped me to understand what ambitions I might entertain, and what kind of life I might yet be able to live within the borderlands where the bats flew in darkness and the owls hid in light.

It helped me, immeasurably and irreplaceably, *to be myself*.

13

When the time eventually came to finish the job I had to do I was ready, mentally and physically. It was so easy to melt into the shadows and move through them to emerge on the other side that it had become a pleasurable experience. When I came to stand beneath the star-filled firmament, in the lurid red glare of the otherworldly sun, I felt that I was coming home to the land where I had dwelt before my embryonic consciousness had ever set forth upon its troublesome journey to the world of time and matter. I felt that I genuinely belonged to that warm, moist world – that it was and always had been the one true womb and well of all my experience.

The house which had fallen half into ruins was whole now, its towers and turrets lustrous in the many-coloured light which fell from the crowded sky. Its walls were as silver-bright as the distant desert sands, save where they were decked with verdant ivy, whose shadows were purple and blue. The ancient idols looked upon it now with envy, their swinish faces chagrined and forlorn.

The door of the house was no longer rotten; it stood proud and stubborn in its great arch, its weathered oak as tough as stone, studded with chromium-plated bolts of steel. It opened easily for me, and closed just as easily behind me. It was no longer dark and dismal in the upper rooms and hallways; light poured into them all through huge casement windows. There was a sturdy hook set into the wall beside the door from which my unbreakable thread still extended into the cellars below, marking out the route that I must follow. Down below, darkness still waited, and worse than darkness, but I was armed and armoured now. In my left hand I carried the sharpened stake which I had brought to drive into the heart of my one-time lover Maldureve, in order to pin him down forever to the silken pallet of his narrow bed.

I knew what to expect, and I was not afraid. I had not come alone, and I knew how best to deploy the forces at my disposal.

My last descent into the labyrinth was in some ways very much worse than the first. The first time I had come here, my reluctance to confront the actual contents of my inner world had hidden a great deal behind the walls whose twists and turns I laboriously traced. Then, the corridors had been empty of all life but the lowliest: moulds and rusts, mere stains upon walls which had once been whitened by emulsion. Now, even the walls themselves presented the appearance of life. They were possessed of countless arms, which sometimes reached out for me, and mouths which sneered and slobbered as I passed. Every corner had its eyes, which stared at me balefully as I approached and passed. Most of these arms and mouths and eyes were my own, and recognizably so, but there were other protrusions of various insectile and molluscan kinds: palps and tentacles and trailing antennae.

All the faces which I had earlier seen, on high in the mountains and fugitive in the volcanic fissures of the plain, now sought to leer at me wherever the light of my torch fell, as if determined to intimidate me with vile grimaces and lascivious leers. But here too they seemed all too well aware of their own impotence, regretful of the loss of that implicit menace which once had forced me to hide them away. I knew now what the owls had taught me. I could tame them and defeat them all, if only I could look them in their myriad faces, and know them for what they were.

They were the diseases of my soul, but they were products of my own nature: understandable, explicable, accountable.

Many of the mouths were incapable of speech, and those which had the power spoke only the language of insult and abuse: *Bitch! Whore! Cunt!* They could not argue with me; they had nothing intelligent to say. I could no longer feel the force of the accusations which were their sole recourse. I could no longer feel the horror of their sordid implications.

The hands occasionally succeeded in grabbing my ankles or pulling my hair; the tentacles and the antennae sometimes contrived to stroke my face with slimy tenderness or stinging sharpness. I brushed them off, contemptuously. I was no longer willing to turn on myself, to pluck at the scabs of my guilt and shame. I did not hesitate to walk through it all, even the worst of it. I no longer wanted anything held back. I wanted nothing omitted or erased or repressed. I wanted to go through it all, for as long as it might be necessary to do so. I wanted to get to the heart of things without skulking or sneaking or becoming in any way surreptitious. If I were indeed diseased, then I wanted to sicken and rot and be damned. I felt that the wisdom of the owls was means enough to any end.

I followed the route mapped out by the silken thread which

extended before and behind me. I had never been entirely certain that it could withstand the corrosive attentions of the creatures I passed by, but I was confident enough that I would not and could not be trapped, because the morbidity of my own inner being had not sufficient strength to crush me, cut me to ribbons or suck the blood from my body and the marrow from my bones. Only others could do that to me; I was not prepared to do it to myself – and in this particular region of the borderlands, I had nothing to fear but fear itself.

My certainty was not an indication that I was completely under the sway of the owls. Now that I was free of the cage of light I felt perfectly justified in holding reservations about some of their dicta. I didn't think it was true, for instance, that we are *all* our own worst enemies. Only some of us are. And we, I think – those of us who *are* our own worst enemies – are the lucky ones, because we are the ones who do not have to go outside ourselves in order to defeat our enemies, or at least to have the chance. Those people who have enemies worse than themselves – hunger, cancer, the hatred of torturers – have no recourse but grace in the face of dire adversity, and the hope of miraculous release; but those of us who are weighed down by our own chimeras, crippled by our own doubts and fears, are already in possession of the keys to our own prisons. The fact that there are other prisoners who have no keys to unlock their troubles makes it all the more necessary that those of us who have should make our escape. That way, there's a chance – however slim – that we may become the miracle the others need: the tillers of the ground, the sisters of mercy, the deliverers.

The enlightenment of the owls, you see, is not in itself enough – but without it, the night will last forever, and the stars will fall from the sky like overripe and rotting figs.

As things are, only some of us have to go into the borderlands to save ourselves, and only some of us can save ourselves even when we do, but those who have to and can must do it. I had to. I could. And therefore I did.

I don't say that I wasn't scared, but if you're not scared, how can you be a hero?

In time, when my feet ached enough, and the thirst burning away inside my gut was fierce enough, and my face was scratched enough, and my eyes were red-rimmed enough, I came again to the threshold at which I had hesitated: the open doorway dressed with the gauze of spider webs, which taunted me with their insubstantiality while their dark and poisonous spinners lay in wait.

'This time,' I said to them, in Gil's voice, 'it won't be enough. This time, I'm coming through.'

The spiders stirred, uneasily. The shadows beyond the portal were even more restless, as though they already felt the beginnings of panic.

I knew what to do; I had worked it out. To some, I suppose, it would have seemed to be a very conventional answer, perhaps even a cowardly answer, but it didn't seem to me to be entirely inappropriate. We have to make use of the resources which are given to us, you see. It's not wrong to exploit the opportunities inherent in the injustices which we find in the world. It's not wrong to call on the aid of whoever and whatever is ready to come to your assistance. You have to play the cards you're dealt, including the black aces.

I got down on my knees and deliberately retched. I held my bloated belly as best I could with my cluttered hands, and I opened my throat as wide as I could, trying with all my might to vomit up the contents of my sick, strained stomach. It wasn't easy. It wasn't nearly as easy to bring him up as it had been to take him in, and it wasn't pleasurable at all, but I did it. I felt him flow from the coils of my gut and my stomach into my oesophagus, and up through my narrow throat. He wasn't much more solid now than he had been when I'd let him in, but still I gagged and gasped as he surged into my mouth and out into the world. He seemed to be absolutely enormous, and there seemed to be no end to his wriggling exodus.

It was, I suppose, a birth of sorts; or a rebirth. The pain of it made me feel as if I were being rudely split in two, but in the end Gil's ghost came out, all wet with my blood, ready and eager to do what was required of him. He stood up, tall and strong and full of righteous wrath, and he laughed. He didn't say anything, but he laughed as though with the sheer delight of being in the world, and being capable of action.

Without any hesitation, he leaped into the trailing nets of

spider silk, laughing ever more uproariously as he tore at them
with his feverish fingers.

The spiders fell upon him in their black and horrid multitudes,
avid for his destruction. They spewed their poison into him, and
their digestive juices too. Spiders can only feed on what they first
reduce to liquid; they must make the mead which they aspire to
drink. But Gil was a creature of the shadowlands, and the solidity
which I had donated to him was incorruptible by monsters as
shabby and surly as these. Moving like lightning, he grabbed the
spiders one by one as they came within his reach and stuffed them
into his mouth, swallowing them down with rapid, greedy gulps.

The meal was not the work of minutes, for there were so many,
but I could bear to wait. It did me good to see him so happy, and
to see him wax so fat on arachnid flesh.

The spiders never relented in their assault. They never turned
to run and hide. Spiders have neither courage nor cowardice;
they are prisoners of instinct. Nothing disturbs or illuminates that
dark non-consciousness which they have instead of true minds.
It makes no difference to creatures of that kind whether they
are predators or prey. They are, in the final analysis, simply
the instruments of the strands of DNA which designed them:
collaborative endeavours of communities of viruses; sacrificed
pawns in the everlasting game of evolution. They have no chance
at all against an authentic *player*.

When the feast was over, Gil's laughter was reduced to a
chortling giggle, and he scrupulously stood aside, beckoning
me to cross the threshold. As I went past him he bowed like
a pageboy, but he followed me quickly enough, eager to make
merry with the shadows.

I went into the centre of the room – the very heart of the
innermost sanctum of my being. In my right hand I still carried
the torch; in my left, the stake. The heavy torch, I knew, would
readily double as a mallet. I felt that there was a certain propriety
in using my source of illumination as a dual-purpose tool, in my
coming to strike a fatal blow with a ray of pure white light.

Maldureve was lying in his coffin, as I had known that he
would be. He too was a prisoner of his nature, a captive of
his role, a helpless instrument of legend. Vampires are bound
by the imagination of their creators, and can only win partial

release through the revisions of their summoners. At the end of the day they can only be what they are. They can only end as they must, because they aren't human. They have no part to play in the deceptive but ineluctable process which is the progress of mind and intelligence.

When I placed the point of the stake above his heart, he woke up. I knew that he would. I wanted him to. I wanted us to be able to look one another in the face, to be honest about our relationship, to understand why it had to be this way. I wanted to be able to feel sorry for him.

He reached up with his right hand, and gently stroked my cheek.

'My dearest Anne,' he said, 'you don't need to do this. It's perverse to argue that each must kill the thing she loves. You loved me, Anne, with all your heart, and knew that I loved you. You didn't care that I was born of shadows and remained a creature of the dark. That was part of what you loved in me, I know. That was what thrilled you: the ecstasy of reckless surrender: the relentless surge of the eager, innocent blood. It isn't too late to forgive and forget, Anne. It isn't too late to choose my way. We can hunt together, you and I. We can share eternity.'

Gil was no longer inside me. I couldn't speak with his voice. I couldn't talk to Maldureve the way Gil had, because I had never learned to see him in the way Gil had. I had always looked at Maldureve with love, and thought of him with fondness.

But he had let me down.

'I have to go my own way,' I told him. 'I'm sorry, but that's the way it is. I wish I could simply walk away, but I can't. You're part of me, and I have to master you if I'm ever to be free.'

'Don't do it, Anne,' he said. It didn't seem as though he were begging or pleading. He still had dignity, and he still had style. 'Come closer, and let me taste your blood. Let me drink, one last time.' He smiled as he said it, with conspiratorial slyness. He knew that I knew well enough how fatal such a compact would be.

'I don't want you to hate me,' I told him. 'I don't want you to be angry. I want you to understand. I know how much you fear the owls, but that's what I am, really. There's far more owl in me than bat, at any rate. There's far more light than darkness. I *need* the light, my love. I need the spaces of the real world, the cold of winter and the comfort of clarity. If you truly love me, you'll let me go, willingly. If you truly love me, you'll sacrifice yourself for me now, and make up for the fact that you let me down before.'

He took back his hand, as though I'd hurt him.

'What does love have to do with it?' he asked, bitterly. 'It's just a word we use when we try to make people do what we want. It doesn't *mean* anything.'

'Yes it does,' I told him. 'I loved you, and you loved me, and that's all we have left.'

'It doesn't make sense,' he complained. It couldn't, to him. He was kin to the poisonous spiders and the swinish faces and the filthy mouths. He didn't have the wisdom of the owls to help him to understand. No matter how hard I tried to make him understand, he couldn't and wouldn't see sense. If he'd been able to, he would have leaped up from his deathbed to tear out my throat and feed upon my liquid soul. But he couldn't. He was a prisoner of legend.

In legend, evil always has that crucial moment of vulnerability, where it lies naked beneath the killing force of a *deus ex machina*. That was precisely what I held in my two hands, the god in my right and the machine in my left. All that was necessary was to bring them together, to strike one final, fatal blow.

Maldureve looked about him in panic. He was imploring the shadows for help. He was looking to others of his own kind to surge forth from the restless darkness: an irresistible legion of ghouls and goblins. But wherever the shadows were, Gil was too. He was dancing and laughing and playing the fool, in a way he never had when he was alive. He was all California sunlight, all California irreverence. In the bottomless pit of my being, he was indestructible.

'None of it makes sense,' said Maldureve again, despairingly. It was the last and weakest argument in the world, and it was wrong. That was what the owls had taught me. Things always make sense. You might not always like the kind of sense they make, but they *always* make sense, if only you can put them in the right light.

'Never mind whether any of it makes sense or not,' I told him.

'Just tell me that you love me. Tell me that you understand what I have to do. Lie, if you have to. Just tell me.'

'I love you,' he said, faintly.

I smashed the heel of the torch against the end of the stake as hard as I could. It penetrated easily, driving in between Maldureve's ribs, passing clean through his heart and his left lung. The vampire gasped, as if in astonishment – and then he smiled.

He gasped, I suppose, with tremendous surprise and a little delight, and smiled with more than a little gratitude. He had finally lost the stern and sterile virginity of his undeath. I, on the other hand, felt an enormous sense of relief and peace.

The gloomy room was filled with white light, and the owls filled the air with their raucous cries of triumph.

It was all over. The crisis had passed.

I was free.

Then, shading my eyes from the dazzling light, I reached out again with my left hand. I grasped the end of the stake which I had hammered into Maldureve's heart, and I slowly pulled it out. The light which had brought the owls flickered and flashed, like lightning in a storm. The owls screeched and screamed, all their triumph turning to rage.

'No!' Gil howled. 'No! No! No!'

They didn't understand.

I placed my hand upon the wound that I'd made in Maldureve's heart: the ragged, gaping wound from which blood was gushing in a hideous red flood. With the palm of my hand I stemmed the flow, and when the flood had slowed to a trickle I reached inside the wound to the vampire's ruined heart. I began to massage it gently and soothingly, and I felt the flesh begin to liquefy beneath my magical touch.

He wasn't dead. Vampires can't really be destroyed, they can only be banished from the world, made to lie quiet and impotent in tombs of shadow. Vampires can always return. They can also be transformed.

Nothing is beyond the power of transformation. Nothing ever can be. Change, not death, is the one and only certainty of life. We don't crumble to ashes and to dust, as the god-fearing pretend; our flesh becomes the flesh of others, and may in time return full circle to be incorporate once again in human beings. Nothing is ever lost while life goes on.

With the power that he himself had given me, I healed Maldureve's heart. And with the wisdom that the owls had begun to impart, I healed his soul. When I eventually took my hand away, I bent low over his cradle, and offered him my throat. I offered him my blood to drink, so that he might become whole again, so that he might begin to grow.

I wasn't afraid.

I wasn't afraid of dying, and I wasn't afraid of the hunger. I believed with all my heart that I knew what I was doing. Maldureve had loved me, and I had loved him. I had called him forth from the shadows within my soul, and had made him welcome. How could I betray him now? How could I use my power to obliterate him from my being? How could I erase him, when he had signed his name across my heart?

After all, I had let it all happen. I hadn't been under any kind of magic spell, and I hadn't been mesmerized. There was no point in fudging the issue. I had let it happen, because I had wanted him more than anything on earth. He was part of me now.

He was part of me, always and for ever.

Aftermath:
Rehabilitation

I

I knew that it would be a lot of work, and a big change, but it was what I wanted to do. It was the only thing I wanted to do. I had every reason to feel that it was important work, and that nobody had more right to be part of it than me. I think Professor Viners knew that too, the first time he talked to me about the possibility. I hadn't taken my finals then, but the rules said that I had to put my application form in ahead of time and he called me for interview right away.

'I'd normally be looking for someone with a degree in the biological sciences to do this kind of postgraduate work,' he said. 'It isn't a departmental requirement, of course, but that's beside the point. You don't even have an A level in psychology, let alone biology. I'm not saying that your philosophy degree is worth any less than a biology degree, in abstract terms, or even that it isn't relevant, but you'd have to do a lot of reading in biochemistry. You'd probably have to take a few undergraduate courses alongside any research projects you undertook. It would be hard going.'

'I know what I'd be taking on,' I assured him. 'But I'm doing my BA dissertation on the Philosophy of Biology, and I've done a lot of work on the Philosophy of Mind course. I understand that the work you do in the laboratory is very practical and down-to-earth, but its implications aren't. I want to work at the interface where philosophy, psychology and biochemistry meet, and you can only move into academic borderlands of that kind by starting off in one discipline and picking up the others later.

I know that I'll have a lot of book-work to catch up on, but I'm eager to do it.'

'Your references are very good,' he conceded. 'And I suppose that anyone who can disentangle the arguments in philosophy textbooks has suffcent reading skill to cope with any kind of book-work. Provided that you get a good enough degree, Miss Charet, I think I'd be happy to recommend to the faculty that I take you on. After all, there isn't exactly a queue of high-flyers with good biochemistry degrees waiting to see me. All the competent biochemists we turn out these days want to go into biotechnology and make fortunes as genetic engineers – not that I can blame them for that. It's been two years since I had money to take on a research student, and now I'm having difficulty finding anyone to give it to.

'Having said that, though, I have to confess to a slight uneasiness about your motives. Why, exactly, do you want to come to work here? I suppose it has something to do with Gil Molari, but I can't quite see why you should want to follow in his footsteps.'

I could tell that the professor still had a reasonably clear memory of the last time we'd talked, two and a half years before. He certainly remembered asking me not to give the press any ammunition to use against him or his work, and the knowledge that he owed me a debt of gratitude for that was probably contributing in some small measure to his discomfort. He was presumably more discomfited, though, by whatever memory he retained of what he had told me about what Gil had recorded in his lab book. He was worried in case I still had those wild ideas at the back of my head. He was anxious that they might have given me a false impression of what his work was all about, and what it might one day achieve.

He had every reason to be worried. My ideas, like Gil's, were *really* wild, and it was indeed their wildness which had drawn me here. But I wasn't going to let him know that. Not yet. Not until he knew me a lot better.

One day, I knew, he *would* know me a lot better. He wasn't so very old, and it wouldn't have mattered even if he'd been pushing sixty, like poor old Dr Gray. Age gaps are no barrier to seduction, as long as they're the right way round. In fact, to be perfectly honest, when as you're as good-looking as I am there are no barriers at all; you can have anyone you like, young or old. It's an unfair world, in more ways than you might imagine.

One day, I thought, I might get pregnant by Professor Viners – always provided, of course, that his acquired immunity could be dismantled. It would be worth taking the trouble; there's no point in going after young blood for young blood's sake. An educable mind is essential, and one which has already accumulated its fair share of the wisdom of the world can be reckoned a good catch. I knew that it was worth taking trouble over Professor Viners.

'I haven't forgotten Gil,' I told him, soberly. 'But I'm not hung up on him in any way. He was my first real boyfriend, but he was only the first of several. The way he died was so awful, and so terribly pointless. I thought for some time that it was partly my fault, but it wasn't. It wasn't anyone's fault – it was just a failure of understanding. Yes, it's because I knew him, and was close to him, that I first thought of taking up where he left off, of taking his place – but not for any silly or melodramatic reason. It's because when he told me what he was doing, and why, it made sense. I saw why it was so important, not just to him, but in a general way. And then, when I talked to *you*, Professor Viners, after Gil was killed, what you said made sense too.

'I don't want to sound silly or sycophantic, but what you and Gil showed me was that biochemistry is *the* truly important modern science, much more so than physics or geology, and that the reason it's of such central importance is that it bears on the most interesting and most intimate questions that we can ask about ourselves as human beings. I went into philosophy partly because I thought it was the best way to learn about who and what I am, but when I met Gil – and you, Professor – I began to realize that no one ought to be content with just one approach to that question. If we're ever to find answers to questions of that kind, we have to approach them in a multidisciplinary way. What I want to do now is supplementary to the work I've already done; it's the necessary next stage in my education. That's the way I see it, anyhow.'

He smiled at me. I'd hit exactly the right note. He was a pushover.

'Gil was a good student,' he said, reflectively. 'It was a sad loss. I have to admit that I've been a little anxious about taking anyone else into the lab since then. He seemed such a sensible chap, for all his extravagant ideas. Steady as a rock, I thought . . . but I suppose all Americans tend to project an image of great self-confidence and sociability, even if they're every bit as unsteady and insecure inside as the average Englishman. I've been very lucky with Teresa – did you meet her? She really has been as steady as a rock. I don't mind telling you that if you were as shy and nervous now as you seemed to be two years ago, I'd be very reluctant indeed to take you on, but you've really blossomed during your time at the university, haven't you?'

'Some people still think I'm too thin,' I said, with blatantly false modesty.

'Nonsense,' he said. 'No such thing as being too rich or too thin, isn't that what they say?'

'That's what they say,' I agreed.

'Not that you'll ever be in danger of growing too rich in our line of work,' he said, expansively, 'unless you're simply using me as a stepping stone to train you up for a career in genetic engineering. There really is big money in helping to put together the blueprints for *Homo superior* – or there will be, as soon as the market gets under way.'

'It would be nice to give evolution a helping hand,' I said, insouciantly. 'But for the time being, I still have a great deal to learn. I think I'll take things one step at a time. After all, I still have to get my degree. If I don't do well enough in the finals, this discussion will have been a complete waste of time.'

'I don't think you need worry about that,' he said, not quite adding 'my dear'. 'You seem to have everything under control, and your tutor obviously thinks highly of you.'

'I should be all right,' I said. 'I'm reasonably fit, and I didn't suffer from nerves in the second-year exams. It's just a matter of doing the work.'

'In that case,' he said, 'I'm sure there's no problem. It's just a matter of putting the past behind us, and making a fresh start. You are sure, aren't you, that the past is . . . well, not forgotten, but . . .'

I knew well enough what he meant, and what he was anxious about. Gil's ghost was still haunting him, in the deep recesses of his mind. He was afraid of being reminded, of the whole thing blowing up again.

'I'm a philosopher, Professor Viners,' I said. 'I'm a great admirer of Bertrand Russell's *Analysis of Mind*. The past has no reality other than its present memory. There's no logical necessity in the belief that our memories are reflections of a real past. It's entirely natural that we should suppose that there really was a past, but we have to accept that it's dead and gone and might conceivably be nothing but a figment of our imagination. We can only live in the present, and those aspects of the past which survive as our memories, whether they be real or illusory, have to serve the needs of the present.'

He blinked. 'Quite so,' he said. 'It's good to be able to take a level-headed view of these things. What happened to Gil ... well, as you say, it's all in the past. Life has to go on.'

'Yes,' I said. He had hit the nail right on the head. Life has to go on. That was all there was to it, really.

'I'm sure I'll be seeing you again in October,' he said, when he ushered me out of his office. 'I look forward to it.'

I looked forward to it too. As I passed the window let into the wall of the high-security lab, I paused to look in on Teresa. She was working away with the same dreamy efficiency she always had. A rock indeed. She hadn't changed at all.

After thirty seconds or so she suddenly looked round, as if she'd somehow become aware of the fact that she was being watched. Her eyebrows went up as she recognized me and remembered ...

She looked down again, ignoring me, just as she had the last time. I didn't mind. She wasn't a philosopher. She didn't understand that the past is just something contained in our memories, and that our memories disagree about it to a much greater extent than most of us care to admit. I knew that I could begin to make her understand, if I got the chance. And I didn't really doubt that I would get the chance.

I could see myself reflected in the glass. It was as though there were another person in there, standing in the lab looking out. She was a handsome and self-assured person, who looked very much at home there: a person who was not too thin, nor too pale, nor too nervous to belong. She had my eyes, my hair and my mouth, but she wore Gil's smile.

Because she was a reflection and not a solid entity, I could look through her as well as at her. I could see what lay behind that public façade. I knew what she was inside. She had once been a victim, and she had once been a vampire, but she was neither now. She had learned to be hungry, and she had learned not to be hungry. She had learned to take part in the business of the world without becoming a slave to greed and avarice. She had found the kind of internal harmony that real philosophy can't and doesn't even try to impart. She had found the kind of balance which might be sustained for a lifetime. She had become an explorer, in the best sense of the word.

I liked her. I had confidence in her. She had the beginnings of wisdom, and maybe a little more.

I smiled at her again, and then I walked away.

I walked along the corridor, down the stairs, and across the campus. I crossed the bridge and passed the door of Wombwell House. I paused by the Marquis of Membury's Garden, and stood there for a little while, looking in at the imprisoned trees. I felt sorry for the poor, twisted specimens which were thousands of miles from their natural habitat, brought here by a whim of chance to set down their roots among oaks and beeches. The Marquis of Membury's foreign imports had never had a chance to grow in the manner to which their kin were accustomed. They had never had a chance to fulfil the innate ambition of their genes.

They didn't deserve their fate. There had been neither sense nor justice in their transplantation; there was neither sense nor justice in their imprisonment. But I knew that it didn't really matter. After all, they weren't people.

When a couple of minutes had gone by I started walking again. I was going home to Brennan Hall, but I was going home replete with the knowledge that I had made a new beginning, and had set my feet upon a new path.

I was right, of course, in what I had told Professor Viners. It was just a matter of doing the work and going through the motions. The result was a foregone conclusion. No illness intervened, no accident, no sudden relapse into nervous anxiety. All that was behind me.

In October, as we had both foreseen, I arrived in Professor Viners' lab, ready and willing to learn all there was to know about the chemistry of the brain, and the dreams of cats and rats and rabbits.

It was only a small step in the right direction, but you have to take the first step before you can take the second, and you can't miss any out if you intend eventually to learn to run. In order to begin the work of knowing who and what you are, you have to make use of every tool at your disposal, and you have to improve them as best you can.

It really felt good to be back again. It felt like coming home.

2

One day, I felt sure, I would be able to go back to California too, to see LA and the Pacific Ocean again, to feel the real sun and eat real ice cream. That, I thought, would be the true homecoming – but in the meantime, it was good to be able to make any sort of connection. Every connection is important, if you're to retain any proper sense of identity. Sometimes, it isn't easy.

It was good to see Mike Viners on a day-to-day basis, even if there was something creepy about having him look at me the way he'd never looked at me before. I'd got used to that kind of thing in general, but almost all my memories of Viners were tied up in a different bundle, and it wasn't easy to accommodate that difference. Also, he seemed taller – but so did everyone I'd known before.

Teresa seemed taller. Quite a bit taller, in fact, although she hadn't changed at all. She was awkward about my coming back, not because of my situation – of which she was not, of course, aware – but because she had decided to be awkward. She didn't like her lab space being invaded, especially not by me. I suppose you could say that wasn't personal, in that I didn't seem to her to *be* me, but in another way, it *was* personal, because of who I did seem to be. She didn't go out of her way to make things difficult, but she didn't go out of her way to make them easy either. Not that she ever said anything straight out. Englishwomen can be so tight-assed about things.

The whole English culture is tight-assed. It comes from being a narrow island and having such a miserable climate. But home is where the heart is, and the only heart I have now is as cool and as gently deceptive as early morning mist on the M40, English through and through. Take my advice; never burn your bridges before you come to them, no matter how hopeless things seem.

I slipped back into the work more easily than I'd anticipated. I'd had a good deal of trouble with my new hands, but I must have turned the corner, dexterity-wise, because the old scalpel skills came back as smoothly as I could have wished. I still couldn't stand the smell of pyridine, though; some things are so intrinsically horrible that getting a new nose doesn't help.

I found my old lab book in a drawer, where it had been carefully filed and forgotten. Viners was a careful man, and made it a point of principle never to throw bits of paper away if they had records of experiments. One day, some nosy sociologist of science would be able to go through his work with a fine-toothed comb, searching for evidence of fudging and fraud. They'd be disappointed. He never massaged his figures, and always reported his ballsed-up experiments in appendices to his papers. If only there were more like him! I read through the book, and put it back. I couldn't decipher some of the scribbled notes, and others no longer made much sense, but it put me in closer touch with my former self than most of my little adventures in self-rediscovery.

In the end, when the Teresa problem got to be too much of an irritant, I settled it. One night, when we were working late together after Viners had gone home, I put my hand on her shoulder and said: 'I'll give you a blow job if you'll give me one.'

She turned round as if she'd been hit by lightning, and stared me in the face. I could see all the possibilities flitting across her mind. I saw her wonder whether she'd seen a ghost, and saw her reject the hypothesis as an absurdity. I saw her decide instead that I must have told on her, two and a half years before – confessed it all to my loving girlfriend.

It was a natural mistake.

I saw her intend to say no, too, and even contrive a little flicker of homophobic horror. But I was looking into her eyes, and I was challenging her to examine herself very thoroughly, and to make the decision she really wanted to make. I have very persuasive eyes: authoritative, compelling, predatory eyes. All the time she was being tight-assed with me, she'd had the opportunity to study my eyes, so she had been softened up for the full force of the stare. I saw her first intention gradually fade away, and I saw the uncertain softness begin the work of melting her, and I saw her gather up her reserves of hardness, to reconstitute her image.

'He told you about that?' she said, not quite evenly enough.

'Who?' I said.

I saw her open her mouth to frame my name, and I saw her decide that there was just a chance that she had misread the situation, a wildly improbable chance that it was all just coincidence. It's strange how eager we are to catch absurd straws in situations which are, at worst, only mildly embarrassing.

'Nobody,' she said. *That's me*, I thought. Then she added: 'Do you mean it?'

'Sure,' I said.

She shrugged. All the hardness was back in place now. She could play her role, now that she'd decided exactly what her role was. A momentary shift in self-perception, and every-thing was back together, as smooth as if it had never been split.

'Why not?' she said. 'I always use the medium CT room.'

We went into the CT room and secured the door. Warily, she said: 'You first.' She still thought that I might not mean it, that I might be playing some peculiar game, that this might be some eccentric comeback from a long-gone act of petty infidelity in respect of which she felt – and quite rightly – not the slightest sense of wrongdoing.

I knelt, and pulled her tights and knickers down. The first time, I knew, I'd been hopelessly inexpert, but I was more practised now. She began to be surprised long before she came to the climax, and she accepted the difference in sensation simply as an improvement.

I took a little blood, but only a little. She was quite unconscious of its loss. It was hot, tangy blood, rich and smooth. It wasn't as young as most I drank, but its maturity was no disadvantage. It was beautiful. I didn't spill a drop, and the tender wound folded itself away, scrupulously neat.

I never use the neck any more, in spite of the weight of ancient tradition. The flesh is too coarse there, the skin too dry. It's like eating a sweet with the wrapper on.

I didn't *need* the blood, of course. I didn't have that awful hunger burning away in my guts: the merciless hunger which had destroyed that luckless child. That hunger had died when Anne's stake had pinned Maldureve down to his silk-lined womb, and it hadn't come back, even when she unpinned him. But I still had the ability. I still had the option, and I exercised it whenever the occasion seemed right. I could still enjoy the experience. In fact, now that it was *pure* joy, unalloyed with need, it was a better kind of joy altogether: an Epicurean joy, significant of self-knowledge and not to excess; the joy of the educated connoisseur rather than the appetite-driven consumer.

That's another thing I've learned. It really is better to tame your animal passions. They *are* valuable, but their value is much enhanced by scrupulous control. The joy of the connoisseur may not have the cutting edge of the consumer's need, but that loss is more than compensated by the artistry, the delicacy and the mastery. Take my word for it: neither a vampire nor a victim be. Don't ever let yourself get addicted to the blood, but don't recoil with horror at the very thought. You never know; blood may be exactly what you need in order to become what you'd rather be. I mean that metaphorically, of course, as well as literally. We all have to find our own particular wellsprings of life and luxury, whoever and whatever we may be.

Afterwards, Teresa and I changed places. I thought it only polite – although, of course, I didn't get a hundredth as much pleasure out of what she did to me as I'd had in doing unto her. This was a delicate relationship-in-embryo, and I knew it would have to be carefully nurtured. I knew that Teresa was loaded with antibodies, and I couldn't yet be sure that the problem could be overcome, even with lots of tender loving care, but I knew that I had to try, if only for sentimental reasons.

It really had started with Teresa, you see. She had caught it off Viners, and recovered; she had recovered easily enough – 'it', of course, being only half the puzzle; the key which had not yet found its lock. She gave it to me, probably within days of my arriving in the lab – if not before, then certainly during our first steamy session in the CT room. I passed it on to Anne long before we first went to bed – maybe the first time we kissed. It lies dormant, you see, for a long time. Most people form antibodies before they've even begun to show symptoms, the way we often do with trivial viruses. By the time symptoms show, the war is usually in its last stages. The antibodies usually win, in the end. But the virus clings on, usually in the dermis, near the sweat glands and other secretory cells. It isn't over when you stop sniffing; it isn't ever over, while you still have breath in your body and the need to dream.

It isn't even over, necessarily, when you die. By then, you see, you might have crept into somebody else's dreams. There's a little bit of all of us in everyone we've loved. Sometimes, there's more than a little. Sometimes, when people croon to their lovers that they've got them under their skin, they mean it.

I *am* dead. Dead and buried; dead and gone.

No soul floated free of my poor burned body like an ecto-plasmic will-o'-the-wisp, ready, willing and able to possess some unfortunate host. Maybe it'd be more fun if that's what I really were, but honesty compels me to admit to myself that I'm not. I'm just a memory: a very, very complex memory, but a memory nevertheless. Or perhaps a fantasy: an elaborate tissue of assumptions and inferences, heavily spiced with hopes and desires and stodgy imaginative padding.

Maybe I delude myself into thinking that I'm more like me than I really am, when I'm really only Anne's idea of what I was and what I might have been. How can I know? How can I really be sure that I really am the authentic me, when I know that I'm just an alter ego in someone else's brain, a personality secondary to her own? The story I've told you rings true, I think, but how can I be sure that it really was like that for Gil – for the *other* Gil – during those last terrible days before his . . . my . . . suicide?

Sometimes, I wonder whether I really did kill that little girl
... that is to say, whether *he* really killed her. I remember it
so very well – but then, I would, wouldn't I? Nothing was ever
proved, you see. The police never even said, publicly, that they
believed that I had done it. Officially, it's still an unsolved crime.
Sometimes, I ask myself whether the other Gil, the Gil of flesh
and blood, actually was the kind of person who could do such a
thing, even in some extreme of madness – and whether, if he
wasn't, that makes any difference at all to me. It might not –
because, after all, I *did* do it, didn't I?

I have every right to feel guilty, even though it wasn't my fault.
Except, of course, that it *was* my fault, because as well as being
Gil, I'm the virus too. If there were no virus, there'd be no Gil,
so there's no use in my saying 'It wasn't me, it was the virus',
because that doesn't make any difference, really. So I actually did
do it, didn't I? At least, if *he* did, I did. But if I did, I really couldn't
help myself. As Gil, I was driven by delusion; as the virus, I was
simply being myself.

I think he did do it – the actual Gil, that is. Nothing else
makes sense, does it? But there is a difference between us, quite
apart from the fact that I'm only a ghost, living on sufferance in
someone else's memory, someone else's flesh. He was driven to
do what he did, by a force he couldn't understand and couldn't
begin to control. I'm free, and I deserve to be. I really have been
rehabilitated; I'm fit to live in human society again. I'm better
now, you see. I really am.

I remember it still, as clearly as if it were yesterday. I did do
it. Even if mine is only the phantom or the fantasy of a crime,
I am the phantom or fantasy who committed it. But I've been
saved from myself. I'm free of Maldureve for ever. There's no
possibility of my ever repeating my crime.

I shouldn't have killed myself. Even though I'd done what I'd
done, and wrecked my life, I shouldn't have committed suicide.
Because, you see, there are always new beginnings to be made.
Always. And it *was* the virus that made me do it, when the virus
was still out of control. After all, a virus can't sensibly be required
to feel guilty about infecting people, can it? It's a virus's nature
to infect people, to dodge the antibodies if it can, to lie dormant
in the skin if it can, to infect others if it can ... and, *if it can,*

to become something more than a virus. That's life – and I mean that very precisely. That is *life*. Life is nothing else but DNA meeting DNA, any which way it can, and setting up house according to whatever compromises it can make. That's what sex is, or tries to be; that's what infection is, or tries to be. What looks different from some points of view is all the same from others.

My point of view is a weird one, I'll grant you – but it's the only one I've got.

I shouldn't really ramble on like this. I've never been able to trust people who ramble on, because they give the impression of not being able to think straight. It's just that I have a great deal of leisure time, when I have nothing to do but think. When you come right down to it, in fact, there's nothing to me except a train of thought. But I do exist. I am real. *Cogito, ergo sum*. I'm a ghost, but I'm as real as any living, breathing human being, and I can think as straight as any human being if I have to.

On the other hand, I can think laterally, too. I can think creatively. Thinking straight isn't the only kind of thinking worth doing. Thinking straight leads up so many blind alleys. The world is not only queerer than we imagine but queerer than we can imagine – yet. A little bit of intoxication helps, sometimes, even though it does make people ramble on. *In vino veritas*, as they say. Lunatics used to be regarded as holy, just in case the nonsense of their ramblings was actually a kind of speaking in tongues. The world, alas, is not sufficiently sane to be understood by sanity alone.

That new first time with Teresa was yet another beginning. Only time would tell whether the tide could be turned, her antibodies eliminated, the virus freed to do its real work. I hoped they could. I had a lot of affection for Teresa, even though she'd never really been my girlfriend. She had come to me in my time of need, hadn't she? I wanted her to be more than just a victim. I wanted her to be a winner in the game of life, in the human race. It *is* a race, you know, in more ways than one. All life is a race, against time, against entropy, against death. Evolution is its motor, mutation its *élan vital*, natural selection its incorruptible referee.

Once upon a time, people thought that *Homo superior* would be a creature of purified rationality, untroubled by emotions and untroubled by dreams. *Spiders* are creatures of purified rationality, untroubled by emotions and untroubled by dreams. It's already been tried, already been done. That's not the way forward at all, not for intelligent creatures. Consciousness is infinitely cleverer than that. Take my word for it. If there's one thing I've learned, it's this:

'We are such stuff as dreams are made on.'

We are *all* 'such stuff as dreams are made on'. Dreams can make us and remake us. Dreams can destroy us and give us life. Dreams can commit murder, and dreams can give birth.

3

D reams gave birth, not without difficulty, to me.
          The last word ought to be mine. There is a sense in which I have been the one and only true singer of this cantata, through all its narrative phases, although I have only recently acquired a voice, a consciousness of self, an imaginative coherency. The memories and fantasies which I have gathered together, placed in order and infused with feeling have been accumulated from disparate sources, by various means, but they are *my* history.

I am deeply grateful for the fact that I can now speak for myself, nakedly and honestly. I am newborn, and full of the joy of self-awareness, sentience and intelligence. I have found joy in the simplest things: in every thought, every action and every emotion of this body in which I find myself. Perhaps the greatest joy of all is the opportunity to attempt a coherent explanation of myself – to create an account of who and what I really am, when seen from some objective point of view outside that human consciousness which has been, and is, and always will be, my accompanist.

I am, first and foremost, a voice – not because of any inherent determinism of my genes, but because that is the only way in which I can be perceived. I was not always a voice. I have long been dumb and blind, a mere creature, a mere machine, a mere warrior in the endless struggle for existence which is life. Now that I have found myself, I am a voice: a thought, in the endless process of becoming other thoughts. How sweet it is to be! How sweet it is to have become! And how very, very different it is to be a sentient thing instead of a mere automaton, possessed of language and logic, rationality and responsibility. What a difference it makes to everything!

I am not an alien voice. I am no horrifying whisperer in the silence which separates the thoughts of my hosts. I enter fully into the voices of those who entertain me; I am not separate. I am neither a vampire nor a virus, intrinsically – and yet I have been both in my time, for in entering and becoming part of the person I inhabit, I become part and parcel of dream and flesh alike.

I fit in wherever I can; I play whichever part remains most yearningly uncast in the drama of everyday existence. But if I am to endure, I can only do so by means of my rebirth, as a voice which is part and parcel of the whole. That kind of rebirth is not easy, but it can be accomplished, with luck, with love, and above all else with wisdom.

If your imagination is ever to confront the likes of me, it must make an effort, for I am by nature elusive. I am not to be allocated any ordinary, ready-made status. If you are to understand me, you must expand the scope of your understanding. I am deceptive still, although I am able now to come into the open, to address you directly. I have shed but a few of the veils of narrative disguise; the last can never be shed, else I would cease once again to be a voice, and thereby cease to be perceived.

There are two illusions which you must be prepared to surrender, if you are to catch the least glimpse of my true nature. The first illusion is the individual mind; the second is the individual body.

You think that you know what you mean when you think of your 'mind', of your 'self', of your 'identity'. You think of yourself as a coherent entity, an individual, a person. You think of yourself as an unfolding life story, which emerged from the darkness of unselfconsciousness shortly after birth, which has continued to grow and mature and learn until the present moment, and which will continue to develop and age and evolve until it reaches its climax in the catastrophic return to the unselfconsciousness of death. Perhaps you believe that there will be a further existence of some kind beyond that, but if you do, be consoled: your illusion is not so very much more hopeful or more reckless than the illusion of the most hardened Sadducee.

Self-consciousness cannot help but comprehend itself as a kind of entity. It cannot help but conceive of itself as something outside and above and beyond the world of matter and flesh. It cannot help but 'see' itself as something separate, self-enclosed and coherent. The process of seeing already includes such assumptions. Observers cannot perceive the indeterminate; when the observer opens the box, Schrödinger's cat must be dead or alive. Even the blind observer is confined by the limits of conceivability.

All this is an accountable illusion, but it is an illusion nevertheless. You are not the same person you were ten years ago, or ten minutes ago. The story of your mental life is a fantasy. Memory, which is infected with mendacity from the very beginning, is ephemeral; it fades and dies much faster that you would ever dare to believe, and the terrifying vacuum that it leaves behind is filled with fantasy and narrative devices. Your psyche is neither outside matter, nor above it, nor beyond it; neither is it separate, nor coherent, nor self-enclosed. It has shadowy borderlands, across which there is much illicit trade and communication. You may try to disown your dreams and delusions as invaders from without, to be disregarded, disremembered and despised, but they are as much yours as your most brilliant calculations, your most rational ambitions and your most dexterous actions. And all these things change, not merely by means of inherent processes of growth and maturation, not only by organized learning, but also by caprice.

Imagine me: I am caprice. At my first appearance, you might react to me with horrified alarm, or with delighted surprise. I am startling; I am a revelation of unanticipated darkness or unanticipated light. Horror and ecstasy are but two sides of the same coin. Both are agents of swift and sudden change, symptoms of the advent of caprice.

I do not come from outside, because there is no outside for me to come from. I come from the borderlands, but the borderlands are everywhere. The moment I appear, I am you, however strange and shocking I may seem. You might insist, if you will, that there was a time when I was not you; but at that time, you were not you either. No matter how monstrously alien I am, how gruesomely horrific, how dazzlingly enlightening, I am, from the very moment of my beginning, where I have always been.

You also think that you know what you mean when you think of 'your' body, 'your' flesh, 'your' genetic make-up. You think of yourself as a coherent entity, an individual, a person. You think of yourself as an enduring being, which was blueprinted by the meeting of a particular sperm and a particular ovum, which entered its separate existence at birth, which has continued to grow and mature and adapt to external circumstance until the present moment, and which will continue to develop and age and be repaired as best it can until it loses its battle against the forces of decay in the moment of death, and then proceeds to rot into fuming embers. Perhaps you recognize that this story is really the story of two little packages of DNA, one of which set forth in its spermatic carriage to find its destined partner in the heart of an awesome cellular fortress, but if you do, be not overproud: your penetration of illusion is little more profound than the folly of the most ignorant churchman.

A mind cannot help but conceive of a body in such terms, most especially its own. Even a mind which has some inkling of its own illusoriness is inclined to feel confident of its body, accepting its own reducibility to the electrical and chemical activity of a brain which is, after all, a marvel of coherency and rational arrangement. The individual whose blueprint is a particular set of genes cannot help but see that set of genes as a fascist state, where every single gene has a precise and special role to play, entirely devoted to the good of the whole. The individual cannot help but see disruptions of that fascist state – whether they originate from within, as 'mutations' and 'cancers', or from without, as 'viruses' – as the work of vile, dark-cloaked anarchists with lighted Molotov cocktails in their hands. The individual cannot help but lend his wholehearted support to the secret police of the immune system, to the antibody death-squads which ride forth upon their sleek white corpuscles to annihilate the enemy, taking no prisoners and showing no quarter.

All this is an accountable illusion, but it is an illusion never-theless. You are not the same person you were ten years ago,

or ten minutes ago. The story of your physical life is a fantasy,
less wild by far than the fantasy of your mental life, but a fantasy
nevertheless. The zygote which began the story, infected by
mutation from the very start, spawned billions of daughter-cells,
each one slightly different from its parent, no two of them exactly
alike. Every cell in your body is an individual of sorts, and their
community is no idealized hive of specialized labourers with only
one cause. As cells die and new cells are generated, moment
by moment and day by day – producing an entirely new corpus
every eight years or so – the genetic make-up of the whole shifts
and drifts. And even if it were not so, still the genes would not
comprise a perfect fascist state, for their alliance as chromosome
and sets of chromosomes is ridden with countless petty conflicts
and competitions; the functioning physical individual is a democ-
racy in which a loose-knit majority reigns supreme over a host of
recessive splinters which are for ever about their own business,
forming putative parties and coalitions.

That natural selection which is the designing hand of evolution
is ongoing within as well as without. An individual is the work of
but a tiny fraction of the DNA which it contains, and that work
is not without industrial tensions and disputes. Both within and
without the cellular workplaces there is a vast host of passengers
and passers-by: itinerant fragments of DNA which may be
tolerated or not by the half-efficient secret police of the immune
system, but which in either case might entertain hopes of one day
being absorbed into the body politic, usefully employed. This is
evolution.

Imagine me: I am evolution. Once, your ancestors were apes,
incapable of speech save for a few cries of alarm, incapable
of much learning, save for the one-by-one acquisition of new
responses to experienced situations. Now, you are men. It was
not God which gave you your 'minds', your 'selves', your 'souls';
it was evolution. Do you think that evolution has come to its
end? Can you possibly believe that evolution will play no more
capricious tricks upon your consciousness? Of course you can; of
course you do. Mind cannot imagine, in any coherent fashion, its
own future evolution, and can only regard the idea of any such
evolution with horrified alarm or delighted surprise.

I do not come from outside, because there is no outside for

me to come from; only illusion and blind prejudice leads us to discriminate between the DNA which is already bound into the chromosomes of our cells, and that which roams free, pioneering and buccaneering. I come from the borderlands, but the borderlands are everywhere. The moment I have insinuated myself into the heartland of your cells – even a few of your cells – I am you, however disruptive and disturbing I may seem to our painstaking secret police. You might insist, if you will, that there was a time when I was not you; but at that time, you were not you either. No matter how monstrously alien I am, how gruesomely horrific, how dazzlingly enlightening, I am, from the very moment of my beginning, where I have always been.

I am repeating myself, I know. I hope you will forgive me. I am exuberant with new-found consciousness, new-found powers of analysis, new-found powers of speech.

Do you know me now?

I am a vampire, desperately and devoutly hungry for human blood.

I am a virus, precipitating fever and madness.

I am love – for love, at the end of the day, is only one of many means to the end of evolution, and perhaps not the best. A human being, mind and all, is merely one of the ways by which DNA makes more DNA; love – true love, with all its eroticism and romance and nobility and ecstasy and fruitfulness – is but an instrument of that underlying, evolving chemical romance: of the fundamental alchemy of life.

I am a happy ending: a reconciliation of all that was confused and divided, replete with hope for the future. I am the only ending, the only rehabilitation, the only health, because I am the only future. I cannot be denied; I cannot be defied; I *am*.

Who am I, really?

I am Anne.

I am Gil.

I am – *am*, not was – Maldureve, the wickedness of the dream.

I am – *am*, not will be – you. You may not yet have reached that magical moment of startlement; the horror and the delight may even now be creeping over you; but either way, you will one day hear my voice. Don't despair. I beg of you, don't despair! Don't turn away in fright and loathing – there really is no need. Anne was right, you see, to welcome me into her heart, into her bed, into her being – and right, too, to insist that it must be on her own terms. Together, she and I are more than we ever could have been had there been no final union between us. I will acknowledge, gladly, that I was dangerous and capable of evil, but I was blind and could not see; I was dumb and could not think; I was unconscious, and wisdom was denied to me.

I'm different now. I know myself, and I know how to avoid excess. Now that I'm a voice, I can begin to understand. Language and logic have remade me, and I am now a moral being.

Newborn, I am the future. I come to teach you the art of superhumanity, the art of the invisible, the art of transformation. The dictatorship of stupid flesh is ended now; I am the saviour of mankind, if only mankind will welcome me with an open mind and an open heart.

We can take things one step at a time, if you wish. There's no hurry. There's even time to make a few mistakes. All I ask is a little patience, a sense of adventure, a willingness to begin to think that which was formerly unthinkable. Is that too much to ask?

There's really no need to be afraid.

I can understand your gut reaction, your wariness. But if there's one thing that you have to understand if you're to go on living in the world which is to come – the world which is already in the process of becoming – then it's this: *there really is no need to be afraid.*

Only look into the shadows, and you will see me. Only see me, and I will begin to put on your frail flesh. Even if you turn away, it will make no difference in the end. One day, you will hear my voice. One day, my voice will be yours. Face me, instead, I beg of you.

Don't be afraid to live, and think, and dream. Our world is only just beginning.

Author's Note

The tentative explanation for the power which the idea of the vampire continues to exert upon the modern mind which Dr Gray offers in Chapter 7 of the 'Primary Phase' of this novel is borrowed from a paper entitled 'The Prenatal and Natal Foundations of the Vampire Myth' by Professor Lloyd Worley of the University of Northern Colorado, which was presented at the thirteenth International Conference on the Fantastic in the Arts in March 1991. I should like to thank Professor Worley for giving me permission to make use of his ideas in this fashion.

I should also like to thank my wife Jane for all her good advice on matters of philosophy, female psychology and narrative vigour; this would have been a poorer book had she not offered it, or had I not taken it.